No Gentle Slopes

No Gentle Slopes

Barrie Anderson

A Square One Publication

First published in 1995 by
Square One Publications,
The Tudor House
Upton upon Severn, Worcs WR8 2HT

© Barrie Anderson 1995

British Cataloguing in Publication Data is available
for this title

NO GENTLE SLOPES

ISBN 1 872017 89 4

Typeset in Palatino 10 on 12 by Avon Dataset Ltd, Bidford on Avon, B50 4JH

Printed by Antony Rowe Ltd of Chippenham, England

This novel is dedicated to all members of Alcoholics Anonymous, which was founded in June 1935; with special thanks to all those members (and those Al Anon members) who permitted me entry into that fellowship, so to learn and understand . . .

Prologue

Georgette carefully placed the folding chair in the centre of the floor. Slowly she settled down upon it and looked around the empty room. Her eyes stopped at the window as the rain that had been threatening all morning started to fall. The rivulets seemed to run into one another as she watched, and gradually her tears matched the raindrops, trickling downwards as her memories flooded back . . .

PART ONE

Georgette – The Early Years

Chapter One

Paris. It was difficult to remember exactly when she had realized what an odd life they had lived, she and her parents, Elizabeth and Henry Delire. But it must have been when they were based in the Vendôme Hotel. Paris was *the* place to visit in the early 1930s of course, for all the 'top' people – foreign rulers with titles such as Emperor, or Maharaja, European Royals, sometimes with their children, passed through the hotel. On a few occasions, Georgette was invited to join them on a picnic, or some outing, but they were few and far between. Elizabeth spent her time sewing exquisite clothes for herself and her daughter – she had no need to shop or cook since – as the wife of the hotel manager – she had only to pick up the telephone to order their meals . . . Henri, an undemonstrative man, put his work first, acknowledging his daughter with a restrained smile and a nod as he came and went in his dark grey suit, stiff collared and immaculate . . .

In 1934, when she was twelve, and she wouldn't be thirteen until the last day of November, still a good few months off, Georgette, a chubby child, learned that her father had been promoted general manager of the hotel group's 'flagship'. That meant the family returning to their homeland – Belgium, to Brussels, and the Hotel Leopold.

Once there, instead of placing Georgette back into the private school she'd attended before that Paris posting, she was sent to an Ecole Professionelle, because Elizabeth was annoyed that her offspring had yet to master needlework. If she felt unloved by her parents, and she did, soon Georgette came to realize that she was despised by the other children at the school, who considered her stuck-up with what they called her 'airs and graces'; something Georgette had not known until they told her was that her paternal grandmother had been nothing more than a laundry worker, so how could she think herself any better than they were?

After a year, with her daughter's needlework markedly improved, Elizabeth readily returned her to private education, where she was happier.

When Georgette was fifteen (and now very slim and quite beautiful), her mother became unwell, and took her growing child with her to the Vallee de l'Ourthe, to rest at the hotel group's Castel de Dinant, where Georgette felt the first stirrings of love, for Gideon, the son of a Scandinavian ambassador who was staying at the hotel. She had been aware of her own awakening sensuality for some time, and it had all channelled itself into her feelings for Gideon; initially, with guarded looks, then days later came a shared swimming lesson, a walk, and happy laughter.

But on that same joyous afternoon she'd had to return to Brussels: her maternal grandfather, Jules Harley, had suffered a severe stroke, dying even as they were travelling the road to his bedside.

Two years earlier she had watched from a Leopold hotel window the state funeral of Queen Astrid who had been killed when the car driven by her husband the King had hit a tree, and she had been terribly emotional even though she had never known the Queen. When Grandfather Harley, a banker, died she felt ashamed that instead of feeling grief, her mind was preoccupied with thoughts of Gideon – the tears that flowed were not for grandfather, but for her lost love, as she sensed that they would not meet again . . .

By the summer of 1938 it became obvious that her mother Elizabeth was very ill, and as her condition worsened it was decided that with school-leaving exams coming up, Georgette should, for the time being, become a weekly boarder at her Roman Catholic school. Except in Maths, she passed well in all the subjects she had to take. Then, willingly she eventually became a full-time nurse to Elizabeth.

It was then that she became aware of Andre, son of the head porter at the hotel. She had always thought him very dashing in his smart blue page-boy uniform, he really stood out from the others with his fair hair and blue eyes. Now he was seventeen, a porter, and very handsome. When he joined the Army, Georgette thought she would never see him again, but he was posted to a regiment in Brussels and when he was home he came up to the flat at the hotel.

'I've called to see how your mother is,' he explained and Georgette could feel her heart beating as she looked at this attractive soldier. But her parents hadn't approved at all. This was not what they had in mind – a romance with the son of an employee. But gradually Andre's visits had become accepted and whenever they were alone together he gradually became more daring until one afternoon, he kissed her on the mouth. She revelled in his embrace and hoped it would go on for ever, he was arousing feelings that she could not explain . . . When he was posted away she thought her heart would break . . .

She remembered the ghastly weeks during which her mother's pain became unbearable – and the sense of blessed relief when finally, Elizabeth lay still.

After the trauma of nursing her mother, Henri arranged for Georgette to visit the Castel de Dinant for a change of scene. She enjoyed the beautiful scenery; and took to reading the newspapers and talking to anyone who was around. There was plenty to talk about. The year was 1940. Though as yet, Belgium was not, much of Europe was at war.

Belgium was neutral, and had been since the first hostilities began elsewhere, in 1936. In that year, with characteristic lightning speed, Chancellor Hitler sent troops to occupy a previously demilitarized zone of Germany, the Rhineland, making France's border vulnerable. The French Government believed that their reaction should be nothing short of mobilization, but an election was pending and they were afraid of losing power. They did nothing.

The following year, anxious to distance his country from the 'quarrels of its neighbours', a nervous King Leopold reneged on the French/Belgium Alliance his father Albert had signed in 1920. In his desire for Belgium to return to its pre-1914/18 War neutrality, he didn't care that his action made France's defensive Maginot line as good as useless.

Thus it was that, when the conflict between Germany and the Allies began, following Germany's invasion of Poland on 1st September 1939, Belgium was but an observer.

Friday 10 May 1940. Whitsun weekend. Georgette was staying with her paternal grandparents, Beatrice and Albert, who lived humbly on the southern outskirts of Brussels. Into the quiet of the early morning came a strange sound, the rac-a-tac-a-tac of a machine gun. They reached the window in time to see a Stuka 90 with enormous black crosses on its wings pass low overhead . . .

All she could think of was Andre, away at the front, in danger . . . She decided to return to the Leopold where she found her father facing the owner of the hotel group, M Dubois, and his wife, who

5

were about to leave Brussels and head for Spain. Georgette told her father that whatever he decided to do, she was staying where she was. 'It's like abandoning a sinking ship!' she said. 'I won't run away.' 'We stay,' her father said quietly to M Dubois.

The small convoy of hotel staff left without them. Over the next few hours the sound of bombardment could be heard in the distance. Georgette thought the matter was settled, but the following morning they were warned that as the Allies had been staying at the hotel the Germans would probably conclude that they had been helping them, in which case they would be shot.

'If you are in danger Papa, you must go,' she told him. He replied that he and two friends were going to try to reach England to fight the Germans from there, and an hour later he and his companions were ready to leave. Henri insisted that he and Georgette take their farewells inside the hotel, not come to the tram stop, by the Gare du Nord, so Georgette went to the roof of the hotel, able to see the tram leave from there. Then came the unexpected. Aimee Carbarat, the woman in charge of the vitrines at the hotel, appeared below and made straight for Henri.

Although she barely knew Aimee – she'd first seen her at the Vendôme in Paris – Georgette had never liked the woman. She had a good figure but there was something about her face. It reminded Georgette of a toad.

To Georgette's surprise and dismay, Aimee flung her arms about Henri and kissed like the lovers in the films Georgette had seen.

'It's disgusting – and I shall tell her so!' she decided, then changed her mind – she'd say nothing.

A tram trundled up and Henri and his companions scrambled aboard. As Aimee ran back to the Leopold in distress, Georgette watched the tram cross the bridge. No sooner had it done so than there was an almighty WHOOSH and the centre of the bridge disintegrated. She gazed at the devastation and felt a sense of pride: saboteurs had deliberately destroyed the bridge rather than allow the Germans a free passage into Brussels. At least someone was fighting back! She had begun to wonder whether the Belgians were courageous at all!

The next few days were spent in a fever of preparation for the coming German invasion. In the absence of her father, Georgette, though only eighteen, was the figurehead to which the staff turned; their decision-maker and protector. All the valuable paintings and carpets were taken down to the cellars, which were then bricked up. She gradually realized that the management had not abandoned the

Hotel from cowardice, but simply because they were Jews and could see what was coming.

While many people were fleeing the City, one evening saw soldiers returning by the train-load from the Eastern front. And although she had no formal training, Georgette found herself at the Gare du Nord helping hard-pressed doctors to care for the many wounded disgorged on to the platforms. Here it was that she recognized a friend of Andre's and the somehow remote happenings solidified into a dreadful personal grief when he told her that he had seen Andre killed. Her true first love. Dead. Gone for ever. Returning to the hotel she dissolved in a paroxysm of tears before she realized that she had a duty to perform – she must visit Andre's parents and commiserate with them . . .

They sat in their overcrowded parlour as Georgette listened to their reminiscences of Andre as a boy. They gave her a photograph taken in uniform. She had not appreciated just how handsome he was. His mother told her that he had confided in her that he was very much in love with Georgette but had been afraid of proposing because she was his boss's daughter. 'I would have married him,' Georgette responded firmly and meant it . . .

On 25 May Henri returned to the Leopold under cover of darkness. She was shocked at the sight of him – slim and tanned, clothes tattered yet retaining his natural elegance, she understood for the first time why her mother had married him. He told her that after a long, hot and tiring walk he and his companions had eventually reached Ostend only to find that the last boat had just sailed for England, and they had no alternative but to return to Brussels.

On 28 May, King Leopold commanded his forces to cease all resistance. Then he, himself, fled to Flanders, the Germanic area of Belgium, and thus into the protection of the enemy.

Shortly afterwards, returning home late one night, Georgette heard a regular sound. Blump! Blump! Blump! The noise grew louder, came closer and suddenly there was a dark green shape moving steadily towards her, like spreading lava. The Germans had arrived . . .

Chapter Two

The winter of 1940 was very cold and living in the spare room with Beatrice and Albert was spartan to say the least. But Georgette enjoyed staying with them, the Germans not wanting her living at the Leopold, now they'd taken it over. And Henri, who'd been retained to manage the hotel, would arrive for supper occasionally, bringing 'real' bread – with no sawdust in it! – about which no questions were asked. She had persuaded him to let her start at commercial college and found to her surprise that her earlier studies now stood her in good stead. She sailed through the finals and when she produced her certificates showing her pass grades, for the first time in her life, she found that she was really in her father's good books.

Although Henri was adamant that she would never work, the Germans played into her hands by declaring that all women in Belgium between the ages of eighteen and thirty-five excluding married women and those already working, had to sign on and could then be sent to factories anywhere in occupied Europe. It was the chance she needed.

'I must take work quickly, Papa. If I don't I could be sent to Silesia, or somewhere like that. Would you want that for me?' Naturally, Henri did not.

As one of the top students from the college, Georgette soon found a good post as a secretary to a managing director of a paint manufacturing company, in an office an easy tram ride away from home. In no time she found herself involved in a lively social set and found that she was particularly attracted to Maurice Le Blond, a Swiss/French lad, a year younger than Georgette but far more mature. Tall, blonde and good-looking, his blue eyes burned when he looked at her.

After a coffee with him one evening he suggested that she follow him upstairs, saying that he had a room above the cafe. She was too naive to see that the room could be used simply by having a quiet word with the barman . . .

She had always pretended that she had already had some sexual experiences and she somehow felt that this was not the moment to admit the truth. She had of course seen statues of naked men in galleries and museums, but, faced with the real thing, she was quite unprepared for the sight that now met her eyes . . . He led her gently to the bed and parted her legs – she had no time to say anything before he thrust upwards and she screamed with pain.

'Oh my God, what have I done?' he blurted out, and his eyes filled with compassion. 'I am so sorry, ma petite. I had no idea,' he said lovingly and held her close. 'You silly girl, why on earth didn't you tell me? Look, let's get dressed and we'll go and have another coffee.'

She was furious with herself that now he would no longer want anything to do with her, but as time passed she accepted that they were simply good friends. He suggested one evening that they go for a walk and by way of reparation he gently explained the facts of life to her so that she should never again be in such a situation through ignorance. On her part, she realized that he was a natural philanderer and that marriage had never entered his thoughts. Despite the turmoil in which she found herself, it was a happy time for her. She was doing a job, and doing it well. She had a father with whom for the first time in her life, she got on well; grandparents who loved her, and a good circle of friends. In fact, everything seemed set fair.

Then her boss retired, and the new managing director arrived.

Chapter Three

Gregoire Watneeteix and Georgette took one look at each other and fell in love. It was as simple as that. Or as complicated, depending how one looked at it. Gregoire was handsome, with a thatch of black hair and startling green eyes. He wore superbly cut suits which enhanced his trim figure. At forty-two, he had been head-hunted for the post of managing director. Two weeks after his arrival he decided that he needed his secretary's desk to be moved into his own office. The tongues started to wag.

Georgette was so much in love that she flew to work in the morning. The love light in her eyes was clear for all to see. She knew that he was married, and she could feel daggers in her back, but she didn't care. She could think of nothing but Gregoire. He tried to keep his distance, knowing the dangers of an office romance, but after some weeks of growing frustration he could stand it no longer.

'Georgette, I am going to take you to lunch tomorrow,' he announced, handing her a piece of paper on which he had written an address, and directions for getting there. 'You take the tram, I will go separately and meet there,' he said.

She never did remember what they ate at that first lunch together. But she never forgot the first time that he took her hand in both of his, turned it palm upwards, and gently and sensually kissed it. She had never felt such excitement in her entire life . . . Later, he told her that he and his wife were practically strangers now and that he intended to divorce her and make Georgette his 'little wife'. For the next two or three weeks, he wrote to her each day, tucking the letter in amongst papers he placed on her desk. She would reply in the same way, and writing to him became the most important part of her day.

Several weeks passed until Gregoire's usual letter was quite different. He told her that he must see her alone and was making arrangements to be out of town on the following Friday. He suggested that she pretended to have a cold so that by Friday she would need no excuse to stay away. They would meet at 'their' restaurant and have lunch first . . .

Sitting at her desk, she read the letter several times. She understood his intentions completely and she tried to grapple with her conscience, but before she could stop herself she looked up, and found his green eyes looking directly at her. She felt her knees go weak. 'I'll attend to the matter straight away,' she said cryptically, and within a few hours she started sniffling into her handkerchief . . .

Right from the start, she knew that this was to be an entirely new experience. The day was hot, and they didn't close the windows of the hotel room, nor did they draw the curtains. A slight breeze ruffled the trees outside and played gently through the room. He took her in his arms and kissed her face and neck repeatedly, murmuring endearments between each kiss. She was waiting for him to make straight for the bed, as had Maurice, but he began to unbutton her dress, his lips following his fingers, slowly stripping her, kissing every new inch of her body as the clothes fell away. She became aware that they were both naked and that he was holding her closely to him and that she found it entirely pleasurable. Slowly his experienced fingers aroused her.

He had known almost immediately that she was inexperienced, and he used all his skills to build her excitement. He wanted to set up house with her and knew that sex could be a powerful force on his side if he handled it well.

'This is marvellous, my darling. We won't go any further now. We'll leave that for the next time.' Immediately he felt the tension leave her, and knew he had made the right decision. 'Are you happy?' he asked her.

'I cannot believe that I feel such ecstasy! I never knew that such feelings existed!'

'Then live with me, Georgette. We would be so happy! I want you to become my wife, and have children by me. Please agree, Georgette – please . . .'

'But I . . .'

Another kiss and caress, and another, and another. She felt she was going out of her mind. She was moaning and writhing and it was all he could do to hold back, but he kept telling himself that self-restraint now would pay dividends in the long run.

Finally she gasped, 'All right Gregoire! All right! I'll do anything you say!'

He sighed with relief. After she had calmed down, he told her that he would start to look for a suitable flat, and that he realized she would need a few days to break the news gently to her grandparents. Georgette had no idea how she was going to broach the subject, but

11

she knew she could no longer live without him. As it happened, the solution was presented to her, in no uncertain terms, only two days later.

Returning from morning Mass, she sensed the atmosphere in the kitchen as soon as she entered. Henri was sitting at the table, in front of him the large brown envelope in which she kept all Gregoire's letters.

'What's all this about?' he demanded fiercely. Georgette guessed immediately that the only person who could have found the letters was her Aunt Pauline. Not an aunt at all really, but a relative of Beatrice's elder sister's late husband. But she'd had a rough time in 1940 in La Panne, and Beatrice had felt sorry for her and invited her to stay a while.

'How could you?' Georgette blazed. 'You dreadful woman!'

Pauline reacted by saying that she had acted in Georgette's best interests as she was still only a child.

'I am twenty years old!' Georgette shot back.

Henri interrupted. 'I take it that the Gregoire is Monsieur Watneeteix, your new managing director?'

'Yes, Papa.'

'You are a disgrace! You must be aware that he is a family man. What on earth do you think you are doing?'

'I love him, Papa,' she replied simply.

Henri snorted. 'I hardly think "love" is the right word! You are infatuated with him and he is no gentleman to take advantage of the fact.'

'That isn't true! He is sweet and kind and . . .'

'Georgette, you're a woman for lovers, no more that that,' Pauline interjected sniffily, and Henri was left in two minds to tell her to keep her tongue.

'Enough!' snapped her father. 'I have no intention of continuing this discussion. Georgette, you will immediately break off this relationship and hand in your notice. Or you will have no place here, under the roof of my parents.'

'Very well Papa. If that's what you want, I shall go. Should I leave right now?'

Chapter Four

Her removal transport was a rickety old cart hitched to a shire mare. Henri was not there to witness the scene. When he had arrived for lunch that dreadful day he had expected to hear that she had seen the error of her ways and was startled to find that she was still determined to disobey him.

Georgette had resigned from the office not only because most of the staff already realized what was going on but also because Gregoire had now found them a flat and had decided that he wanted her to be there when he came home from work. Over the last few days, whenever her resolution had begun to slip she had remembered that fantastic lunch hour, and the memory had warmed her and strengthened her resolve.

The flat was on the first floor. It had several rooms, reasonably sized, and also use of the cellar.

They settled down into life together, and with the help of a cook book and some personal tips from Madame Binet, their landlady, she quickly learned how to make good meals despite the wartime shortages. Gregoire handled their sex life together with great care, taking a whole week before he gently coaxed her to relax and to open her body to him, overcoming her fear and finally starting to enjoy their lovemaking.

A few days later Therese Distel called on Georgette. Therese was a cousin on her father's side but they had never been close and Georgette wondered why she came to call. The truth emerged very soon. Henri had sent her to ask for his wife's jewellery, which he regarded as his property. Georgette was deeply hurt. She adored her mother's jewels but reluctantly she handed over all the pieces that she knew did really belong to her father, trusting that he would look after them. She never saw any of it again and learned that he had had the gold melted down and made into a hideous modern engagement ring set with an enormous diamond bought from the proceeds of the remaining jewellery. The ring he gave to Aimee Carbarat on the morning of New Year's Day.

* * *

Shortly before her twenty-first birthday Georgette was paying Philippe Pillot, the local pharmacist a call when a small boy burst into the shop crying that his father had been arrested by the Germans. When the lad had gone, Philippe told her that the father was the man who helped him out by delivering prescriptions. Thinking of the many hours she spent alone at the flat, Georgette volunteered to take his place. To her surprise, Philippe seemed reluctant to accept her offer, and it slowly dawned on her that the job was not as simple as merely delivering prescriptions. She pressed him gently, and he admitted that it did sometimes include delivering packages to the Resistance, and that it could be dangerous. The thought of being of help to her beloved country thrilled Georgette. From then on she called at the pharmacy at some time every weekday – she could not manage weekends without Gregoire knowing and Philippe made her swear that she would tell no one, not even her 'husband'.

Christmas 1942 was the happiest Georgette could remember. Gregoire spent the whole period with her. It was very cold outside but they were warm, really warm. Black Market coal blazed in the grate while they ate Black Market sardines and potatoes for lunch, followed by a few silver-wrapped chocolates, washed down with a bottle of champagne. That evening, they made love in front of the fire no less than three times. By the New Year, every day was like a sexual layer cake – sex before and after breakfast, sex before and after lunch, sex before and at least twice after the evening meal. Gregoire might have been in his early forties, but he had a terrific libido. And none of their enjoyment was limited by precautions.

All that was expected of Georgette she did, with great happiness. She cooked for him, cleaned for him, made love with him and, once or twice a week, went out for a meal with him. She thought it all idyllic and it never occurred to her that anything would change.

One day in March Gregoire arrived home with a present: a long-haired russet-brown Belgian Papillon, a breed named for its butterfly wing ears. A very elegant and affectionate lap-dog which she adored at first sight.

'I shall call her Lina.'

'Actually, it's not a bitch!'

Georgette giggled. 'I'll still call him Lina! What made you buy such a wonderful present?'

He ran his hand over his lips before replying. 'I thought the pup would be good company for you,' he said.

The following day when she returned to the flat from her errands for the pharmacy she had to face that in her absence, her world had been turned upside down.

On the mantelpiece was a letter from Gregoire.

'My darling little wife,
Forgive me, my dearest. It is with sadness that I have to return to my wife and son. The pressures on me to do so have become too great. My job was to be taken from me on the grounds that our relationship was affecting my attitude to my work. And without an income I would not be able to live, far less support you.
Enclosed are the laundry and dry-cleaning tickets for your things and some money to help you over the next few weeks. Be brave, my darling! I have to leave the nest for both our sakes, but my heart remains forever on the pillow of our love. God bless and keep you. I will love you always.

Your Gregoire.'

Georgette was stunned. For a long time she could only stare unseeingly out of the window, lost in her shattered world and bitter reflections. The Papillon sensed that something was wrong and rubbed his tiny body against her legs, whimpering for attention. She bent down and picked him up, cuddling him in her arms while the puppy licked the salty tears from her face . . .

She spent the next couple of days considering her future. She had no money apart from the few francs Gregoire had left her. Where could she go? She hated the thought of crawling to her father, and in desperation she decided to call on Therese, even though they were not really friendly.

Therese was not sympathetic. 'It was bound to happen – we all knew that,' she said. 'But I suppose you had better move in with me for a week or two until you get a job and a flat of your own.'

'May I bring my dog?' asked Georgette. And that was the end of that suggestion, because Therese's landlord had a 'No Pets' ban, though Therese said there was a large attic in which Georgette could temporarily store her things.

One of the consequences of the Allied bombing was that many people had moved out of town into the country, and Georgette found that actually there was no shortage of furnished flats to let in the centre of Brussels. When she went in to see one of them she took Lina with her, leaving him tied to a post in the street while she called in to a grocery shop on the way. To her horror when she emerged, he was gone, and though she searched for more than an hour she had to admit that he had been stolen – probably for meat in these days of food shortages. He had been a comforting companion over the past few days but although she grieved for him she had to admit that, in reality, his disappearance added little to the already overcrowded catalogue of her miseries.

Once again she visited Therese with the sad news, but the reaction was practical. 'At least you can now move in here,' said Therese.

The old boy with the horse and cart transported Georgette's possessions the few miles to the new address, but this time his passenger had no joy in her heart and was as taciturn as he.

The next step was to find a job, and Philippe Pillot told her that a dentist friend of his was looking for a temporary dental nurse to help in his surgery. He said he would see what he could do, though privately he thought that with Georgette's looks she would stand a very good chance . . .

Claude Badin was fleshy. His stomach tipped disturbingly over the black leather belt at his waist as he came towards Georgette, his head nodding from side to side. His tight black hair was combed forward, to hide a receding hairline. One look at Georgette and the job was hers. He issued her with a smart white coat and a pretty little white cap. Although the receptionist was an attractive girl, she looked plain beside Georgette. Claude was delighted to find that she was clever as well as pretty, and she soon learned the job far in advance of his expectations.

After a few weeks Claude suggested that he might take Georgette to dinner? Over the following month it became common practice for him to take her to fine restaurants where they ate well, showing the power of real money on the Black Market.

Inevitably came the night when he took her back to his luxurious flat above the surgery. He poured glasses of red wine for them both and in her intoxicated state she found his kissing and cuddling quite pleasant . . .

Living with Therese seemed to work out well and by mutual consent there was no further talk of looking for lodgings.

Chapter Five

June 1944 and the atmosphere in Brussels was euphoric. The Allied Forces had landed on the beaches of Normandy and people felt that their longed-for freedom was soon to become a reality. The Resistance were in a frenzy and Georgette was spending more of her spare time each day doing courier work for Phillipe. She did not care for the consequences, but was proud to be associated with such people, in however small a way.

She learned from her grandparents that her father had married Aimee on 8 June and although she felt rejected and wondered if the breach between them could ever now be healed, she was pleased for her father despite her dislike of Aimee.

Engrossed with this news she was unaware of the air raid warning and, immersed in misery, she was only vaguely aware of the drone of bombers overhead and the sound of German ack-ack guns on the roof of a nearby building retaliating, until she felt something thump into her chest, the impact propelling her backwards. Pain hit her, and she passed out. When she opened her eyes she saw Phillipe, standing in a crowd who had gathered around. He looked at her dress, drenched with blood, and fought his way to her, helping her to her feet and half carrying her to his flat over the shop. He sent for Yves Serret, a retired doctor who was these days in much demand. He told her that a piece of shrapnel, most certainly from the German guns, had hit her sternum, luckily missing her heart, leaving a wound that would require a few stitches but no permanent damage. Phillipe insisted that she stayed in his spare room until the stitches were removed and she had recovered. He held up the piece of metal. 'Do you want to keep this, or shall I throw it away?' he asked.

'I want to keep it – that's a souvenir!' she replied.

During the next few days a stranger with an unmistakable air of authority called to see Phillipe. Phillipe would tell her nothing about him until a day later, when he produced a single sheet of paper. 'Do you know anyone on this list?' he asked.

One name was familiar. 'Cecil Merlier!' she replied. 'He was a friend of my mother's. I stayed with him when I was small but the last time I saw him was at Maman's funeral. He's a builder and lives in a village called Vierre, near Tournivel.'

'Why don't you go and stay with him for a while to recuperate from the shock of your injuries?'

'Are you serious, Phillipe? I don't know him well.'

'Deadly serious – and I mean that literally, Georgette. He's a collaborator and we need to know about his dealings with the Germans. You are in an ideal position to get information for us. Will you do it?'

She was thrilled. She was actually being asked to be a spy!

'Of course! Shall I ring him now? Give me the phone number . . .'

The midday sun was scorching as Georgette came out of the station at Tournivel. Monsieur Merlier drove into the yard in his large grey Citroen. He looked healthy and well fed. 'Good journey, Georgette?' he asked.

'Surprisingly uneventful Monsieur, though rather tiring.'

'Call me Cecil, please.'

As she bent to pick up her suitcase he noticed that she winced and asked if she was all right? She explained what had happened, omitting only that she had stayed with Phillipe.

'Good lord! No wonder you need a break,' he said as he helped her into the car.

The childless Merliers were living in clover and didn't know the meaning of 'shortages'. He was clearly 'Number One' in the district and proud of it. He showed her plans of buildings he had erected for the Germans, boasting that some of them were military installations, and she fumed inwardly but showed no trace of her real feelings.

She stayed for a month, finding it increasingly difficult to conceal her distaste for both Cecil and his wife and hating to feel indebted to them, especially as they were very kind to her. She gathered information, storing it in her head and by the time she left, in late July felt she had significant news for Philippe. When she returned to Brussels Phillipe was delighted with her report.

'Well done, Georgette! Our saboteurs will be able to destroy some of the Germans' key installations and, when the war ends we'll get Merlier himself!' He put a friendly arm around her shoulders. 'There's more good news,' he said. 'Your father wants to see you.'

She was startled, but couldn't wait to get to the Leopold, where Edouard who was at the porter's desk beamed with delight. She was shown to her father's office and guffaws of laughter could be heard as the door opened and two German officers came out and strode off down the corridor.

'What was that about?' she asked.

'Oh, some joke about a Jew,' replied Henri. 'But things are going badly for them now and soon the joke will be on them. Sit down, Georgette.'

A little awkward to begin with, their conversation eased and Henri said that he was sorry she had not been asked to the wedding. 'It was childish of me. I wanted you to be there, but I didn't think you would come.' Georgette found his sincerity rather surprising, but a small glow of joy invaded her . . .

Chapter Six

At seven a.m. on 3 September 1944 Georgette rose early; the sky was promising a beautiful day. She was now without a job – Claude's qualified aide had replaced her and she had not minded one bit! A neighbour came to say that the enormous Law Courts building was ablaze and had been burning right through the night. Georgette rushed there – it was an appalling sight for the many Belgians who had gathered to watch. Some time that afternoon the dome caved in and Georgette unashamedly joined many others in tears.

Then someone shouted 'The Allies are coming!' Liberation was nigh. 'The British are coming! Oh, isn't this marvellous!'

Instead of a sea of green, as in 1940, there was now a sea of khaki and an escort of powerful British tanks . . .

During that exciting night Georgette made a new friend of about her own age, Monique Fourmeaux, a cabaret artiste until the German invasion had halted her career.

The day after Liberation, Monique took Georgette to a cellar club where people sang their own songs and recited poetry. She loved the atmosphere and commented 'I wouldn't mind being on the stage.'

'Seriously?' responded Monique. Georgette nodded vigorously. She was attracted to the theatre by its glamour and the desire to be admired and envied, to be the centre of attraction.

She could have continued to live with Therese but felt that it was time to move on. Returning to the Leopold was not viable because of Aimee, and she could not return to her grandparents' house because she had simply outgrown the luxury of their loving arms.

The solution was suggested by Monique. Why not move in with her mother and herself? They had a large basement flat, and although they had only met a couple of days earlier, they both felt as though they had been friends for years.

Once more the man with the horse and cart was summoned and, with great enthusiasm, Georgette loaded up her chattels for the move.

A day later Monique returned to the flat bubbling with good news. Not only was she to compere a Stars in Battledress show, she also had a singing spot in it. As if that weren't enough, she had an invitation for all three of them to go to a party held by some RAF officers at their hotel, that night.

The three women turned heads when they arrived at the RAF party. Georgette wore emerald green with her brown hair tumbled around her shoulders. Monique and her mother wore red, that accentuated Monique's long, shining black hair and her mother's equally attractive silver locks. Long hair was a symbol of pride nowadays: proof that one hadn't been a collaborator . . .

Georgette sat at a table surrounded by a group of young officers who were very attentive to her, buying her drinks and asking a lot of questions about how she had fared in the war. One officer in particular attracted her eye, a squadron leader; a young, lean, good-looking Australian called Simon Tait. At her request most of their conversation was in English and she was enjoying the practise. Then a sandy-haired officer with broad shoulders and four blue and white bars on his epaulettes came over, a wide smile directed at her. Group Captain Ralph Rusby accepted authority with consummate ease. He smiled at his subordinates, then offered Georgette his hand. 'I'm delighted to meet you, Mademoiselle Delire.'

Georgette blushed. 'You know my name?'

'I asked about you.'

He went on to tell her that he had learned to fly before the war, in the volunteer Reserve, but that he was too old to be a fighter pilot now, at thirty-eight. He also told her that he had heard she had worked for the Resistance. She replied that she hadn't really done very much, appreciating at the same time that her inflection implied the opposite, which alarmed her slightly.

He suggested that she might let him escort her for the next few evenings, and since, with the exception of a dalliance with Claude, she had not dated anyone since Gregoire had left her, her confidence needed a boost, she thought that an innocent flirtation with this pleasant man could do no harm.

From the first, Ralph was more attentive to Georgette than to his other guests. He had sent his driver to fetch her and Monique from their flat to drive them to whichever night club was that evening's rendezvous. On both evenings he arranged a table for two slightly away from the main group. He presented her with a corsage, but behaved like a perfect gentleman and as soon as she realized that she was not being pressurised to go to bed with him, Georgette relaxed and enjoyed his company.

Ralph showed her photographs of his two children, but when she referred to him looking forward to living them again he frowned and said that was not at all certain, as he and his wife had divorced just before the war. He offered no further explanation as to why they had divorced, and she did not ask.

The ENSA show was a great success. Ralph had hoped that Georgette would accompany him, but Monique had asked her to help her backstage with dress changes and pronunciation of the English cards which described the different acts. He therefore took Madam Fourmeaux, which delighted her!

One particular artiste attracted Georgette's attention, a tall, dark-haired Londoner named Colin Brian, who played trumpet and clarinet with an amazing range. She was bowled over by him, and she certainly caught his eye! When after the show, there was a party for the performers at their hotel, he invited her. She was given a large gin, which she downed quickly and found it tasted better than it smelled, so she accepted another, and another after that. By the time people began to leave, Georgette felt more than a little confused, and when Colin proposed that they should go to his room, swept along on the magic of the evening, she agreed. Through the alcoholic haze which surrounded her, she was only vaguely aware that they were making love . . .

Ralph was dominating Georgette's life. Lunching at his hotel became a routine. He was thinking of becoming a freelance journalist in peace-time and was proposing to write a book about wartime in occupied Europe, he told her. Daily she provided him with details and in return, he gave her flowers, chocolates and cigarettes – for she was now smoking. Then, towards the end of September, something didn't happen for Georgette when it should have done – her period was late. She knew immediately that something was wrong. The days went by with no sign. She became sure that the unthinkable had happened and that she was pregnant. After the kind of sex-life she had enjoyed with Gregoire without taking any precautions at all, she found it difficult to believe that just one night with Colin Brian could turn out like this! He had made no secret of the fact that he was married, so there seemed little point in trying to contact him now that the show had moved on. She knew vaguely that it was possible to get rid of unwanted babies, but she had no idea of how to go about it. And in any case, she didn't like the idea. But, the disgrace! Who could she tell? Certainly not her father! Nor Therese.

'I'm going to have to get married,' she confided to Monique.

'Well, Ralph's the obvious candidate,' said Monique without

hesitation. 'You could do a lot worse. He's unattached, he must be comfortably off, and he's dotty about you. Why not encourage him a bit and see what happens?'

Ralph had already brought up the subject of marriage once before, and she didn't think it would be too difficult to get him to do so again.

'I know what I'm planning is not very nice,' she said guiltily to Monique, 'but Ralph obviously misses being married so, in a way, I'll be doing him a favour, won't I?'

Monique felt this piece of self-justification needed no answer.

It was not at all difficult. Georgette confided in Ralph her worries about her future in Belgium. He took the bait without a second's hesitation. 'My darling, if you are so worried about the future, why not come back with me to England when peace comes?'

'My father would not approve of such an arrangement,' she replied after a long silence.

'Oh my dear girl – you misunderstand! I want you to be my wife!' he exclaimed. There was love light in his eyes, and sincerity in his voice. Georgette could sense the tenderness in him and, for a few moments, she forgot all about the baby and loved him back.

'I will marry you, Ralph, and I'll try to make you happy!'

Now that she was committed, Georgette wasted no time. The next day she took a delighted Ralph to meet her father. Henri greeted the news with enthusiasm – a high ranking British officer was willing to take *his* daughter's hand!

They arranged to be married almost immediately, before Ralph's imminent move to Paris to be nearer to SHAEF, which suited Georgette admirably...

They were married on 1 October, with only some of Ralph's RAF colleagues and Georgette's small circle of friends as their guests. Squadron Leader Tait was best man.

That night they slept together in the Leopold's newly refurbished bridal suite. Although Ralph had been working under stress for so long and was absolutely exhausted, his beautiful young bride was resolute that the marriage should be consummated without delay, and finally they achieved their objective and she was able to relax...

The following day, Ralph left for Paris and Georgette returned to the Fourmeaux's flat to wait until he should send for her.

Nearing the end of October Georgette set off to join her husband at the requisitioned hotel, on the Avenue de l'Opera; keen to see Paris, though she knew its atmosphere sadly would not be as she remembered from childhood.

Ralph's tired eyes lit up at the sight of his beautiful young bride as she entered the hotel foyer. 'You've made it in time for lunch, thank heavens! I'm afraid I must go back to work afterwards but Corporal Daniels will drive you to the quarters I've chosen – I hope you'll like it there.'

Ralph's billet was in a beautiful Napoleonic house no great distance from the Charlton. The Duviviers, the French family to whom it belonged made Georgette extremely welcome and a routine quickly became established whereby Ralph would return home – often at midnight – while Georgette amused herself in their quaint accommodation and made friends with the family, especially the older son Boma Duvivier an artistic homosexual, apart from the occasional lunch times when she was able to join Ralph. It suited her admirably and by early November she knew that it was safe to tell him that he was to be a father. He was cock-a-hoop and called for champagne all round that lunch-time. Shortly before Christmas, Ralph decided that it would be best if Georgette returned to Brussels. V1 and V2 flying bombs were being launched from the north-east of Belgium, still a German stronghold.

'I think it would be best, my love,' he told her. 'I'm going to be around even less from now on and after tonight I have to sleep at HQ.'

'Very well, dear, if that's what you want. When shall I leave?'

'Tomorrow. Simon Tait is going there on leave and will pick you up in the early afternoon.'

She was secretly delighted that she would be home for Christmas. She could hardly wait for the next day, and to see her family and friends again.

Aimee's reception was very cordial, but Georgette felt an underlying resentment and was sure that her stepmother was putting on an act. How different the hotel looked now that the Germans had gone!

The highlight of Christmas was the arrival, with Daniels carrying it, of a large box from Ralph containing her Christmas present – a beautiful fur coat. It looked magnificent on her, and she gloated in Aimee's look of pure jealousy . . .

Chapter Seven

In the early days of 1945 Field Marshal von Rundstedt advanced so far that his forces effectively separated Belgium from France. Georgette asked Ralph if she could return to Paris, but he said that was quite out of the question.

'But I miss you, darling! What shall I do until you get here?'

'I miss you too! Terribly! But please stay in Brussels. If you're not happy at the Leopold, get yourself a flat and I'll arrange with HQ to pay for it. You'll be safe there. It won't be for long.'

That couldn't have suited Georgette better. She found a small neatly furnished apartment in the centre of the city. She felt in clover.

It was April when Ralph told her that SHAEF HQ was leaving Paris. 'We're off to Germany sweetheart, but don't worry about me – take care of yourself and the baby, darling!'

On 30 April 1945, Adolf Hitler, that evil genius of the Third Reich, committed suicide. Everyone knew that that meant the end of the war in Europe was in sight at last, and on 8 May the proclamation was made.

It was late that evening when the telephone sounded. It was Ralph. 'Darling, we're on our way to England!' he proclaimed jubilantly. 'So telephone whoever you need because I'm afraid you won't have time before we go to see anyone in person. I shall be picking you up tomorrow at eight-thirty a.m. Can you be packed and ready by then?'

'Of course darling! But I'm so excited I won't be able to sleep a wink tonight!'

Ralph arrived almost to the minute of his e.t.a., spick and span and more relaxed than Georgette had ever seen him. With his gold-braided peaked cap tilted slightly forward and his medal ribbons on his chest, he looked every inch a hero. Georgette almost fell into his arms, she was so pleased to see him, suddenly happy that she was this man's wife.

The 'plane that was to carry them to England was a small Oxford, old and rickety-looking. 'Will it get us there in one piece!' she asked him nervously.

'Why not ask the pilot, darling?' She turned round and there, climbing from the object of her distress to make exterior flight checks was the familiar face of Simon Tait.

'As I'm coming with you, it had better!' he quipped.

As, from the Oxford's cockpit, she watched the white cliffs of Dover approach a range of emotions surged through Georgette that she could not begin to analyse, and she found tears streaming down her cheeks.

'I never thought it would upset you so much to leave Belgium, dearest,' Ralph said, concerned.

'You don't understand, Ralph. They're not tears of regret. I was just wondering how on earth the Germans failed to get there – here. How did you ever get saved from Occupation? The journey is so very short!'

Ralph reflected a moment, then said laconically, 'They made mistakes.'

PART TWO

Georgette – The Middle Years
May 1945 – April 1955

Chapter Eight

London was everything Georgette had ever imagined. The Houses of Parliament, the Tower of Big Ben, Buckingham Palace, even bomb-battered still held their heads proud. But the moment she really fell in love with it was when she and Ralph walked into the Bond Street Tea-Rooms. She was captivated; it was so refined, so very English! They ate delightful, thinly cut cucumber sandwiches, served by waitresses in beige dresses wearing little hats, and aprons edged with lace. They looked like lovely little parlour maids as they glided amongst the wicker tables.

Now eight months pregnant, Georgette discussed with Ralph names for their soon-to-be child. They decided on David Henri – David was Ralph's choice and Henri because Georgette wanted her father to be included. If it was a girl, it would be Barbara Elizabeth, one name from each of their mothers.

After only a few hours in England, she felt safe and she knew that the awful years in Belgium would have no counterpart in this, her new country. She would always think that the English were just wonderful, even when they were soon to vote Churchill out of power in a General Election. How could they, she wondered, when he had been their wartime leader? She didn't understand it at all.

The first cloud on their horizon came next morning when, with Danny at the wheel, she and Ralph left London behind them and Ralph was explaining to her that Kent was called 'The Garden of England'. He pointed out hop fields, orchards of fruit trees, corn fields, animals grazing, the roads becoming narrower with banks and hedges bordering them.

Ralph told her that a great friend of his who was killed in the Western Desert in 1942 had lived here, and they were going to visit the fellow's parents for a couple of days and look for temporary accommodation while they found a house to buy. Georgette was not at all pleased at the prospect. She was a townie! Horrified at the thought of being buried in the country! But she decided to say nothing for the time being, after all, he was going back to Germany soon.

Dennis and May Hammond were warm, friendly people and she

liked them immediately. After a more than adequate luncheon the men left to play a round of golf and Georgette and May cleared up the kitchen and then settled down to get to know each other over a very English pot of tea. May told Georgette that her son David and Ralph had been inseparable friends and Georgette realized why Ralph had chosen that name for their child. May also told her much about Ralph that Georgette had not appreciated – how he had felt rejected by his first wife Stella, and how he desperately wanted to become a novelist but felt rejected in that direction also, and how she had left him with her two children to live with an under-writer in Surrey. While May was telling her all this, and especially a comment that Stella had married Ralph on the rebound Georgette reflected guiltily that she had married him for an even worse reason . . .

They found a flat above a grocery-cum-everything shop in a village called Baterford St. Mary. Mr and Mrs Miles, the owners, were used to holiday letting, and they clearly liked the idea of having the wife of an RAF officer staying in one of their properties. Weeping willows adorned the village green, and Georgette put her doubts on one side as they inspected the flat. It had both a telephone and a radio and was bright and comfortable. Over a drink in the local hostelry the business arrangements were made and Georgette moved into her new flat the following Saturday, the day Ralph started his journey back to Germany . . .

During the week following Georgette decided that life in England did, indeed have much to recommend it, notably the pleasant people and the excellent food. Admittedly it was still rationed, but she didn't get a kick in the shins while she queued, something that had happened to her on occasion in Belgium and France. She found that small treats often found their way into her shopping basket and thought how kind it was of people to spoil her because she was pregnant. She didn't know that May had let it be known that Georgette was a Belgian Resistance heroine who had been wounded . . .

But all that aside, she was soon bored. Life in the country was so dull. Even when Ralph came over on leave and found particulars of houses for sale she could raise little enthusiasm, since they were all in the country. One of the things they sorted out was a doctor for Georgette's confinement, and he recommended a nursing home as it was her first child. When on the afternoon of 27 June she started in labour, the doctor arrived in person to drive her to the large grey mansion that housed the nursing home. Everyone but her, of course, thought it had arrived early, but not so early that suspicion was aroused . . . The birth was straightforward, a beautiful boy child, and Georgette loved all 5lb 7oz of him. Ralph flew in from Germany the next morning to see his wife and newest son.

Ten days later when Ralph and Dennis Hammond arrived to take them home, Georgette was surprised when at the village green, the car swung off to the right instead of left towards the flat. Georgette's heart sank as they travelled deeper into the countryside, seemingly into the middle of nowhere. 'Where are we going?' she asked. 'It's a surprise!' replied Ralph. But she had guessed – it was to their new home. This was to be life in the wilderness, indeed . . .

'Here we are, one and all!' proclaimed Dennis as he slowed the car. He turned into the drive of a large house, with a garage attached. Chimneys sprouted from a succession of tiled roofs. The brickwork was mellow with age and she commented that it must be very old. 'Some three hundred years, darling,' said Ralph. The gardens were lined with herbaceous borders along a path leading to the solid oak front door. 'Now darling, hand little David over to Dennis for a moment. I want to carry you over the threshold!' which he did, to squeals of laughter.

Ralph spent the next week mowing lawns, trimming hedges and organizing deliveries of coal, but all too soon he had to return to Germany, saying he would be back in a month's time for David's christening.

The nursing home had recommended a middle-aged midwife called Emily Enley. She wore a black raincoat and nanny's hat all the time during her daily visits. Wispy white hair trailed from under the hat and she rushed everywhere in a tiny Austin car. She led Georgette gently into the ways of motherhood, and her visits saved the day both for little David and for Georgette.

After three weeks, Emily asked Georgette if she thought she could cope with little David on her own now? 'Oh yes,' answered Georgette.

'Good. Then I won't need to come again.'

Georgette was saddened, although she had spoken nothing less than the truth, but after Emily's departure, loneliness grew in her, particularly at night, when she desperately missed conversation and had to be content with either a book or the radio.

'What a dreadful penance I'm having to pay for making Ralph marry me and become the father of a child who is not his!' she concluded, and for the first time she felt truly ashamed of her conduct. She made up her mind not to complain to Ralph, or anyone else, and in fact she made a good job of that pretence when he came home for the christening. Ralph's parents, elderly but very distinguished looking, and May and Dennis Hammond, were the baby's godparents and Georgette not only liked her in-law parents but felt that they also approved of her. And Ralph's youngsters, Dougie and Helen, seemed to approve of her too, enough to want to stay a week with her later that month, at Ralph's suggestion.

When their visitors had gone, Ralph dropped a bombshell. 'Georgette, I have to tell you something. I'm staying on with the RAF for another three years.'

'Ralph, how could you?' she exclaimed.

Ralph ignored her and went on. 'They've asked me to and as I see it, it is in our best interests. Three years is not a lifetime, after all.'

No, thought Georgette. Not for you, stuck in the middle of nowhere, isolated from everyone.

Ralph felt guilty. He knew he should have consulted her, but he also had known that she would oppose his plans.

Georgette realized that she had been presented with a fait accompli. She raised her glass. 'May the three years pass very quickly, Ralph.'

Three days later, 15 August 1945 saw the end of hostilities in the Far East. Celebrations were not on the scale of VE day a few months before, but there was a general feeling of relief that peace had finally arrived.

One Friday in late September, just as Georgette felt she would go mad if she were alone for another twenty-four hours, the phone rang and to her surprise and delight, it was Simon Tait. He said he had been posted to London and was inviting himself for the weekend. He said that Ralph had said he trusted him, and Georgette said she was delighted.

He drove down in a three-seater Sprite sports car, with the hood down. He tidied the garden and generally made himself at home and she realized how much she enjoyed seeing him around the house. On his third consecutive weekend visit she knew that she wanted him, and she made it obvious.

'I won't make love with you, Georgette,' he told her gently, though he wanted to, dammit! Thanks to her allure, he had himself a full erection now, if she did but know it. 'So stop that! Ralph's a friend of mine.'

She accepted his rebuff, even respected him for it, but that afternoon, lunch cleared away and David asleep in his cot, suddenly, surprising even herself, she burst into tears, a release of the frustrations and loneliness of the past months which had built up inside her. Simon pulled her to her feet, and hugged her close until her sobs quietened.

'Oh Simon, what am I to do? I'm so unhappy. I feel as though I'm living in the middle of the Sahara! All my life I've been at the centre of things and I want to be where it's all happening. I can put up with Ralph being away for another three years, but not here!'

'I should have guessed,' he said thoughtfully. 'Friend or not, I think Ralph's behaving badly. Georgette, leave this with me. Ralph told me to look after you and I intend to do just that, so keep your chin up. I think I might have a way out for you.'

Simon's flat was in Grayson Mansions, off London's Victoria Street. Strictly speaking its lease belonged to his parents, who lived in Australia. His neighbour, Martha Cremorne, mentioned that she was thinking of letting out a room and Simon immediately thought of Georgette. There was of course, a snag. Mrs Cremorne was not keen on babies, but suggested that he might be put in a nursery. At first appalled, Georgette talked it over with Simon and gradually it started to seem a good idea. She would be able to work and the money would pay for a really first class nursery. May looked after David while she travelled to London to look at possibilities – Mrs Cremorne recommended an agency in Oxford Street and Georgette made that her first stop. Accompanied by a member of the agency staff, she went to inspect a nursery in a large Victorian house in Beckenham. It was spotlessly clean and bright and the Matron and her staff were warm and friendly. This was just the right home for her darling David, she concluded.

Three days later Simon drove Georgette and David to Beckenham. She felt the wrench of parting with him dreadfully and deep down she felt that she was abandoning him. But she would visit him every weekend, and she would keep her sanity. If Ralph didn't approve, that was just too bad! She had written to him with her new address but as yet had heard nothing from him.

As she locked up Ralph's house and handed the keys to Dennis and May, she felt as though a heavy burden had been lifted from her shoulders.

Georgette was offered a temporary job at the Belgian Embassy but after only two weeks they suggested that she come on the permanent staff. She was exhilarated by the linguistic demands made on her as well as enjoying the company of the other staff, and of her diplomat boss. Each Saturday she spent with David, catering for all his needs until evening when it was time to take the train back to Charing Cross where Simon would meet her and take her either to a theatre, a cinema or a smart restaurant.

Ralph's RAF allowance, combined with her own salary, proved more than enough to cover her expenses and she became very contented with her lifestyle. The only cloud on the horizon was Ralph's continuing silence but she assumed he was simply sulking . . .

That Christmas, Henri sent an air ticket for Georgette to spend the holiday with him at the Leopold. Their visit was a great success and Henri simply adored his little grandson. The charming baby even won the affections of Aimee, and they were all delighted that she was so happy in her adopted England. Not one person asked after Ralph, and Georgette knew they must be aware there was a problem but she didn't feel able to discuss it with her father.

Not long into the New Year, Georgette began to realize that her landlady was getting more and more difficult. There was no trace of the pleasant woman she had once seemed to be, and Georgette didn't see that the root of the problem was jealousy, both of her lifestyle and of her friendship with Simon. He had taken Martha out a couple of times, and his 'Happy New Year' kiss had been seen as more than just that . . .

Arriving home one evening Georgette picked up a letter in the hall and knew it was from Ralph. She felt in turmoil, and put off opening it for as long as she could, wanting to read it and not wanting to know what he said. Simon called in and greeted her with a friendly kiss, wanting to talk to her about his more than usually harassing day at the Air Ministry, but he broke off as he looked at her face, and at the letter she was clutching.

'What's that?' he asked.

'A letter from Ralph, I think,' she said, starting to open it. As she read it, Simon watched the colour drain from her face.

'Strewth, Georgette! What's the matter?'

Silently, she handed him the letter. He read it through and looked at her with a shocked expression. 'I wish we were having an affair!' he said vehemently. 'Ralph asked me to keep an eye on you and that's all I've done! I know who's behind this!' he added fiercely. 'Martha Cremorne, it has to be!'

'Do you really think she wrote to Ralph? How would she have known where he was?' Georgette said, still appalled by the contents of the letter. Simon told her that c/o The Air Ministry would have found Ralph, and that he had been aware for some time that Martha was seeing more into their relationship than he had intended. He was convinced she was behind this. Georgette said that she couldn't possibly stay on in the mansion apartment and started to pack her things. She could afford to stay in a hotel for a day or two while she found new lodgings.

She had finished packing and Simon picked up her suitcase, but as they closed the door on the flat Martha Cremorne was coming along the carpeted corridor. Simon blazed at her and it was quite obvious that she knew exactly why Georgette was leaving. Georgette's emotions were frozen. Thanks to this woman, Ralph was asking for a divorce. What would happen now?

There was a good atmosphere about Sandings. It was homely, quiet, clean and very respectable hotel. Georgette had taken a small room with a metered gas fire.

The manager recommended a solicitor who was a friend of his, a Mr Halin, of Holroyd and Dillon.

He listened impassively. Finally he said, 'You want to contest, Mrs Rusby, I take it?'

'I certainly do. I am innocent and I don't want a divorce if that means I would risk losing my child.'

'Oh that's not likely. The mother almost always gets custody you know. You say adultery has not taken place and I cannot see how he could prove you to be lying.'

'He can't, because I'm not lying!' she said indignantly.

'Quite.' He said it as though it mattered not a jot to him whether she was or not, if it couldn't be proved.

When the case came to court some months later, Mr Halin dissuaded her from attending, saying that he felt her 'voluptuousness' would make it difficult for the judge to believe in her innocence. She twigged that he was stating his own belief, but she had left it too late now to find someone else and reluctantly she followed his advice. She missed Simon Tait, who had left the Air Force and gone back to Australia to help with the family's catering business when his father had had a slight stroke a few weeks earlier. Mr Halin had not thought it necessary to recall him.

She waited on tenterhooks all morning, unable to think of anything other than what might be happening in court. When she reached the solicitor's office her worst fears were realized. Ralph had been granted both the divorce, and custody of David. It was clear that Halin had totally failed to anticipate the case that would be brought against her. Much had been made of the war hero still serving his country abroad, who had foolishly trusted his best friend, a colonial (therefore uncivilised) with his wife (a foreigner, therefore untrustworthy) and had been rewarded by his son being dumped in a home so that they could be free to satisfy their base desires. Clearly the woman was totally unsuited to be a mother. Mrs Cremorne had even testified that when she had returned unexpectedly to the flat she had found Simon and Georgette together, naked, on Georgette's bed. This could not be challenged since the defendant was not present.

How could she have been so stupid? Would David never again lie in her arms?

She walked back to Sandings, blinded with tears, her brain numb with disbelief. She got there in a daze, let herself into her room and collapsed in a sobbing heap on the bed. For the first time she wondered if there was some other woman in Ralph's life.

Months later, she was to learn that this suspicion was correct. Word reached her through the grapevine, that Ralph was to re-marry and the woman was Thelma Wallington, who had been his secretary since he first went to Germany. 'Well, there you are then,' she murmured resignedly when she heard the news.

The following day, feeling completely washed out, she took the train to Beckenham, every mile in torment that the baby might already have gone. But when she arrived the Matron greeted her as warmly as ever and over a cup of tea Georgette told her what had happened. 'What can I do?' she asked. 'I want to do what is best for David, but I don't know if I'm even supposed to see him, let alone what's going to happen in the future.'

The Matron looked at her with compassion. She gently told Georgette that in her opinion if Ralph re-married it was more than likely that his new wife would wish to bring David up as their own child. 'It is terribly confusing for a small child to have two mothers,' she went on. 'I know it's a dreadful thing to say, my dear, but if you are asking for my opinion I do feel strongly that it would be far better for David, possibly even for you, to make a clean break now. He is young enough now to forget quickly and will accept the woman who brings him up as his mother, and be happy with her.'

Georgette walked over to the window and with unseeing eyes, stared out. She considered what the Matron had said and reluctantly came to the conclusion that the advice was sound. But her heart was breaking at the thought of losing her beautiful baby and tears coursed down her cheeks as she made her decision.

She had lost the battle, and there was no point in going over it again and again, that would change nothing. She decided that this must be her last visit.

'I want to see him one last time,' she said. As she picked up her son and held him close she was aware that already her subconscious was throwing a shield around her maternal instincts. Nevertheless, she hugged and kissed her little son until he opened his eyes and smiled at her, then he yawned and fell back to sleep as she placed him gently back in his cot.

By the time she arrived back at Sandings, she thought the worst was over. Then she caught sight of David's photograph on the mantelpiece and collapsed in a fit of uncontrollable weeping, clutching the frame to her breast in total desolation, racked with guilt at the realization that none of this would have happened if she hadn't deliberately led Ralph to believe that he was the father.

'Oh my baby! My baby!' she wailed aloud. 'May God forgive me!'

Chapter Nine

She tried hard to bury herself in work – her boss and her colleagues knew what had happened and were all very kind but nothing helped her depression. Then when she picked up the phone in her room she was told that someone was waiting for her in Reception. The 'someone' was ex RAF Flight Lieutenant Richard 'Dickie' Barestone-Tailour, whom she had met at Simon Tait's farewell party. Tall and of spare build, she remembered him immediately. She had found him very interesting and thought that the look in his dark brown eyes showed that he reciprocated, but he had a very attractive girl with him and it had seemed clear that they were a well-established couple.

She went down, intending to tell him to go away but somehow found herself instead agreeing to dine with him. He had traced her through the Embassy, pretending to be an old friend who had lost touch with her.

Over dinner, Georgette learned that Dickie's father had been killed on the Somme and that his mother, a wealthy woman, had spoiled Dickie outrageously. As far as she could make out he was really little more than a playboy until war came and he joined the RAF, which he actually had taken seriously. He didn't like dining alone and had remembered the attractive girl at Simon's party. His current girl friend had gone home to her parents in County Wicklow and he was not about to tell Georgette that it was because she had spurned his proposal. Georgette's company was just what he needed, and he was aware of her unhappy divorce so it seemed that she needed him, too.

After rather a lengthy silence Georgette became aware that she was not good company and said so.

'Nonsense! You're a delightful companion! But I'm sorry you've had such problems Georgette. I would be only too happy to help in any way I can. I do hope you will let me be your friend?'

'Thank you Dickie, but I don't know whether I'm coming or going at the moment.'

'In that case, I think you could do with a weekend away. What do you say?'

She decided that this man was unbelievable even as she heard herself accepting. Not only was he devastatingly attractive, but also kind and incredibly understanding.

Over the next few weeks Georgette spent more and more time with Dickie. He was attentive and took her to places she had never dreamed of – introducing her to marvellous characters. There was Carmella Hambledon, with her beautiful Victorian house on the Thames where they spent their first weekend away. Georgette was amazed by the lushness of her bedroom but it never crossed her mind that the place was actually a high-class brothel until Dickie told her much later, and she realized why the other 'guests' had spent more time in their bedrooms than in the gardens . . .

Then there was 'Strawberry' and 'Cream' who gave a cocktail party at their Regent's Park house. Strawberry (on account of his 'boozer's' nose) was in fact Wing Commander Achilles Cressingborough and Cream (on account of the white powder she perpetually used on her face) was his older sister, Mildred. They held parties every night except Sundays and, once accepted, you didn't have to wait for another invitation . . .

Georgette found the Ritz stuffy, but she liked the Berkley. She was glad she had inherited so many lovely dresses from her mother, and no longer regretted the long hours as a girl learning to sew, because she could now alter her wardrobe as need demanded.

It was a wonderful summer. One night in early September they went to the Savoy and, by the time he drove her back to Sandings it was four o'clock in the morning. As he kissed her she felt a passion that she had not experienced in him before.

'You know,' he said reflectively, 'there's really no point in you continuing to pay rent here nor in me collecting you from Sandings every day. It would be much more sensible if you were to move in with me. Everybody thinks we are sleeping together anyway, so your reputation won't suffer and I promise I won't force myself on you.'

'Yes, I think that's a good idea,' Georgette heard herself say dreamily, though slightly woozily. She had drunk more than her usual quota of champagne.

'You are saying "yes" then?' Dickie's voice rose in delight.

'I am.'

Dickie lived in a small three-bedroomed mews house near Lancaster Gate. He kept his word, and told her she could have either of the spare bedrooms, but that Saturday afternoon they made love on the double bed in his bedroom. He was very gentle, and very caring. It had been so long since she had made love and she told him that he was a wonderful lover, and meant it. Although their love-making lacked the passion she had known with Gregoire Watneeteix, making love with Dickie was something that gave her great pleasure and she decided that she would share his bedroom from then on.

A couple of weeks later Dickie's mother arrived for afternoon tea. She had rung a few days earlier to let him know and he had been on edge ever since, but he greeted her with an affectionate kiss and made a great fuss of her. Georgette had imagined a comfortably off widow but he had not prepared her for the chauffeur-driven Rolls Royce and her still stunning looks.

It was not an enjoyable visit. She obviously disapproved of her son living with a foreigner and made no pretence about it, and scattered pointed remarks throughout her stay, nagging Dickie about not getting a job so that it was with a feeling of relief that they watched the Rolls reverse out of the mews.

'She doesn't approve of me,' said Georgette.

'Nonsense.'

'Oh Dickie, you must be blind! She couldn't have made it more obvious. And what on earth did I say wrong when she arrived?'

'Nothing, really. It's just that I should have told you she's not *Mrs* Barestone-Tailour – she's Lady Margaret. My maternal grandfather was the 7th Earl of Whetslane, so she has a title in her own right. A distant cousin has the title now, but mother has the money, rather a lot of it.'

'You should have told me before.'

'Sorry. It isn't something I consider important, apart from the money. You see I will be stinking rich when the old girl pops off. So I can't see the point of working my guts out, but I might just take a job if something interesting comes up.'

A few weeks later on one of their visits to Strawberry's cocktail parties the Wing Commander mentioned that an air traffic controller's job was coming up, in Malta, where Dickie had already spent some time during his war service. A few days later when Georgette arrived home from the Embassy Dickie greeted her with the news that the job was his – it suited him down to the ground as it was only three days a week. He wanted Georgette to go with him and she knew that he was unreliable but she wasn't willing to let him get away from her. He was the person who had consoled her over the loss of her child and had shown her how wonderful life could still be. It would be a gamble, she knew that, but what had she to lose?

'I will come with you, Dickie,' she said eventually. 'Oh my darling, that is splendid!'

The very next day she received a letter saying that her divorce was now final. She hoped it was a good omen . . .

Chapter Ten

Georgette admired the ancient buildings which had survived the German bombardment, built by the Knights of the Order of Saint John in the defence of Christendom and as a cathedral of their faith. But after only three weeks on the George Cross island of Malta she had to conclude that it was not for her. She missed London and the clubs she had enjoyed so much, and apart from a boat trip to Gozo or water sports there was little else to do. She would have been happier if she'd been able to get a job, but Dickie didn't want her to and she didn't feel inclined to argue as she really was more than a little in love with him.

One thing that Malta did offer however, was extremely cheap alcohol – lots of it . . . Georgette found that time passed more quickly when she was 'happy' and she rather liked the feeling she got from rather a lot of gin. Dickie didn't disapprove, laughing at her and she didn't realize that of course he was himself 'happy' on drink on the days he wasn't working.

She learned for the first time that drinking and making love did not often go hand in hand but she enjoyed being with Dickie and she decided that the sexually undemanding nature of their relationship was one of the things she enjoyed about it . . . As their bouts of drinking grew, Dickie's ability to keep the working days separate from the drinking days started to blur, and his work inevitably suffered.

'God I'm bored,' he said with a sigh almost daily as he downed his first whisky. At the beginning of June he made a mistake that might well have cost lives, and he was sacked. He couldn't have cared less.

'Silly fools!' was all he said.

The day before they were due to leave Malta, Dickie became suddenly fearful that she might not want to go back to London with him, having become very aware of the close friendship she had formed with Hugo, a dashing friend on a similar contract to his own. 'The chap's a real womanizer and out to bed Georgette, for sure,' Dickie thought, concluding truthfully 'if he hasn't already done so . . !'

'Don't be silly darling,' she said to him. 'Wherever you go, I go!'

'Even to the altar?'

Georgette gazed disbelievingly at him, not daring to believe her ears. 'Is that a proposal?'

'I suppose it is, old girl,' he replied. 'I mean it. Will you marry me?'

'I accept,' she heard herself say dreamily.

With studied concentration, Dickie recharged their wine glasses. 'To the two of us,' he said softly, thinking 'Good Lord, she's accepted me!'

When they had left for Malta Dickie had put the mews house with an agent to be sold, and the proceeds were enough to look for a new home. Georgette needed to find a job and decided to try the Embassy again – not surprisingly her old job had been filled but there was a need for another bi-lingual secretary and she was asked to start the following Monday.

Dickie was pained, but he knew she was right. He had found them a home in Whittington Gardens which was offered at a very reasonable price because it needed a lot of work done on it. Georgette was horrified at the state of it when he took her to see it but she agreed that it did have possibilities . . .

He wasn't looking forward to telling his mother their news but with a bad grace she accepted his decision and the engaged couple were invited to her home, Grace Hall, for the following weekend. The house stood on a hill overlooking the picturesque village of Titchfield in Hampshire. If she had felt frozen out when Dickie's mother had called at the mews house, she felt it even more here. She also found it quite sickening to watch Dickie fawning over his mother because he desperately needed her money and, therefore her approval for his marriage.

On the Sunday morning as Georgette made her way to the dining room, Dickie appeared with a wide grin. 'For you my beloved!' It was an exquisite ruby and diamond ring and obviously worth a fortune. 'It's one of the family heirlooms and signifies your acceptance into the family,' he said with satisfaction.

He also waved a four-figure cheque at her. 'And she's given us an engagement present,' he said smugly.

'How kind,' said Georgette. But she had to accept that it would make the revamping of the flat a great deal easier.

'Now that Mother's accepted things, let's get married as soon as we can arrange it, and to hell with them all!' He was jubilant. Three weeks later they were married at their local registry office, the only witnesses were the photographer and a woman they asked in from the street, who thought it all very romantic.

They both enjoyed the next few months. Georgette helped with the decorating and Dickie spent hours wiring and re-plumbing, and combing auction rooms for furniture. The finished product pleased them both, and to make their happiness complete Georgette's New Year present was to tell Dickie that she was pregnant. He was over the moon. After all, he was forty-two, and this was to be his first child. The next months were a cherished time for Georgette. Dickie shopped and did all the housework, waiting on her hand and foot and proving a much more domesticated person than she had thought possible. It was a wonderful partnership.

'My husband's brilliant!' she thought contentedly.

Lady Margaret had been told of Georgette's pregnancy and had twice called in for afternoon tea. She was quite affable on both occasions and presented Dickie with a large cheque without even waiting to be asked.

They had another stroke of good luck when they were introduced to an interior decorator, Humphrey Manley, who they met at one of Strawberry's parties. They invited him to dinner at their flat and he was very taken with what Dickie had achieved there, and when the evening ended and he was about to leave, he suggested that Dickie might be interested in working for him? 'I really could use someone with your ability,' he said. Dickie protested that he was only an amateur, but Humphrey insisted that in his opinion Dickie had great flair. After a visit to Humphrey's office the following day, Dickie rushed home to tell Georgette that he had been offered a generous salary and on the first day of September he was to become a professional interior decorator.

His restlessness vanished almost immediately – he had finally found his niche in life.

A few days after Dickie had embarked on his new career, on 7 September 1948, Susan Elizabeth was born to Georgette (née Delire) and Dickie Barestone-Tailour.

Henri was surprised and delighted with the news. She had not told him of her pregnancy, not wishing to tempt fate. She hoped now that this new baby would help her, finally, to get over her loss of David. Susan had the same large round brown eyes and dark brown hair, and by the time she was three months old she was already a sturdy child. Georgette took her to Brussels to show her off to her father and grand-parents. She had hoped Dickie would be able to accompany her, but he was busy with a new contract and she didn't want to deter him from working. There would be plenty of other times, she told herself.

Her four days in Belgium flew by, catching up with family and friends, many of whom had made their way to the Leopold bringing gifts for the baby.

She had been dreading Christmas with her Ladyship but it was far better than she had anticipated. As she said goodbye to 1948 and greeted the New Year, Georgette prayed that her wonderful partnership with Dickie would last the rest of her life. She had never been so contented with her lot.

Shortly after Susan's third birthday the doorbell rang while Dickie was at work. The short, stocky man standing there doffed his hat to reveal a thinning head of sandy hair.

'Good afternoon – Mrs Barestone-Tailour? My name is Donald Kerr. Friends tell me Dickie lives here. I'm an old chum of his.'

She liked the man and invited him in to await Dickie's return, when Georgette witnessed the reunion of two friends who had lost touch with each other. They were quickly back into the closeness that only good friends can pick up after an interval of years. Don stayed to dinner and as he was leaving Dickie told him that he was always welcome and was to feel free to visit whenever he wanted to.

It was an invitation that Don accepted often and in no time at all he seemed to be always with them. He found himself a job and a room but apart from working and sleeping it seemed that he spent virtually all his time with them. The two men seemed never to tire of talking about old times, the City and politics and there were times when Georgette felt excluded from this male bonding. She liked Don very much, but didn't want him there all the time!

Her sex life with Dickie was still enjoyable, but there was no longer any excitement in it. Don was a rogue, but an attractive one, and she knew the attraction was mutual. Deep down, she knew that if there came a time when he made a serious play for her, she might not be able to resist. But she didn't want that to happen. She was very happy with Dickie and had no intention of rocking that boat. It was obvious that Dickie trusted Don absolutely but she sometimes wondered how he could be quite so blind. Don was always brushing up against her 'accidentally' and finding an excuse to touch her.

When Dickie had to spend a few days in Scotland on business, she told Don that he was not to visit her until Dickie's return. 'Oh, all right,' he said, seeming to accept the situation. And he did keep away until the following Friday.

'Dickie is not due back until tomorrow or Sunday,' she said unsmilingly. 'You know that perfectly well, so please go away.'

'I just don't understand you!' Don's tone was exasperated. 'You know you fancy me and I can't sleep for wanting you. What harm can it do if we make love?'

'I'm a happily married woman,' she snapped, 'and my husband is foolish enough to trust you because he thinks you are his friend!'

But he persisted with his arguments. He seemed to have an answer for everything and in the end he threatened to throw himself off the roof of his home unless she let him in. 'Believe me, I will!' he said with his eyes fixed on her menacingly.

Georgette didn't really believe him, but suppose she were wrong and he did mean it? How would she ever forgive herself?

She stood irresolutely, then he began to cry! What on earth would he do next?

'You had better come in and have a coffee,' she said. But they didn't get as far as the kitchen. As the door of the flat closed behind him, he took her in his strong arms and kissed her passionately until she began to respond. Soon her scruples were swept aside by her physical excitement.

Afterwards, they did make some coffee. Then he left.

Dickie arrived home the next morning. She wanted to clear her conscience by telling him, but she didn't. She could hardly pretend she had been raped, and what good would it do?

A couple of hours later the telephone rang. 'Come to dinner,' she heard Dickie say.

'Mon Dieu! Here we go again!' she thought.

Their old routine was resumed just as though nothing had happened.

Shortly before Christmas, Georgette found she was pregnant once more and, to her horror, realized that she didn't know who the father was – it could be either Dickie or Don!

Dickie was wonderful to her, pampering every whim which wasn't easy as with this pregnancy she developed a craving for pineapple sandwiches. It was not a fruit readily available in 1952 but Fortnum's as usual came to the rescue. Georgette and Dickie now employed a French au pair, Brigitte, and although she was very helpful Georgette never grew close to the girl, but she wanted her children to grow up bilingual and agreed to employ her for the two and a half years she wished to stay while she learned English.

Georgette's new baby was born on 17 August 1952, while the nation was still recovering from the death, in February, of King George VI. The commonwealth now had a new Sovereign, Elizabeth II who was to be enthroned in June 1953.

The baby was a boy: Alexander William, twelve days early and very small and delicate. But he was healthy and everyone was delighted.

The first year and five months of Alex's life passed contentedly. It seemed as if Don's 'one night stand' had satisfied him, for he made no further overtures to Georgette. He had found a flat and no longer spent all his time with them.

In mid-January, Dickie came home from a couple of days working in Essex and suggested to Georgette that she might like to spend a few days in Belgium. He said that Henri would like to see Alex and that he and Brigitte could cope with Susan.

Georgette was thrilled and he said he would book a flight for her the next day.

'Such generosity,' thought Georgette.

When she returned a few days later, Dickie seemed different. She couldn't put her finger on it, but something was not quite right. He seemed reluctant to go to the office and started to grumble about the reports he had to write up after each house visit.

'What on earth's wrong with you?' she asked.

'I can't help the way I feel!' He was pouring whisky into an iced tumbler and she noticed that it was an extremely generous measure.

The next thing was that he suggested to Humphrey Manley that he work from home, rather than going to the office each day and for a while that seemed to ease Dickie's apparent depression. A couple of months later, Dickie's drinking began again and he would often sit in sullen silence for an entire evening. Then he began to criticize Georgette's cooking, making arguments which were embarrassing for Brigitte, who didn't want to be drawn into them, and for Don who still joined them for their regular evening meal.

What Dickie's problem was she really had no idea. He was now drinking more than he'd done for years and his behaviour in the evening became a ritual that was frightening to watch. At intervals of ten to fifteen minutes (she began to time him) he would walk all the way to the dresser in the dining-room, carefully pour a large measure of whisky into the tumbler and add twice that volume of water to it. He would return to his chair sighing heavily and drink in silence. Ten to fifteen minutes later the process would be repeated and would continue usually until the decanter was empty. He didn't get hopelessly drunk, didn't even appear to get hangovers, but it was a joyless pastime.

'Dickie dear, why don't you put the decanter and water jug on the table by your chair?' she once asked him.

47

'Why don't you mind your own business?' was his only response.

Georgette became increasingly unsure of herself and, for a while, she began to join him, drink for drink. But she didn't get any closer to him, and she became fed up with having an almost constant hangover and let him get on with it alone.

One Saturday in August she could keep things bottled up no longer and when Don was giving her a lift to the shops in Kensington she confided that she just didn't know what to do. 'Has he given you any idea of what's wrong?' she asked Don.

'I'm just as puzzled as you are,' he replied. 'Can't say I haven't noticed a change because I have. He told me the other day that he has to go on working now because Lady Margaret won't help him out any more. Perhaps he blames you for that?'

They chatted about it for some time and Don could see that she was clearly distressed. He had always felt guilty about his behaviour that night when Dickie was away and had behaved himself ever since, but his feelings about Georgette were still the same and he wondered if a bit of sexual activity might not brighten up her life a bit?

He drove to Bayswater and parked outside his small flat. She went in with him and when he put his arms around her she felt the loneliness Dickie had forced on her over the past months begin to lessen.

Every Saturday after that they would do the shopping and then go to Don's flat for an hour or so. These regular sessions helped to release the tension within her and she was better able to cope with Dickie's verbal abuse.

Often these days his criticism was about the way she was bringing up the children. 'I give them more love than you do,' he remarked coldly one evening, 'And I dread the fast approaching day when Brigitte has to leave us. If it weren't for her, my children would be deprived of a woman's love.'

On one point Georgette was in agreement: Brigitte's imminent return to France. She hadn't been over fond of the girl but she couldn't fault her work and it would be difficult to replace her. When she had visited Henri she had mentioned that they would be looking for someone else later in the year, and a few mornings later out of the blue Georgette received a letter from Therese, suggesting that she could come herself to look after the children. Although it seemed preposterous at first, the more they thought about it the more feasible it seemed. Her fiance Thierry was no longer on the scene, and although the language would be a problem Georgette felt that she owed her some return for the kindness shown to her during the War when Therese gave her a home when she needed one.

In due course she arrived and worked for a day alongside Brigitte so that the transition was achieved very smoothly with the children seemingly quite happy with their new guardian. A few days later Dickie drove Brigitte to the station and saw her safely entrained for France.

Some days later Georgette was horrified to find Dickie in a heap on the sofa convulsed by sobbing. 'Darling, what on earth is the matter?' she blurted out. Slowly he calmed down, took a gulp of his whisky and looked at her. 'You're not going to like what I have to say, old dear,' he said hesitantly.

He went on to tell her that he had been having an affair with Mary, a girl who worked at the local pub. Georgette was flabbergasted. She knew the woman and didn't think she would have been at all Dickie's type. It was now her turn to burst into tears. This was so unexpected that Dickie threw his arms around her. 'Please forgive me,' he pleaded. 'It's all over now, I won't be seeing her again.'

'I do forgive you,' she said gently. 'I just wish you had told me earlier, but I do understand.'

How could she not forgive him against the background of her own illicit liaison with Don?

Dickie kissed her lightly on the forehead, then slumped back on the sofa and picked up his drink.

But the following Saturday when Don picked her up as usual for their 'shopping' trip she poured her heart out to him when they reached his flat. 'There's something so terribly wrong between Dickie and I now,' she confided, and went on to tell him about Dickie's confession. Don's comment was that after all, most marriages had their ups and downs, but Georgette responded that nowadays it was one continuous down, and the confession was almost the last straw. She felt now that life with Dickie was so strained she was seriously thinking about divorcing him, taking the children with her and leaving.

Don was quiet for a while and then remarked, 'I suppose I have seen this coming, but I never thought that Mary would be part of the cause. Look my dear,' he said, giving her a hug. 'If you're really serious about this you should talk to a solicitor and find out where you stand. Speak to Nathan Carleigh before you make any irrevocable decisions. It can't do any harm and he may give you some good advice.' He wrote the name and telephone number and handed it to her and even though she was thinking that the last solicitor she had didn't do anything for her at all, she put it thoughtfully in her purse.

Nathan Carleigh was much younger than she had expected, a little under thirty she guessed. He invited her to take a seat and with a warm smile, he suggested that she tell him 'all about it'.

He did not interrupt her, simply took notes until she came to a halt, feeling emotionally drained.

'Oh Mr Carleigh, I am so frightened that something awful is going to happen, but I don't know what. What shall I do?'

'You say that Commander Kerr went to the public house and asked the woman directly, but that she flatly denied any such liaison?'

'Absolutely. She just laughed at the idea. And even before that, I found it difficult to believe that there could be anything between them. We came to the conclusion that my husband must have named her to protect someone else, but we have no idea who, one of his clients, we think. And although he said that it was all over, I don't believe him. Even if he isn't seeing her at the moment, I'm convinced that he has every intention of resuming the affair as soon as he can.'

Carleigh looked at her carefully and then calmly summed up what he saw as the relevant points.

'You want a divorce on the grounds of adultery but you have no idea who your husband's mistress is and can produce no evidence of his misbehaviour; and you want custody of the children although you have no money of your own, because you consider your husband unreliable as a provider. Is that correct?'

She agreed, although she felt it sounded hopeless. He told her that it was important to find out whether or not the affair was still going on, and that she was in fact the best person to do so. 'First things first,' he said. 'You must go home now and behave as naturally as you can whilst keeping your eyes and ears open and try to get some indication of the woman's identity. Let's give it a month and see what you can turn up.'

Georgette actually quite enjoyed her role as private investigator and soon realized that Dickie's movements were quite easy to identify. Every morning he received a phone call from the office at about 9.30.One morning it dawned on her that she had no proof that it *was* from the office and she arranged to be in the bedroom when the phone rang and gently lifted the extension. It was Miss Harper, Humphrey's secretary and when they had finished talking about appointments she heard her say, 'That's it for now Mr Barestone-Tailour, I'm afraid there's nothing in the post.'

'I see. Thank you, Miss Harper.' The disappointment in his voice was unmistakable. Georgette replaced her receiver. 'There's nothing in the post.' Why had that statement made Dickie sound so disappointed? She followed the same routine for the next three mornings and each time the comment was the same, followed by the same disappointed note in Dickie's voice. It dawned on her that he was expecting something particular delivered to the office, and that if it was, she ought to get it first. . .

Two days later the secretary told him that his letter had arrived. Georgette put the receiver down, and as soon as Dickie left the house she slipped out of the front door and ran down to the main road where she flagged down a cab. She guessed that she would have the edge on Dickie who had to negotiate the garage doors and start the car.

It was no problem to collect what proved to be an air mail letter. Saying that she was picking it up for her husband, an office junior handed it to her, then Georgette made her way to a telephone box to ring the solicitor's office, where she arrived an hour later with it still unopened in her pocket. Nathan Carleigh had asked her to first take the lift to the fourth floor of the building and deliver the letter to a Mr Gilfish. Feeling puzzled, she did as instructed, finding Mr Gilfish to be an insignificant-looking man to whom she handed over the now slightly crumpled-looking letter. He was obviously the person who 'arranged' evidence for divorces by finding people *in flagrante delecto*, producing photographic evidence for the court. He viewed it with some satisfaction and said mysteriously, 'A most considerate little envelope! Thank you Madam. Good morning.'

More bewildered than ever, Georgette made her way downstairs to Mr Carleigh's office. They made polite conversation for a while, and she was grateful for hot coffee, finding her hands shaking after the cloak and dagger atmosphere of the morning. A short while later they were interrupted by a girl who handed Nathan a tray on which was an open air mail envelope and a letter. 'How very fortunate that you are here,' Nathan said to Georgette. 'This letter addressed to your husband appears to have gone astray and has been delivered to the detective agency upstairs. It would appear that the envelope was very poorly glued too, as the contents seem to have come out – perhaps you had better check that they are in order before you re-seal it?'

The letter was making an assignation to meet Dickie in Paris, the writer had booked a room for two nights with a Madame Roux and would meet him there in ten days' time. The letter was signed 'With fondest love, your Brigitte.'

Georgette arrived home in the afternoon. Therese was out with the children in the park and Dickie was alone, a glass of whisky in his hand when she walked through the door.

'Why did you take my letter?' he demanded.

'I wanted to know who you really had the affair with. I knew it couldn't be Mary, and now I know it's Brigitte, from the writing on the envelope. Here's your wretched letter,' she said as she threw it dismissively into his lap.

'You didn't open it?' he said, obviously both surprised and relieved.

'No, I didn't, though I was tempted.'

'I do love you, you know.'

'Oh really! I can only say you have a strange way of showing it. But at least I now understand some of your behaviour. Now if you don't mind, I want to lie down for a while.'

In fact, she needed to sort through her jewellery and decide which pieces could be spared to hand over to Nathan Carleigh to pay for Mr Gilfish's trip to Paris . . .

Georgette's pride had been deeply hurt when she had learned the true identity of her rival. The thought that it had happened under her own roof, and that they had obviously gone to bed together while she was away in Brussels. How could Dickie possibly have preferred the French girl? She was awaiting his return from 'Scotland' but which she herself knew to be Paris. The grey miserable evening well suited her mood as she heard him come through the door. Susan ran towards him and his face softened for a moment as he picked her up and gave her a big kiss. 'Hallo poppet! I'll talk to you later.' Waiting till she had returned to playing with Alex and keeping his voice low he spat at her, 'That was a dirty trick!'

'What did you expect me to do?' countered Georgette hotly.

'Sending someone all the way to Paris to spy on me!'

'And I was right to do so!' Georgette slammed back. 'What I don't understand is what you could see in her!'

'She gives me love.'

'I've given you love!'

'No Georgette. You've let me love you – there's an essential difference.'

Georgette could see no difference and took the comment only as a barb. 'I want a divorce and you will be hearing from my solicitor shortly.'

'I won't contest it,' responded Dickie quietly. 'I want to be free as much as you do. But I want to keep the kids.'

'We'll see about that!'

Nathan Carleigh toyed with a pencil while his beautiful client listened, trustingly.

He established with her that she really did want to go on now to the next step, that of actually divorcing Dickie.

'I must, Mr Carleigh!'

'Very well. Now that you have evidence of your husband's infidelity, it might be construed as condoning his conduct if you stayed under his roof. You must therefore find somewhere else to live as soon as possible.'

'With my children, you mean?'

'No. Just you.'

'But I can't leave my babies!'

'I cannot promise to help you if you don't follow my advice.'

'But won't I lose my rights over them if I leave them with Dickie?'

He assured her that that would not be the case, but that it would take about six months for the case to come to court. That would be followed by another wait of about the same time for the decree to become final. He suggested that she use the time to find a good job so that she could find a suitable home for herself, the children and a nanny.

'The question of custody won't arise until after we get the *decree nisi* so you have six months, but when the time comes you must be able to show that you are ready and able to care for the children without the aid of your husband.'

She left his office with her mind in a whirl. She felt desperately unhappy. How could she leave her babies? How could anyone expect her to do that? Yet she was paying Nathan Carleigh to advise her and to make sure that she got her divorce and custody of the children. If she didn't take her advice, what else could she do?

The atmosphere at home now was unbearable. Dickie virtually ignored her and Therese was obviously thoroughly disapproving of Georgette, telling her that she was mad even to consider leaving. 'Don't you care about your children?' she asked. 'Dickie says it's only a fifty-fifty chance that you'll get custody of them if you do leave.' But the more Therese lectured her, the more determined she became to prove that she could go it alone and make a home for her children without Dickie.

Although Nathan had warned her not to continue her liaison with Don, in case Dickie changed his mind and decided to file a counter-suit, she felt that Don was a family friend and as such, when he rang to invite her for lunch she felt it was quite in order for her to accept his invitation.

They arranged to meet at Mervyn's, a Tudor-style restaurant where you could almost feel your money depreciating as soon as you went through the door.

She arrived smartly dressed in a white silk blouse and a suit which she knew made her look terrific. Don was waiting for her and told her that they would be joined by Tom and Nancy Flowers, Don's boss and his wife. Tom was looking for a temporary secretary and though she wasn't too keen on the 'temporary', Georgette found that from the first moment, she hit it off with both of them. She was quite honest about her situation, the impending divorce and the fact that she was looking for somewhere to live. By the time they had reached coffee they all knew that she had a job, and by the following Monday she found herself familiarizing herself with her new job.

Nancy was in the office with Tom when she arrived, and Tom said that they had been talking things over and thought they had a solution to her immediate housing problem. They had a country home, and a flat in Chelsea, and had heard that a furnished flat in their block would be available as from the following week.

The flat was marvellous. Central heating, two bedrooms, all that she needed for the moment. When the time came, she'd sleep on a camp bed in the living room, the children could have one bedroom, and Therese the other. It seemed too good to be true.

Dickie was taking the children to Grace Hall for Christmas, but Georgette refused to accompany them. She told him to take Therese. It wrenched at her heart but she managed to keep thinking that it wouldn't be for long. She couldn't cope with his mother's disapproval when she learned about the divorce.

She hugged Susan and kissed her, grateful that Alex was fast asleep.

Don called on her that evening and they toasted her new life. But he left after only half an hour. Deliberately.

On New Year's Eve he took Georgette to Trafalgar Square to welcome the arrival of 1955.

After two and a half months had passed Georgette was told that the girl she was temporarily replacing would be returning to the fold and it was time for her to start job hunting in earnest. Tom recommended Mrs Melody, the head of an employment agency he'd used on occasion. It paid off, and Mrs Melody got her an interview with a company called Global Business Equipment. They were American based, and keen to get started on selling their business machines in the UK. Though Georgette felt nervous because she had no experience of selling, which is what the vacancy was about, Mrs Melody told her that they had their own sales training force. The basic starting salary was seventeen hundred pounds a year, which Georgette thought was a fortune, and realized she had little hope of getting the job.

On the day of the interview, she spent a lot of time looking efficient as well as attractive. Looking her best in the suit she had worn when she met Tom and Nancy, but with a small black clutch handbag and a hat she had spied in a shop window the day before, she set off with confidence to GBE's head office off Davies Street.

Mr Saint was about fifty, with a brush of golden hair set around a lightly tanned face. His questions were searching, but she was honest and when he asked why she wanted to work for them, she answered 'I need a well-paid job in order to bring up my children.' She went on to tell him about the divorce and that she felt she had to be ready to assume a man's role and to earn a man's money.

'I also want to take out private medical insurance for myself and the children. The National Health Serivce is wonderful for poor people, but I prefer to stand on my own two feet and pay for the best.'

'Commendable,' said Mr Saint, then he explained that she could either work on a salary and commission, or no salary and double commission. When he asked her to choose, she plumped for the double commission.

'It is taking a risk,' Mr Saint cautioned. 'You'd get nothing at all if you failed to sell.'

'Since I can see that that depends on myself, Mr Saint,' Georgette replied spontaneously, 'I will make sure I succeed!'

'I believe you,' he said. 'You've got the job. I'm convinced you'll be one of the best!'

'You really think so?'

'I wouldn't say so if I didn't. I have seldom seen anyone who sold themselves so well!'

'Oh, thank you!' Georgette was amazed at his confidence in her. But if a man who had been in sales for thirty years thought she would be good, who was she to question his judgment?

She walked down Davies Street with wings on her heels. 'I'm going to sell business machines! I'm going to sell business machines!' she endlessly chanted in her head.

That evening Nancy came to call; with the Flowers for neighbours her friendship with Nancy had blossomed. Georgette gave her the good news, adding that she would be sorry she wouldn't be working for Tom any more and hoping that they would all stay in touch.

'Of course we shall. We think of you as a friend,' said Nancy, adding, 'Georgette, let's collect your children and take them down to our country home for the weekend. Tom and I would love to have them.'

'Will I be allowed to?'

'My dear, you still have access to them, surely?'

'Oh yes.'

So Georgette rang Nathan Carleigh, and he said 'By all means take them out. By all means.'

Dickie put no obstacles in her way and Georgette had a wonderful weekend with Susan and Alex at the Flowers' country home.

PART THREE

Georgette – The Middle Years
April 1955 – Feb 1971

Chapter Eleven

In mid-April, at the age of thirty-three, Georgette started her career with Global Business Equipment. Along with seven men and one other woman, she had three weeks of training ahead, learning all about the machines and how to sell them.

The training room had once been a private living-room and it had ornate alcoves and a decorative ceiling. Office furniture had been set down on heavy duty carpet and a comfortable wooden chair was tucked under each desk. There were ashtrays on every desk, together with a folder of literature and a small tool kit, and everyone was soon smoking like a chimney. Some were doing so out of nervousness but Georgette's reason was self-protection – she found the smoky atmosphere less oppressive when she was contributing to it herself.

Les Dykes, the instructor, was quite marvellous in Georgette's eyes. He was middle-aged and as smooth as his Brylcream. Like Mr Saint, he was English but had been with GBE for many years. He taught the trainees ethical salesmanship, which made them want to do the job.

'Where we are lucky, ladies and gentlemen, is that no one in this country really knows what an electric typewriter is and we have no opposition except the potential customer's own prejudice against change! So our main task is to educate him. He's likely to say: "I've never heard of such a machine – it looks complicated to me!" You'll say: "It isn't nearly as complicated as it looks, just give me a couple of minutes and I'll show you what it does." Curiosity will be on your side in most cases – people like to see new gadgets even if they have no intention of buying them. Your job, ladies and gentlemen, is to use that demonstration time to overcome their sales resistance and persuade them to buy at least one machine.'

Georgette clung to Mr Dyke's every word, taking copious notes in shorthand, so that she could go over it all again at her leisure and absorb everything of importance.

Two of the male trainees quickly got out of their depth and left voluntarily at the end of the first week. The other female trainee was happy with selling techniques but left at the end of the second week, when she could not master the mechanics of the machines themselves.

It became clear that, to survive the course, the trainees had to be the cream of the cream and the six who were left were just that. They had to have a good appearance: clean, tidy, smart and up-to-date – 'a modern appearance to sell a modern product' said Les Dykes. They must be neither pompous nor over-pushy – 'friendly helpfulness works best'. Nor must they deprecate other people's products. They should just concentrate on showing that GBE's machines were new and different. They might cost more, but they were well worth the extra in terms of improved efficiency, and the long wait for delivery would be amply rewarded.

'And therein lies the only real snag, lady and gentlemen. At present there is a wait of about six months for the Paragon typewriter and even longer for the Paramount – almost a year!' Mr Dykes gave the facts firmly. 'Customers won't like that, so you'll have to be first-class salesmen, won't you? If you, yourselves, don't believe in the product, you won't be able to sell it. Nobody can sell anything unless they believe in it. Even if it's Heinz sauce. Any questions?'

'Yes, Mr Dykes,' said one of the trainees. 'Wouldn't it have been better to postpone the launch until there was a good stock of machines ready for immediate delivery?'

'Good question. In some ways you're right, of course, but it was decided that the disadvantages of waiting outweighed that single advantage. If we waited a full year, until the Paramount were ready, we might find that other electric typewriters were on the market and we would have lost the valuable element of curiosity, as well as having competition. By starting our launch now, we hope to have a secure hold on the market before our competitors arrive.'

Georgette believed in the product. She absorbed all the mechanical details of GBE's models and was able to take them apart and put them together again quite expertly by the end of her training. She also absorbed everything she was taught about selling techniques – and, just as importantly, the theories that lay behind them. She did not want to sound like a parrot by reciting well-rehearsed lines. With the exception of one or two key phrases, she intended to make up her own sales spiel as she went along.

The cost of the Paragon model was £156 which was at least three times the cost of a manual machine and the Paramount at £224 was more than the price of a reasonable second-hand car. So they were not cheap. The trainees were told to make the secretarial staff their allies before they approached the money men. It should also be easier, as Mr Dykes pointed out, to get an interview with the managing director's secretary than with the big man himself.

They were also told to concentrate on one small part of their territory every day, so as to waste the minimum of time in travelling. 'In other words, start at the top of, say, Bond Street and call in everywhere on the right, then walk back along Bond Street on the left. Just keep walking up and down!'

Suppressed laughter followed that last statement. Didn't Mr Dykes know that prostitutes walked up and down Bond Street? Even Georgette knew that. He did, of course, but remained the picture of innocence.

On the last day of the three-week course, the six remaining trainees were given their territories by Mr Saint. Georgette was assigned part of London W1, SW1 and WC2, plus Surrey. 'We don't cover Sussex and the south coast routinely yet, but you're the one who will go there if we receive any requests for demonstrations.'

When all the territories had been allocated, Mr Saint addressed them all. 'You don't have to keep time sheets – all I'm interested in is results. So you can allocate your time in whichever way you find most productive and if you want a day off for personal reasons, that's fine – just take it. But, for your own sakes, it would be foolish to abuse the privilege. GBE won't carry dead wood and our standards are high – you have got to sell. I'd like you to come here once a week and give me a written report on the previous week's calls and orders – I'll speak to each of you individually to arrange a convenient time – and I'm always available if you have any problems you wish to discuss. Please come here at nine o'clock on Monday so that Les Dykes can give you your kits and final instructions. Good luck to you all!'

Six people to cover the whole of the south-east of England, and no sales staff at all elsewhere in the country yet. Georgette felt she was in at the beginning of something with tremendous potential, for surely expansion would come in due course.

Since Georgette had opted to be paid only by commission, she had received no money while training and she realized that she would have to survive for another few weeks before money started coming in. It had been agreed that half her commission would be paid when an order was confirmed and the other half on delivery of the machine. But the first half, and any expenses, would be paid at the end of the relevant calendar month. Which was fair enough, but did mean that she would have to wait a while before she received any pay at all. Until she had built up enough money in the bank to keep her going, therefore, money would be tight. She decided to give up smoking again, and all other luxuries, until she did have a financial cushion. She was glad that, in the meantime, she still had jewellery to pawn – enough to keep her going until her pay cheques were arriving on a regular basis.

'First impressions are of the greatest importance,' Mr Dykes had stressed, and Georgette had spent some time considering this. She had decided she would start each day by taking a taxi to the area she intended to cover. It would be a bit expensive, but would ensure that she began her work looking and feeling fresh. She had seldom used the underground and, when she had, she had emerged feeling absolutely filthy. The buses were all right, in themselves, but the queuing and jostling made her feel jaded. So she felt that expenditure on taxis was justifiable, even though her expense account was based on public transport, except when she had to carry a machine with her for a demonstration.

The typewriters were very heavy and demonstrations would, when possible, be given in the Sales office, but it was inevitable that some clients would require a demonstration on their own premises. So the trainees had each been given a special carrying case, and had been shown how to pick it up, carry it and put it down without injuring themselves.

Fortunately, on most days, they had to carry only a briefcase containing descriptive booklets, order pads and other literature. That was heavy enough, Georgette thought, but it would enable her to carry a couple of spare pairs of white gloves, a spare blouse and a cloth to polish up her shoes from time to time, so she could avoid looking grimy as the day wore on. She felt nothing created such a good impression as a pair of really clean white gloves and she had purchased a dozen pairs.

Like excited youngsters, the sales team gathered at the office on their first sales morning, a Monday. London was bathed in sunlight and a beaming Mr Dykes gave them a final pep talk. Then, fired for action, they wished each other luck and set off to conquer their various territories.

As part of the West One postal district was one of her territories, Georgette had decided to start in Brook Street, which was just around the corner from GBE's office, so no transport was needed.

Bubbling with enthusiasm, her briefcase in her hand, she walked briskly and was soon staring at a series of name-plates outside a three-storey building. She wrote all the names down on a file card, put it in her briefcase and headed for the top floor to make her very first call.

She was not at all nervous as she rang the bell of a door marked 'Best Textile Importers'. She saw herself as Mrs GBE, and she was proud of her company.

The door was soon opened by a middle-aged lady, quite prim in demeanour.

'Good morning, Madam,' Georgette was on her way. 'My name is Mrs Barestone-Tailour and I represent Global Business Equipment. May I speak to the managing director's secretary, please.'

'I am the managing director's secretary, Miss Daliday.'

'Then may I have a few moments of your time to talk about electric typewriters, which I feel will be most beneficial to you.'

'Electric typewriters? That sounds interesting!'

Georgette was admitted to the office to explain about the machines and show samples that GBE typewriters had produced. 'The roller will accept enough carbons to give you up to twenty copies, all legible in this pica type-style.' With a flourish, Georgette removed from her case twenty identical letters that the machine had produced.

'Most fascinating, Mrs – er . . .?'

'Barestone-Tailour, Miss Daliday.' (Hadn't Mr Dykes said, 'Always remember the customer's name first time'? He'd also said, 'Behave as if the order's already certain.') Georgette took out her diary. 'Will Wednesday morning be convenient for the demonstration? Our office is just around the corner.'

'Well . . .'

'No obligation, of course. But it is the machine of tomorrow, today!' Ten-thirty on Wednesday was duly agreed for Miss Daliday to visit GBE with her boss.

Georgette left with her heart singing – how easy it was! The firm on the first floor didn't want to know, nor did the one below that, but she wasn't deterred – that was bound to happen sometimes, and she made notes on her file card to return at a later date and ask for different people.

At the end of the first day, Georgette almost burst into Mr Saint's office with the wonderful news.

'I've made eight calls and five of the firms are coming here on Wednesday for demonstrations!' And, when they did, all but one signed up. Subsequent days were less spectacularly successful but Georgette was never to have a real setback. Her enthusiasm for the product, coupled with her personality and the brilliance of the machines themselves, carried her forward so fast that she quickly out-paced the sales of her colleagues.

By early July, Georgette's skill and diligence had earned her over £1,500, a staggering sum by any standards. She had yet to receive the second half of the money, of course, but she now had a reasonable bank balance, far more than she had anticipated at such an early stage of her career, and every prospect of making a lot more. Then the company announced a change of policy: in future she and her colleagues would be paid a set salary plus single commission.

'You'll bankrupt us at this rate!' said Mr Saint with a laugh. 'I'm sorry about the change but, to compensate you, I have been authorized to increase your basic salary to £2,500 – I think a rise of £800 after only two months with the company should be acceptable?'

Georgette had to agree. Although she could make more on double commission, £2,500 per annum plus single commission was still a great deal and she thought her solicitor might approve of her having a secure regular salary.

Nathan Carleigh was, indeed, delighted by her progress. 'You've done amazingly well, Mrs Barestone-Tailour. Just when I can tell you that your *decree nisi* has come through. I feel the time has come for me to ask your husband's solicitors to instruct him to deliver the children into your care pending the custody hearing. Will your cousin – er, Therese – come with them, or will you have to hire a full-time nanny?'

'I haven't actually asked her, but I'm quite sure Therese will want to come with me. Dickie won't need her when the children leave and she has nowhere else to go.'

'Good! You definitely need someone to look after them on a full-time basis and now you can afford to put the whole thing on a business-like footing by paying her a regular salary!'

Therese did agree and Georgette learned from her that Dickie had been furious when the solicitor's instructions reached him, but he had to obey. So Therese, Susan, Alex and his cot were delivered to

Dauphin Circus at five o'clock on the last Friday in July, a date and time she would not forget, she promised herself. What joy she felt at the reunion! She had truly achieved something and could go on doing so, thanks to her inexplicable ability to sell – even she did not quite know how she managed to do so much better than her colleagues.

Nancy had helped Georgette prepare jelly and cakes for a special welcome tea, and everyone happily sang songs and played games. Only Therese was aloof. As she admitted to Georgette that same evening, she was somewhat bewildered by events, as she still thought the children should have stayed with Dickie.

'They really like being with him,' she explained, almost as an afterthought. But Georgette didn't really take in the implication of the remark. She was already thinking about what the next week would bring her by way of sales.

Chapter Twelve

Eleven days later, on a Thursday morning, Global Business Equipment received a call from a precision instruments firm based near Cobham in rural Surrey. When Georgette arrived later that day, ready to give a prospective client a demonstration, she was called to Mr Saint's office.

'We're getting known, Mrs Barestone-Tailour! A firm in Surrey wants us to pop down and give them a demonstration. Grant Controls. Don't know how big they are, but they make temperature measurement and control equipment. The owner, Mr Grant, wants to see you personally, so ring his secretary to make an appointment.'

The trip was arranged for the following Friday. Georgette had, by now, purchased three new business suits, but the original blue one remained her favourite. She wore it on this occasion and was confident she was looking her very best.

GBE had negotiated a special rate with a taxi driver who agreed that he would wait for Georgette until she was ready to make the return journey. Following instructions provided by Mr Grant's secretary, the vehicle used the A3 to the outskirts of Cobham before turning off and driving a few miles further to reach a complex dominated by an enormous sign – 'GRANT CONTROLS'.

The factory was large and the adjoining office block impressive. The cab pulled up by some steps that led up to the glass entrance doors. As soon as Georgette had dismounted, the elderly cabbie drove the short distance to a designated car-park, produced a thermos of tea and settled down with a book.

Georgette was left to struggle unaided, with the briefcase and the precious typing machine, up the concrete steps. The receptionist was expecting her and, minutes later, Mr Grant's secretary was showing her into his office.

As she walked over the powder blue carpet of the huge wood-panelled room towards his impressive desk, Jack Grant rose to greet her and Georgette was struck almost physically by the force of his personality. She thought she had never met a more dynamic, exciting person in all her life.

He was a good-looking man with a beautiful head of straight silvery-grey hair that flowed back from what could only be described as a noble brow. His penetrating blue-grey eyes enveloped her, almost mesmerizing her. He was tall and urbane, immaculately clothed in a light summer suit. She thought him every inch the quintessential English gentleman, and he was everything she found attractive in a man!

His eyes were alight with amusement at the sight of her trying to look calm and collected while struggling with the weight of her demonstration typewriter. He came forward, took the machine from her and placed it on his huge leather-topped desk, which was remarkably clear of papers. Only then could they shake hands.

'Hi! I'm Jack Grant.' The accent astonished her.

'But you're American!' she blurted out involuntarily.

He chuckled. 'Guilty! And, judging from your slight accent, I'd say you were French?'

'Belgian – I came here from Brussels the day after V-E Day.'

'To get married?'

'No, with my first husband. We got married in Brussels during the war, in '44.'

'Take a seat.' He indicated a chair, asked his secretary to arrange some coffee, and settled into his own swivel leather chair.

'Thank you, Mr Grant.'

'It seems we have something in common. My wife is English. She didn't want to live States-side, so I had to agree to come here before she would marry me. I started this business and I've been here ever since – that's more than thirty years now.'

'My word. Do you ever feel homesick?'

'Not any more.'

'Are you from New York?'

'No. Not with my Southern drawl! I hail from Surfside. That's near Miami, Florida. I guess you've heard of that place?'

Georgette nodded and they got down to business. Jack Grant really wanted to know about the machines, and asked some very searching questions. Georgette was thankful that she was so well briefed, and her presentation went like a dream. Grant seemed satisfied. He called his secretary back in, then sent for the woman who was in charge of the typing pool. The three of them witnessed Georgette type a letter with twenty copies, and were impressed. Then the two women tried it out. They made rather a mess, but were convinced when Georgette told them it would not take long to adjust their technique.

'It really is the best,' Georgette stressed.

'It's an American product,' Grant said, a twinkle in his eye, 'What else would you expect?' He dismissed the two women before the discussion continued. 'I'm sold on the machine, all right, but I am concerned about the long wait for delivery.'

'I'm afraid that can't be avoided, Mr Grant. It's a case of demand exceeding supply. But, as you have seen me demonstrate, the machines are well worth waiting for.'

'Hmm!' Grant fell to thought, then suddenly he leaned across his desk. 'All right, Mrs Barestone-Tailour, I'd like three of the Paragon typewriters and one of the Paramount model. Can you handle an order like that?'

Could Georgette handle that? She couldn't believe the size of the order, but she was determined not to show it. 'Certainly, Mr Grant. That's no problem at all,' she said calmly, then drew out her order forms from the briefcase and filled one of them in.

He signed with a flourish, saying, 'Anything you can do to hurry them up . . .' Then he eased his frame out of his chair and came round his desk to sit in an armchair facing her.

'Now tell me, Mrs Barestone-Tailour, I'm absolutely fascinated by something. I hope you won't think I'm being too personal – we Americans are renowned for our frankness, you know, and I can never adjust to the reticence of the Brits. You are obviously very good at your job, so no criticism is intended, but I really cannot understand how someone like you came to do this sort of thing?'

'But I love the job, I really do, and I had to do something for a living. I am divorcing my husband, you see.'

'That'd be your second husband, would it?'

'Er, yes.'

'I see. Go on!'

'I have two small children to support and this job came along just when I was wondering how to do it. It's that simple.'

'Well, I think it's very enterprising of you! Now I know about your job, would you like to know something about mine? May I take you round my factory and show you what we do?'

'There is the taxi . . .' Georgette began hesitantly.

'We'll pay his waiting time, give him a good tip. I'll see to that! And, in the meantime, I'll get someone to take your typewriter and briefcase to the front door, ready for when you leave.'

He called his secretary in to arrange all that, then gave Georgette a conducted tour round the factory.

As they got back to Reception, Grant was told there was an urgent long-distance phone call for him, so he bade Georgette a hasty farewell and returned to his office.

As promised, her briefcase and typewriter were waiting by the main door. Without a thought, Georgette lifted one in each hand, and carried them safely down the steps. The driver saw her emerge and drove over. As she leaned forward to put the typewriter onto the floor of the cab, she felt a stab of pain in her back. It was gone in an instant, however, and she gave no more thought to the incident.

The taxi set off for London with Georgette in euphoric mood. She could hardly wait to get back to the office and tell Mr Saint the good news. Four machines sold to one customer! Even she had not previously managed more than two.

'Treats, poppets!' Georgette called out as she walked through her front door, holding fresh cream cakes from a Chelsea bakery. Susan came running into the hall and flung herself into her mother's arms in greeting. As she swung her daughter up into the air, Georgette felt another twinge of pain in her back but, again, it was momentary and she dismissed it from her mind. Alex followed his sister. He was a handsome little boy, with a mass of straight black hair, and his once blue eyes were now brown.

'I've sold four machines today, isn't that wonderful?' she asked them. 'Hasn't Mummy sold well?'

'Mummy sold well! Mummy sold well!' Susan began, and Alex picked up the chant. The two of them continued singing it through the flat as Therese transferred the cakes onto plates.

They ate happily, smearing cream everywhere, then Georgette played with them, still high on adrenalin from her magnificent sale and still thinking about Jack Grant.

'Oh, you're wonderful Mr Grant, you really are!' kept swimming dreamily through her head. He was still very much on her mind when she finally fell to sleep that night.

The next day, Georgette awoke with a searing pain in her neck. She expected it to go, thinking she must have slept awkwardly, but it persisted.

Nevertheless she kept her promise to accompany Therese and the children to a local fete, where Susan and Alex had a lovely time. They especially enjoyed hurling wet paper sponges at the face of a fat man sitting in some stocks. Then Georgette found she couldn't face walking any longer.

'I'm sorry, poppets, but I'm afraid we are going to have to cut our outing short. Mummy's neck hurts so.'

'Oh, Mummy!' Susan was close to tears. 'We're having such fun!'

'I know you are, sweetie, but it's time to go.'

'But we only just got here! Why do we have to leave?'

'I've already told you why, Susan. I'm sorry, but that's all there is to it. I want to get a taxi home – now!'

Trailed by two miserable children, Georgette led the way to the road.

'Are you really in pain?' Therese's concern was more for the children's disappointment than anything else. 'You're not just tired? After all, you have been working very hard all week.'

'I am in pain!' Georgette snapped. She was in no mood for one of Therese's lectures. 'If you weren't my cousin . . .' She managed to choke back the rest, and continued more calmly. 'Maybe I just need to lie down for a while.'

Georgette really thought that would do the trick. But it didn't. By Sunday morning she was in a worse state. She could hardly move her arm, let alone her head. Just getting off the divan to answer a call of nature caused her real agony and Therese realized something was seriously wrong, so she rang an emergency service for help.

A young doctor arrived in the early afternoon. He was obviously rushed, but gave Georgette a brief examination.

'Have you recently tried to lift anything heavy?'

Only then did Georgette remember the moment of pain when she'd lifted the typewriter into the taxi. Floating on bliss, she had forgotten the instructions on safe lifting that GBE had given her. Now, she realized, she was paying the price for her carelessness.

'Easily done!' The doctor said airily. 'I don't think you have dislocated your collar-bone. Possibly you've done no worse than rick your neck. I'll give you some sedatives and you must rest for at least twenty-four hours. It may be all right by then. If not, you should contact your own doctor.'

'But I have to go to work tomorrow!'

'No, Mrs Barestone-Tailour. That really is out of the question. I'm afraid you must remain in bed – phone your boss and explain. I can give you a medical certificate.'

* * *

'I'll try and come in tomorrow,' she told Mr Saint on the telephone. But, by Tuesday, she still couldn't move. What worried her most was that her lack of sales might result in her dismissal. She had not forgotten how three trainees had been encouraged to leave because they weren't up to standard, nor how Mr Saint had said that all GBE were interested in was results.

But Mr Saint accepted the situation very calmly. 'Don't worry. All you have to concern yourself about, my dear young lady, is getting better. Your job will still be here when you're fit again!'

That evening, at about six o'clock, the door bell sounded. Therese answered it. The caller was Mr Saint, no less. Georgette was in bed.

'You sounded so worried on the phone that I thought I'd call and talk to you face to face,' he explained.

'I am sorry, Mr Saint!'

'Don't be. These things happen. I just wanted to reassure you about your job. We're not so short-sighted that we would let our star saleswoman go just because she is temporarily unable to work! What I want you to do is to stop worrying and concentrate on getting yourself well. The advantage of having a set salary is that it will continue to be paid while you are ill.'

'But what about my territory?'

'Any enquiries will be covered by one of us, and if one of your colleagues brings in a new customer on your territory, you will split the commission for that sale with him. I think you'll agree that's fair?'

Georgette did, and Mr Saint continued. 'You've got medical insurance, haven't you? I remember you saying at your interview that you were going to take it out.'

'And I did, Mr Saint.'

'Then don't you think this is a good time to use it? If you don't feel a great deal better by tomorrow, I think you should consult a specialist. I suspect that you should be in an orthopaedic ward with proper medical supervision.'

Mr Saint took his leave and Georgette felt much less worried. As usual, it was left to Therese to voice what was now her biggest fear – that she wouldn't recover sufficiently to carry on with her job. 'And then what happens, Georgette? How will you bring up the children then? Dickie could be caring for you, if you weren't so stubborn!'

The next day Georgette was no better, and took Mr Saint's advice.

By the afternoon she was safely installed in a small private hospital in St John's Wood.

Mr Perry wore glasses as though he never wanted them near his eyes, so they rested on the end of his nose and he peered over them. He was in his fifties, with a dour face. His high forehead was made to seem even higher by a fast-receding hairline. He had a grey pallor that made him appear in need of a doctor himself.

'No doubt about it, it's a slipped disc,' he diagnosed. 'We may have to take it out.'

'Oh no, doctor!' Georgette was most emphatic. 'I'm not having that! I have heard people can be crippled as a result of that operation, in ninety percent of cases.'

The white-coated consultant was more amused than annoyed by that retort. 'An exaggeration, my dear, but I'd only do it as a last resort. For now, you are going to be out flat on a board, and we will see what that does. We'll give it a week.'

Georgette found herself laid, aching, on a sheet-covered board. She couldn't even move her fingers without inducing pain. She couldn't eat, because she couldn't swallow. The nursing staff fed her liquid through something not unlike a little teapot that first night – a mercifully short-lived state of helplessness that terrified her while it lasted.

Visits were permitted and, once she could move enough to use it, a pay telephone was placed by her bed. Therese had informed Henri and he rang, his worry making him angry.

'I don't know what you are doing, taking on work like that! You are a trained secretary and you are good at it. That's a respectable job. Walking the streets, selling machines, I don't understand it!'

'But, Papa, I have to bring up the children, and I earn very much more by selling than by working as a secretary!'

'You shouldn't be working for a living at all! What you should be working at is your marriage!'

'Dickie loves somebody else.'

'Maybe he does at the moment. But men seldom leave their wives for their mistresses unless they are pushed into it. If you stuck it out, he would, sooner or later, tire of this woman and turn back to you. All you need is patience and understanding. Furthermore, I can't see you lasting in this job. If you're going to be constantly incapacitated, you won't be in a position to keep yourself, much less anyone else.'

'I'll manage,' she said defensively.

'That remains to be seen. Who's looking after the children now? Therese?'

'Yes, Papa. I pay her a full nanny's wage, you know. I can afford to pay her that out of my own salary. I really am very good at my job, Papa!'

'Well, I've said all I've got to say on the subject. You always would do things your own way!' But he sounded mollified and, just for a second, she thought she caught a hint of paternal pride. 'Look after yourself and get well soon. Let me know if I can do anything to help.' He was almost tender.

Tom and Nancy Flowers called, so did Don Kerr. Dickie sent flowers with Therese, who brought the children to see her. Susan was very sympathetic but little Alex was bewildered, not understanding what was going on. One afternoon, Bob and Geoff, two of her fellow salesmen from GBE, came round with their arms full of magnificent flowers. 'We got 'em all off the tables at the company lunch today,' Bob explained – the lunches were held once a month to congratulate that month's top salesman. 'It was you again, so we all agreed you should get the flowers. Pity we haven't any lemonade to pour on them. They'd last longer, then.'

The next day she received a letter from the company's managing director: an American in his mid-thirties, who had learned his craft at business school. Georgette had met him once, at the very first salesman's lunch. He was writing to confirm all that Mr Saint had told her about the arrangements for her salary and commission while she was off sick, and knowing that it was all official really helped her to relax.

That night, while she was trying to get to sleep, the offending disc just slipped back into place, the feeling comparable to when one sucks a whole plum into one's mouth. She immediately felt incredibly relaxed and dropped into a comfortable sleep, not stirring until she was awakened at the usual early hour hospitals employ.

The acute pain was replaced by an overall soreness which she was told would fade, given rest and time. Then Mr Perry realized that all was still not well. 'I'm afraid that you have three other discs slightly out of joint, beneath the main offender.'

'What does that mean?'

'Basically that you must not do anything remotely strenuous for at least a month, Mrs Barestone-Tailour. Not even then if you feel the slightest twinge. But, on the good side, another day of complete rest here and I think we can send you home.'

'But I can't do nothing! I can rest for a month, if that's really necessary for a complete recovery, but after that I shall have to get back to work, Mr Perry. My employers are being very reasonable but they won't wait forever. My work involves a lot of walking and I have to carry a fairly heavy briefcase all the time. There's no way around that.'

'I'm sorry, Mrs Barestone-Tailour, but I really cannot be responsible for the consequences if you choose to ignore my advice!' A few pleasantries, then he swept from the room with his small entourage, off to see his next patient.

But what now? If she couldn't sell GBE business equipment any more, as Therese and Henri were both saying was possible, she'd have to let the children go back to Dickie. No other job for her would be so well paid. She was engulfed in self-pity.

Then the telephone rang. She composed herself and answered it.

'Mrs Barestone-Tailour?'

'Speaking.'

'Jack Grant here.'

'Good heavens! How nice of you to call.'

'And just what are you doing in hospital? Don't tell me, I know! I rang your company to see if there was any chance of an earlier delivery of my machines, and they told me. We've got to do something about all this, haven't we?'

'What do you suggest? They tell me I must do nothing but rest.'

'I'm sure they do. But me – I think conventional medicine has its limits and I have got the most marvellous osteopath! He's a man by the name of Rosen. Samuel Rosen, and he's based in Wimbledon. As soon as you get out of there, will you allow me to send my car to fetch you, and take you to see Mr Rosen?'

'It's very nice of you, Mr Grant, but they're letting me out tomorrow and say I should be all right in a month.'

'But maybe you won't!' countered Grant firmly. 'And why should you have to wait a month to find out? I'm going to have Sam Rosen look at you. He'll tell you if he can help you. The number of people who walk into his surgery almost crippled and come out healed is quite remarkable – so why not you?'

'I can't thank you enough for your kindness, Mr Grant, but I'm sure I shall be all right.'

'Well, take a rain-check on it.'

'Sorry?'

He laughed. 'It means the offer will stay open – let me know if you change your mind.'

The next day Georgette went home and was only too happy to follow the consultant's advice to spend most of her time in bed because, though she was no longer in agony when she moved, she was still very sore and her back felt wrong in some indefinable way.

Therese was as comforting as ever.

'It will never be completely cured, you know. Back problems never are. Once you start picking things up, you'll be crippled again!' That was her genuine belief. 'So your best course of action is to do what you should have done in the first place – let the children go back to Dickie.'

'I don't want them to go back to Dickie. All I want is to have my children with me, come what may.'

After a few days, Georgette struggled onto her feet and returned to the office. Her back was still felt very sore but she assured Mr Saint that she was capable of resuming work.

But she found that, by the end of the day, she was in a lot of pain. By the end of the week it was obvious that she could not continue to work her territory so hard. Everything took longer to do. Stairs were like mountains and when she couldn't take the lift she had to rest for a while on every landing to get upstairs at all. She could barely hold the briefcase and began to lean forward like a cripple with every step – hardly an image to inspire confidence.

She sold only two Paragon machines during the whole of that week, and knew that things would get no better, so she went to see Mr Saint. 'What do you think of osteopaths?' she asked.

'You must try something, Georgette. At this stage I can't see that you have anything to lose.'

'You don't think it's all quack stuff?'

'I've heard it called that, but I've also heard people say it works, so I have a completely open mind on the subject.'

With a sense of relief, Georgette told him about Jack Grant's offer.

'My dear girl, take it up! Ring him now. Be my guest,' he swept an expansive hand towards his phone.

Georgette dialled Jack Grant, and there was no disguising the delight in his voice. 'I happen to know Sam Rosen is not there right now. Give me your home number and I'll call you back this evening.'

She hung up with a sense of relief. Grant's enthusiasm had her believing that Samuel Rosen was the answer to her problem.

'Now,' Grant stressed, when he made that evening telephone call, 'it's all arranged. But I insist on one thing – I've talked you into this treatment and I shall pick up the tab, so you needn't worry about the cost.'

Georgette protested, but she had been a little worried about the cost – as she knew her medical insurance did not cover treatment that was not recognized as legitimate by the medical profession – so she allowed herself to be overruled.

Grant's was the second call that evening. When she'd reached home, the phone had just started to ring and, surprisingly, it proved to be Monique Fourmeaux, calling from Brussels.

'I've got a cabaret job for three weeks. Guess where?'

'Not London?'

'Yes! At Castella's, in Piccadilly. I start Monday week, 12 September.'

'But how marvellous! How did that come about?'

'Castella's owner saw me working here and invited me. I've just received the contract. Oh, Georgette, isn't that just fantastic?'

'It certainly is, Monique! You deserve a break – just think, my friend's becoming an international artiste! It will be so good to see you!'

'Can I stay with you?'

Georgette agreed without hesitation. Tom and Nancy possessed a fold-up bed which they had said she could borrow any time she had a visitor.

'Who was that?' Therese asked, entering the living-room, wiping her hands on an apron.

'Monique!'

'What did she want?'

'She asked how I was feeling,' replied Georgette guardedly. She wasn't sure why she had replied in such a way. But some instinct suddenly made her distrustful, and she deferred telling Therese of Monique's forthcoming arrival.

It was the same feeling of caution that made Georgette ask Jack Grant to send his chauffeur, Steve, to collect her from GBE's office instead of from her own flat. Therese was bathing Alex when Jack's call came through and Georgette told her boldly to mind her own business when she asked who it was.

Driving a shining Daimler, Steve, a tubby man of medium height, duly arrived at GBE's office the next day and drove Georgette to Wimbledon for her first appointment with the osteopath.

Samuel Rosen was a dour little Jewish gentleman who, with his wife and son, had fled from Hitler's tyranny in the thirties. In Germany he had been a flower seller. On arrival in England, he was interned on the Isle of Man and spent the war developing his osteopathic skills. In the ten years since, he had built up a successful practice. His four-bedroomed home, a delightful natural-brick building with a large garden, bore mute witness to his success.

'It is true you have a few discs out of joint,' Rosen delivered his verdict in a heavy accent. 'Two, three visits before we get it absolutely right, but I can help a little immediately.'

Georgette settled on his surgical couch and,with a practised hand, Rosen began to push her spine here, and pull her spine there, with a deftness that gave her total confidence in his actions: 'I'm releasing all the muscles and nerves that are trapped,' he informed her.

By the end of that session, for the first time in weeks, Georgette was able to breathe easily. She walked out of his surgery straight, not with the gait of a cripple.

Steve was impressed. 'Mrs Barestone-Tailour that is some improvement!' He commented with a wide smile, as he held the car door open for her. 'Back to your office, is it?'

It was Saturday and no one was at the sales office, but Georgette hailed a cab as soon as the Daimler had gone. Therese and the children were out when she got home, so she rang Jack Grant to tell him the good news and thank him.

He said, 'I have already spoken to Rosen, and he told me that you have another appointment next week. Correct?'

'That is correct.'

'Steve will be at your office, as before, to collect you and bring you back.'

'Mr Grant, please, there is no need for that. I feel much better already and I shall be able . . .'

'Steve will be there, Mrs Barestone-Tailour. It's all arranged. Goodbye for now.' The telephone went dead. Grant had hung up.

'What an incredible man you are, Mr Grant!' Georgette spoke her mind into the dead phone.

That evening Georgette was relaxing on the divan as her cousin sank wearily into an armchair, having tucked the children up for the night. 'I've something to say,' Therese announced dramatically. Georgette had sensed something building up over the last few days and now said nothing.

'I've decided that I am going to leave you. We really don't get on very well, and you're not going to get anywhere like this. It's obvious that your back is not going to recover and that you will not be able to support the children, so I have made up my mind to go back to Dickie.'

Georgette stared at her cousin and realized that, subconsciously, she had been waiting for something like this to happen. She had become aware, from odd things that Therese had let drop, that Dickie was being kept informed of everything she, Georgette, said and did, and she was sick to death of harbouring a spy.

Slowly, evenly, Georgette said, 'Very well, Therese, you must do what you think best. Now Susan's at school, I can probably manage her without help, and it won't take long to find someone to look after Alex. When do you plan to leave?'

That stunned Therese, since she hadn't seen herself going anywhere without the children and she didn't see how she could go back to Dickie without them. 'But . . . but I meant I'd take Susan and Alex back to their father!'

Georgette looked at her cousin coldly. 'Whatever made you think that *you* were in a position to make decisions on behalf of *my* children? But I agree that we do not really get on and I can see no reason why you should not leave. Your resignation is accepted – would next Saturday be convenient for you to go?'

Therese tried to wriggle out of the hole she'd dug for herself, but Georgette would not allow her to change her mind, and the following Saturday was agreed as her departure date.

Georgette went into the office the next day and Mr Saint was delighted to see the improvement in her. But he cautioned her not to do too much immediately and suggested that, for the next week or two, she should work only part-time – stopping as soon as she began to feel tired.

Before she left the office she rang Nathan Carleigh. He listened as she told him the latest developments, then he said, 'Mr Barestone-Tailour's solicitors have been asking for the children to be allowed to visit him for a while, so I'll arrange for them to go to him for a month while you get your strength back and find a new nanny.'

Then Georgette went back to work happily, and secured orders for three Paragon machines before she felt too tired to carry on and headed for home.

Saturday dawned bright and sunny. Dickie came to the flat to collect the children and enough clothes for a month away. The meeting between them was concerned with practicalities and reasonably amicable. Georgette noted, with a degree of pleasure, that Dickie had few words for Therese. Her usefulness was over.

When the hour came for Therese to take her leave, Georgette's farewell was brief. 'Thank you very much for your help with the children – goodbye.' So far as Georgette was concerned, that was that. She vaguely assumed Therese would return to Belgium, but she neither knew nor cared.

The excitement of Monique's impending arrival from Brussels the very next day filled Georgette's mind, and she did not even grieve at being separated from her children once more. With Therese gone, Monique could have the comfort of a real bed, and Georgette hummed happily as she prepared the bedroom for her friend.

What a blessing Monique Fourmeaux's visit proved to be. As she was working only in the evenings, she took it on herself to accompany Georgette during the day. She assisted her up and down stairways, when necessary, carried her briefcase all the time and, most importantly, insisted that Georgette sat down for a while and had a rest whenever she began to show signs of strain. As a result, they spent quite a lot of time chatting over cups of tea and coffee between calls.

Georgette didn't fret about the precious selling time wasted, because she enjoyed Monique's company so much. After a while, she realized that this routine meant that, although she was making less calls a day, she was at the top of her form for all the calls she did make, and her sales figures were climbing again.

Her lightened work load also gave her body a chance to respond fully to the osteopath's treatment, and she was feeling stronger with every day that passed. For the rest of her life, tears would come to Georgette's eyes whenever she remembered Monique's unselfish help over this period.

After only three visits to Samuel Rosen's surgery, Georgette was feeling back to normal, but he cautioned her to be more careful in future, as a recurrence was always possible.

'I repeat, Mrs Barestone-Tailour, that you should not lift anything heavy unless you really have to. When you cannot avoid doing so, make sure that you follow my instructions and do it in such a way that you put the minimum strain on your back.'

'I will, Mr Rosen!' Georgette assured him. She was grateful for everything he'd done for her and was determined to follow his instructions to the letter.

'You will be a bit sore for a while, but that will pass. I hope I will not need to treat you for anything serious again, but do get in touch with me immediately if you have any problems. A massage can help, for instance, if you feel you are becoming over-tense.'

That night, for the first time since her disc had slipped, she felt well enough to go out for the evening and told Monique that she would, at last, be able to watch her perform. She hadn't seen much of Don recently, but he responded readily to her plea for an escort to Castella's.

Georgette was amazed by the high standard of Monique's act. Her singing and presentation had become very polished since she had last seen her perform, and she had been good even then. No wonder Castella's had booked her! And the audience really lapped up her performance. If Georgette was any judge, her teasing remark would come true and Monique really would become an international cabaret star!

After Monique returned to Brussels, Georgette felt lonely. She had greatly enjoyed her friend's visit. Dear Monique – if she hadn't come and forced Georgette to behave sensibly, the future scenario might have been very different. As it was, everything looked rosy.

She was on her own for most evenings now, although she saw a fair amount of Tom and Nancy Flowers. But her back was still in need of proper rest at the end of each working day, and she knew that relaxing at home was a good thing and would hasten her complete recovery.

Lying in a hot bath the evening after Monique had left, to soak away the aches of another successful work day, it suddenly dawned on her that her nine-month lease had not long to run and it was time she did something about finding a more permanent home.

She had also done nothing about finding a new nanny, and the children were due home in a week's time!

She rang Nathan Carleigh, explained that she had let things slip in the worry about her health, and asked if he could arrange for the children's stay with Dickie to be extended by a week, to give her a little more time to get organized. That proved to be no problem.

Chapter Thirteen

As soon as Georgette told the estate agent what she wanted he said he had the ideal thing. She took this with a pinch of salt; but it turned out to be true and Georgette knew that the place was for her as soon as she saw it. It was a top floor flat in Sparrow Hall Walk, a quiet residential turning off a narrow road that led directly from Fulham Road to the Chelsea Embankment. Before the solidly-built three-storey houses had sprouted, sparrows had been known to congregate there, hence the name.

The flat had a lot of character. The large sitting-room had a delightful carved ceiling and an Adam-style marble fireplace. French windows led onto a large balcony that was covered in clinging foliage, and looked out over small gardens to the neat backs of other Georgian houses. The gardens were mostly paved, but mulberry bushes and some scattered shrubs provided splashes of green.

'What a joy to be able to come straight out of the living-room into the sun and fresh air,' she commented to the house owner, Mrs Maddock, as they stood on the balcony. 'I shall put flowers everywhere.'

Mrs Maddock had only recently finished converting the large house into three self-contained flats. She and her family had moved down to Sussex to live in a property her husband had inherited. The flat had a newly installed and neatly tiled bathroom. The kitchen window overlooked the garden and an old oven was still in place. There were four bedrooms, three on the small side and one large. Each contained a single bed, though the place was supposed to be unfurnished.

'We didn't need them, so I thought they might as well stay,' Mrs Maddock explained, 'but I can dispose of them if they're not wanted. The same goes for the settee in the living-room and the old cooker – there's nothing wrong with it. I'm leaving the living-room carpet, too. It's good quality but the wrong colour for the new place. Have you got any furniture?'

'Very little – just a divan, a cot and some rugs. I intend to go to the Army and Navy Store in Victoria. They have auction sales of furniture every week.'

Mrs Maddock was offering Georgette a twenty-five year lease. The cost was high, but within Georgette's means, and she considered it was good value.

The survey was satisfactory and the other formalities went smoothly. Contracts were exchanged in record time and Georgette took possession.

Tom and Nancy gave her ample curtains for all the windows, and a couple of chairs as well. Georgette bought some wonderful stuff called rubberized flooring for all the bare boards, and a man came to lay it for her. She had enough rugs to put one by the side of each bed and she organized her work so she could be in Victoria on the preview day of the Army and Navy Stores sale. She managed to get everything else she considered essential on her first visit there – enough to keep the children happy until she could get the other things she needed to make the place really comfortable.

In between doing her job and getting the flat organized, Georgette had been interviewing nannies. Nanny Trotter seemed ideal, and she was a reasonable French speaker, too.

She habitually dressed in the image of her calling. At fifty-three years of age, her hair was white, but she was tall and still slim. She hailed from Derbyshire and her references were impeccable. She had served only three families in her years of service, all of them from the upper classes, and Georgette felt as if she was the one being interviewed. After inspecting the new flat, Nanny had pronounced herself satisfied – with one proviso: 'I will be left completely in charge of the children, won't I, Madam? I can't be doing with interference!' Her voice was precise.

'That is how I wish it,' replied Georgette decisively.

'Very well.' Nanny Trotter knew, from photographs of the children, that she would like them. Georgette just hoped that they would take to this rather formidable woman. But she needn't have worried – towards her charges Nanny displayed none of the ferocity she directed towards their parents. With children she was firm, but very loving. She moved into the flat the day before the children were due, and took them under her wing as soon as Dickie dropped them off – both loved her on sight.

From then on, Nanny Trotter did all the shopping for the children, cooked for them as well as herself, took Susan to school and brought her back at the end of the day, accompanied Alex to kindergarten twice a week and looked after him the rest of the time. She also saw to their weekend exercise. Knowing 'Madam' was a busy lady, she even bought the clothes for her charges, often saving her employer a lot of money by going to a shop where people would leave perfectly good clothes that their offspring had outgrown.

Georgette had absolute confidence in her and soon upped her wages to £7.10s.0d a week, on top of her keep. Nanny Trotter was delighted and Georgette had peace of mind to pursue her career.

Thursday was Nanny's day off and she usually left the house immediately after breakfast and returned fairly late at night. On the rare occasions she returned early, she would go straight to her room and remain there for the rest of the day. Both Susan and Alex understood that she was not to be disturbed on these occasions. She was a reticent woman and never volunteered any information about how she'd spent the day and Georgette, respecting her privacy, did not ask.

Georgette had also engaged a daily cleaning lady, a friend of the woman who obliged Tom and Nancy at Dauphin Circus. She said she would be very happy to fill in for Nanny and look after the children on Thursdays – 'Make a nice change from cleaning, and I love kids!'

Mrs Daisy Brown was a cuddly little woman with a heart of gold. She was in her early fifties and had brought up three boys of her own – 'Couldn't seem to manage a girl, now it's too late.' After Daisy had given the children their tea, she would bath them both and put Alex to bed, then play with Susan until Georgette got home from work. Georgette fell into the habit of using Thursday evenings to write up her weekly report, so she had only to add Friday's sales before handing it in to Mr Saint on Monday morning.

Georgette was content with this routine and the only cloud on her horizon, at present, was that the battle for custody of the children was still being fought. Dickie might have given up by now, Georgette thought, but Lady Margaret was fighting a determined rearguard action.

But there was nothing Georgette could do to influence the matter either way at this stage, except to ensure that her own behaviour was beyond reproach.

At one point Her Ladyship and Dickie both wrote to Georgette to say that she (Lady Margaret) would be happy to help her out by paying for the children's education.

Georgette nearly fell for that ploy but Nathan Carleigh was having none of it. 'Refuse the offer straightaway. You can afford to pay for everything yourself, can't you?'

'Yes, Mr Carleigh.'

'Then don't accept any help from Lady Margaret. Do not underestimate the effect her title can have on some people! If you did take anything from her she could quite truthfully tell the court that she was supplementing your income, and that might influence the judge to let her have some say in the children's upbringing.'

That was the last thing Georgette wanted and the lesson was learned. Further offers of help were rejected out of hand.

On the Saturday before Christmas, a most enormous bunch of flowers arrived for her at her new flat in Chelsea. The card read: 'Happy Christmas from Jack Grant and all at Grant Controls.'

With great care, Georgette removed the cellophane from around the mass of chrysanthemums and carnations, their reds, whites and yellows sure to brighten any room.

She diligently prepared each stem and placed them in two large crystal vases, a present from Dickie in happier times. She filled them with lemonade, remembering the tip she had picked up from Bob and Geoff while in hospital. Georgette wanted these flowers to last, partly because they were from Jack Grant and partly because it would be good to have them brightening up the living-room right over the Christmas period. So she thought it was a good time to test the lemonade theory.

The flat was now fully furnished. It wasn't luxurious, but it was comfortable and homely.

While Georgette was arranging the flowers, Nanny was out with the children, seeing to haircuts at a salon in Kings Road.

'They must look smart for Christmas,' she had prefaced the visit.

By the time they got home, Georgette was relaxing on the settee. They all ate tea together, then set about decorating the Christmas tree, which added to the anticipation of the coming festivities. Nanny had turned down Georgette's offer of time off at Christmas. Though she had a younger sister she could have gone to who was married she and her husband had no children, so Nanny preferred to spend it with Susan and Alex. 'Christmas is for children, isn't it, Madam? I think it's all rather pointless without them.'

* * *

On Christmas Day the children took a telephone call from their father and Granny, which seemed to upset them. Georgette thought Lady Margaret must have said something tactless. It didn't occur to her that it was simply that they were missing their father.

But they were soon bright again, Nanny had produced some presents of her own for them: a little wooden engine for Alex and a skipping-rope for Susan. Then she played with them while Georgette put the finishing touches to their traditional Christmas lunch.

After the meal, which was consumed with relish, they listened to the Queen's speech. Then the adults, who both felt they'd eaten too much, took it in turns to have a nap.

As she watched her children playing with their new toys on the rug in front of the blazing coal fire, Georgette felt very content with her lot. Her back was no longer troubling her that much; she was happy in her new home and had perfect staff to help her run it; and her sales were excellent again, so her income was more than enough to cover all her needs. It couldn't be much longer until her divorce was finalized and she was looking forward to a happy 1956.

New Year's Day arrived and, while quite a few people were compelled to work, Georgette had been advised not to. GBE felt it would be counter-productive for their sales force to work on that day because so many of their prospective clients were liable to be suffering from hangovers.

Georgette was one of the sufferers, having celebrated rather too freely with Don, Tom and Nancy. She was still in bed, awake but loth to move, when the telephone rang in the living-room. Susan answered it and came to her bedside. 'Telephone for you, Mummy.'

'Who is it darling?'

'It's a man. He wants to speak to you.'

With great reluctance, Georgette rose from her bed and slipped on a quilted dressing-gown, a Christmas present from Tom and Nancy.

'Happy New Year, Mrs Barestone-Tailour!' There was no mistaking the American accent.

'Mr Grant – Happy New Year to you!'

'How are you? Did you have a good Christmas?'

'It was quiet, you know, but we enjoyed it very much.'

'That's splendid! Did the children get all the things they wanted?'

'It seems Susan wanted a big doll, not the small one I got her, and

Alex would have liked a teddy bear, I now realize. But apart from that . . .'

'That's children!' Jack chuckled. 'I'd love to meet them. May I?'

Memories of her time with Gregoire rushed to the fore and alarm bells sounded in Georgette's head. She was very attracted to Jack Grant, but he was a married man and she was reluctant to have anything to do with anybody who was married.

'Yes, of course. You must – some time. But I'm very busy at present!'

'I know – selling those typewriters! And I get my three Paragon models this month, don't I?'

'Yes, Head Office have assured me that the size of your order has given you priority and you will get a delivery a month earlier than usual.'

'Splendid! Give me a ring when they come in.'

In the middle of January the three Paragon typewriters earmarked for Grant Controls arrived at GBE's offices. So, unexpectedly, did the Paramount he'd ordered – nearly six months early! Georgette unpacked and tested each one, and was more relieved than normal that all four machines functioned well.

She rang Jack Grant.

'That's splendid, my dear! I'll tell you what, I'll send Steve up to London to collect the machines. I remember you said that you would be coming with them, to make sure everything is in order. Will this Thursday suit you?'

'Certainly, Mr Grant.'

'After you've shown my girls how to use them, I'll take you down to my golf club for lunch.' It was a statement, not a question.

'Thank you, Mr Grant. That would be lovely!' She meant it. After all, she couldn't come to much harm over lunch.

'You are certainly enjoying that!' said Jack Grant, with satisfaction, as Georgette tucked into an excellent fillet of prime scotch beef. It was cooked rare, exactly to her liking, and her pleasure was obvious.

'It is absolutely delicious! I can't remember having a better steak!'

'You deserve the best,' Jack declared, grinning from a face that was deeply tanned. 'He's been abroad,' Georgette concluded, but she did not choose to comment, considered it not her place to be so familiar. 'Your training session this morning was most impressive,' Jack continued, when it looked like a silence would fall forever if he didn't.

'We like to be sure that the operators can use the machines correctly, and so get the best out of the typewriters.' Georgette's mind was still on the steak and she delivered the company line automatically, and rather woodenly.

Grant laughed. 'And I'm sure we will. When is it your birthday, Georgette?' He used her first name so casually, so naturally, that she barely noticed.

'November thirtieth.'

'I've just missed one, then. Care to tell me which one?'

'I was thirty-four.'

'So old, yet still so dynamic!' he teased. 'And so beautiful, so adorable!'

Georgette blushed, sensing that he hadn't meant to voice that last thought.

Just then the sun broke through the slate-grey clouds and spread its rays over the wintery landscape, which was still draped in a heavy frost – picturesque from the warmth of the golf club's panelled dining-room.

'The sun!' Georgette commented unneccessarily, to break the sudden silence between them.

'Quite!' He laid down his knife and fork and leaned confidentially towards his guest. 'I want to see you again, Georgette!'

'You will, Mr Grant. As part of our normal service I will be calling on you at intervals over the next few months, to make sure the machines are being used properly and that every user is getting the best out of them.' A happy customer places new orders, but that motive for the follow-up service was, of course, never uttered.

'That's not what I mean, Georgette, and well you know it!' There was just the faint trace of irritation in his voice. 'I want to see you socially. I want to get to know you, and your children. I want for you to get to know me.'

'But you are a married man, Mr Grant. Surely you love your wife?'

'Jack – my name is Jack. Call me that, please!' He was not going to respond to her comment, and Georgette knew it. Somewhere, deep inside, she was glad.

The whole idea of getting to know him better was tempting. After all, there was no man in her life at present. Don was good company, but he was no longer her lover and his visits to her had become infrequent recently. From what Nancy had said he'd found himself a woman and she was pleased for him.

But Jack Grant – she wasn't at all sure he should be allowed to inveigle himself into her life. He had already proved a good friend, and she was undoubtedly indebted to him, but she could not pretend that their relationship would remain platonic. She found him devastatingly attractive and was under no illusions about his feelings for her. So far he had behaved very properly but she was sure that it was only a matter of time and was equally sure that, when he made his move, she would be unable to resist him. He was a man well used to getting what he wanted. But he was married – so a liaison was out of the question she reminded herself firmly – and yet . . .

'Will you at least think about it?' His words penetrated her thoughts.

'That I promise!' she heard herself respond, and Grant seemed content.

Steve drove Georgette back to London as the cloak of dusk was rapidly changing to the dark of night. As they drove along the Kingston-By-Pass, Georgette told Steve she had decided not to return to her office and he could drop her off at her home. That pleased him: Chelsea was closer and he wouldn't have to go all the way into town.

'What a day!' she exclaimed, as she entered her flat and flopped into a fireside armchair. Daisy Brown was playing with the children, tickling Alex into one of his infectious bouts of giggles. 'Have you had a good day, Mrs Brown? Have the children been good?' She kissed them both.

'Little angels! Susan, show your mummy the paintings you've done while I make us all a nice cuppa.'

Tom and Nancy came to dinner a few nights later, and Georgette told them about Jack Grant. 'You make him sound very nice,' concluded Nancy.

'That's it – he is! But he's married, so I don't want to have anything to do with him.'

'You don't mean that, old girl. I can tell.' Tom corrected her.

Georgette blinked at that, then sighed heavily. 'You are right. One side of me knows that I should keep him at a distance, while the other . . . I like him so much!'

'You say he is married. But does he still live with his wife? Do you know that?' asked Nancy.

'Yes. Something he said made that obvious. He doesn't mention her much, but he must love her. After all, they've been married for some thirty years.'

'In that case,' reasoned Nancy, 'he may just want to know you as a friend.'

'I wish I could believe that, Nancy, but I don't! I believe he's as attracted to me as I am to him, and I feel in my bones that he is fated to play a large part in my life. When I'm with him it's as if an invisible magnet is drawing us together – I felt it the moment we met and, although I've tried to fight it, I'm sure that nothing I do will make any difference in the end! He's very subtle, but also very strong, and I truly feel that the situation is out of my control!'

'What about children – has he any?' asked Tom.

'I don't know. I only know he wants to meet Susan and Alex and I don't know if I want him to. I suspect his desire to meet them is just a way of getting closer to me.'

'Seems to me that would be the best way, too,' Nancy agreed.

'Would you like me to have a word with him, warn him off?' Tom offered.

'Oh no!' The words slipped out involuntarily, surprising Georgette by their vehemence.

'Then all I can suggest is that you wait and see what happens,' said Tom.

'He may just love children and, because he likes you, be wondering what yours are like,' said Nancy. 'We did, when we were talking about you after our first meeting.'

That thought hadn't occurred to Georgette, and she wanted to believe it was true. Surely it would be ungracious of her to refuse such a simple request from someone who had been so very kind to her? She decided she would agree if he asked her again.

A few days later, Jack Grant was on the phone, his manner breezy. 'I just wanted to know how you are? I've been thinking of you.'

'I'm very well now, thanks to your Samuel Rosen.'

'Splendid! Have you thought any more about letting me meet the kids?'

Georgette had thought of little else. 'When would you like to call, Mr Grant – er – Jack?'

'How about four-thirty tomorrow afternoon? Will that be all right by you?'

'I'm sorry, no – I have to see someone tomorrow. Could you make it the day after? You'll be very welcome then.'

'Business before pleasure, every time! Friday it shall be. I look forward to it!'

Georgette still had her reservations, but at least Nanny would be there as a chaperon.

What Georgette chose not to tell Grant was that, on that Thursday morning, she was due in court. The custody case was finally coming to a conclusion. To her relief, the judgement was in her favour. Dickie was to have access to the children, but guardianship and all major decisions concerning them were hers. Additionally, Dickie was ordered to pay her a monthly sum for their maintenance.

So it was a really happy Georgette who welcomed Jack Grant to her door the next day. He had brought a huge doll for Susan – 'You did say she wanted a big one!' – and a large teddy bear for Alex. He also presented Nanny with a bottle of excellent sherry and Georgette with an enormous bunch of summer flowers that must have cost him a fortune at that time of year.

He made a real fuss of the children, showing a genuine fondness for them. He might be fifty-two but he had that rare knack of being accepted by children as one of themselves. As ever, Georgette felt a twinge of envy, knowing she lacked that ability.

He took his leave after only an hour, with the children begging him to stay longer. They thought him quite wonderful. It was obvious that Jack was equally reluctant to leave, but he was determined not to outstay his welcome. Georgette saw the unfeigned fatherly warmth in the smile that he gave the youngsters as Nanny dragged them away to their bath.

'It's been a wonderful afternoon, Georgette, please may I come again?' He asked as she saw him to the front door.

'Of course you may, Jack! You are so very good with children – do you have any of your own?'

'No!' he said, almost fiercely, and she realized it was a sore point. Then he gave her her a wan smile and went down to his waiting Daimler. As she closed the door, Georgette chewed thoughtfully on her lip. She had undoubtedly said the wrong thing, but was not sure why.

After that, Jack dropped in at least once a week to see the children. Both Nanny and Daisy Brown adored the man, so he always received a warm welcome.

'And I think he is just charming, too,' confessed Nancy, having come round with Tom for drinks one evening and met Jack briefly as he was about to leave.

'I could never stop him coming,' Georgette told them. 'He brings such happiness to the children. Can it be right for him to spend so much time here though?'

'We can't judge that, can we dear?' Tom's question was addressed to Nancy.

'No,' she concurred. 'But I can tell you one thing, Georgette. If he does have ulterior motives, you should be flattered! No man ever went to so much trouble to win my favour – certainly not Tom!'

Georgette concluded that they thought it shouldn't be happening as, in all honesty, so did she. But, so far at least, he had made no improper suggestions to her at all – had not even tried to be alone with her – so how could she possibly object to his visits? Sometimes he even came when he knew she would be at work, and she began to wonder if she'd misjudged him. Maybe his interest was more in the children than in her. She didn't know whether that would be a cause for relief or disappointment.

Arriving home from work one day, she saw the Daimler and hastened her pace. A wave to Steve, sitting in the car, and she was up the front steps and letting herself into the house. As she entered her flat, the children were standing outside Alex's bedroom door, their ears to the woodwork.

'What on earth's going on?'

She was hushed to silence.

Nanny came up. 'Mr Grant is talking to Big Chief Wallah Wallah Span Span, to see if the children have been good enough to have a gift from him,' she explained in hushed tones.

'Oh! How exciting!' said Georgette. She put her ear to the door, too, and could hear talking on the other side.

Shortly afterwards Jack emerged, a hand deep in his pocket. 'The Chief says you have both been good papooses today, so you can have a present,' and he produced two shiny threepenny coins and gave them one each. He did that often, Georgette learned, and the children expected him to if they had been good. But if Nanny had ticked one or other of them off for being naughty – gosh, the Chief always knew it!

Jack saw Georgette. 'My, you are home early! How nice!'

They shook hands, as always, rather formally.

By May, Jack was regarded as part of the family, an important part of the children's lives. Georgette knew that they would be heartbroken if the visits stopped. If Jack was conducting a campaign to win her heart, he had certainly won the first round.

One day Georgette did not get home from work until after seven o'clock and, stepping from her taxi, she was surprised to see that Jack's car was still there. He normally left much earlier. The children were in bed, and Jack was being entertained by Nanny Trotter, who tactfully withdrew to her room as Georgette came in.

He rose and gave Georgette a light kiss on her cheek. 'Here you are at last!'

'Difficult customers! But I did sign them up for the Paramount model!'

'Good business, that's the ticket! I had to stay until you got in because I haven't seen you for a while and I have something to put to you.'

'Oh!' She was noticeably weary as she sank into her favourite armchair and waited for him to continue.

'Let me pour you a drink,' Jack proposed. 'Whisky isn't it?' He was quite at home as he fixed the drink and handed her the glass. 'Don't get me wrong now, Georgette, but will you please allow me to spend a bit of money on this place?'

Georgette immediately went onto the defensive. 'No, thank you, Jack. You're very kind but I can afford to do it myself. I just haven't got round to it.'

'There – I knew you'd say that!'

'I do earn enough, you know.'

'I don't doubt that, my dear, but you work so hard that I don't think you can afford the time to consider what you want done. This place badly needs decorating properly, cries out for the best. All the wallpaper is thin and nasty and the paintwork is of appalling quality – obviously the owner used people who were cheap and spent only the minimum necessary in order to lease the place.'

'I'm sure you're right.'

'I know a very good decorator, who is also a quick worker. He could do the whole thing in two or three days and it would make a hell of a difference! Will you please let me organize it for you?'

'I'll think about it,' Georgette was weakening.

'Don't think about it, Georgette. Just say "yes"! I get so much pleasure from coming here, and want to express my appreciation by spending a little money on you.'

'You do enough for the children!'

'Very little, and I get as much pleasure as they do. I want to do something that will benefit you directly!' He paused, then said, 'I've told Phyllis about you, if that's what's bothering you.'

'Oh, yes? Why did you feel that necessary?' rejoined Georgette suspiciously.

'It wasn't necessary, but I don't lie to her about my movements. She knows how much time I spend here and I wanted her to know how marvellous you are!' There was sincerity in his voice.

'I don't think I'm marvellous, Jack.'

'I do! That's why I want to do things for you! I know Nanny Trotter is taking a few days holiday next week. To visit her sister in Scotland, she told me. And Susan and Alex are to stay with their Granny while she is away. So that would be a convenient time for some decorating to be done.'

Suddenly it seemed churlish to deny his wish. The man was lonely and he was touching things in her that nobody had ever touched before. Perhaps she shouldn't fight him quite so much.

'Very well, Jack, and thank you. I'll tell Daisy not to come and I'm sure Tom and Nancy will put me up for a couple of nights, so the decorators can have the place to themselves.'

Jack beamed. 'Great! I'll organize it immediately. You needn't worry about your things. My people are both honest and careful, so nothing will come to any harm or go missing.'

When Georgette returned to her home, it looked marvellous. It was obvious that Jack had employed workmen of the highest quality, and that his instructions had been along the lines of: 'Expense no object, get on with it.'

He had been waiting for her when she arrived, and grinned when he saw her reaction. 'You are pleased with what has been done, aren't you?'

'You know I am!' The only problem was that her furniture now looked decidedly shabby, a fact that had not escaped Jack's attention. 'Maybe I could finish the job by getting you a bit of new furniture? It would make me very happy!'

'No, Jack! Absolutely not! That's for me to do. Later this year I'll see to it.' This time she was firm. There really was a limit to how much she could accept from him.

Georgette would have liked to re-furnish the living-room immediately, but her illness had made her wary and she did not want to reduce her nest-egg in case of some other emergency. Dickie had, so far, made only one maintenance payment. He was presenting a series of excuses to Carleigh to explain the non-payment of the rest.

Eventually Carleigh said to Georgette. 'The basic problem Mrs Barestone-Tailour, is that your ex-husband does not have the money to keep up the payments. He is still employed by Humphrey Manley Associates, but is doing less. My impression is that he feels that he would be working hard merely for your benefit and is not prepared to do so. The co-respondent in your divorce is now living with him and I understand that they will be getting married in the immediate future. That is unlikely to improve his financial situation and I really feel that pursuing your claim at this time is simply sending good money after bad.

'So there are two possibilities: we can just let the matter drop until he either settles down to earning more or inherits from his mother – or we can sue him for non-payment, with the possibility that he will go to jail.'

Georgette recoiled at that. 'I can't even contemplate sending my children's father to jail, Mr Carleigh! So I would rather forget the whole thing. It isn't as if I can't cope without his help. I have, after all, planned my life on the assumption that Dickie would not be contributing.'

'Yes, Mrs Barestone-Tailour. I now understand why you were so determined to be completely independent. You were absolutely right and I must apologize for doubting your belief that your husband was unreliable.'

So that was that for the time being. But there remained the hope that one day, when Dickie inherited his mother's estate, he could be forced to make good all the back payments – and to pay compound interest on them. As a business woman, she now knew about these things.

* * *

The decision to take driving lessons had come to Georgette quite suddenly. At Easter she had secretly enrolled with a driving school in the Kings Road. To her astonishment, she took to the wheel like a duck to water. She took the test in July and passed first time. That had to be an asset to her company as well as herself, and she decided to buy a car immediately.

If she had her own vehicle, she could cover her Surrey territory with much greater ease, as well as using it to answer any calls she might get from Sussex and the south coast. Her expense account would cover petrol and other routine running costs, and she would have the car for pleasure trips, too.

Jimmy, her driving instructor, recommended a reputable dealer in the Edgware Road, and dropped her off there on his way back to base.

'A Vauxhall Velox is the thing for you, Madam,' said the slim youngish salesman, who was dressed in slacks and a blazer that had the Navy badge on the breast pocket. 'It has a three-speed gearbox and is very economical to run.'

'You have such a car here?'

'We can let you test-drive one right away, but the actual delivery will be about a month – two months at the outside. Good makes like the Velox are worth waiting for, though, because I can assure you, Madam, when you have taken our model for a spin you will think the wait worthwhile.'

Georgette smiled inwardly. 'You could be selling my typewriters!' she thought. She noticed how he dodged her queries about the cost of the car, as he expounded the virtues of the model he had recommended.

'What are the colours?'

'The most fashionable is metallic silver-grey. Step in, Madam, and I'll take you for a little drive and show you its operating characteristics. Then I'll let you drive for a bit.' Although she largely ignored his sales pitch, Georgette was completely satisfied with what she saw and experienced: the Velox seemed to glide effortlessly along the busy road, handling well, and she felt comfortable behind the wheel.

'So, how much did you say?'

He told her.

'Oh, dear!'

'That includes purchase tax, of course,' he said hastily. 'You can, of course, buy the car on hire purchase, Madam. Have you considered that?'

She had not.

'Oh, yes, Madam!' he said eagerly. 'You pay only forty percent down and can spread the balance payments over twenty-four months.'

'With interest, of course?'

'But very reasonable interest! And it's tax deductible if the vehicle is to be used for business.'

'All the same, I think I would prefer to put sixty percent down, to reduce the interest on the balance.'

'That's perfectly acceptable.'

'You will, of course, deliver the car to my house fully ready for the road?'

'We'd be delighted to do so, Madam, and with a tank full of petrol!'

Towards the end of August, the Vauxhall Velox was ready for delivery and Georgette took a day off work to receive it.

When the doorbell sounded, Georgette was preparing a salad for lunch. She went to the bedroom window and peered down. There, in the road below, she could see her beautiful gleaming new car.

'Children, come with me. Nanny, you come too. I've something to show you all – a big surprise!'

It was follow-my-leader down the stairs and into the street. The excitement when they saw they had a car of their own was a delight to Georgette.

'A ride, Mummy, a ride!' demanded Susan.

'A long ride,' put in Alex, now a bright four-year-old.

'Where do you want to go?'

'Windsor, Mummy!' decided Susan.

'Windsor, Mummy!' echoed Alex, although he had no idea what that meant.

'Is that all right with you, Nanny?'

'A wonderful idea, Madam. I have not been there for a long time.' Nanny was chuckling, too, infected by the cheerful mood.

'Then it's unanimous. We shall go to Windsor straight after lunch!'

Chapter Fourteen

As the Vauxhall Velox drew near to Windsor, Georgette's back began to ache very badly. She had awakened that morning with a twinge, but that wasn't unusual and the pain generally eased before long. But not today. Being behind the wheel of a car and a new car at that, with the children in the back and Nanny at her side, instead of an instructor, induced unexpected tension. The prospect of traipsing around Windsor Castle no longer held any appeal for her.

They left the car in a car-park and, when they were gathered at the top of Thames Street, which led down beside the castle, Georgette made a decision. She turned to Nanny, 'I'm sorry, but I have to say it: my back needs a rest. If you could take the children on alone, I'll rest in that nice little tea-shop over there, and you can all join me for a cup of tea when you've finished exploring.'

The children protested, but Nanny understood and whisked them away.

Even the short walk to the tea-shop jarred her spine, and Georgette knew she'd made the right decision. She entered the pleasant little place and found it was empty of customers, enjoying a lull after a busy lunch-time, so she had her choice of tables. She opted for a straight-backed chair by the window and ordered a pot of tea and some cakes.

The place had an air of quiet dignity, with a hint of awareness that its near neighbour was none other than Windsor Castle!

Idly, Georgette watched the passers-by ambling along, enjoying the warm, sunny day, and dwarfed by the backdrop of the imposing stone facade of the castle.

As she raised a teacup to her lips, a man walked by with a glance in her direction. Their eyes met momentarily, then he was gone, leaving Georgette staring after him in disbelief – surely she knew that face!

She felt peculiar and her hand shook as she settled her cup back on its saucer. She tried to rise, suddenly determined to pursue the man, but the sudden movement produced a sharp pain in her back and she hastily resumed her seat.

She couldn't run after him to make sure and she told herself she must be wrong. It was eleven years since she had last seen that face, and its owner had then been only fourteen. Could it really have been Dougie Rusby, once her step-son? She had really liked Dougie, and could recall his adolescent's face very clearly – and that person certainly had looked like an older version of him.

In that moment she wished she could have stayed in touch with Dougie and, through him, learnt of David's progress through the years. But the man had continued up the hill, so either he had not recognized her or he did not wish to acknowledge her. After all, she had been married to his father only briefly, and there was no real tie between them.

With an effort, Georgette shook off her growing melancholy, and told herself it was not Dougie she had seen, though something inside her still insisted it was. She drank some tea then, with deliberation, lit a cigarette. She drew heavily on it, and was returning the lighter to her handbag when a man's voice said, 'Madam, please forgive the intrusion, but is your name Georgette?'

Georgette looked up – and it was him!

'Dougie! How wonderful to see you!' She looked at him fully and admired the dashing appearance he cut in his two-piece grey/green mohair suit.

'You remember me!' He took a seat, amazed that she was still so beautiful and remembering vividly his adolescent desires. He had hesitated to come into the tea-shop while he considered the wisdom of acknowledging Georgette. But curiosity, and a desire to meet her again, had overcome his caution.

Blessedly, their meeting was without awkwardness.

'I saw your face in the window, and it rang a bell, but it was only when I was well past that I placed it. I just had to come back and see if it really was you!'

'How kind of you to take the trouble! I was just thinking how like you that person looked! But I had decided I must have been mistaken – I'm so glad that I was not!'

'What brings you to Windsor, Georgette?'

'I was going to take my children round the castle, but my back was giving me some trouble – a slipped disc, you know – so I told Nanny to go with them.'

'I'm sorry to hear you have back problems. Are you feeling all right now?'

'Perfectly, thank you. I just needed a bit of a rest after the drive.'

'You married again, obviously. How many children do you have?'

'A girl and a boy.'

'And your husband?'

'We're divorced.' She outlined her story.

'So that's how you got your bad back, eh? Lifting these machines you speak of?'

'I'm afraid so.'

'Poor Georgette! Gosh, it's really good to see you again, you know. Truly it is! It can't be easy for you, bringing up children and working.'

'Oh, I'm doing very well, Dougie. I love selling.'

'Forgive me, I did not mean to imply . . .'

'No, I know that! But tell me about yourself. How is it you are in Windsor?'

'I'm stationed here. I'm in the Army. I have been for six years.'

'You wear those tall fluffy black hats that the soldiers wear at the castle?'

Dougie laughed. 'Bearskins, Georgette, that's what they are! No, that's not us, that's the foot guards. I'm in The Life Guards.'

'Oh! Are they the ones with the shiny breastplates and helmets and plumes?'

'That's right, with red tunics.'

'And you ride with the Queen?'

'Well, the ceremonial regiment does that. I've yet to be posted to Knightsbridge. I work with armoured vehicles.'

'It is a career for you, the Army?'

'Very much so! I'm a captain now.'

'And you are married?'

'I'm still single. I live in the Officers' House at Combermere Barracks, which is behind the castle. My first posting was there, as a troop commander. It always is for new officers. For the last four years the Regiment has been in Germany, and we've only just come back, to find a completely new barracks complex has been built on the site.'

'You make it sound as if you don't like the change?'

'I think you can say we will miss the untroubled Victorian calm that the old buildings had. Certainly the old Officers' House will be missed. It was a grand building that opened up onto a cricket field, which is now the barracks square. The Officers' House itself has been demolished to make way for the other ranks' cook-house. But we'll get used to the new buildings in time, I expect. At the moment the whole complex is still a criss-cross of trenches for power cables, heating pipes and so forth. However, it's not all bad. The old stables and riding school are intact and I can still get my horse shod there.'

'You have a horse? How nice! But, if there is no cricket field, where do you play cricket? You do still play cricket. I imagine?'

'Very much so! Luckily the Queen has given us the use of Home Park and, thanks to the groundsmen, we have got a bloody good wicket – we're winning on it!'

'Do you like your men?'

'They are the finest soldiers in the world, Georgette! We're very lucky. The whole regiment is rather like an extended family.'

Georgette studied the assured young man seated beside her, and knew he was happy.

'It might be the life for David one day?' she ventured tentatively.

'I wondered when you would get around to asking about him! Actually, I don't think he will want to join the Army. He's more likely to do something academic, as he's very bright and rather sensitive. Thelma adores him and it's mutual. Father dotes on him, of course, and we all love him. By "all" I mean me, Helen and little Emma.'

'Emma?'

'Of course, you wouldn't know – Emma's our half-sister, Thelma's daughter. David's a happy child and popular at school. Father's put him down for Winchester and his masters say he's certain to get a scholarship.'

'I'm so glad! Does David know anything about me?'

'He knows you exist, of course, but he doesn't ask about you. Thelma is very much his mother. He was told simply that you and Father had split up when he was a baby, and I think he's under the impression that you returned to Belgium. I'm sorry, Georgette, but I'm fairly sure he considers you abandoned him and has wiped you from his life.'

'I never wanted to give him up, Dougie, never! I loved him so very much!' Georgette's voice was cracking with emotion. 'He was such a beautiful baby!'

'He's a very good-looking boy now. I could send you a photograph if . . .'

'No, I don't think that would be sensible, too much torment! I don't want to intrude on his life, but perhaps, from time to time, you could write to me – just to let me know he's all right? I'll write my home address on the back of my business card.' She acted on her words and handed it over.

'I'll do that, Georgette, and gladly! I've often wondered how you were getting on – you must know how much I liked you when we came to you in the holidays that one time – so did Helen. But I fear she must have forgotten you now. After all, she was only young, then.' Dougie slipped the card into his wallet. 'You can always write to me care of The Life Guards.'

'Does your father get on well with Thelma?'

'How can I answer that? They are right for each other, that's the truth. My mother thinks that, too.'

'Is Ralph still in the Royal Air Force? Did he stay on longer than those three extra years?'

'No, he is now running a very successful public relations company in Maidstone. We still live in the house he bought that you lived in.'

More tea was ordered and they talked on for some time, then Dougie checked his watch. 'Sorry, Georgette, but it's time I was getting back to barracks. I'm truly delighted to have seen you again, and I promise I'll keep in touch – so you'll always have a link with David.'

They kissed goodbye, and shook hands at the same time. Both knew this meeting would remain their secret and that they would be most unlikely to meet again. But, for Georgette, it was enough to know that the occasional letter would let her know how her beloved first-born was progressing.

As she sat alone, a tear travelled slowly down her cheek and settled by her chin. Elegantly, she dabbed it away with a table napkin, and poured a further cup of tea.

As he had withdrawn, Dougie had taken his teacup and had placed it on another table, and Georgette silently thanked him for that consideration. She wouldn't have thought to remove it and Nanny would have been certain to spot the additional used cup, even if the children did not.

Happily there was time enough before the children and Nanny came back to compose herself, shake herself free of melancholy. Any residue of emotion could be put down to her back pain.

Susan and Alex came running in excitedly, full of their visit to the royal castle. Trailing in their wake came Nanny, glad of a rest.

'It was wonderful Mummy! You should have come!' said Susan.

'I know, my darling poppet!' But if she had . . .

They hadn't been home from Windsor more than an hour when Jack paid a call, and, while Nanny made a bath ready for her charges, the children rushed to tell him all about their drive to a grand castle in Mummy's new car. That led to them dragging him downstairs to view the vehicle.

Jack showed delight in front of Susan and Alex but, as soon as he was alone with Georgette in the living-room, his attitude changed.

'So you have spent your hard-earned money buying a car? Why?'

Georgette was startled by the hostile note in his voice. 'Why ever not, Jack? I need a car!'

'Of course you do. But I was planning to buy you one!'

'But Jack, I didn't know that! Anyway, you don't have to keep giving me things. You've done enough for me already.'

'I don't *have* to do anything, Georgette,' his voice was harsh. 'I *want* to give you things. It makes me happy to give you things. It gives me a kick every time I look at this flat now. It's beautifully decorated, and the right setting for your beauty – except for the furniture, of course! Since you've deprived me of the pleasure of buying you a car, I insist you now let me furnish this place!' His voice was slightly softer, but it was clear he would brook no argument, and Georgette gave in as gracefully as she could, still a little awed by his original ferocity.

A few days later, Georgette and Nancy dined at a little restaurant in Claygate, Surrey. It was a beautiful summer evening and, as Tom was in Paris for a couple of days on business, Georgette had taken her friend for a drive in the Velox. While they were waiting for their queen's pudding and cream, Georgette poured out her concern about Jack's conduct.

'It sounds to me as if he's lonely,' declared Nancy.

'I think you're right, but I don't know why he should be. He seems to have everything, except . . .'

'Except you, dear?'

'Except happiness, I was going to say.'

'Then you must give him happiness.'

'I must?'

'No! I mean . . . don't take that the wrong way! I meant to say that it obviously gives him happiness to indulge you. So why not let him? I can't see that letting him give you things will do anybody any harm.'

'But he's a married man – I keep telling you that!'

'Yes, dear, but his wife must know about you, or he could not be with you so much, and he obviously has enough money to look after you both. But something is missing from his life – being married doesn't automatically mean that one is happy. Were you happy when you were married?'

'Touché. But Nancy, don't you see, I don't understand Jack. I don't know what makes him tick. There was something rather frightening about the way he enthused over the car to please the children and then turned on me as soon as they were in the bath. He was like two different people!'

The meal over, Georgette dropped Nancy off at Dauphin Circus and got home at about ten-thirty.

As she turned into Sparrow Hall Walk, Georgette saw Jack Grant's Daimler parked outside her door. He'd never visited her this late before. Steve was dozing behind the wheel and Georgette didn't disturb him.

As she entered the flat, Nanny appeared, concern on her face. She said, 'I'm sorry, Madam, but I didn't know what to do. Mr and Mrs Grant are in the sitting-room. They arrived about ten minutes ago.'

'Are the children asleep all right?'

'Yes, Madam.'

'Then that's all right, Nanny. Thank you. You go to bed.' Nanny, relieved, retired to her quarters.

Georgette entered the living-room. There on the settee sat a very sweet-looking woman, small and neat, with grey hair swept back off her face. Jack was in the armchair he seemed to have adopted. It was clear he had had plenty to drink, but she wasn't sure he was drunk.

'Here you are at last!' he greeted her with a firm handshake, but proffered no kiss. 'Phyllis and I have been to our favourite restaurant, in Lower Regent Street. Wonderful meal, wasn't it, darling? I wanted you two to meet.'

Georgette smiled at Jack's wife, as she rose courteously and came forward to shake hands.

'You are very welcome. Sorry I was out. I was at a restaurant, too.'

'With Nancy Flowers, Nanny said.'

'Would you like a cup of coffee or something?'

'Actually we helped ourselves. Nanny approved it!' said Jack.

'Mrs Grant, I really am pleased to meet you and have a chance to explain. I hope you do not misunderstand all this, because . . .'

Mrs Grant put up a hand to silence her. 'Don't worry, my dear. I do understand, and I don't blame you at all. I know that you haven't encouraged Jack but, when he wants something, he is a determined man. He's been so happy since he met you and the children!' It wasn't intended it should be detected, but there was hurt in her gentle voice and it cut Georgette to the quick.

She was bewildered by the turn of events. What was all this about? She'd been trying desperately not to let her relationship with Jack develop, simply because he was married and she had no desire to create problems with his marriage, and now he had brought his wife to her home to meet her! Furthermore, as Nancy had said, Mrs Grant seemed fully aware of what was happening and seemed to accept the fact that her husband was infatuated with another woman, even to condone his behaviour. How could Jack do that to his wife?

Jack came forward and put a hand on Georgette's shoulders. He was silent, but his eyes said it all. From the first time she had seen him, it was his eyes that spoke, drew her to him. They seemed to see right through her, and know her feelings for him. They were all-enveloping. Jack Grant looking at her like that made her feel utterly defenceless.

She tore her eyes away. 'Honestly, Mrs Grant, I promise you I haven't willingly done anything to encourage him. And, whatever it may look like, we are not having an affair – our relationship is platonic, I swear! Tell her, Jack!'

But Jack said nothing.

Mrs Grant smiled, a little sadly. 'I do believe you, my dear, really I do. Jack and I have been married for thirty years, well, I expect you know, and I understand him better than he understands himself. I know that you will have little choice in how your relationship progresses. You may think of it as purely platonic but I know that Jack does not – whether or not you have actually made love is rather immaterial, don't you think? He is undeniably in love with you and there's really not much else to be said.'

Georgette had to agree. The couple left a few minutes later, Mrs Grant offering Georgette a firm handshake and Jack a good-night kiss on the cheek.

The French windows onto the balcony were open and Georgette ran out there and wept, not sure whether her tears were for herself or Phyllis Grant.

The clink of milk bottles rattling in their crates on the milkman's float played no part the next day in awakening Georgette from her night's slumbers. She was already awake, having had only a fitful sleep and seen the light of day begin to thrust its way through the light curtains in her bedroom. She wanted to roll over and rest her eyes for a while longer, but she had to get up. She still had her living to earn, and this was a working day. During the restless night, she had decided to speak to Mr Saint before she started her day's canvassing.

The happy sounds of the children getting ready for the day did something to cheer her up as she saw to her own preparations.

As a gesture to comfort, on the back of GBE's growing prosperity, Mr Saint now had a thick pile carpet on the floor of his office and he was sitting in a deep leather chair. He was always at his desk early, and always ready to spare time if his staff had any problems they wanted to talk over.

When Georgette had finished pouring out her story, Mr Saint remained in deep thought for a moment.

'You're saying this situation began on the day you sold him the machines?'

'I think he fell for me that first day. That may have been why he bought so many machines – or any machines at all.'

And Mr Saint thought ruefully, 'In his position, I might have done the same thing!' But what he said was: 'Well, I'm glad you haven't allowed his attentions to affect your sales figures. They're still very good.'

'I'd never deliberately let my sales fall, Mr Saint! That's my job!'

'Quite.' And he wished all his salesmen thought that way.

'But I am finding this new development a problem, Mr Saint. I really don't think he's going to take "No" for an answer but, if I accept his offer, I shall be so beholden to him that it will be difficult to refuse his advances. The only answer I can see is to go somewhere far away! Is there any chance I could be posted to Australia, or somewhere?'

Australia had been her first thought during the night, encouraged by the prospect of renewing her friendship with Simon Tait. She had received no Christmas card from him last year and hoped that was not an indication that he was forgetting her.

Mr Saint gave her an old-fashioned look. 'Do you know who his father is?' His question was rhetorical. 'Grant Marine Incorporated. I found out that by chance.'

Georgette looked blank. The revelation meant nothing.

'That's a vast multi-national firm. Grant Marine make marine engines all over the world. Jack Grant's father founded the business in Miami and he still runs the firm from there, despite the fact that, officially he could have retired years ago. They have contacts absolutely everywhere and running away will not help you.'

'Then what on earth can I do?' she pleaded.

Mr Saint paused before answering, then said, 'I don't know if I should say this, Georgette, because, although I'm always happy to listen to problems, I don't really think it's a good idea for employers to give their staff personal advice. But, since your problem arose because of your work . . .

'From what I've heard of your Mr Grant, he is a man who won't give up. He has a reputation for being remarkably tenacious and, once he's made up his mind to something, that's it – you may recall that he managed to get early delivery of his typewriters, the only UK client who has ever managed that! I followed your request to put through a routine request for early delivery to Head Office in New York but I was expecting a flat refusal. I have learnt, since, that he contacted them direct and pulled a few strings – hence their co-operation!'

'Couldn't he have got his typewriters directly from the States, through Grant Marine, quicker?' Georgette interjected even as the notion occurred to her.

'Undoubtedly, I should think, except he didn't! ('Because of you, that's certain,' he reasoned.) So . . . If you are correct in saying that he has his sights fixed on you, I don't believe that you will achieve anything by leaving the country – he'd trace you wherever you go, and I believe that he will do just that. So you might just as well accept that as the situation and learn to live with it.'

Georgette was aghast. 'But you are saying I'm trapped, Mr Saint!'

'It would seem so. But infatuations do die, you know – and that's all it is in my book. If you hold out long enough, he may simply lose interest.'

'And if he doesn't what do I do then?'

'I'm not a psychiatrist, Georgette, I'm just your boss, and I'm afraid that is a decision for you alone. You must understand that my job is to look at these things only in so far as they might affect your work.'

Even as she took her leave of Mr Saint, Georgette's heart told her she didn't want to give Jack up and, since there seemed to be little she could do to deter him, she decided she might as well give in gracefully.

It had been a long time since she had had a real boy-friend and, apart from Nancy, she had few female friends. She was lonely and, clearly, so was he – and his wife appeared to accept the situation, so why should she continue to resist him?

Chapter Fifteen

The next time he saw her, Jack instinctively knew that Georgette had surrendered, but he made no move to advance their relationship, just continued to enfold her in affection.

He made Georgette's thirty-fifth birthday memorable by giving her a beautiful shimmering red evening gown and laying on a little lunch party in her flat. On his instructions, she took the day off work. Jack brought in caterers to prepare, serve and clear away a delicious lunch, so that the guests could be free to relax and enjoy themselves. The guests were Tom and Nancy Flowers, Nanny Trotter, Daisy Brown and the children, plus Jack himself, but Georgette was the guest of honour and loved all her presents. It was a delightful afternoon.

Later, when the children were in bed and the guests, other than Nanny, had departed, Jack took Georgette out for a quiet candle-lit dinner. They went to his favourite restaurant, in Lower Regent Street, where the best wines complemented each dish. Jack knew she liked trout, and trout they ate, with all the trimmings. The dessert was simple: fresh marinated fruit with double cream.

'This has been a most beautiful day for me, Jack,' Georgette confessed, as they took coffee with an excellent cognac. 'I never thought a whole day could be so nice.'

'Every day can be delightful when you are with people who love you. And I do love you!'

'I love you, too!'

'Then isn't it sad that most of our time is spent, necessarily, in the company of people we do not love?'

Georgette recognized that as a thought of her own. 'But doesn't the separation make the hours when we are together even more precious?'

'Very precious, Georgette! I've decided to take you on holiday soon. You will come?'

Happily relaxed, Georgette responded without hesitation. 'Oh, yes, Jack – where shall we go?'

'Florida.'

'America!'

'Why not? I go to Miami every year. Indeed, I rang you from there for last New Year, but I don't think you guessed that. I want you to meet my father.'

'But what about Alex and Susan?'

'Do you think I wouldn't consider them? They are with you for Christmas, are they not?'

'Yes.'

'Then they go to their Granny's, with their father, for a couple of weeks – coming home just in time for Susan's new term in mid-January?'

'Yes.'

'Well, that's when we go to America, just after Christmas. I believe Nanny will be going on holiday then, too, to visit her sister in Scotland.'

'You have it all worked out?'

'That's my way.'

'But I have to work, Jack.'

'Your office tells me you are owed time off. You haven't taken your holiday this year.'

'Well, I had so much time off last year, when my back was bad, that . . .'

'That was sick-leave. What kind of passport do you have – British or Belgian?'

'British.'

'Good, then I don't think you need a visa. But I'll check it out.'

Jack's mind was clearly made up and, with America beckoning, Georgette didn't feel inclined to argue.

The Viscount airliner was on its controlled descent into Miami airport. As the tarmac became less of a ribbon and more of a runway, Georgette, seated in a window seat of the aircraft, gazed out of the porthole at the scenery below. All of it was so flat, with less than incisive water inlets. It was land reclaimed from mangrove swamps, as she understood it, but it was not quite how she had envisaged it would be. By her side, Jack Grant was still resting his eyes.

The plane touched heavily down on the runway and jerked as the brakes were applied, squealing in agony as they connected with the wheels. The strato-cruiser that had carried them overnight from London to Nassau had not done that; it had dropped like a feather onto Bahamian soil, so that Georgette scarcely knew they had actually made contact with terra firma. Then she had felt weary, despite the comfort of the aircraft, and they had taken their sleeping bunks.

Now she felt only excitement. For the first time in her life she was entering another continent, the glamorous world of the United States of America!

It was not until she and Jack were queueing to go through immigration that Georgette began to feel apprehension. Jack sensed her concern, guessed its cause. 'Don't worry. My father is really going to like you – how can he not?'

Georgette gave a weak smile, and felt better as, gently, his fingers entwined in hers. But that couldn't alter the fact that Jack had a wife back in England, and thoughts of Phyllis persisted. Georgette could not help feeling that this was a trip on which Jack should have brought his wife, rather than his mistress. But she pushed her feelings of guilt aside, for Jack had told her, during the flight, that Phyllis had always refused to accompany him on trips to Florida. She had been there once, shortly after their marriage, but, since then, she had always come up with some excuse, and told him to go alone.

'She's never said why, but I think it's because she didn't take to my father – and didn't want to hurt my feelings by saying so. He's a self-made man, you know, and there is a very ruthless side to him. I guess she sensed that and it put her off. It worried me at first, as I've always tried to spend the New Year at home. Surprising as it may seem, my father has never set foot outside the States – always sent some minion to set up the overseas branches and refused all my invitations to come to England. I guess he couldn't spare the time when travel was by sea, and just doesn't fancy long journeys now he's getting on a bit. Anyway, Phyllis never objected to my annual visit and, after a while, I just stopped asking her to accompany me.'

Through Immigration, through Baggage Control, through Customs, all without delay, and suddenly Georgette and Jack were in a corridor, one flank of which was made up of greeters, peering anxiously at every emerging person as they sought the familiar faces.

It was practically four-thirty, Eastern Standard Time, the flight a little later in than scheduled. The temperature was well into the seventies, with humidity to match. And this was winter!

Then Jack was talking animatedly to a fleshy man in a grey suit.

'Georgette darling, meet Gene. He's here to drive us home. He and his good wife, Ellie, look after my father.'

'We certain sure try!' responded Gene. 'Pleased to meet you, Ma'am.' He smiled, discreetly showing his approval of her.

Attended by porters, Gene led Jack and Georgette to where he had parked the car. Once out of the airport buildings, Georgette basked in the caress of the sun's warmth, as she had when crossing the tarmac after leaving the aircraft. She had thought she might find it too hot to take, but not so; though she was glad of the sunglasses Jack had bought her, which saved her squinting against the glaring sunlight.

Georgette was astonished by the shiny limousine Gene took them to. It was a black Cadillac and she giggled as she spoke confidentially to Jack: 'I think my car would fit with ease into the back!'

Jack laughed. 'Remember, Georgette, everything is bigger in America. We have the space.'

'And you have the money, too,' thought Georgette, not without a trace of cynicism.

With her legs stretched out from the comfort of the back seat of the car, Georgette noted that the journey to Surfside, Miami, where Ben Grant lived, was not nearly as heavy with traffic as she had reckoned, nor was the skyline crowded with skyscrapers. She commented on all that to Jack.

'It used to be quieter than this. Now travelling is becoming easier and, given another thirty years, I doubt if I'll recognize the place! It's changed a lot already, since I was a small boy, I can tell you. Like us, people from northern states like to vacation here. It's so much warmer, takes them away from their cold winter.'

The Cadillac began to slow and Georgette saw that they were driving parallel to a high brick wall. This led to huge ornamental gates with sculptured pillars either side, each pillar topped with a large concrete pineapple.

'My, it's a jungle either side of us!' Georgette exclaimed, as Gene drove through the gates, which had been quickly opened by an estate worker.

'It's called "hammock",' explained Jack, who had anticipated she would be enthralled by this unexpected sight. 'It's found only in parts of southern Florida and my parents insisted it should be preserved.'

The driveway to the house took a deliberate meandering path, so that the sub-tropical jungle could be enjoyed to the full by visitors. Then the Cadillac was out of it, its wheels gliding over a stone forecourt towards the house, which was impressive. Made of solid concrete, it had green carpet running up the flight of steps that led to the front door, which was under a pillared porch.

'How many acres have you got here?' Georgette asked, after Jack had helped her step from the car. She was drinking in the carefully-planted royal palms and ficus trees, and the manicured lawns beyond.

'Not more than eight acres. Others have more, of course, but it's enough for Father.'

'It's all so lovely!'

'You like it?'

'It's a delight! The house – it looks so old, but it can't be?'

'No, my parents had it built forty-odd years ago. In Europe we take antiquity for granted, but America does not have real antiquity, so it creates it. The house is the way they wanted it, with a lot of Italian influence, and we've some fine antiques from Italy, too, as well as from England. No formal gardens here, though – we're more English that way. On the other side of the house there's an inlet from the sea.'

The tall, white-painted front door opened at that moment and a bear of a man, dressed in a cream cashmere jacket and blue cotton slacks, hurried down the steps. He had to be Jack's father, Georgette concluded, but she knew he was eighty-three and he didn't look anything like that old.

She stood by shyly while the man hugged and kissed his son, obviously pleased to see him and full of parental affection.

'So you are Georgette!' Ben's voice was a gravelly southern drawl. He smiled warmly, through features that deeply resembled Jack's. He had the aura of a man accustomed to being obeyed.

'Yes, sir.'

'Call me Ben. I insist.' He took her hand, and it disappeared into his enormous palm while he shook it. 'Well, you're most welcome, Georgette. Make yourself right at home. It's the quick and the dead here – if you get hungry or thirsty between meals, go find the kitchen. Don't wait to be asked – you won't be! Let me show you to your room. Then I'll give you the grand tour.'

'He's taken a shine to you, I can tell,' Jack whispered the aside to Georgette, and there was an unintended hint of relief in his voice.

Ben led the way into the house which, with the exception of a 'wheel-house' built to provide a good view of the sea inlet, was all on one level: raised slightly above the ground.

The long marble-floored hall was decorated with painted and lacquered wall panels that had been copied from an eighteenth century design, while the large dining-room was adorned with genuinely old oil paintings. Next to that was a large breakfast room and a well-equipped kitchen, where Georgette met Gene's wife, Ellie, who was small and plump, with a kind face. The staff quarters were reached from the kitchen, but their privacy was respected and Georgette's tour did not include their rooms.

The main reception room was enormous, and filled with priceless objets d'art. In one corner was a spiral staircase that ascended to the 'wheel-house' and, through the french windows which formed one wall could be seen a patio garden with a few delightful statues of cherubs and goddesses. Ben's private suite was through a door from the reception room, and consisted of a den, bedroom and bathroom. He explained that the den had originally been his wife's dressing-room but it was now very masculine – the sort of room Georgette imagined would be found in one of those gentlemen's clubs in St James's.

She was surprised to be shown an elegant music-room ('my wife's favourite retreat') and an airy tea-room ('It's not true that we Americans drink only coffee, you know, and my wife liked to give tea parties')

The five luxurious guest-rooms were at the front of the house, and all had *en suite* bathrooms. Georgette had been allocated the principal guest-room, complete with four-poster bed and drapery. The seating consisted of antique gilt chairs. The wardrobe and chest of drawers were both of mahogany.

Having freshened up, rejuvenating herself in a warm, oiled, bath, Georgette was ready for Jack's knock on her door, when he came to escort her to the tea-room.

When they entered that airy room, which gave the illusion of being even bigger than it was due to the fact that enormous glass doors led out to the open area surrounding the sizeable swimming pool, Ben was already standing by those doors.

'Had these fitted since you were last here, Jack,' he said, without preamble. 'Good and strong, and look at that bevelled glass. One man hung these doors, too. Some craftsman, eh, Georgette?'

Georgette smiled her agreement. She was still a little shy of him.

'You like to swim, Georgette? There's the pool. Just dip yourself in, any time.'

'I will. I like the glass swan swimming on it.'

113

'Ah, she does a valuable job, helps to keep the pool clean! You see she holds the chlorine, lets it out a little at a time.' Then he caught sight of Ellie, hovering at the hall entrance to the room, bearing a loaded tray in her hands. 'Ah, Ellie, come on in. Put the tea down there.'

Ellie did so, exchanged a little banter with Jack and Ben, then withdrew to 'see to dinner'.

'Didn't think to ask – do you like Earl Grey, Georgette?'

'I drink it a lot.'

'That's what we've got. Take a seat, both of you. Shall I pour?' Ben acted on his own suggestion, and poured out the teas.

'Jack, were you planning on doing any sea-fishing this trip?'

'No, I'm not feeling energetic enough to try for the big fish this time.' But he would have liked to have done – he always did – and Jack sensed that his father was going to say so, and added quickly: 'I thought I'd fish off the jetty, though.'

'Okay. Only I let Judge Holdiman have the fishing craft. You know Theo – he found he had time free and wanted to take me up on my promise to lend my boat to him. But I could get you one in, if you want it?'

'No, that's fine.'

'Good! The trumpy's in dry dock. Did I say that in my last letter? It looked time for major preventative maintenance, so it's having that now.'

'What's a trumpy?' Georgette asked of Jack, almost in a whisper, but it was Ben who answered. Nothing wrong with his hearing!

'It's our motor yacht, my dear, designed and built by J. Trumpy & Sons, back in '41. We had it from new. It's usually moored out the back here. We also make boats ourselves, of course, but not in that range. She's named *Bejama*, same as the house. Did you see that name as you drove in?'

Georgette recalled seeing a wrought-iron name-plate on the wall by the right-hand pillar. 'I don't know what the word means, though,' she admitted.

Ben looked conspiratorially at Jack. 'Shall we tell her?'

'Sure.'

'I'm Benjamin. My dear wife, Jack's mother, was called Marilyn. Between us we had Jack.'

'Ah – the first two letters of each name, with Jack's in the middle.' Georgette cottoned on fast.

'Bright girl!' Jack teased her.

'Jack, take Georgette down to the dry dock tomorrow to see her, why don't you?'

'That's a good idea.'

'That way, Georgette, you can see where I started my business – over sixty years ago.'

Grant Marine's dry dock was on the Miami River. Entry to the yard was through a pair of tubular framed gates, covered, like the perimeter fence, with chain-link wiring.

Driving a red Buick, one of four cars Ben Grant owned which were garaged next to the house, Jack drove into the dirt and gravel enclosure, shifting dust in his progress. It was not yet nine o'clock but the sun was already very hot. Georgette was wearing a cotton blouse and slacks, Jack a white shirt and Bermuda shorts. Was it only yesterday that they had been wrapped in heavy clothes and shivering in London's cold air?

'There's the *Bejama*.' Jack pointed her out, as he parked beside some open-backed Chevrolets and Fords: workers' trucks. 'And you're privileged – not many guests get to see her bottom!'

They walked over to her and stood peering up at her hull, for the motor yacht was high and dry, towering above them. Georgette could see quite a few men moving about on her – all doing important work, she was sure.

'She's enormous!'

'It's only because she's out of the water that she looks so big. The *Bejama* is only seventy-six feet long. We can handle boats up to one hundred and fifty feet here. Do you want to go aboard to take a look?'

'I think I would not make it up the ladder. It's a bit too high a climb for me.'

'Fair enough! You can always tell a trumpy. It's got a straight bow, which enables it to cut cleanly through the water. And you see the fretwork scrolls on either side of the bow? You only get those on a trumpy.'

'Morning, Mr Grant. How are you?' A voice hailed from the *Bejama*'s deck.

'Hi there, Howie! How's it all going?'

'Great, just great! You looking for Chuck Boward?'

'Yes, when he's free.'

'Should be any time soon. He's got a problem in No. 2 wet storage shed.'

'Those have to be the massive buildings behind us,' Georgette reasoned.

'They can get Chuck over the tannoy, if needed,' continued Howie, wiping sweat from his brow with the back of a greasy arm, his eyes appreciatively on Georgette.

'Okay, Howie, don't worry. We'll hang around for him in Reception.' Jack gave a parting wave, and Georgette followed in his wake as he made his way to the office area, back near the car. 'We can get a coffee there,' he told Georgette.

'Who's Chuck Boward?'

'The superintendent here. He and I were boys together and he's worked here all his life, worked his way up from the bottom. What he doesn't know about boats isn't worth knowing.'

The offices were a collection of interconnecting prefabricated cabins, everything functional rather than luxurious; low ceilings, wood partitioning, solid floors – and all a bit grubby to Georgette's eyes.

While Jack and Georgette took chairs, the young receptionist rushed off to get them coffee.

The reception area was lighted by fluorescent tubes and the centre-piece was a table made from an old capstan wheel. The wheel was horizontal and raised up to coffee-table height by four legs, each consisting of three large links of anchor chain welded together. A piece of thick plate-glass was spread over it all.

'Do you like that, Georgette?'

'It's marvellous!'

'I helped Father make that when I was a lad. Well, I like to think I did – I held things for him! And this is where his business empire all started, as he said yesterday.'

Jack stood up and went over to one of the many framed photographs adorning the walls, mostly of yachts the company had worked on. He took it down and handed it to Georgette. 'This was the original site, as it was when Father took it over.'

Georgette eyed it keenly. It was a very peaceful river scene, and she said so.

Jack concurred. 'All these buildings he's had to raise since, in order to handle eight hundred to a thousand boats a year.'

Georgette was suitably impressed.

Jack replaced the photograph and started, lovingly, to survey the various pictures of yachts. 'I know many of these boats. Here's one I remember well. She was one hundred and fifty feet long, but went down in a hurricane – must be twenty years ago. No one survived.'

Coffee arrived at that moment, just as a raw-boned man, with crew-cut hair and clothed in greasy grey overalls, darkened the entrance. This was Chuck Boward. He saw Jack. 'Hi, how you doing? Heard you were about. Good to see ya. Bring your coffees into my office. Nina, can you get me one, too, please?'

Once in the office, the two men embraced, real pals, then Jack introduced Georgette.

'Welcome to Florida, Ma'am. How are you liking things here?'

'Very much!' Georgette replied, intrigued by the striking shape of Chuck's head, which could be likened to an electric light bulb – and the grin he gave her did light up his whole face.

'What do you think of Miami?'

'We only got in yesterday, Chuck!' Jack protested.

'Okay ... then you won't have seen much yet. You're from England, I guess?'

'Yes, but I was born in Belgium.'

'Interesting. We have quite a few Anglos working here, and Swedes and Irish, but no Belgians.'

The phone on his cluttered desk rang. He answered it casually. 'Hello? ... Oh, Jason Cassidy! What's the guy's problem now? ... Okay, let's get his boat fixed up in a hurry, so he can bring it back again next week!' Jack settled the receiver with a thump, then grinned round at Jack and Georgette. 'There's another member of the "hard aground" club!'

'What's he done?' Georgette was perplexed.

'Banged up his propeller like a mushroom, by getting into shallow water and dragging along the sea-bed. He's a "weekend warrior", as we call 'em, and to them vacation time's money!'

'What will you do?'

'Fit him a new propeller, check for other damage.'

'And if it's a good "mushroom",' Jack came in, 'the boys here will mount it and present it to him.'

Georgette thought that very funny and was giggling when Nina brought in Chuck's coffee. He drank it rapidly.

He and Jack chatted awhile, then Jack asked, 'You're busy, Chuck?'

'All of that.'

'Then is it al'right with you if I show Georgette around the dock?'

'Go right ahead, Jack.'

So Georgette spent almost ninety minutes wandering about the boat-yard. The whole place was a hive of activity: welders attending to propellers or fixing plates to hulls, carpenters making panels and replacing deck planking, painters and varnishers creating a beautiful finish and mechanics sorting out engine problems.

Everything in the yard was huge, bulky: the cranes, cables,

117

winches and massive shoring blocks, variously shaped to hold boats firm once the winches had hauled them out of water. There were thick piles, made of wood or concrete, to support the walkways either side of the dry dock spaces. And the smell of the oily river water seemed to Georgette to add to the weighty masculine atmosphere of the place.

If she felt a little awed, out of her depth, she noticed that Jack was really revelling in it all – a different man to the one she knew in England. He became particularly animated when he found not one, but two, 150-ft yachts among the vessels moored in the wet storage sheds, awaiting attention.

Standing on the concrete jetty fronting the river, Georgette suddenly wondered how the vessels got to the boat-yard, and away again. 'They must come from that way?' she asked, pointing.

'Mostly not,' Jack answered lightly, 'because the sea is the other way!'

'But there's a very low bridge that way!' Georgette objected.

Jack looked amused, but realized she was serious and explained quietly. 'It's a drawbridge, Georgette!' They both burst out laughing.

As they were finishing lunch, tiredness overcame Georgette: jet-lag had got to her.

Jack wasn't surprised. 'Well, that's all right,' he said, his voice now more American than ever. 'Relax up by the pool for the afternoon. Have a little snooze, why don't you, while I do a spell of fishing off the jetty. Ellie can bring you tea out there. You can do the same tomorrow, if you feel like it. We don't have to be out doing things all the time. Maybe we'll have a walk round the grounds tomorrow, too.'

That is what they did, with Georgette finding the gardens absolutely enchanting. Ben was bringing along a fine rose-bed, and was pleased by her praise. Over a salad lunch, he asked Georgette, 'Ever had stone crabs?'

'No, I don't think so.'

'No, you wouldn't have, most likely. They're ornery-looking critturs that ain't to be found no place else but Florida Keys. They're real good, and you've gotta try some. Do you feel up to going out tonight?'

'I feel just fine now.'

'Great!' Ben turned to Jack. 'It's Ellie and Gene's night off, how say we go to Joe's tonight?'

'Al Capone sat right where you are sitting now, Georgette,' Ben proclaimed solemnly, as she, he and Jack took chairs at a wooden table in the corner.

'Then this must be some place,' concluded Georgette instantly.

Ten minutes or so earlier, she had thought Jack joking when, having taken the Buick down Biscayne Street, he began to brake near to what looked like nothing more than an old shack with palm trees around it, saying, 'This is Joe's.' And it was!

'Al Capone ... this very chair?' she was enthralled by the prospect.

Ben issued a belly laugh. He was enjoying himself, very relaxed. 'To be honest, honey, I don't know where he sat! But he certainly has eaten here. So have royalty and film stars.'

Dining at Joe's was on a first-come, first-served basis, except Ben's party waited no more than a few minutes for their eight-fifteen table. Ben had influence somewhere along the line. He had said what time he was coming to eat and that was, almost, when they did eat.

'You can only eat stone crabs in season, between October and April,' Ben informed her, putting aside his jesting.

'Rather like pheasant-shooting in England in that respect,' Jack put in. 'And with these crabs you eat only the legs. The body is wasted.'

'And you don't need to use dinky little oyster forks here, unless you want to. Just use your fingers,' was Ben's advice.

'That's how you get the meat out?'

'You'll see. They smash the shells with a wooden mallet before they bring 'em to the table and, because they're boiled so well, the shell just slides off the meat – or should do!'

It did, and Georgette relished that meal of leg after leg of jumbo stone crab, eaten with melted butter, slices of lemon and a plate of hash browns. It was like no dish she had ever eaten before.

Ben enjoyed her pleasure. 'We sure didn't make a mistake bringing you here, did we?'

'I love such surprises, Ben!'

'Now that I'm glad to hear!'

* * *

Georgette had practically forgotten that New Year's Eve was on the morrow. Ben hadn't, of course. He had laid on a pool party that was to start with brunch and continue into the first hours of 1957. Caterers were brought in for the occasion, to serve food and drink throughout the proceedings. Ben had a fondness for traditional jazz and a group played all afternoon, under a gazebo by the top of the pool.

The Grants had many friends and some fifty people enjoyed themselves dipping in the warm water, including Georgette. Although they were perfectly polite, Georgette was aware that they had little real interest in her, the women being more interested in the latest gossip about their own set and the younger men absorbed in business talk – the older men's consuming interest appeared to be golf.

In the evening, some folks had to go, but the majority stayed on to see in the New Year. The jazz band left and was replaced by a small dance band that played on a rostrum in the main reception room.

Jack mentioned to someone that Georgette had been a Resistance fighter in the war and, suddenly, she became interesting to know. From then on, she was chatted to with respect and curiosity, and was delighted to be regarded as a heroine again.

Just before the witching hour, corks were popped on the imported champagne and glasses were charged. Ben called everyone to order seconds before the grandfather clock in the hall gave out the Westminster chimes. Then, as the first stroke of midnight sounded, he proposed the usual toast: 'Happy New Year!'

The band struck up 'Auld Lang Syne' and glasses were temporarily abandoned, as the ritual of holding crossed hands with the person next to you was performed and the traditional song was sung. At its finish, Jack slipped an arm about Georgette's waist and squeezed her gently. 'I'm so glad you are here with me, darling!' he whispered sincerely into her ear, and his eyes were moist. 'Happy New Year!'

'Could you live here forever?' Jack asked her, when they had taken seats after a time dancing.

Georgette knew her answer, and said, 'I think, if I did, I would not appreciate it all nearly so much. Living elsewhere, I shall long to come here again.'

'That you will do, Georgette. That you will, every year now, with me!' It was said almost as if she had no choice in the matter, not that she detected that truth in his voice.

Ben Grant came up and, raising his voice above the hubbub of merriment about them, said, 'I thought you kids might like to go down to the Torch Ramrod Channel for a couple of days?'

'What a funny name!' said Georgette.

'Surely not as funny as Piddle, or Piddlehaven in England!' Jack reminded her, chuckling. 'And I'm sure Belgian place names can sound just as odd.'

'Whaddya say, Jack?' Ben wanted an answer now.

'It's a great idea!'

'Good! You can fish off there real peaceful. It's all laid on, anyways! Young Bo Goddard's bringing the flying boat down later this afternoon. Georgette, you must want to see something of Florida. What better than the Keys, and from the air? Then, after Torch Ramrod, you go on to Key West. I've got rooms booked at the Casa Marina.'

'Does the idea appeal, Georgette?' asked Jack, knowing that it would.

'Oh, yes! Please!'

'Well, that's right – you don't want to be hanging around here all the time with an old man!' Ben winked, and Georgette knew he really liked her, was not just being polite for his son's sake.

She might have felt less comforted by this thought if she had known that he had also liked Phyllis very much when he had first met her. One day Phyllis had been lounging by the pool while Jack was out deep-sea fishing and Marilyn was visiting a sick friend. In those days there were no live-in staff, so Ben and Phyllis were alone in the house and, despite the fact that he loved his wife, he had been unable to resist the temptation to make advances to his daughter-in-law.

Her initially ladylike protestations and attempts to draw away from him, however, served merely to increase his lust and he launched himself at her in a serious physical assault. Phyllis was no fool, and knew she was no match for him, so she pretended to faint.

Ben pulled back slightly, in surprise, and some instinct made her raise one knee sharply. It caught him in the groin and he rolled away in agony, screaming words of abuse. The foul language shocked Phyllis, and helped her to get over her fright. She put on her towelling robe and sat down calmly, waiting for him to recover.

When he stopped writhing and swearing, she informed him icily that she did not wish to hurt either Marilyn or Jack, so would not mention the incident to either of them provided that he never laid a finger on her again. She added that she would never set foot in his house again, and would break her silence if he ever suggested visiting her in England.

With that, she swept off to her room, and remained there until Marilyn returned to the house. Phyllis and Jack were to return to London the following day, but the remaining few hours were very strained and Jack concluded that his wife and his father had fallen out, though both denied there was any problem, and his mother was unaware of any disagreement between them.

Once he had recovered from the pain, Ben had been deeply ashamed of his behaviour, but Phyllis ensured they were not left alone together for the rest of her stay, so he had no chance to apologize – and had never laid eyes on her again. He had tried to phone her a couple of times, when he knew that Jack would be at work, but she had hung up as soon as she heard his voice, and he did not dare write, in case Jack saw the letter. In the end he'd given up any attempt at a reconciliation.

But he was older now, and much wiser, and, although his libido was still very strong, he had no intention of jeopardizing his relationship with Georgette.

It was Jack who was to pilot the flying boat down to Torch Ramrod Channel.

'While I still have my licence, I will fly!' he responded tetchily, when Georgette expressed her surprise on learning that detail. Such a gruff reaction was not what she had expected at all, but she didn't dwell on it.

'All right, Jack! I'm not criticising you – I just didn't know you could fly aeroplanes. That's all I meant!'

Jack realized his mistake, and said thoughtfully. 'Of course you didn't! I've never mentioned it, have I?' His good humour restored, he grinned broadly, and kissed her lightly on the forehead.

Their luggage stowed, they set off from the jetty shortly after four o'clock. Soon they were flying low over the water. After a while, Jack jabbed a finger down at the sea then, loudly, above the drone of the engine, he spoke. 'The Gulf Stream. I had to show you that – its position varies according to the time of year. Right now, it's here. Some of my happiest days have been spent fishing in that water.'

He drifted into introspection, a smile forming on his lips. 'The start of the Keys,' he announced eventually, 'Key Largo.'

'I saw the film – Humphrey Bogart and Lauren Bacall.'

'That's the island. See that road down there? That's US1: runs right through to Key West, over forty-two bridges that join the little islands together, in about a hundred-mile stretch. And, as we are travelling now towards Torch Ramrod and Key West, the Mexican Gulf is on the right and we are flying above the Atlantic.'

'What a lot of blues there are in the sea,' Georgette noted happily.

'That's right. When you are at sea you need to know those hues. The deep blue is the deep water, the less deep it is the paler the water. So that pale turquoise stretch means that it's very shallow there.'

'Oh look, Jack! Deep water right next to shallow water!' Georgette observed, a short while later.

Jack gave a half laugh. 'No, my darling! *That* dark water is a seaweed bed!' She laughed with him, and they flew on in companionable silence for a while.

'Look to your right, and ahead, Georgette. See that white hut?'

'I see it – by the water's edge?'

'That's your home for the next couple of days, and where I'll fish.'

Jack landed the sea-plane smoothly on the channel between Torch Key and Ramrod Key and gently steered it, engine chugging, towards the dock by the hut. Even as they were heaving to, a middle-aged man came running out of the place to help make the craft fast.

Jack and the man, who was probably two stone overweight, exchanged warm greetings, then Jack introduced him to Georgette as Frank.

'He and his good wife look after this place,' Jack explained, and breathed in the good air.

'You'll like your room, Ma'am,' Frank assured Georgette, even as they neared its door, 'and this whole place.'

She did.

Her room had a rural look, with a well-sprung double bed next to a rocking chair. The view from one window was of the sea and the view from the other was of woods. The place itself, surrounded by a veranda, was charming. Built on stilts ('We don't want to get wet feet unexpectedly!'), the whole construction was of wood, including the roof shingles – which were painted white, like the rear of the place, to deflect the sun. After *Bejama*, The Hut felt cosy: just three bedrooms, one bathroom, one reception room and quarters for Frank and his wife, Millie. Under it all were two garages. Some hut!

Millie was tall and cultured. A practical woman, she undoubtedly ran the place, and Frank obeyed. To go with a welcoming pot of tea, she had prepared English muffins, and they were quite scrumptious. For dinner, she had made key-lime pie.

Given the relatively short time Georgette had been in Florida, she had quite a tan developing and, over the next couple of days, she cultivated it – stretched out on a lounger on the pier, succumbing to the air of somnolence. She felt utterly relaxed, and was perfectly content to be idle for hours on end, watching Jack fish: seated in an old canvas chair and casually dangling a rod.

She sometimes wondered what he was thinking, but not once did she feel apart from him. She knew that he loved her, and she felt right with him, that they did belong together. She couldn't say she understood him, exactly, but then, did he really know her? One puzzlement: so far Jack had made no move to sleep with her, to make love to her. She was longing for him to do so, and sensed he wanted that, too. Perhaps when they reached Key West?

Jack flew the sea-plane from Torch Ramrod over to the Naval Air Station near to Key West, where it had been arranged it could be parked for a couple of nights for safe keeping. Then, after drinks in the officers' mess, one of the hotel's courtesy cars came to transfer Jack and Georgette to the Casa Marina. The hotel's red-barrel Cuban tiled roof glinted in the sun as the vehicle pulled up at the main entrance, which was protected by a porte-cochere.

A flurry of courteous attention followed, as they were escorted into the fortress-walled hotel and up the main staircase from the colonial-style lobby to their two communicating rooms overlooking the Atlantic ocean.

But not once during their stay did Jack make any attempt to make love to her. Each time he entered her room, to escort her to meals or to the white sandy beach and shady palms, he knocked first. It was as if he was anxious he should not catch her in an indecorous state. He kissed her and cuddled her, but that was all he did: the perfect gentleman!

After spending each day on the beach, reclining on loungers, with the salt-laden air fanned by the trade winds enhancing the depth of their tans, Georgette and Jack would watch the spectacular sunset before going to their rooms to change for dinner. The red-ball sun seemed to drop at some speed into the ocean in its last visible moments, as if anxious to cool off before heating up again to brighten Africa, Europe and places beyond.

Georgette knew she would never have a holiday so wonderful again, however many times she might come back to America.

They left the hotel grounds only once during their three days there, to look at Ernest Hemingway's house and his watering-hole, Sloppy Joe's Bar, because she had once read the book "A Farewell to Arms".

– 'Oh, such a romantic, if doomed, love affair.'

'Now you will have to read "To Have and Have Not",' Jack declared, as they took a taxi back to the hotel afterwards.

'Why?'

'It's another classic of his, and it's set around here.'

They dined each evening in the elegant and comfortable decor of the hotel's restaurant, which was like stepping back into the 1920s. The dining tables were set in intimate alcoves backed with mirrors in arched dark rattan frames. The restaurant was called Flagler's, and Georgette commented that it was an unusual name.

'Henry Flagler was an unusual man,' said Jack.

'He was?'

'He was a private citizen who conceived, and carried to completion, a railway line over the sea and islands to this place. He intended to build this hotel, too, but died before it got started – in 1912. Well, he was eighty-odd by then, and had worked darned hard all his life!'

'You showed me no railway from the air.'

'There isn't one any more, only a few old bridges. A hurricane demolished it in 1934 – the same hurricane that took down that ship whose photograph I showed you back at Dad's boatyard – and no one has thought it worthwhile to build another. But Flagler did also organize the railway from New York to Miami, shortly before the turn of the century.'

At their last dinner in the Casa Marina, Georgette put to Jack another query, something which had puzzled her all the time they had been in America. 'You love Florida, you love fishing, you love boats, you love being at *Bejama*, you love your father. Yet you live in England and have nothing to do with boats or fishing. Why not?'

Jack sighed deeply. 'And I only fly enough to keep my hours in. Okay, I'll answer you. I was twenty-one. I fell in love with an English girl, who hated Florida and everything it stood for, so we had to settle in England and I soon found that deep sea fishing and boating in English weather left a lot to be desired!'

Georgette couldn't help wondering if, under the circumstances,

Jack's marriage had been doomed from the start but, wisely, she kept her peace. It had, after all, lasted for thirty years.

Steve was at the airport with the Daimler to greet the two very suntanned people. The flights that Georgette and Jack had taken back to a very cold London had been comfortable and uneventful. It was early evening by the time they reached Sparrow Hall Walk. There was still two days to go before the children came back from Hampshire, and one day before Nanny was due to return from Scotland.

They were feeling rather jaded after the long journey and felt a brisk walk would do them both good, so Steve was dismissed, which surprised Georgette – how was Jack planning to get home, or was he proposing to spend the night at her place? The very thought sent an excited tingle high through her.

After they had dumped their luggage at her place and freshened up, she and Jack set off at a good pace to Kings Road. They weren't particularly hungry after all the snacks served on the flight, but found a small place that specialized in soups and salad.

Some ninety minutes later they decided they would also walk home. After the winter sun of Florida, they felt the cold more than usual and their gentle stroll soon became another brisk march. Georgette was beginning to feel very tired and realized she was suffering from jet-lag again. Jack was very quiet and she assumed that he had the same problem.

They turned into Sparrow Hall Walk and Jack pulled her to a halt. 'I want to show you something,' he said mysteriously, and dug into his coat pocket. Out came some keys and he pointed to the building immediately opposite Georgette's flat.

It was another Georgian house that had been converted into flats. This one had an open-fronted garage to one side, mainly tiled, but with heavy black timber supports, in the Tudor style, running across the ceiling. An extension had been added to the first-floor and there was a room above the garage. Georgette thought the overall effect was very odd.

'I'm your new neighbour, Georgette! I've taken a lease on the bottom flat there. So now we can be together in the fullest sense of the words!'

'You have done what? You don't mean that you have left Mrs Grant?' Georgette was aghast.

'She gave me no choice. She said it was time I made up my mind, that I must either stop seeing you entirely or leave her properly – in body as well as spirit. Well, hell! That was an easy decision! She says that she will divorce me, but bears you no ill-will and won't drag you into it. She knows me too well to blame you for my misdeeds!'

He was really cheerful as he said this, and Georgette could have killed him! But what was the point in even trying to argue? She followed him meekly into his new home. It was superbly, luxuriously, furnished.

'Where are your clothes and things?'

'Here – I arranged for Steve to bring them while we were away so that I could move in straight away when we got back.'

'What do I say?' asked Georgette helplessly.

'Nothing, sugar! You knew it was inevitable the moment we met, just as I did, but I wanted everything to be right – no grotty motel, no furtiveness, no grabbing at a few moments while other people were out of the way! Now we're alone together, in our own place, and I've waited long enough to make my claim! Now, my darling, I intend to possess you slowly and completely, to make you my slave forever!'

His quiet intensity sent a tremor through her and, speechlessly, she held out her arms.

As they made love, Georgette knew that this was, must be, what it was supposed to be all about. Jack loved her, as well as her body, and his long-suppressed desire showed in his every action. Even with Gregoire, she had never felt as she did now. She had desired Jack in Florida, yet he had made no attempt to take her to bed, though he could have done, easily, and now she understood why, and was glad that he had waited for the perfect time.

He didn't ravish her, he just did everything beautifully. His loving was sweet and soft and painful and fiery and calm and excited. It had everything in it that she had ever experienced or imagined, combined together, all the various facets of love-making that she had previously enjoyed with different people were combined in him – and he even added a few. She was lost in pleasure, and an ecstacy that was entirely new to her, and knew she could never have enough of him. All she wanted out of life was to stay in bed with him forever!

Prior to this, most of Georgette's love-making had been a form of escapism, often a pleasurable activity, more often a way of exercising her power over a man. This was not. On the contrary, she was the

127

one who was powerless in this partnership. Jack was already exercising mental control over her to a great degree, now he took control of her physically, too, and she was lost. His loving skill, combined with the chemistry created by her own attraction to him, made her faint with desire and she knew she could never achieve such heights of passion with anyone else.

Yet, even as they relaxed after the first beautiful session, Georgette felt uneasy. She didn't think she was a prude, but she knew it was wrong to break up a marriage and how could she pretend she had not done that, however unwillingly? She was no longer the thoughtless child she had been when she had set up house with Gregoire, and how could she be truly happy, knowing that her happiness was at someone else's expense? But she could not help herself – she knew she was Jack's as long as he wanted her – and she prayed that that would be forever.

'Oh, Jack darling, I never knew how long I'd yearned for this feeling – till now I didn't even know that such feelings existed! I didn't know such variety of emotion and sensation was possible with just one person. I want you so much I can't bear it! Please, darling, can we do it again? Right now?'

Jack needed no second invitation. Afterwards he sighed in deep content. 'I have desired you so long, my own little baby, and now you are finally mine! I can't tell you how happy I am, but I promise you one thing – now that I have you, I shall never, ever let you go!'

'That suits me, darling!' murmered Georgette, and meant it. She wanted nothing else, and gave herself up to erotic sensations as he began to fondle her yet again.

Less than a week later, genuine grief intruded on Georgette's happiness: a telephone call came from Henri, to tell her that darling Bonne-maman had died peacefully in her sleep, at the age of eighty-seven.

A grief-sticken Georgette flew to Brussels to attend the funeral.

Jack phoned her every day she was away, and pouring out her heart to him so regularly helped her through those miserable days.

When she returned from Brussels, Jack was at the airport to meet her and she discovered that he had put her absence to good effect. Not only had he done the promised re-furnishing of the living-room, but there was now an enormous fitted wardrobe in her bedroom ('You'll need it for all the beautiful clothes I intend to buy you!') and he'd bought her a proper orthopaedic bed to help her back ('Love-making in my outsize double bed, recovery here!' he joked).

She was touched by his thoughtfulness, but it was a good week before her grief really began to dissipate in the fire of his passion. What she failed to realize was that Jack was becoming obsessively possessive, jealous of any man who came anywhere near her. He even resented time she spent with women friends – Daisy Brown and Nanny Trotter excepted, as they were part of the household and did not take Georgette away from him.

Not only was Jack at her flat every evening now but, more and more, he would leave his office at lunch-time and spend the afternoon in Sparrow Hall Walk, waiting impatiently for Georgette to return – usually playing with Alex in Georgette's flat (Susan was now at school all day, but Alex was still going only in the mornings), but sometimes in his own flat. He spent every weekend with her and the children and showered them all with presents – often including Nanny and Daisy in his largesse. They all regarded him as part of the family and Nanny, although she obviously did not approve, made no comment about the 'goings on' across the road.

Georgette regarded Jack's attention as very flattering. What woman wouldn't? Getting so much attention and such wonderful sex-filled nights, too. Not that they made love every night, of course, but every time they did it was blissful. Their love-making was always at his flat, never hers. He seemed to feel that it should be kept away from the children, and she saw no reason not to humour him.

One weekend Jack took Georgette and the children to see the Changing of the Guard at Buckingham Palace. Alex, now four, was much taken by the soldiers on horseback. 'Me, Mummy, me!' he said, stabbing a little finger in their direction.

'Yes, darling!' Georgette indulged him, motherly, thought it very likely that he would want to be a fireman next week and a train-driver the week after that.

Chapter Sixteen

Alex and Susan had gone to stay with Dickie for the Easter holiday and Nanny had taken the opportunity to visit to her sister in the Highlands. Georgette had been working hard, long hours, and was looking forward to the long weekend break when, on the Thursday morning before she set out on her rounds, Don Kerr telephoned her at her office. She had not seen him for some time, though she knew his movements through Tom and Nancy.

'I thought it was time we had a meal together,' he proposed. 'Can you make lunch today?'

'I can.'

'Marvellous! Mervyn's? One o'clock? My treat.'

It was a splendid treat! She got home from work at seven, rather late because it had been a particularly good day for sales in SW1 and she had wanted to finish writing up her notes that day, so that she would be free of work for the rest of the holiday. As she stood in Sparrow Hall Walk, looking for her latchkey, Jack came striding over from his flat.

'Hello, darling,' she bubbled, turning the key in the front door and not noticing that he didn't reply, merely followed her up the stairs. Only when they were in the living-room did he speak.

'What did you do today, Georgette?' he asked, his voice harsh. There was the smell of alcohol on his breath.

'I worked and had lunch with an old friend of mine and Dickie's, Don Kerr.'

'I know you had lunch with him!' Jack shot back hotly. 'I rang your office and they told me you had gone to Mervyn's! So I rang Mervyn's and persuaded them to tell me who had booked your table. You can't keep secrets from me, you see! But what did you do after lunch? That's what I want to know.'

'I went back to work, of course, and so did Don.'

'How do I know you only did that?'

'What do you mean, darling? What else would I have done?'

'Don't pretend to be innocent – it doesn't suit you! I know that he wanted you to sleep with him, and that you did sleep with him!'

'No!' It was the truth but, even as she spoke, the thought flashed through Georgette's mind that it had once been true – and she reddened, then became flustered. 'No!' she repeated. 'It was as I told you – Don went back to his office and I went back to selling. It was all entirely innocent.'

'Innocent? Of course, the man desired you! He must do! Every man does! Your very presence encourages carnal knowledge! I've seen the way men look at you in your red dress when we go out to dinner. You deliberately wear it to excite them!'

'I don't, Jack! You bought me that dress. That's why I wear it – to please *you*!'

'Well, you will not wear it again!'

He stormed into the kitchen and, from a drawer, withdrew a bread knife. With mounting horror, a perplexed Georgette followed him into her bedroom and watched him take the offending dress from the wardrobe and proceed to rip at it ruthlessly. With the garment in tatters, his rage was apparently spent and Jack became deadly calm. Standing by the bed, he surveyed his destruction, then said reproachfully, 'Why are you unfaithful? Why do you encourage all these men to follow you?'

Tears of bewilderment coursed down Georgette's cheeks. 'Jack, darling, I don't know why you suspect me of such a thing! I love you and you are all I want! Since we met I haven't so much as thought about another man – you must believe me!'

Jack threw the dress down on the bed, the knife after it. 'If that's true, why did you go to lunch with this man?'

'Because he's an old friend, as I told you, and he asked me.'

'So, anyone who invites you out, you will say yes to?'

'Of course not, Jack! That's not what I said!'

'No, I agree you didn't say it – you simply proved it by doing it, damn you!'

'For heavens sake, Jack, be reasonable! All I did was have lunch with an old friend that I haven't seen for a while. What's so wrong about that? There was no hint of anything improper.'

But Jack ignored her and strode downstairs without another word. She heard the flat door slam shut behind him, closely followed by the sound of the street door banging closed.

Then all was still – except Georgette, who was shaking from head to toe. She fell weakly onto her bed and burst into tears. Until now there had been a deep glow within her at being loved by Jack. There had been a feeling of warm security that she could be loved so much by somebody so wonderful. But now that security had vanished. She had been made forcibly aware that there was a dark side to Jack's love and she was both bewildered and frightened. Of one thing she was sure – she would never again go out alone with a man, however innocently. It simply wasn't worth it!

During the night she considered giving Jack up, but she knew she couldn't. The thought of life without him was too painful for serious consideration. By ten o'clock in the morning he was on the doorstep, smiling cheerfully and full of plans for the bank holiday weekend. No mention was made of the previous evening's events and the four days passed very happily.

To avoid carrying more weight than necessary, Georgette had fallen into the habit of going into the Sales office every morning to collect just enough literature to see her through that one day. She had just reached the office on the Tuesday morning when Jack rang.

'Can you meet me at Willard's, in Wigmore Street, at three-thirty?'

'Yes, of course.' Georgette had not visited the establishment before, but knew its reputation as a place that always had an excellent selection of in-vogue garments.

'Splendid! They are expecting us. I am going to buy you a new dress.'

Although he hadn't mentioned it, Georgette assumed that this was Jack's way of apologizing for the destruction of the red dress she'd liked so much.

That afternoon Jack spent sixty pounds on a perfectly-cut low-necked green silk cocktail dress and matching evening bag. With her long dark hair, Georgette looked stunning in it but Jack walked round her with a frown, muttering, 'Something's missing!' Then he dug into his pocket and produced a jewel box containing an emerald and diamond bracelet. It must have cost a fortune and Georgette was lost for words as he fastened it round her wrist and stood back to admire the result.

'You like it! I can see it in your face!' he said laughingly.

'But Jack . . .'

'Just a token of my esteem, darling! You can show it off next weekend, because you are coming with me to a business convention in Blackpool. We leave on Friday.'

'But Jack . . .'

'I've already spoken to your Mr Saint, and he knows you'll be away Friday and Monday.'

* * *

The convention had been arranged by Grant Controls to display the latest developments in their temperature and measurement control equipment, and Georgette found it very interesting. She was full of admiration for the inventive minds of the people Jack employed, and felt that good sales had to result from such ingenuity.

Georgette's role was to act as Jack's hostess, and everyone accepted her as such, and behaved very pleasantly to her. But she sensed that many of them disapproved, considering her a gold-digger, and were polite only because their livelihoods depended on keeping on the right side of Jack.

For the whole of the weekend, Georgette found Jack was an absolute joy to be with during the day and passionate in everything he did at night. They made love at least once each night, and it couldn't have been more perfect in Georgette's view.

She was to accompany him to several more Grant Control conventions. Each time he bought her a new dress, and a new piece of jewellery to go with it, and each time he was sweetness and light for the duration of the convention. It was during the weeks between that he was difficult.

Phyllis Grant was pleading desertion as the grounds for divorce, which meant that it would be at least three years before Jack was free to remarry. But he had no intention of letting Georgette slip away from him during that time, and made it very clear to everybody they met that she was his mistress and not available – even people they met casually in pubs and clubs were left in no doubt about their relationship.

Georgette did not mind that in the least. She was proud to be with him, and had no desire to encourage any other man. Jack's overt possessiveness saved her the trouble of brushing off unwanted advances. It was the private behaviour that arose from the possessiveness that she could not take.

When she returned from work each evening she would look towards Jack's window. If he was not there she knew all was well, that she'd find him playing happily with Alex, and possibly Susan too, in her flat. Then they'd have a pleasant evening together and he would usually go home quite early, knowing that she preferred not to make love when she had to be up early for work the next day.

But sometimes Georgette would get home to find him sitting at his window, waiting for her, and that usually meant trouble. But she knew that going into her own flat would merely postpone the row, and she couldn't bear the thought of going through the evening with it hanging over her, so she preferred to get it out of the way and would go straight over to his flat. As soon as she was inside, he would go into a jealous rage over something – or, rather, over nothing. It was always the same old song – Georgette had been seeing other men. Nothing she could say or do would convince him otherwise.

She never knew what set him off, only that it was in some way connected with drink, since it never happened when he was sober. In the end she came to the conclusion that he felt this insane jealousy all the time, deep down, but that he was able to keep it under control except when he'd had a few drinks. It was the alcohol that lessened both his powers of reason and his inhibitions.

Sometimes he would remember the dreadful scenes he'd created and apologize profusely the next day, begging for forgiveness and swearing it would never happen again. On other occasions he remembered nothing and grew angry at what he considered false accusations.

She learned that walking out on him when he was in one of these moods was not the answer. The only way to stop the argument completely was to get him into bed and make passionate love – he had never had so much to drink that he became impotent and the sexual activity dissipated the effect of the alcohol. But getting him into the mood was easier said than done, and she had to wait for his rage to peak before she attempted to distract him in this way.

She was in despair much of the time and, over and over again, she decided to leave him. But she couldn't do it – she was completely under his spell.

How Therese would gloat, thought Georgette, if she was with her cousin now and could see how low her 'loose ways' had brought her!

Georgette noticed the absence of household bills behind the clock on the mantelpiece when she came into the living-room one day after seeing Susan and Alex off on their summer holidays with Dickie and Brigitte.

'Oh, the bills have gone again, Nanny!' Georgette said resignedly.

'That's Mr Grant for you!' chuckled Nanny. She knew that, once again, Jack had sneaked them away to pay them. She still liked him very much, despite the fact that she was beginning to appreciate the turbulent nature of Georgette's relationship with him – she had never seen him at his worst.

The children were blissfully unaware of their mother's problems. To them 'Uncle Jack' was the kindest of men, who brought them wonderful toys and arranged exciting outings. They were Jack's main joy in life, his feelings for them unsullied by the jealousy he directed at Georgette. He loved them deeply and had never exchanged a cross word with their mother in front of them. Something in him was aware of their presence and held him in check even when he had been drinking heavily.

Two days after the children had gone off with Dickie, Nanny departed for her summer break. She was going to stay with friends in Cheltenham, for a change. While Daisy Brown departed for Blackpool for a week with her husband.

Georgette returned from the office and, unusually, there was no sign of Jack waiting to greet her.

So, in the peacefulness of her empty flat, Georgette listened to the radio while she prepared herself a light meal. Then she had a luxurious soak in the bath, undisturbed by cries of 'Hurry up, Mummy, I want to go!' What bliss it was to be totally alone for once, she thought. She returned to the living-room and settled into her favourite chair, with the warm summer air drifting in through the open french windows, to write up her daily report. It had not been a very good day for sales, only one clinched, but she felt that two of the prospects would need only a little more courting, and intended to contact them again in about six weeks.

By ten-thirty Georgette was feeling thoroughly relaxed and ready for bed. By eleven o'clock she was fast asleep. At eleven-fifteen she was jolted into sudden wakefulness by the sound of glass breaking.

'Oh, my God! That was the door to the flat! Burglars!' Georgette spoke aloud in her fear, her heart pounding, as though speed were of the essence to catch up with the seconds that had gone ahead when she nearly jumped out of her skin!

'Well, they can't get in that way,' she knew, the glass panels were too small to climb through, and her front door had not only a Yale lock but a mortise lock, and bolts top and bottom; and it was these bolts that were stopping entry being gained by anyone just now. Then it suddenly occurred to her that the intruder just might be Jack himself, back from being somewhere where he couldn't take her, and he could have been drinking.

Then the door was rattled violently and she heard swearing – it was Jack's voice! Fearful of what the people downstairs would think, if they were at home to hear (though she didn't think they were) Georgette switched on a light and hastened to pull on a dressing-gown.

'All right, Jack, I'm coming!' she called out, as she hurried downstairs.

'Why didn't you answer your door bell?' he demanded without preamble, his tone accusing, his breath whisky-ridden. 'You're with a man! I'll find him! I'll kill him!' He pushed past her and raced, less than sure-footed, up the stairs.

'I didn't hear it. I was asleep.' Georgette called after his retreating figure, then hurried after him. She reached her bedroom in time to see him on his knees, peering under the bed.

'You don't normally go to bed this early! You must have had some reason for doing so!' He was now searching her wardrobe, throwing all her clothes into an untidy heap on the floor.

'I did have a reason – I was tired! And you were not here, so there was no reason for me to stay up. I thought an early night would do me good.'

'Surely you don't expect me to believe that!' he sneered, brushing past her on his way to Nanny's room. Fortunately she had few clothes and he did not feel it necessary to empty her wardrobe. He rampaged through the flat, going from room to room and peering into every nook and cranny that was capable of concealing a person.

A bewildered and terrified Georgette followed him, shaking in her slippered feet and desperately trying to bring him to his senses.

Finally Jack had no option but to believe that Georgette was alone in the flat. He slumped onto the sofa, puffing heavily, his lightweight summer suit crumpling around him.

'I'm sorry, Georgette! It's just that I can't bear the thought of you in the arms of another man! Just thinking about it drives me insane, because I need you so much!'

'I love you, Jack! I don't want other men!' Georgette, thanking God that his rage had passed, moved slowly over to sit on the sofa beside him.

But suddenly a new thought dawned on Jack, and his eyes grew fierce once more. 'Of course! He must have gone out of the french windows and down the fire-escape while I was downstairs!'

'No, Jack, no!' cried Georgette despairingly. 'There was no man! I was sleeping alone! I love only you! Why do you hurt me this way?'

'Because all men desire you! I know they do! I see them ogle you! Can you deny it? Do you really think you can fool me by saying you resist them?'

'I don't want to fool you, darling! And it's not necessary, because I have nothing to conceal! I love you – you, and only you! How many more times must I say it?'

Without warning, the anger went out of him again. 'If only I could believe you!' he said miserably. Georgette surveyed the slumped figure. It was hardly possible that this pitiful creature was the same dynamic person she had fallen in love with. But she did still love him, even in this state, with all her heart. She hugged him to her as she would have hugged a hurt child. He looked so sad and vulnerable. A lost soul.

Gently she said, 'Come on, Jack, let me take you home. I'll come to bed with you.'

Georgette really did not want to sleep with Jack that night, but she felt that the sex act was the only thing that would be likely to draw him out of the depression into which he was obviously sinking. She went back to her own place just in time to get ready for work, and made time to clear up the mess; she couldn't bear the thought of coming home at the end of her day's work to a less than tidy place.

When Georgette got home that evening Jack was waiting for her. As she threw back the mortise lock of the front door to her flat, prior to using the latch key, Jack saw the broken pane and was horrified.

'My God!' he exclaimed. 'You must have been burgled!'

Georgette looked at him incredulously. 'I've not been burgled. You did it, Jack.'

'What? Don't be ridiculous, Georgette. How could you say I did such a thing? I can't appreciate your sense of humour. Don't touch anything – we'd better call the police.'

Georgette was very confused. He really did seem to believe that he hadn't done the damage, but how could he possibly have forgotten something so drastic? She knew that if she protested he would grow angry, but she certainly didn't want him calling the police! So despising her weakness, she feigned a laugh and 'admitted' that she had said what she had said only as a joke.

'No – that wasn't funny, Georgette,' Jack responded reprovingly. 'So what is the truth?'

'I accidentally shut the door on myself this morning when picking up the milk bottles, and I had to get back in. With everyone on holiday, there was no one indoors.' ('My, what made me come up with that excuse!')

To her relief, Jack accepted that explanation without comment. He called a glazier in.

* * *

The next few months were easier for Georgette. She was determined to give Jack no chance to suspect her of anything and made a point of being constantly with him when she was not at work, even asking him to drive her to such places as the hairdresser, so that he knew her appointments were genuine. She got home as early as possible after work and gave him a blow-by-blow account of her working day. She went nowhere without him, even stopped seeing Nancy unless Tom and Jack came too.

So, gradually, her social life became entirely dependent on Jack and her personality was almost absorbed by him, but she loved him and did not complain. Her plan worked and the rows stopped, so she was content.

She deceived him in only one way. She did not want to lose her Belgian friends, but was frightened to phone them from home in case Jack took the bill and noticed the long-distance calls, so she asked Mr Saint for permission to ring them from the office. He said that was all right, as long as she paid the bills when they came in.

They had a wonderfully happy family Christmas at Sparrow Hall Walk, then the children went to Grace Hall, Nanny to Scotland and Jack and Georgette to Florida. They all enjoyed themselves.

At Easter the children went to Dickie again, Nanny Trotter to Cheltenham, Daisy Brown to a caravan on the Isle of Sheppey, and Jack took Georgette to the South of France for a short break. As always when they were away, he was relaxed and loving and they had a wonderful holiday.

Then, in May 1958, GBE announced that they would be having a convention abroad; three days in Italy the following month. The company had been expanding rapidly throughout Europe and had decided it was time they staged an event which would provide a reward for their top salesmen and act as an incentive to the others.

Georgette was entitled to attend, of course, because she had the top UK sales record, as usual. She wanted to go, but could visualize the rows that would follow her return so, to save herself the agony, she told Mr Saint that she could not make it. He was shocked.

'But you have to go, Georgette! It's not just a junket, you know, although we hope that everyone will have fun. There are a number of official functions and, as our top salesman in the UK, you will be expected to give a short address on your approach to the job. I was about to call you in to explain that, so you would have a chance to prepare the address. Members of the Head Office board will be coming over from the States, too, and want to meet you personally. I'm sorry, but it really is obligatory for you to go – a penalty of success, I'm afraid!'

'Fair enough. I hadn't realized that was the situation, Mr Saint. Of course I'll go.' Georgette could not bring herself to talk to anyone about her subjugation to Jack, because she felt it was so humiliating, and could think of no plausible reason not to go.

But when she finally plucked up the courage to broach the matter to Jack he nearly blew his top.

'But you can't go!'

'Jack, I tried to refuse!'

'How do I know that?'

'Ring the office. Ask them. Ask Mr Saint.'

If he felt chagrin afterwards, he never admitted to it, but Jack did find some pretext to telephone Mr Saint and asked him, seemingly casually, if it really was essential for Georgette to go. Mr Saint, of course, confirmed what he had said to Georgette and Jack had to accept that – but he was far from happy.

Desperately trying to avoid trouble, Georgette suggested that Jack go, too, but he was unable to do so because he had a couple of long-standing business appointments that could not be cancelled at such relatively short notice and were important to his firm.

So Georgette went alone. Steve drove her to Heathrow and Jack came along to see her off, looking pale as he did so.

'You behave yourself, you hear me!' He tried, unsuccessfully, to make the words sound jocular, then gave Georgette a passionate farewell kiss.

'You know I will! I'll phone you every day, darling, so you'll know I'm thinking of you.'

Georgette was thoroughly miserable during those three days in Rome. She attended all the official functions and banquets, but that was it. The rest of the time she stayed resolutely in her room. She refused all the social invitations, pleading a headache one day and an upset stomach the next, and saw nothing of the 'Eternal City'.

In the evenings she phoned Jack, as promised, and told him everything she had done during the course of that day. The conversations were long, and loving on both sides, and she prayed that behaving like this would keep his suspicions at bay.

Her friends in the sales force were sorry that Georgette would not join them, but they did not let her unsociable behaviour interfere with their own fun and Georgette was green with envy when she heard them talking about the wonderful things they had seen and done. But it was worth missing out, she thought, if doing so meant a peaceful time when she got home.

The flight back to London touched down at Heathrow in the early evening and, as they came through Arrivals, Georgette made sure that she stayed apart from the others.

There was Jack, waiting among the greeters, and her heart sank as she saw the peculiar colour of his face. He wasn't white or grey – he was green with anxiety. She kissed him with great tenderness and told him how much she'd missed him, but he did not respond and she could smell the drink on him. He looked as if he hadn't slept for the whole of the past three days.

All during the drive home he didn't speak, so she gave up her attempts to chat and the atmosphere in the car was heavy. She knew she was in for a grilling and might as well resign herself to the fact. By the time the Daimler braked at Sparrow Hall Walk it was dark and the street lighting was on. She knew Alex would be in bed and Susan occupied with her homework, so she did not have to go to her flat and made dutifully for Jack's front door.

Steve was dismissed, and was only too keen to be on his way home. He didn't need to be psychic to know that all hell would break loose once the couple were behind the governor's closed door – and he did not envy Georgette.

'Do you think I'm a fool, Georgette?' snarled Jack, as he handed her a glass of whisky, as generous in size as his own.

'No, dear, of course not.'

'So you accept that I wasn't fooled for one minute by seeing you coming through the Arrivals hall alone?'

'Fooled about what, Jack?'

'Your affairs in Italy!'

'There were none, Jack!'

'I told you, you haven't fooled me! Being out of my sight doesn't stop me from knowing what you get up to – letting all those men fawn over you!'

'But Jack – I stayed faithful to you! I didn't go out with anyone, not even in a group. I swear I didn't. You know I spent most of the evening on the phone to you – how could I have gone out?'

'How could you possibly not have gone out in a romantic place like Rome when there were so many men with you?' He said dismissively. 'I'm not so stupid that I believed you were alone in your room when you phoned me. I know you were with someone, just waiting for the conversation to finish before you went to bed with him! Was it only one man, or a different one every night, I wonder? You are nothing but a whore!'

His eyes were like lasers, boring into her, trying to find some little recess of her mind where guilt was concealed.

The pain of this sort of conduct was something Georgette knew well by now, and she took a deep gulp of whisky, trying to deaden her feelings.

'I love you, Jack! God help me, but I do! I do not need other men, but I just don't know what more I can do to prove it to you!'

'Easy enough to say that you love me, Georgette, but I know it isn't true! I know that you let other men crawl all over you whenever my back is turned! I know you behave like a slut!'

'No, I don't! Oh God, how can I make you believe me?' Georgette was desperate. 'Don't you realize, Jack, that one of these days I'm going to admit to doing something I didn't do, simply to stop you interrogating me like this? Why should I want to be with other men when it's you I love? I've never met anyone who made me feel the way you do! For the first time in my life, I understand what it means to feel like a real woman!'

'Well the trouble is right there, Georgette dear, you've never been loved by a real man before. Now you've acquired a taste for fornication!'

'For God's sake, Jack, stop it! Why do you persist in persecuting me like this? I'm only too happy that you've made me into a real woman but, if you were a real man, you would take my word that I was being faithful!'

He went pale at that and, for a moment, Georgette thought that he was going to hit her. 'Oh, my darling, I'm sorry!' she said hastily. 'You know I didn't mean that – you're more of a man than anyone I have ever met, and I love the glow that I get from knowing that you love me totally. But you weaken me with your love, so that I cannot even think straight.'

'You cannot cope with me?' Jack drained his glass with a gulp.

'Sometimes I feel smothered, as if I can't breathe!'

'Bullshit!'

'Jack, dear, please try to understand. When you love someone truly, you must also trust them a little, I think, and leave them a little freedom.'

'Hah! Freedom to do what, may I ask?' His voice was rising again.

'Nothing evil, darling! Just freedom to be a little independent, to exist as an individual. I sometimes feel that I am just one of your possessions, not a person in my own right!'

'Do I stop you working?'

'No.'

'Have I even *suggested* that you stop?'

'No, never.'

'Do you know why? Because I agree that everyone should be independent in some way. I admire good workers, and you are one. I have no respect for people who play at their jobs. I do respect people like you, who have determination and ability to make good money by their own efforts. So, you see, I give you freedom to do it!'

'Why then do you want to supplement what I earn?'

'Because you are mine and I love you!'

'But you pour money into my place, buy me clothes and jewels, buy all sorts of things for the children, never stop spending money on me and mine. Don't you see that I don't have any personal freedom at all – you're literally running my life.'

Jack was enraged. He lunged out of his chair and grabbed her handbag. 'You're right! I shouldn't spend money on someone so undeserving! Well, I can fix that!' he tipped the bag's contents out onto the carpet and went through them, evidently seeking evidence of some wrong-doing on her part.

He found none, of course, but that didn't lessen his temper. He smashed his glass on the edge of the wooden coffee table then, viciously, used a jagged piece of it to slash the soft leather handbag he'd once bought her into shreds.

The low light from a standard lamp was the only illumination in the room, and it cast a shadow of menace over his movements. Georgette was frightened – what might he do next?

'Tomorrow I'll do that to all the rest of the things I've bought you, see if I don't. Broads like you, Georgette, you don't cheat on me and get away with it! I put you on a pedestal – now you will fall!'

Georgette knew that, by the time morning arrived, Jack would be very different, but that knowledge did not lessen her present dread. Drinking heavily herself now, she had to sit there long into the night, while he persisted in trying to get the 'truth' out of her about how she'd spent her free time in Rome. With each hour that passed he became more and more abusive.

'Why is this happening to me? Why should I have to go through such interrogation?' She cried in anguish, and deliberately drank more whisky to anaesthetize her battered mind.

For another year Georgette endured Jack's strange behaviour. He never hurt her physically, wounding her only with words, but his conduct racked her with distress and stretched their relationship almost to breaking point.

The high spot of that year together was another trip to Surfside in late December/early January. Jack was relaxed there, feeling totally secure on his home ground and with her constantly by his side.

With Jack turning the shape of love into a creeping, strangling, murderous vine, Georgette's job became her only escape. It never knocked her, only rewarded her efforts, winning her continual entry into the Top Ten Club and, with it, the obligation to attend the GBE sales convention, which was to become an annual event.

Fortunately the venue for the 1959 convention was London. Georgette gave Jack a copy of the programme, so he was able to meet her when each official function ended, and trouble was avoided.

Georgette would have liked to visit her father – she had not been to Brussels since Bonne-maman's funeral. Whenever she mentioned the possibility, however, Jack went into a sulk, and her suggestion that he should go with her fell on deaf ears. Eventually she came to the suspicion that she had concluded before, that if he came he reckoned he would have to take a back seat in a place where, inevitably he would be a stranger while she was on familiar territory. So she dropped the whole idea, and continued to keep in touch by phoning Henri and her friends from GBE's office.

Drink became her companion, gradually becoming an integral part of her life, an anaesthetic in the bad times and something to heighten her appreciation of the good ones. For the good times outweighed the bad now she was so seldom out of his sight. When Jack was completely sober he was as pleasant and caring as he had ever been and, drunk or not, he always behaved perfectly when the children were around.

Nanny was fully aware of what was going on by now, and loyally did her best to keep Georgette cheerful, and Alex from under her feet. Susan, now nearly eleven, was spending a lot of time with her schoolfriends and she sometimes spent entire weekends away from home. She seldom asked them back to the flat, however, which worried Nanny – Georgette didn't notice.

Georgette was finding less and less time to spend with the children. After a hard day's work she usually felt really tired, and was almost exhausted by the end of each week. When she got home, her main desire was for some peace while she unwound and she was only to happy to let Jack play with the children or take them out, with or without Nanny, while she took a much-needed rest. Her back still ached from time to time and she was ever-fearful of putting it out again.

Daisy Brown was a great consolation to Georgette. Although now in her early sixties, she was still very fit, and happy to continue with the cleaning. But she had become more than an employee, she was now a good friend. Dear Daisy! Georgette lost count of the times she found release by crying, sometimes literally, on Daisy's shoulder.

How odd, Georgette thought, that she was envied by many women for being with Jack – if only they knew the reality! But so many people thought that she was with him just for his money. If only that were true, then she would be free to leave him. As it was, despite everything, she loved him desperately and could not visualize life without him. She realized she had grown to depend on him totally and had lost any real desire for independence.

Towards the end of 1959, Jack started to deteriorate physically and Georgette discovered that he was dying of cancer. The disease was widespread, but worst in the bowel. As well as losing a lot of weight, he was constantly in pain. His physician, Amanda Freshwood, who was also a close friend of his, did what she could, but that wasn't much because the disease was very advanced.

Dr Freshwood was forty-five and of medium build. Her straight hair was always tied back, making her face severe, schoolmarmish. She had been born in Glamorgan, Wales, but brought up in England, and her Welsh accent was very faint. She had been married when very young, but it had not lasted long – Georgette didn't know the reason for the break-up. In fact, although she'd met Amanda socially on several occasions, she knew very little about her. She was a good doctor, who believed in the National Health Service in principle but preferred her personal dealings to be with private patients like Jack.

Within months he was full of drugs. He did not feel up to visiting Florida for the New Year and in February he took to his bed completely. A team of nurses was engaged to care for him round the clock.

All his suspicions and belligerence vanished and he became very gentle, and grateful for everything that was done for him. Apart from his nurses, he wanted only Georgette with him, but insisted that she should go on working. 'I can't let you give up your career just for my sake, sugar! You'll need it when I'm gone to occupy your mind.'

There was no more fighting and, just as she had done for her mother, Georgette nursed Jack devotedly when she wasn't working. But eventually his legs became so swollen that he could hardly move, and he was in so much pain that it became impossible to look after him properly at home.

He was taken to a private hospital, where he deteriorated rapidly, and it was obvious that he had little time to live. He was adamant that his father should be kept in ignorance of the severity of his condition, as he knew that Ben would feel obliged to fly over, and he didn't want him to do that: 'He's an old man and, fit as he is, I don't think it would be wise for him to make such a tiring journey.' But on one point Georgette was firm: 'Jack, Phyllis wants to come and see you. You must let her!' He reluctantly agreed and Amanda Freshwood arranged it. Georgette stayed away during the visit, not wanting to add to Phyllis's pain as she said her farewell to the man she had lost after so many years.

Despite Jack's protests, Georgette applied to GBE for leave, and it was readily granted, so she was able to stay at his bedside morning, noon and night. He was in a private suite, which boasted a sofa and an *en suite* shower, so Georgette just stayed there. When Jack's doctor realized that nothing would persuade her to leave, he arranged for meals to be brought in for her.

Within days of Phyllis's visit, Jack had weakened so much that his voice was barely audible when he tried to speak to Georgette. She leaned close to him, her hand on his to convey her love. 'What is it, Jack?'

'Georgette, my darling. Forgive me my foolish ways! I know my suspicions were unjustified. I have always thought that you were an absolute brick!'

Tears swept down Georgette's pale face at these words. She had never heard anyone use that term of endearment before and thought it was a lovely thing to say, and it was spoken with so much feeling. A few hours later Jack was dead and Georgette collapsed.

After Jack's death there was a lot to do and, as an executor of his will, Amanda Freshwood saw to it all.

To Georgette's amazement, people rushed to comfort her. Many wrote her the most wonderful letters, for they realized that she had not, after all, been with Jack for his money – the anguish she displayed could never have been feigned.

For the benefit of his British friends, prior to a private cremation, a funeral service was held in St Benedict's Church, Weybridge. It was a beautiful service, with beautiful singing. The church reverberated as the strains of Elgar's 'Nimrod' rang out, the stately flow of the strings and brass stirring pride in the aching hearts. It was a superb recording.

At Phyllis Grant's request, Amanda Freshwood had been responsible for arranging the reception that followed, and there was no ill-will between Phyllis and Georgette, both of whom were numb with grief. Each respected the other's genuine sorrow.

Georgette went through the reception in a daze, then the Flowers took her and the children home. They were in tears, too, because they loved their Uncle Jack. He had taken up a large part of their short lives and they had never before had to face the death of someone they loved. But, with the resilience of the young, they were soon cheerful again and Nanny took them off to the cinema, so that Georgette could be alone to give vent to her feelings.

In accordance with his wishes, Jack's ashes were to be taken to Florida and scattered over the sea. Amanda was to attend the ceremony and Phyllis, as his wife, was to scatter the ashes, and Jack had told Amanda he wanted Georgette to be there, too.

Privately, Phyllis was very pleased that she would not be the only person staying at *Bejama*. She did not anticipate any problems with Ben, at his age, and was, indeed, ready to accept any apology he might see fit to make, but there was bound to be some initial awkwardness and the presence of the other two women should help things go smoothly.

The gleaming trumpy was doing a steady twelve knots over calm seas, cutting a fine bow-wave as it headed for the Gulf Stream, a journey of about two hours from Surfside. But the air of solemnity aboard the *Bejama* was not to be shifted by the fairly strong breeze rolling over the sea – a cool fresh blow usually welcomed by guests when cruising under blazing skies – for today the aft deck was completely enclosed by the roll-up plastic curtains which were intended for less attractive weather. The yacht's captain had taken the initiative, and it seemed proper somehow, so Ben Grant had not seen fit to countermand his action.

Apart from the crew, Ben, the three women and the pastor of the little Surfside church, there were seven other mourners, all men, Joe Boward amongst them. They were privileged to be aboard because Jack had specifically requested that they should be there to witness the scattering of his ashes – each had been deep-sea fishing with him on many occasions over the years and shared his enthusiasm for the sport.

Two were seated on the aft deck, talking together in low tones, but most, like Joe Boward, were ensconced in the elegant air-conditioned mahogany-panelled main salon, with its beautifully carved wooden balustrade on the stairs leading down to the staterooms.

In that salon, to starboard, there was a drinks bar, complete with ice-maker, and some mourners were grateful for that. They felt the need of a stiffener to help them through this last moving part of a melancholy day – a day which had begun with a memorial service to Jack in the pastor's church, filled to capacity with folk keen to pay their last respects. Such was Ben's hospitality that all of those with long distances to travel had been accommodated in local hotels at his expense.

The three women had arrived yesterday, clothed in mourning, and would be travelling straight back to London on the morrow. They had crossed the Atlantic in a private aircraft, chartered by Ben, and each of them had a guest-room in his house.

Georgette was sitting on her own on the after-deck, glum-faced, alone with her thoughts. The two Americans sitting nearby had recognized she wanted it that way, and had acknowledged her presence only with reassuring smiles.

Amanda Freshwood was resting in a stateroom. Though she didn't suffer from airsickness, she had realized, belatedly, that she didn't travel well on water, and she'd taken lunch not an hour earlier! A case of 'physician heal thyself'!

Phyllis was with Ben, and Georgette could see them both relaxing at the bar. From the moment he had greeted the three of them, at the steps of his house, Ben had spent a lot of time with Phyllis. Only right and proper, of course, and Ben had not ignored Georgette in any way, nor any of his other guests.

Georgette did not know it, of course, but Ben had been determined not to miss this sad opportunity to make his peace with Phyllis, pleasantly surprised that she had agreed to attend the American service. Finally he had found a chance to beg that forgiveness, and she *had* forgiven him. It was clear to her that he was truly sorry, and she had felt it would have been churlish not to lay the past to rest after all these years.

Georgette had been shocked by how aged Ben had become in the fourteen months since she had last seen him – for New Year 1958/59.

Although no stranger to bereavement, the loss of his son had hit Ben hard. That Jack would pre-decease him was not something Ben had anticipated, and it was proving hard for him to bear. He had already outlived most of his own generation, and felt that he could not have much longer to go, himself. In fact, Ben was destined to live until he was ninety-three. Apart from substantial bequests to his household staff, he was to bequeath all his wealth, many millions, to charitable foundations.

Clutching her half-empty glass of whisky, Georgette reflected on her time with Jack. Not all of it had been bad, and they had always been extremely happy here in Florida. She recalled that first holiday especially, then the following visits, and recollected their trips in the fishing boat to the Gulf Stream. She had always taken pleasure in seeing Jack's joy when he reeled in a big one, even when he had needed the crew's help to get it aboard.

Last time he'd hooked one, she remembered, he'd needed help, although it wasn't as big as one he'd brought in alone the year before. At the time, she hadn't thought twice about it, but now she knew why.

Then there had been the two cruises on the trumpy, tanning herself in the salty air while Jack played Number One to the yacht's captain, and then letting him help her to catch 'tiddlers' from the spot where she was sitting now. At sunset the yacht would put into harbour somewhere along the Florida coast and, while the crew attended to their duties on board, she and Jack would enjoy a sumptuous evening meal ashore before returning to the trumpy, and to the master stateroom, there to make the most passionate of love. Jack's foreplay, as ever, was so tender, so beautiful, so much desired, that she could respond as fully as he wanted.

Georgette felt a tear course down her cheek; the memories were hurting, perhaps they would always hurt. With her forefinger, she wiped away the tear, and became aware of a change in the sound of the engine; the yacht was drawing to a halt. A suitable stretch of the North Atlantic Drift, Jack's beloved Gulf Stream, had been reached.

A crew member now appeared from the main salon and rolled up the stern curtains. The mourners gathered on the opened deck, Amanda Freshwood finding her way to Georgette's side to offer comfort. The pastor, an elderly man, tall and stout, with curly grey hair sweeping up at the nape, read the prayers for Jack, his tone sombre but mellifluous.

Then Phyllis, who had kept charge of the urn during the whole journey from England, came forward, supported caringly by Ben, and Jack's ashes were spread across the sparkling blue sea. All too briefly, the purpose of all their journeys was accomplished – simply, effectively. Now each mourner set upon the water his or her personal wreath. Georgette's was of red roses.

A moment of silent prayer followed and, in that moment, Ben began to crumple. It was Phyllis who gave him the support he needed, had been trying to deny to himself that he needed. In that moment of mutual grief, the rift between them was truly healed.

As the trumpy was returning to Surfside, it dawned on Georgette that it was probable she would never again set foot in America, never again visit Florida, her haven of delight. Ben might invite her to come again, but she doubted that she would make the journey. Without Jack at her side, vacationing here would lack its magical appeal and would only emphasize her loss. Ben was a man she liked, but she was not close to him, and his presence alone was not enough to lure her back to Florida.

During the flight back to England, Amanda Freshwood – who was one of Jack's executors – informed Georgette that she was a beneficiary under the will, which had already been read to Phyllis. Under the circumstances, the solicitor had thought it would be more tactful to have two readings than to follow the usual procedure of having all beneficiaries present at one reading. So Amanda had made a provisional appointment with the solicitor for the following day, and suggested that she and Georgette should meet him in Jack's flat. Georgette agreed.

* * *

While they waited for the solicitor to arrive, the first thing Amanda did was to give Georgette Jack's wrist-watch. It was a rather ornate one, with a lot of gadgets, which had always fascinated Alex. Jack had asked Amanda to make sure it was given to the boy and Georgette said she would keep it for him until he was old enough to appreciate it. She knew that it wouldn't last two minutes if Alex had it now.

'If there is anything you want from this flat, you must take it,' said Amanda.

'I don't feel I'm entitled to take anything. Jack gave me so much while he was alive, more than I ever needed, but surely everything that's left should go to his wife.'

'Phyllis doesn't want any of this. She knew that Jack would have wanted you to have it, although he didn't actually get around to saying so in his will, and she doesn't want it herself. She said that nothing here is any part of her life and you can do whatever you like with it. It's beautiful stuff and it would be sad to see it all going to scavengers. If you don't want it, then at least let me arrange for it to be sold – I'm sure the money will come in handy.'

Georgette's eyes brimmed over with tears at the thought of strangers invading her love-nest. She certainly didn't want them using all Jack's things, but there was no room for them in her own flat. 'Thank you, Amanda,' she sobbed. 'Please do sell it.'

Amanda came over, from standing by the hearth, and placed a comforting arm about her shoulders. Automatically, Georgette snuggled into the motherly embrace. 'I loved him so much, Amanda!' she confided.

'I know that, dear. And you hated him at times. I know that also.'

Georgette stiffened. 'I didn't think anyone guessed that.'

'He told me everything, Georgette. As his doctor, I knew things about him that were known to no one else, and that encouraged him to confide other things to me, as a friend. He couldn't always remember what he'd done to you, but he used to tell me what you said he had done, and it wasn't difficult for me to fill in the gaps and know how you must be feeling.'

'The worst thing was the insecurity, the not knowing what would come next. One minute it was "Oh, my little darling, I love you!" and the next, when under the influence of drink, he'd abuse me and destroy things he'd given me. That's when I hated him, but I never didn't love him – if that makes sense to you?'

'It does. When you are continually on tenterhooks like that, it's what we call a love/hate relationship.'

'I find living so hard, Amanda,' Georgette then confessed in a tone of wearied resignation.

Amanda reacted sharply, and as though echoing a phrase long ago learned and now wise to the truth of it. 'Georgette! It's the same for us all – there are no gentle slopes on the way to Paradise.'

A startled, chastened Georgette pondered on that pronouncement for a moment and found it strangely calming and decidedly reassuring – 'so everyone suffers!' She nodded her acceptance of that wisdom, then asked, 'Do you know why Jack took to drinking so heavily in the first place, Amanda? You do, don't you? Can you tell me?'

'It began when he learned from me that he'd contracted cancer, and there was nothing anyone could do to stop it.'

'He never even told me he was suffering from cancer! Not until it became too bad to be hidden.'

'He couldn't be persuaded to tell anyone, not even his wife. Indeed he was prepared to die, at first, glad that he had time to organize his affairs. It was about six months after the disease was diagnosed that he met you, and then he wanted to live forever. He loved you from the first day he saw you in his office. He came to me to beg me to save him, but I had to tell him I couldn't – that no one could. I told him that he could have treatment that might postpone the inevitable, but that it would not alter the outcome. Incidentally, I'm not breaking a confidence by telling you this. He said that, once it was all over, he wanted you to know everything – he hoped that the knowledge would help you to understand and forgive him.'

'I do!'

'I haven't finished the story yet, Georgette. Jack loved you very much but, in a different way, he loved your children even more! He came to think of them as his own children, the children he could never have – he was infertile, you see. That was at the root of his insecurity, an insecurity that caused him to become what we call a psychopathic alcoholic. When he was sober he loved you absolutely. When he was drunk he hated you, because you were capable of bearing children. That made him jealous and his jealousy overflowed to every man you met, because any one of them could do what he could not: make you pregnant. He lived in dread that some other man would make you pregnant and you would pretend he was the father – in a perverse way, I think he sometimes actually hoped that would happen. But, even in his blackest moods, he still had to love you – because you were the mother of the children he adored and regarded as his own!'

'Poor Jack! I never realized he was so complicated! He must have been terribly unhappy!'

'He was, Georgette. Now you understand why, you forgive him?'

Georgette was choked with emotion and could only nod, vigorously.

'He didn't even want you to work, in truth, although he admired you for it, because you were away from him while you worked. He allowed you to continue only because he knew he was a dying man and, when rational, he knew that you would need your career in the years ahead, to occupy you, when he couldn't look after you any more.'

'Oh, poor Jack! I loved him so much when he wasn't in a rage. We had a wonderful time when we were doing something with the children, and when he took me on holidays, and when we went out to dinner or to pubs frequented by his friends, with people like you, Amanda, and when we were spending a quiet evening alone together. All of that was marvellous, but when he'd been drinking alone I couldn't say or do anything without arousing suspicion! You obviously knew him very well, Amanda. May I ask you a personal question? Did you love him?'

Amanda laughed. 'Yes, I did – but not in the way you mean. I loved him as a friend, nothing more.' She gave Georgette an affectionate hug and kissed her on the forehead. 'I'd like to be a good friend to you now, if you'll let me.'

At that moment the door bell sounded. It was the solicitor, an elderly, blustery, chubby man in a grey suit. He puffed his way into the living-room, briefcase in hand, bemoaning the heat of the day with the same intensity he would have used had it been a cold day. He wasted no time on pleasantries.

The bulk of Jack's estate had been left to his long-suffering wife, and Georgette was glad about that. She was also delighted to learn that he had set up a trust fund for her children that would provide them both with a boarding-school education until they reached the age of nineteen. Not having to face that expense would be an enormous help to her.

Dickie and Bridgitte had been married for nearly four years now and he was once again working better as an interior decorator for Humphrey Manley, but though his relationship with Georgette had become quite cordial, which made life pleasanter, he had never made good the maintenance payments that he owed her, and she in her wisdom decided to let sleeping dogs lie.

Jack had also left Georgette a few thousand pounds in her own right, and some shares. It was all, she felt, much more than she deserved. She held back her emotions until the solicitor departed, then broke down, grateful for the comfort that Amanda offered.

'I feel so drained! I stayed totally loyal to him and all he did was persecute me! I understand now why he behaved as he did, and I do forgive him, but he dominated me so completely that, somewhere along the way, I lost my own personality and became nothing more than a part of him! He took me over so completely that, without him, I don't seem to have any being!'

'We'll find you again, my dear. It may take a little while, but don't forget I'm your friend now. Please believe me when I say that I fully understand your problem.'

Chapter Seventeen

Amanda Freshwood proved to be a delightful companion to Georgette during the dark days following the death of Jack Grant. Tom and Nancy Flowers, Nanny Trotter and Daisy Brown did all they could to keep her cheerful, but Amanda was the only person who had really known Jack for what he was and could appreciate Georgette's confused feelings about him.

Georgette's whole way of life changed, of course. For about three months she did little more than exist. She buried herself in work, to take her mind off her grief, and worked herself practically to a standstill. She had to seem cheerful when with customers, and found that terribly difficult, but it was excellent self-discipline.

She was drinking far too much, and perfectly aware of the fact, but it helped her get through this difficult period and she told herself that she would stop when the pain of her loss abated.

On most days Amanda Freshwood would ring up for a long conversation, or call round to see her. Often they just stayed at home and chatted, but sometimes Amanda would persuade Georgette to go out with her for a meal or to a show. Georgette was happy to be organized in this way, and never objected to anything Amanda suggested. She knew her friend was deliberately leaving her with as little time as possible to brood.

Had any man shown her the attention that Amanda was currently devoting to her, Georgette suspected that she would have gone to bed with him by now, but there was no man on her horizon at present – and she was disinclined to look for one.

One hot July afternoon, Amanda and Georgette were in swimsuits, relaxing on loungers on the balcony and sipping at long drinks while they soaked up the sun.

'I thought we might go to a club I belong to this evening. Do you fancy that?'

'Why not?' Georgette replied breezily. 'What do I wear?'

'Just look good. I'll call for you at eight. It's not far from here.'

'Not far from here' proved correct. Though Georgette had had no idea the place existed, it was within walking distance of her flat, just off Kings Road. From the street all that could be seen was a rather smart restaurant. Once inside the main entrance, however, Amanda ignored the glass door into the dining-room and led Georgette through a side door marked 'PRIVATE'. They walked along a narrow passage, then down some carpeted stairs and into another life: a twilight world.

The place was full of women, many of whom stopped talking to stare at Georgette. She felt rather uncomfortable but Amanda, in an undertone, told her not to worry – it was just that she was a newcomer to the club. To Georgette's relief, they soon returned to their gossip.

'Hallo, Marjory,' a young blonde girl called out and Amanda replied. Georgette was not surprised, because Amanda had told her that it was a quirk of the place to use only first names, and false ones at that.

An elderly, slim woman came forward and gave Amanda a peck on the cheek. Evidently she was expected. 'Marjory, darling, how nice to see you so early! And this must be your friend, Erica?'

'Indeed it is, Isobel.' She turned to Georgette. 'Erica, this is Isobel. She owns the club.'

'Welcome, dear.' Spindly fingers reached out and briefly shook Georgette's hand. Isobel took Amanda to one side, and they completed whatever formalities were required for a guest, then Amanda and Georgette took a table. The evening was spent drinking, dining and dancing – the lot, but never a man in sight. Georgette didn't like the idea of dancing with a woman and refused all offers to go on the dance floor, which was very dimly lit.

She would have liked to watch the dancers, but her attention was claimed by a continuous stream of ladies who came to their table, ostensibly to exchange a bit of casual conversation with Amanda. But Georgette guessed that she was the magnet. Obviously they were curious about this newcomer to their club, but most were fairly discreet with their questions and she didn't object.

What did puzzle her was that the women obviously came from all walks of life and were of all types. They seemed to have very little in common, and she had always thought that clubs were set up for the benefit of people who shared a common interest of some kind.

Around midnight they strolled back to Sparrow Hall Walk and, before she got into her car, Amanda asked, 'Did you enjoy the club, Georgette?'

'It was very interesting. It's different, isn't it? I found it rather restful, not having to contend with men all the time.'

Amanda smiled. 'That's one way of putting it. Would you like to go again?'

'I think I would. I thought some of the members were very nice.'

'I'm so glad! I hoped you would see that there can be a good life without men.' She paused, then added quietly. 'It can even be fun to go to bed with a woman.' With that, she got into her car and drove off.

Georgette stared after the car, startled. The thought had never occurred to her. She had heard of lesbians but had never met one before as far as she knew, and had certainly not recognized Amanda as being one. She had never suspected that the woman's kindness to her had been anything other than sympathetic friendship. Suddenly she wished she had paid more attention to what had been going on around her at the club, for she had no idea how lesbians behaved and was curious.

Male homosexuals, yes, she knew a fair amount about them. Those days in Paris, after its liberation, had introduced her to many, thanks to dear Boma Duviviers, and she had come across them since and rather liked them. They tended to be sensitive people who understood women's feelings and made good friends. Most of the ones she had met had been in show business and she knew some who had even had injections of glycerine in their chests to give them breasts for their drag acts.

But she had never thought very much about what they got up to in private, and had given no thought at all to women who behaved in a similar manner. A few days later they dined at Amanda's house, and took plenty of wine with their meal. Not quite sure how it had come about, but suspecting that curiosity had played some part in her compliance, Georgette found herself in bed with her friend.

Ever since they had met, Amanda had always been very much in control of the situation. Without Jack, Georgette had been looking for someone to direct her life, and Amanda had done so. In her lesbian relationships, too, Amanda had always played the dominant role and it was she who lured Georgette into bed. Once there, however, something surprising happened and, suddenly, it was Georgette who was in command. In retrospect, she concluded that she must have had some sort of reaction to being so much under Jack's influence sexually and, subconsciously, decided that it would not happen again.

However it happened, Georgette was the one in charge right from the start. Amanda was putty in her hands and everything Georgette did made the doctor behave like a woman, a role to which she was unaccustomed. Georgette, not knowing what was expected of her, just fondled her friend as a man might have done: whatever had been done to her by men she did to Amanda, and the woman was absolutely transfixed by what she termed Georgette's 'power'.

For her part, Georgette quite enjoyed the experience, because she derived a sort of satisfaction from her dominance. But she found that, sexually, it was a complete waste of time for her. Out of kindness, she pretended a physical pleasure that she did not feel. She would much rather have been with a man – any man, since she couldn't have Jack. 'Dear, darling Jack, would you have thought this performance very funny? I rather believe you would, you old devil!'

The outcome of that night was that Amanda fell deeply in love with Georgette!

She told Isobel how marvellous 'Erica' was, and word soon spread through the club. 'Marjory's' reputation in the lesbian community was that she knew her onions, so her word was accepted and whenever Georgette descended those carpeted stairs into the club it was as if royalty were arriving. She became the centre of attention, and was continually turning down approaches from other members. She considered it all very silly, because she really could not understand how two women could derive satisfaction from being together in 'that way'.

She continued her relationship with Amanda simply because it was the line of least resistance. Whenever she began, tactfully, to suggest that they part, Amanda became so distressed that Georgette let the matter drop. But, after about six months flirting with lesbianism, Georgette was very bored with the whole thing.

One evening 'Vera', a very attractive blue-eyed young blonde, accosted her in the club while Amanda was in the powder room. A little squiffily, Vera took a seat at Georgette's table, waving her elegant silver cigarette holder.

'Oh, Erica,' she pleaded, 'for God's sake leave Marjory and be with me!'

Georgette didn't like the woman and looked at her coldly. 'Leave Marjory? What are you saying?'

'I'm in love with you! I want you to dominate me! Leave Marjory and come with me – name your price!'

That Vera could afford to be generous, Georgette did not doubt, but did the woman think she was some kind of prostitute, to be bought off?

Georgette had learned quite a lot about the other members over the months and she knew that Vera was rolling in inherited wealth, and decidedly out of the top-drawer socially. Among other things, she owned two Rolls Royces and a couple of houses, one in Mayfair and the other in the country. No one in 'outside' life knew that Vera was a lesbian. Georgette had discovered there were many such people at the club, women leading double lives and unsuspected of being sexual deviants.

'But Vera, sweetie, I'm not "with" Marjory – nor anyone else.'

'Then you can come with me – please!'

'You misunderstood me, Vera. I mean that I am not emotionally or sexually attracted to any woman.'

'But you come here!'

'I come here as Marjory's guest, nothing else.'

'But you make love to her! I've heard about you!'

Georgette wanted desperately to issue a denial, but to do that would have betrayed a friendship. Whatever her reasons, Amanda had been a friend in her time of need, and was worthy of loyalty.

Mercifully, Georgette was saved from replying by Amanda returning, her face clouded, for she guessed the reason for Vera's presence at the table, and her jealousy was obvious.

But that encounter convinced Georgette that it was time for her to get out of her relationship with Amanda, and she determined to do so as kindly as possible.

Over the next few weeks she tried to do some match-making between Amanda and some of the younger girls, who had taken to clustering round Georgette whenever she went to the club. As Georgette gradually withdrew her 'favours' Amanda did go off with one or two of the girls, but they were of no real interest to her and, after each of these encounters, Amanda came back to Georgette, practically begging for some time in bed with her.

Georgette decided her only option was to be forthright. One evening Amanda was setting the dining-table for two, declaring that the meal, a lamb casserole, wouldn't be ready for another quarter of an hour. Georgette decided that this was the moment to speak out. She took a deep breath.

'Amanda. I'm very sorry, but I want you to let me go! Our relationship does nothing for me and it has become too serious. I don't want to hurt you, but I cannot go on like this any longer!'

Amanda let the rest of the cutlery fall onto the dining-table. 'Georgette, what are you saying?'

'Everything about our relationship is, I feel, dangerous to me.'

'No, it's not! No!' There was desperation in the cry.

'I think it is very unhealthy for me. I am not a lesbian – and I am glad that is the case, because I see so much misery in it. I mean, all these women are so sad – their lives are a lie from beginning to end.'

'Not all the time!'

'There are moments of joy, I grant you, but only when they're together. It's all based on nothing, and has no place in the real world. Maybe the world will change one day and things will be different but, as it is, a blind man could see how miserable they are most of the time. What they enjoy, it's . . . well . . . I'm sorry, but there's no other way to say it – it's not natural!'

'You are talking about me when you speak like this! I'm one of those unnatural hypocrites! The truth is, most of us are born to feel greater love for women not men.'

The comment went straight by Georgette, but she realized that she had said more than she'd intended. 'I'm sorry, Amanda. I didn't mean to offend you. But I cannot deny that what I said is what I feel. I don't condemn you for what you are, don't think that. I'm also grateful for the way you helped me over Jack's death – I don't know how I should have managed without you! But this is not the life for me, and I can no longer pretend that it is.'

'Couldn't we just be together, not go to the club, if it's that which upsets you.'

'No, Amanda. Please understand. It's not the club – that's just a place where things surface. The whole lesbian scene frightens me. At first I thought it was just a harmless bit of fun, a game to prove that women can manage without men, but I've come to realize that nothing about it is a joke. Those little girls at the club – and women like Vera – I feel like one of those awful Roman spectators getting fun from watching the lions eat the Christians. I'm completely detached from the whole thing and just playing around with something that means their whole lives to them, and that's a cruel thing to do.'

'You do not see it, dearest, do you? But you are cock of the walk! They do not think you are playing around with them. They love you – as I do.'

'The longer they go on playing lesbians in exclusivity the more pathetic they'll be!'

'But it's not playing, Georgette. It's what they are. It's what I am!'

'But that's the whole point, don't you see? I agree that it's what they are, but it's not what they really want to be. It can't be! That's why it's so tragic! Can you honestly tell me that you wouldn't be happier if you had normal sexual tastes?'

Amanda didn't answer.

'It isn't that I don't like you, Amanda. I do – and most of them, too. But I find it terrifying! I mean, I've been playing for a few "chips" since you introduced me to this life but these girls are playing with their whole lives! I did not know the mentality of these people at first. Now I do, and I . . . I pity them.'

Amanda was silent for a long time. 'All right, Georgette, you've made your point. I thought, at first, that you had lesbian tendencies – or I'd never have seduced you – but I've known for some time that I was wrong. I know I can't keep you with me against your will.' To Georgette's dismay, Amanda burst into tears. She'd lost lovers before, but never anyone she'd cared for so much, and her pain was great.

'Oh, Amanda, I didn't mean to hurt you!' Georgette was genuinely fond of Amanda, and it distressed her to see the supposedly tough woman in this state.

After a while Amanda's tears ceased. 'What I didn't see in you originally was that you are a naturally dominant person. Jack must have suppressed that side of you. I wish I had seen it earlier – you only thrive when you dominate.'

'I don't see that.'

'You wouldn't. I do. That is you. I accept it. The girls who have fallen for you see it, too, and they want you to dominate them.'

'Oh, how awful!'

'And I need you to dominate me, too.'

'Amanda, you don't! You're just saying that!'

'It's true, dear. I used to play the masculine role, but that no longer satisfies me: on that day we first went to bed I changed. You didn't mean it to happen, but you made me take the passive role and I found that was much more satisfactory. I don't think I could change back now.'

'I'm sorry.'

'Don't be. It wasn't your fault. I seduced you and now I'm paying the price. I've lost my way. I want only to be passive now. I tried it with Vera, but she brought out in me none of the sensitivities you extract. You're a good lover, Georgette and I shall never forget you – but I can accept that it's over, that you don't want me.' She stood up abruptly. 'I've got to go to the church for a minute,' she said, and left the room.

Georgette stared out of the window at Amanda's retreating figure, somewhat surprised by this announcement, but relieved that the scene was over. There was a church only a few doors down the road, but Georgette assumed that Amanda was going there to pray and would be gone for some time.

In fact, she was back inside seven minutes. She went straight to the sideboard and picked up a silver candlestick that flared out to hold two candles. Setting it down on the dining-table, she produced two plain white candles from her pocket.

Georgette was shocked. 'Surely you didn't steal those from the church?'

While she placed the candles into position and then lit them, Amanda replied nonchalantly. 'Whenever I run out of candles, I go to the church and bring a couple back. But don't worry – I always put more than enough money in the box to pay for them.'

That struck Georgette as very funny. 'I thought you had gone to church to pray!' she giggled.

'What makes you think I didn't?' asked Amanda. 'Georgette, I . . . This is difficult to say, because I do regard you as a friend, but I don't think we should see each other again after tonight. I don't think I could bear to go on seeing you, knowing that we could never again be together properly. So do you mind if we make this our last meeting?'

Chapter Eighteen

The naked woman looking back at Georgette had definitely put on weight since she had started drinking heavily, and a recent indulgence in chocolates and ice-cream had compounded the problem. But Georgette did not bemoan her weight gain. She felt her beauty had been a drawback as often as an asset and that, now it was fading, she might be able to lead a more peaceful life, loved for herself instead of for her body. She looked away from her reflection and attended to the task of getting ready for work.

The previous September both children had gone off to boarding-school. Dickie had wanted Alex to go to his old prep school, and Georgette saw no reason to object, but Susan immediately said it wasn't fair – that she wanted to board, too. Jack's trust fund was sufficient to cover the cost, so Georgette agreed.

Nanny Trotter, now sixty, had gone into well-earned retirement and, unsurprisingly, had chosen to go and live in the Scottish Highlands to be near to her sister and brother-in-law. So apart from Daisy Brown's daily visits, Georgette had her flat to herself and, without Amanda's comradeship, she was lonely.

As she dressed, Georgette's thoughts turned to Brussels. A few mornings before she had received a letter from Henri, informing her that 'Tante' Pauline had died. He had known that Georgette had never liked Pauline and would not wish to attend the funeral, so there had been no rush to pass on the news to her and Pauline was already in her grave when he wrote.

With Jack gone, there was nothing to stop Georgette from visiting Brussels whenever she wanted, so why didn't she go now? She felt she was getting into a rut and thought a brief change of scene might do her good.

By the time she reached the office Georgette had made up her mind, and she decided to ring her father without delay. Henri was delighted. 'Come on the twenty-first. Your usual room will be free then.'

Then Georgette began to think about Maurice Le Blond. She had been without sex with a man for over a year now, and wanted to

162

expunge the experience of being with a woman. But she was a bit wary. Most of the men with whom she had slept had ended up hurting her emotionally, but she knew where she was with Maurice. He was still single and still wanted her – or had the last time they had met – and she had never quite got him out of her system, but she knew better than to suppose that a sexual liaison between them would lead to anything, so she could just treat him as a loving friend and not be hurt when their relationship did not change. The more she thought about it, the more attractive she found the idea, and finally, from home, she rang Maurice.

'I'm coming over soon. Officially I'm arriving on the twenty-first, and will be staying at the Leopold, but I could arrange to arrive on the twentieth, if you feel like making some arrangements for that night?'

'You're teasing me, Georgette!' Maurice was laughing, but she caught the undertone of excitement.

'No, Maurice, I mean it. I thought it was time we tried again. If you ring my father and say that you'll meet me at the airport on the twenty-first, he'll be none the wiser if you drop me off at the Leopold then, after we've spent the night together. I really do want to sleep with you!'

'This is marvellous, Georgette!' He made no further effort to disguise the excitement in his voice, a feeling which his body was reflecting at the mere thought of being in bed with Georgette again. 'Let me know when you've fixed your flight and I *will* meet you at the airport.'

So, a few days later, she took a late afternoon flight and they met at Brussels Airport, the first time they'd seen each other since Bonne-maman's funeral. Maurice Le Blond could not help but notice how plump she had become, but he liked a bit of flesh to get hold of – and, if anything, his desire increased.

'Honey, you're looking swell!' he jested, with an American accent, as they motored to the hotel he had booked. 'But gorgeous with it!' he added hastily, in case she took his joke the wrong way.

'While you are as slim and handsome as ever!' Georgette responded lightly, taking no offence and warmed by his admiration.

'I've not changed my ways, either. As you know, I'm still not married – and won't be changing that!'

'Don't worry, Maurice! I've had enough of husbands for the time being. So you're quite safe with me. My only designs are on your body!'

The adrenalin rushed through him at that remark and he could hardly wait to reach their room.

They arrived at the hotel and checked in. A page-boy deposited their cases on the rack, took his tip and left. Maurice reached out and eagerly pulled Georgette to him but she had no intention of missing out on her evening meal. 'We've waited for years, Maurice, an hour or so more won't harm us, and I'm hungry,' she said firmly, giving him a brief kiss to be going on with, and delighting in the way his body showed his desire before she pulled away from his embrace. That erection was for her!

They decided to eat in the hotel dining-room. Over the food they caught up with each other's news, though Georgette couldn't bring herself to mention the nature of her relationship with Amanda Freshwood.

'You've certainly learned a thing or two about life since my early lecture on the birds and bees! Now let's see what else I can teach you!' The time had at last come for them to retire for the night, and Maurice could hardly wait. His impatience was obvious and Georgette smiled, already feeling very feminine again, and revelling in the fact.

What Amanda had said about her liking to dominate crossed her mind, and she could not deny that part of her enjoyment of the evening, so far, had derived from the way she had imposed her will on Maurice. She wanted him very much. The thought alone of just holding his proud penis was sending shivers of delight through her; but making him wait, against his will, was making her feel powerful – and that was a great feeling.

But the time had come for the teasing to stop. Together they went upstairs, a compelling sense of closeness bonding them. Entering their room, they found someone had invitingly turned down the sheets of the well-sprung double bed – an invitation they accepted immediately.

Their long-suppressed sexual hunger for each other was evident in the passion of their caresses, each moment producing an emotional ecstasy in both. 'My God! You really have learned things, haven't you!' Maurice moaned, through her increasingly demanding kisses, unable to control his desire any longer and giving up any attempt at finesse.

After they had recovered from that initial surge of animal lust, their true fondness for each other was allowed to surface and, from then on, it was erotic fun in the bed that night. Sleep came only an

164

hour before dawn, but neither felt they were suffering from lack of sleep when they vacated their room at eleven o'clock.

As they left the hotel and retrieved the car from the car-park, for Maurice to drop Georgette at the Leopold, how glad they both were that Georgette had dared to add those extra hours to her Belgian itinerary.

But Georgette should have timed her arrival at the Leopold better. Henri knew airline schedules, and her arrival did not coincide with any of the flights from London.

Maurice helped her carry her bags up the steps. As they entered Reception, Edouard hastened forward, signalling to a porter to take over the burden. How old Edouard was looking, thought Georgette, as she greeted him with an affectionate kiss on the cheek, little knowing that Edouard was thinking along similar lines about her.

Henri saw them arrive. Maurice caught his knowing look and quickly took his leave.

Georgette turned to her father and said, 'It's good to be back, Papa!' Although in no position to throw stones, she was sorry to see that the weight was back on him again – he was even more spherical than she remembered him being in her early childhood. But he was getting on for seventy, she reminded herself.

'If you are going to spend a night in town before coming here, you might time your arrival better!'

Georgette reddened, then thought, 'Oh hell! I don't care what he thinks!' But Henri had made his point, and the matter was never referred to again.

Georgette had an enjoyable stay and all her friends made a fuss of her, so the week passed very quickly. Monique was starring in a local cabaret and Georgette went to see her twice, with Maurice as her escort. They did not sleep together again on that trip, by mutual agreement, but their shared night had brought them that feeling of closeness that exists only between caring lovers, and they laughed a great deal at silly little incidents. For the first time since she had first started going with Jack, Georgette was really relaxed and happy.

Then came the time when she had to return to England where, she supposed, she belonged. She had never questioned that before and, thinking over the matter seriously, she was not all that sure she wanted to return. But it was her home now – her children were there, and so was her job.

Her friends in Belgium had been delighted to see her after so long, and more than happy to put themselves out to entertain her for a week, but they had their own lives to lead and would not rearrange their affairs so much if she were around all the time. Certainly Maurice would not always be available as an escort, for he was not the type to confine his attentions for long to just one woman, even one as special to him as Georgette. He was, in any case, thinking of migrating to Canada. He had relations in Quebec who had been trying to convince him that Canada was the land of opportunity, and he was tempted.

Georgette was still very close to Monique, and knew that nothing would ever change that, but the nature of Monique's work meant that she kept odd hours and tended to mix with members of her profession who were in the same position. She was, anyway, in some demand these days and often away from Brussels – mainly elsewhere in Belgium or in France, but with occasional bookings from other European countries.

Georgette felt very much alone, suddenly appreciating that, apart from Daisy Brown and the Flowers, all of whom were much older than Georgette, she had few real friends in England, either.

It was a heavy-hearted woman who took her leave of Brussels.

Georgette concentrated on her work and, when not working, drank heavily. She spent a lot of time in The Mitre, the nearest pub to her office, and in The Grapes, which had been her local when she was with Jack. She knew a lot of the regulars in both places and was often invited to parties. She quite frequently held parties, too, and made sure that there was always plenty of alcohol in the flat.

Something within her insisted on regular nourishment, however much she had been drinking, so she did not skip meals and remained capable of buying and cooking good food.

She still liked clothes, and spent quite a lot on them, as she seldom found time to sew these days. She also bought a washing-machine and other electrical gadgets that caught her eye.

But drink was her main expense, and there was never anything left over from her earnings these days.

As time passed, Georgette became dissatisfied with her life-style and decided it was time she settled down with a man again. But this time she didn't want her heart to be involved – she wanted someone she could control, so that she could avoid being hurt again. And she had just the man in mind, a regular at The Grapes. He had been an acquaintance of Jack's, so she had known him casually for some time and knew that he fancied her.

Martin Ashley was an account executive with a large advertising agency, so he should be reasonably affluent. He had been divorced for some time, so was available, and had a teenage son at boarding-school, which should mean that he would be able to cope with her children. He was about forty-five, she guessed. A tall man, he was very slim and gave the impression of being a little effeminate, but she was sure that was misleading, for she had seen the way he looked at her. He had receding fair hair and blue eyes. She was not that attracted to him, but nor did she find him repulsive. One way and another, she thought he would be very suitable.

One evening, therefore, Georgette took particular care over her appearance and went to The Grapes early, and stone-cold sober, in the hope that Martin would be there. He was, and wandered over.

'You are on your own tonight, Mrs Barestone-Tailour?' he said diffidently. He was used to the English-rose type and thought Georgette very exotic. He was also very impressed by her business ability, about which he had heard from Jack. Although he was completely smitten with her, Georgette knew that he would need encouragement to make the first move, and she had decided to give it to him.

'I am, Mr Ashley.' She replied demurely. 'I've been for a walk and worked up a bit of a thirst. So I came here. I hoped there would be someone here I knew, because I don't like drinking alone.' Not strictly the truth, anymore, of course. 'If you are alone, too, Mr Ashley, perhaps you would be kind enough to join me?' He needed no second invitation and the evening culminated in them dining together.

Over the next few months, they met often at the pub and then went on somewhere together. Georgette found him pleasant enough company, and he was undemanding sexually. She slept with him once or twice, usually when they'd both had a bit to drink, and feigned more passion than she felt. But most of the time she kept him at arm's length. He would always take 'No' for an answer without too many problems.

They never went anywhere flashy, but Martin seemed to know a lot of places that were both good and reasonably priced. From time to time she offered to pay the bill and he always seemed a little relieved. She began to wonder if she'd been right in supposing that he was well paid. He didn't run a car, which was unusual, and never gave her presents. But, whenever she tried to find out his financial position, he became very secretive and she finally gave up.

Then one cold Saturday night in June, as she and Martin huddled over a single-bar electric fire, and drank champagne cider whilst listening to Brahms and Beethoven, after having made love but a while earlier, it dawned on Georgette what she hadn't seen before. Martin wasn't poor – he was just extremely mean!

But he'd said he loved her, and he did seem to, so maybe she could change him? In the next instant she answered that question for herself in the negative, knew there was no future in a marriage to him.

Back in her own flat, she wrote to Martin that she did not feel she was the girl for him, and even as she penned the words she had begun to wonder if she was the right person for any man to marry – both her husbands had gone on to be much happier in marriage with other women. So perhaps that was what 'Tante' Pauline had meant when she'd declared her 'a woman for lovers'? What perception!

A few weeks later Georgette was horrified to discover that she was pregnant!

'Well, this is the end!' She fumed to herself. 'One night of drinking champagne cider and I end up like this!' There was no doubt Martin Ashley was the father, for she had slept with no other man since she had started going out with him.

In a panic, she rang Nancy. 'Well, I can't say I'm surprised! That's bound to happen, sooner or later, when you don't take any precautions.'

'But what am I going to do? I can't have the child!'

'No, I can see that. Don't worry – I think I can sort something out for you.'

Nancy had a friend called Dr Bestlove, who was the senior gynaecologist at a London hospital and also the consultant at a private nursing-home. He examined Georgette and declared her in need of a D&C.

'I feel that, in your case, it's the most sensible solution,' he said firmly, 'and you will need only a few days off work.' Georgette acquiesced without hesitation. So, right or wrong, she received a legal abortion and was sterilized at the same time.

Alone again, Georgette spent the next two years drinking more heavily than ever before, although she never had her first drink until the evening, and seldom had a hangover. So her sales were unaffected, and she continued to work very hard, maintaining her position as GBE's top sales-person – as she was called now, although she had never objected to being called a salesman.

Although she saw little of them, Georgette felt she was doing all the right things for her children. She made a point of going to their separate Sports Days and Open Days, and special events like that. Luckily the dates never clashed. On these visits she gave them both an elaborate display of affection, never pausing to consider that she might be embarrassing them in front of their school-friends.

They spent few days at home, just enough time at the beginning and end of holidays to unpack or pack their trunks, with Daisy Brown's help, and get ready for the holidays or the return to school.

Since Georgette was so busy working, the children's holidays were organized so that they spent the minimum amount of time in London. They always went to Dickie, Brigitte and Lady Margaret for a while, and Georgette also arranged for them to go on escorted trips to various parts of Europe, thinking it would be good for them, as well as enjoyable, to learn a little about other countries.

She thought the children must love her for all this liberty and foreign travel and they did enjoy their holidays very much, but both wished they had a mother who would spend some time with them and give them natural love, instead of being all over them one moment and sending them away the next. They never quite knew where they were with her.

One day the telephone rang very early, just after seven in the morning. It was Aimee!

'Bad news, Georgette. I'm afraid your father died last night!'

Georgette was stunned, awakened from sleep.

'That's very sudden, isn't it?'

'He'd been ill.'

'How long had he been ill?'

'Nearly ten days.'

'And you did not let me know?'

'I didn't realize he was going to die.'

'What was wrong with him?'

'Er – a blockage of the kidney.'

'He was in hospital?'

'He would not go to hospital.'

'Papa was always pig-headed! I suppose he refused to listen to the doctor?'

'That's right. He just got worse and worse, and must have been in great pain, but he wouldn't admit it! Not until the very last.'

'When is the funeral?'

'Next Wednesday afternoon. I imagine you'd like your usual room?'

'Yes, thank you. I'll fly over early that morning and return on Thursday morning, so it'll only be for one night. I'll take a taxi, so you needn't arrange for me to be met.' Georgette wanted as little fuss as possible.

As she hung up she realized that, other than the hated Therese and other relations so distant she didn't know them, she no longer had any family. She was an orphan! Although she had seen him seldom since she grew up, Georgette had always felt Henri was in the background and the thought had been vaguely comforting. Now he was no longer there and she felt a terrible sensation of absolute loneliness. She wept.

Georgette told the children, of course, but Grandfather Delire was only a name to them and it would have been pointless for them to go with her to the funeral.

She flew to Brussels knowing it was probably the last time she would stay at the Leopold. A new manager would be appointed and life would go on. There would be no reason for her to visit the place which had been her home for most of her formative years. Even dear Edouard was no longer there, having retired shortly after her last visit.

All through the service, she felt no emotion. She was just there, beside Aimee, who sobbed without stopping and was obviously very much in distress. Whatever she might feel about Aimee, the woman had made him a good wife and it was obvious her feelings for him had been genuine. Of Therese there was no sign.

After the church service, a procession moved slowly to the cemetery where Henri's first wife and her parents, and his parents were already at rest.

It rained at the grave-side, quite heavily. Georgette's eye started to itch, and she brought a gloved hand to it to ease the problem. A little old lady Georgette did not know, who was standing by her, dressed in black as they all were, placed a hand on her arm and said, 'See, even the angels are crying for him!'

'Which is more than I am!' thought Georgette, momentarily encased in guilt for thinking such a thing. But she had wept away her grief when first told of her father's death, and had no tears left for him.

Before she left the cemetery, she visited the adjoining graves of Elizabeth, Beatrice and Albert. Then she looked upon those of Grand-maman and Grand-pere Harley, and paid her respects to them, too.

To Georgette's surprise, Philippe Pillot was among the mourners at the funeral, having come from Liege especially. She had not been aware he knew her father well enough to make the journey, but was delighted to see her old friend after so long; hadn't worked it out that he had reasoned it a chance to see Georgette just once more.

'Dear Philippe!' she said at the reception afterwards. 'I don't know how I would have got through my early life without you! I wasn't very mature in those days, was I?' ('And maybe it is I still am not,' the thought crossed her mind). 'But tell me about yourself, your wife, your life in Liege. There's so much to catch up on!'

It had suddenly dawned on Georgette that her friend was now in his seventies and, although he seemed well, she had a feeling this might be their last meeting. There were tears in her eyes when the time came for them to part.

She saw her whole visit as marking the end of an era.

Chapter Nineteen

The children came home for Christmas and Georgette was surprised at how grown-up they were becoming. Susan's adolescent gawkiness was vanishing as she became an attractive young lady. She was busy preparing to take eight subjects in the General Certificate of Education examinations. Alex had suddenly shot up and was now about the same height as Georgette. His mind was also on exams as he was getting ready for the Common Entrance Exam to Wellington College.

After Christmas Dickie and Brigitte came over and took them off to their grandmother's for the New Year, before seeing them off to Austria on a skiing trip. It was to be Lady Margaret's last Christmas. Six weeks later she passed away in her sleep and, at the age of fifty-eight, Dickie finally came into his long-anticipated inheritance.

A year later, Brigitte was to give birth to a son and they were a contented couple. Even Georgette no longer thought about the disparity in their ages, and she hoped that she was as gracious to Brigitte as Phyllis Grant had been to her.

The excessive drink she was still consuming was beginning to have an effect on Georgette's personality, although she couldn't see it. She was gradually becoming uninterested in everybody about her, growing more and more selfish. If something didn't affect her directly, then she couldn't be bothered about it. She felt she had too much on her own plate to worry about other people's problems. Her true lack of concern showed through, even when she pretended to be interested.

GBE's growth was continuing. The UK headquarters was now housed in a new office block in Lewisham, South London although the offices off Davies Street were retained as the base for the sales force. Being so central, it was also a good place to give demonstrations of their machines.

Apart from causing her to start work late in the mornings, drink was not noticeably making Georgette's work suffer. She was not quite as sharp as she had been, and her appearance was less of a help to her, but those facts were more than offset by GBE's growing reputation and Georgette's natural ability, coupled with her total knowledge of all her lines – she had heard all the questions so often before that she could have answered most of them in her sleep.

So she continued to earn a great deal in commission and was often asked to take a trainee along with her to see how the spiel worked in action. Since that meant she had someone to carry her briefcase and, if necessary, one of the machines, she was only too pleased to co-operate. Since they were mostly young men, who were unattached and had a very low salary while they were training – all so different from her own first days with GBE – she often ended the day by buying them drinks or taking them to a restaurant or night-club.

After a while, however, Georgette could not fail to notice that some of these young men, who had joined GBE long after her and had nothing like her experience, were becoming managers. While she, now forty-two, was still out on the road. Her sales ability was held up as a shining example, but no one ever mentioned the possibility of promotion.

Georgette felt that success and long service should be among the main criteria for becoming a manager. She considered that, because of her experience and recognized achievement in one field of the company's activities, she was automatically entitled to a managerial position. She couldn't see that she lacked any of the qualities of those young men so, if they were management material, why wasn't she?

Then she learned that the people who were becoming managers had been sent on management courses and she became really resentful. She'd never in her life failed any course (except maths at school, and that wasn't relevant), not even her driving test, so she was absolutely sure that she'd have no problems at all with this one.

'Why shouldn't I be going on these courses?' she'd mutter into her glass of alcohol, alone in her flat, too proud to voice these thoughts publicly. 'I mean, if management came naturally there wouldn't need to be courses. Since it has to be taught, I can learn it! I became a salesman by having my salesmanship brought out in me, so why shouldn't I become a manager by having my managerial qualities brought out?' She came to the conclusion that the only possible explanation was that she was a woman, and that wasn't good enough, but she didn't see what she could do about it.

Her sales figures were beginning to show a slight drop, and that worried Georgette, although she knew that it didn't reflect on her personally – the rest of the sales force were in the same boat. GBE had figured that their profits would be higher if they employed more people and gave each a smaller territory. This policy did result in more sales overall, but no individual sales-person could bring in quite as much business as had been possible in the old days. At the same time, competitors were becoming established and GBE no longer had the market to themselves.

These facts, combined with the fact that she now disliked the physical effort involved in selling, made Georgette want to be office-based. She was sure that she would find life less burdensome as a manager.

GBE's range now included dictating machines, switchboard systems and photocopiers. Georgette learned everything about each new machine as it came onto the market, and her knowledge was unrivalled within the company.

But she was getting older. She was by far the oldest person in the sales force – and she felt it! She was constantly tired and felt misunderstood, unappreciated, hard done by. She tried talking the matter over with Les Dykes, who was now Sales Director. He'd just taken over from Mr Saint, who had taken early retirement.

'But you're too good at sales, Georgette. What would we do without you?' He made it clear that the subject was closed.

Despite her pride, as the months passed without any sign of promotion, she began to complain to other people in the company whose opinion she valued. They offered sympathy, but none told her the truth – that there was no question of her being made a manager because, whatever else she might have to offer, her drinking habits would prevent her from having the respect that a good manager needs from the work force.

So she went on selling, becoming increasingly moody as her disaffection increased. Her sales dropped as her enthusiasm waned and, of course, her commission also decreased. Meanwhile her cost of living seemed to be increasing daily and the Swinging Sixties were certainly not swinging for her. She always had good food in the house, and still ate well, but whisky had become the single most important item in her budget and she knew by heart the telephone number of her nearest off-licence.

Some of her colleagues at GBE were seriously worried about her by this time, including Les Dykes, and he was forthright. 'You're such a nice person, Georgette, when you're yourself. But recently, when you've had a couple of drinks, you change completely and become quite impossible. You really should take it easy.'

Georgette refused to listen. 'Oh, Les, don't tease me like that! As if I'd change! Anyone would think I drank too much! How silly you are!' After a few more attempts, Les saw he was getting nowhere and he might just as well save his breath.

But Georgette's attitude to work was deteriorating all the time and her sales began to fall much faster than the general circumstances made necessary. She often rose very late, after sleeping off the drink from the night before, and her work reports (now requiring her to state the hours she worked) concealed the fact, by stating that she'd spent longer with prospective customers than she actually had.

She did still manage to sell as much as everyone else in the sales force, even when actually working less hours than any of them, but she was no longer number one. She had to really psych herself up to do five or six calls a day, but she did make sure that they were really good calls. That took all her energy and, afterwards, she was completely worn out.

Les Dykes was asked about her falling sales, and had no option but to tell the truth. He pointed out that her results were still a little above average and that there was always the possibility that she was going through a bad patch and would pull herself together.

She began to row with people when in her cups, and seldom remembered doing so. Over and over again she would greet someone cheerfully in the morning, only to be cut dead. Bewildered, she would tell someone else what had happened and they would tell her that the previous evening she had said something hurtful, if not unforgivable, to the person concerned. She would try to apologize, but it was difficult when she had absolutely no recollection of the incident, and she became aware that some people tried to avoid being in her company. But she didn't stop drinking – with every month that passed her desire for alcohol was becoming more overwhelming. It was the only thing that overcame her loneliness.

Susan had passed all eight of her GCE 'O' level subjects, but had decided that she didn't want to go on to take 'A' levels and then go to university. She wanted to become independent as soon as possible, so she had left school and gone to live with Georgette, planning to take a full-time secretarial course at the local technical college. Before the first term had started, however, she had realized what was happening to her mother. Her first instinct had been to run to Dickie, but she had felt it was her duty to do whatever she could to help, so she had enrolled in evening classes for shorthand-typing and got herself a day-time job as a shop assistant in a West End department store.

Alex was still at school and too young to cope with Georgette's moods. He pleaded with his father to let him spend all his school holidays with him. Georgette could no longer afford to send him abroad and was relieved that Dickie was taking over the responsibility of looking after him. Thank God, Jack's money was still meeting the school fees, so she could pretend to Dickie that she was earning more than she was.

Georgette began to wet her bed. Drink and her recurring back pain had begun to affect her bladder. After it had happened a few times she bowed to the inevitable and bought herself a rubber sheet. She soon became adept at changing the bedding and was thankful that she had gone to the trouble of having a washing-machine installed.

Samuel Rosen had retired but she found a new osteopath, with a surgery not far from her home. Jeff Castle, a spindly little man, was pleased with the new business, but Georgette would often reach his surgery obviously the worse for drink and that annoyed him. 'Look here, Mrs Barestone-Tailour,' he said one day. 'You must know your back would be much better if you never touched alcohol.'

'I don't see any connection.' She said airily.

'I should have thought it was obvious. When you are drunk you don't take care how you move, and you're always putting an unnecessary strain on your back and undoing my work.'

Georgette didn't like what she heard, so she pretended to ignore it. But she was desperately afraid of being bedridden again and did not dare take the chance that he would refuse to treat her, so thereafter she made a point of remaining sober when she had an appointment with Castle.

Alone at home one evening, as Susan was at her shorthand-typing class, Georgette was in her dressing-gown and had just finished her first whisky when the doorbell sounded. She went to the door. A couple she had met in a pub recently were standing there. 'Why, how nice to see you!' she greeted them.

'Georgette! You're not dressed!' the woman blurted out.

'I relax better this way when I'm alone.'

'Oh!' exclaimed the woman. She glanced at her husband, then said, 'You asked us to come to dinner tonight.'

'Oh my darlings! So I did – I'd quite forgotten! It was a tough day at work and I was so busy thinking about my sales that it quite slipped my mind you were coming! Can you forgive me?' The truth was that she had no recollection at all of having asked them – her mind was a complete blank on the subject. She dismissed it as middle-aged forgetfulness, never put it down to drink.

'Anyway, it doesn't matter – I've plenty of food in the house and can quickly produce something. Come on in!' And she saw to it that the meal was very good – her cooking ability was totally unaffected by her drinking – and they all had a pleasant evening.

The next day Georgette could remember them arriving, could remember beginning to prepare the meal and could remember them leaving. But nothing at all in between. This was fairly typical – a 'blackout' as she took to calling it, would usually hit her without warning and there would be no surface indication of them having occurred. They'd descend around the time she finished her first drink of the evening and the length of the amnesia would vary – sometimes, but only sometimes, the mist would clear sufficiently for her to remember some of the late evening. Now, she could understand, all too well, Jack's lapses of memory.

The drink was affecting her body, as well as her mind, and she was getting increasingly tired at the end of a day's work. She seldom drank in the day, except at weekends. But in the evenings she usually had a drink immediately after work – and once she'd had one drink she couldn't stop, she had to go on having more.

Sometimes, inexplicably, Georgette would lose the taste for drink and be dry for weeks on end. This led to her kidding herself that she could stop drinking completely whenever she wanted to. During these periods Susan would find peace at home and begin to hope that her mother was on the road to recovery.

But, sooner or later, the day would come when someone in the office would say, 'Fancy a quick one on the way home?' and Georgette would accompany them to the local and, once there, she would be off the wagon as soon as the first round was ordered. Sometimes it would occur to her to call Susan, to say she'd been delayed. At other times she simply got home late. Either way, she was the worse for drink when she did arrive, and Susan would brace herself for the criticism that came her way more often than not:

'Susan this plate is filthy! You're supposed to have washed it. How can I dry it in this condition? I suppose you think you are too important to wash the dishes properly now you are a working girl?'

or:

'I asked you to peel a few potatoes, Susan. I should have thought even you could have managed that, but you leave great chunks of peel on them that even a blind man could see. You are useless! God help the man who marries you!'

There were many variations on the theme and Susan didn't know how to cope, how to answer, for she knew only too well that, in these moods, her mother was not rational. So she bit her lip and suffered in silence.

She was now a qualified shorthand-typist, working as a 'temp' for a local employment agency. What she wanted was for Georgette to take more care of herself, but all she could do was watch helplessly as her mother's condition continued to decline.

When Georgette got back to the flat one evening she was surprised to find Susan had returned from a stay with Dickie and was busy at the sink, preparing some vegetables for their dinner.

'Hi, Mummy. Had a good day?' she asked.

'You're back early, aren't you, sweetie?' Georgette asked, wondering if she'd got the dates wrong.

'Yes, Mummy. The agency rang me at Daddy's and asked if I could work from tomorrow morning. Apparently Mr Pillinger of Rice, Hawkins, wants me again – asked for me especially!' Georgette was familiar with the name, which was that of a prestigious firm of accountants, but she could not recall Susan working for them before.

'That's very flattering, sweetie, but you should have insisted on having the week off as you'd planned. There's not much point in being a temp if you don't have that sort of freedom.'

'But I don't really mind, Mummy. I wasn't doing anything special, after all, and I don't want to upset the agency. I have to earn as much as possible, remember?'

'Yes, dear,' Georgette hadn't a notion why, but assumed that her daughter was saving for something and she didn't want to admit that she couldn't remember what it was. She couldn't even remember what had prompted Susan to visit Dickie in the first place. But this sort of memory lapse happened so frequently nowadays that she shrugged it off. 'When you're good at your job, people always want you, dear,' she said vaguely, as she poured herself a large drink.

Alex was now fifteen, tall and favoured with a strong physique. But Georgette was sad to see the loss of his childhood beauty and innocence. She thought he was very grown-up, but he was not mature enough to understand his mother's problem fully. He just knew she drank too much, and was unpredictable and embarrassing, so he stayed away from her as much as possible.

Dickie insisted that Alex contact Georgette whenever he was in London, but he never spent longer with her than he could help. How thankful Alex was that all his holidays were now based at Grace Hall with his father, Brigitte and little Jocelyn (known as Joss), now an active three-year-old who was into everything.

Georgette had not visited Alex at Wellington for over a year. He had made it clear he didn't wish her to and, although she was hurt by his attitude, she was relieved that she didn't have to make the effort.

The only times he visited her voluntarily were when he needed a bed for the night because he had to be in London early the next morning, to meet friends or go shopping in Carnaby Street with money supplied by his father.

He had become, by anybody's standards, an attractive boy, but he was not at all academically inclined and was having to work very hard to be sure of passing his GCE 'O' level exams next year. His childhood desire had never changed – he still wanted to be a soldier. On one visit to his mother, he found she was sober for once and reaffirmed his intention of becoming a military man.

'But I don't want to find I've made a mistake, Mummy, so I'm going for a short-service commission.'

'Have you a regiment in mind?'

'Mummy you know I have! If they'll have me, I want to try for The Life Guards. They're a wonderful regiment, aren't they?'

Georgette practically choked on the chocolate she'd just popped into her mouth. It was bad enough that he wanted to be a soldier, but a Life Guard! It looked as if her past might be about to catch up with her. If Alex were to be commissioned into The Life Guards he would be sure to meet Dougie, sooner or later, and what would happen then?

Dougie would probably say nothing to the boy. But what if Alex started wondering about Dougie? He knew she had been married to someone called Rusby before she'd met Dickie, and it wasn't a very common name. Neither Susan nor Alex had any idea that David existed, and she didn't want Alex to find out accidentally, but she couldn't bring herself to tell him about his half-brother at this late stage.

She decided that, if he were to be accepted by The Life Guards, she would write to Dougie and ask him to ensure that Alex and David would not run into each other.

'Mummy?'

She realized that she had been silent for rather a long time and Alex was wondering why she hadn't answered his question.

'Sorry, darling – that was a caramel and rather chewy! I don't know much about the Army, but don't you need a lot of money to join a regiment like that?'

'No Mummy, I don't need private means. I've been assured of that. Anyway, I'm sure Daddy would cough up if I did, because he wants me to be in a good regiment.'

Alex had his shoeless feet up on a coffee table as he spoke.

'Just take your feet off my table, Alex. You want to be a soldier, do you? Good – the discipline is just what you need. The Army'll soon smarten you up!'

Why did she always have to demean him? Alex held his tongue.

Over the next year Georgette's work deteriorated alarmingly, as Les Dykes noted with sadness. He could see that, for the very first time since she had joined GBE, she would fail to make the Top Ten Club. If she continued on her present path, it was probable that he would soon be instructed to dispense with her services altogether. He had become fond of her and did not want that to happen, but there was a limit to how far he could cover up for her shortcomings, and he certainly wasn't prepared to risk his own job.

Georgette's once-excellent salary had not increased in line with inflation, since GBE's policy had changed again and they now preferred their sales staff to rely mainly on commission. Since her commission was shrinking, the day came when she had to begin to supplement her earnings with her savings, and her capital was dwindling.

She had started taking taxis again, because she now found it tedious to get into her car, make the effort to drive somewhere and then go through all the bother of finding somewhere to park. Nor could she cope with the physical aspects of selling any more. Even filling in the daily reports seemed to her to be hard work.

One day in 1969 Alex rang Georgette to say he was coming up to London the next day and could he stay the night?

'Of course, sweetie! I'll make sure I'm home by five o'clock.'

Typically, Georgette didn't think to ask her son what was bringing him to London.

She got home just before he arrived and he told her that he had an appointment the next morning, with an Army school's liaison officer at Whitehall.

Georgette's heart sank. But she smiled as brightly as she could and asked Alex to be sure he let her know how he got on. 'Can you pop in here tomorrow evening, before you leave town?'

He was somewhat surprised by what was obviously genuine interest, and promised he would.

True to his word, the next evening he arrived at the flat shortly after Georgette, and was delighted to find that she was stone-cold sober, so he went into some detail.

The fact that his first choice was The Life Guards had seemed to please the officer who had interviewed him initially. This interview was a fairly boring affair and he was asked all the usual questions. 'What school do you go to? What does your father do? Why choose the Army?' etc.

The answers Alex gave had seemed to satisfy the inquisitor and, in what seemed no time at all, he was being ushered along a warren of corridors to meet the Lieutenant Colonel commanding The Life Guards. 'He's a full colonel, Mummy, and is known as "Silver Stick in Waiting" because, on ceremonial occasions, he waits on the Queen and he always carries a silver-topped stick.'

'Very nice.'

'He and his adjutant put the same questions to me the liaison officer had put; but these guys really made me feel at ease.'

'Well, they would. Have you eaten?'

'I was taken by them to lunch at Knightsbridge Barracks.

Afterwards we went back to Silver Stick's office and he offered me a short-service commission in The Life Guards, which I did not hesitate to accept!'

'So you're an officer, just like that?'

'No Mummy, it is not quite as easy as that! I don't start till August next year, then it's intensive training for a while. First of all I have to do eight weeks of training with the Brigade Squad at Pirbright, to see if I'm any good at soldiering. Then, if I get through that, I have to satisfy the Regular Commissions Board that I'm officer material – that consists of three days of assessment at Westbury – that's in Wiltshire. If I get through that, I'm almost there, but I still have to go to Mons for twenty weeks to earn my commission.'

'Belgium? Whatever for?'

Alex laughed. 'Not the place, Mummy! But it is named after that famous World War One battle there. "My" Mons is an officer cadet school at Aldershot.'

'I thought officers went to Sandhurst?'

'Not short-service officers.'

'It'll be a lot of hard work by the sound of it.'

'But it's what I want, Mummy, so I'll do it very happily.'

'You really are passionate about the Army, darling!'

A little later Alex left, to catch his train back to Titchfield, and Georgette settled down to write to Dougie. She did not touch a drink until her letter was finished.

One evening not long after Alex's visit Georgette got home late, and drunk. Susan was relaxing on a huge cushion, watching television. Her heart sank when she saw the state her mother was in and she prayed that Georgette would not be in a belligerent mood. Susan was now an attractive long-legged twenty-year-old, and had a delightful personality that seldom emerged in the presence of her mother.

'Pour me a drink, sweetie, will you? And do turn the box off. I cannot stand that noise tonight.'

Susan obeyed, peeved – she had been enjoying the film.

'Do you want anything to eat, Mummy?'

'No dear, I'm not hungry. Please pour me a drink.'

She vanished into the bathroom, while Susan obediently poured a large scotch. 'Did you have a good day?' Georgette called out from the bathroom, having left the door ajar while she sat on the loo.

'Very good, Mummy. I'll tell you about it when you're ready.'

After what seemed to Susan a very long time, Georgette returned to the living-room, settled into her chair and reached for her glass.

'I've good news,' Susan said hurriedly. She wanted to get it off her chest before Georgette started drinking.

'You have, dear?' Georgette sounded only mildly interested.

'I've been accepted for Australia! I told them I'd rather fly than go by sea and they said I will not have long to wait.'

Georgette had had only a couple of mouthfuls of her drink and she was jolted into full attention. She put the glass down. 'Australia? What are you talking about, sweetie?'

Susan sighed. She had been expecting something like this. 'I'm going to migrate there, Mummy. I want to see something of the world, and that seems like a good place to start.'

'First I've heard of it!'

'No, Mummy, it's not. We have discussed it several times.'

'I don't remember, dear.'

'Daddy thinks it's a great idea, too. I only have to stay for two years. After that they give me back my passport and I'm free to leave if I want to. But I don't want to arrive penniless, and that's why I've been saving up.'

'I didn't know you had been.'

'Mummy, I explained it all! Because of the assisted passage, it is only costing me £10 for the journey, but I don't want to end up in one of their transit camps, so I need enough to put down a deposit on a flat when I arrive and to keep me going until I can get a job. I want to take as much as possible so that I have something for emergencies. I believe things like dentists cost a fortune there. Daddy offered to help, but I'm starting a new life and I want to do it properly, and be independent right from the start.'

Georgette was silent, realizing that Susan must have told her all this when she was in a blackout. But she was horrified that she could have forgotten something so important.

'Mummy?'

'Sorry, darling, I was lost in thought. Which town are you going to? Is anyone going with you? Do you have any contacts there?'

'Oh for goodness sake, Mummy! We've discussed all that already. Please do try to remember! You know I've done a lot of work recently for Rice, Hawkins, the accountants? Whenever they needed a temp they ask for me, and I've got to know one or two of the top people quite well – I'm actually working for them this week. They are an international concern, with offices in Sydney, Melbourne and Perth, so I asked them if they would give me a letter of introduction. My present boss is from Perth and he says they are expanding there and he's very confident that they'll be able to offer me something – he'll phone a couple of people if I let him know exactly when I'm going. He said he'll also write to his sister, who still lives there, and ask her to put me up while I look for somewhere to live. So I'll really be getting off to a good start and should be able to settle down very quickly.'

'That's all very well, but I don't want you to leave!' Georgette said bluntly.

'Why ever not?'

'Because I love you, and I don't want you going off to the other side of the world so that I'll never see you again.'

Susan was aghast. 'Oh for Christ's sake! Sorry, Mummy, I know you don't like me to swear but, honestly, who are you kidding? You're so wrapped up in yourself that you're barely aware of whether or not I'm here even when I'm living with you! I've been telling you my plans for months, keeping you informed of every new development, and you haven't listened properly to a word I've said. Now, when everything's coming to a head, you suddenly say you don't want me to go! Well, I'm very sorry, Mummy, but I really don't care what you want! I've tried very hard to be a good daughter, and I've stayed with you, instead of running off to Daddy like Alex, but I'm sick to death of living like this and I can't wait for my travel documents to come through. And, in case you've forgotten, you have already signed a form giving your consent – as a minor, I needed your written permission. The sooner I'm out of here, the better!'

Georgette flushed. Was this her daughter talking? Had she really been such a bad mother that both her children hated being with her? 'But darling, I may not have spent as much time with you as I would have liked, but that's because I've always been so busy trying to survive and to provide a good home for us all,' she said weakly. 'I've always loved you.'

'Not us, Mummy. It's always been your work that you loved. It's been everything to you. That's all Alex and I have ever seen, your love of business. And the drink! Mummy had to be left alone. Mummy was tired. Mummy was always bloody tired! I gave you love. Alex gave you love. But you gave us nothing back – nothing but lip-service to the idea of love!'

'Sweetie, it wasn't a child's love I wanted – it was a father's!' The words came out unbidden and astonished Georgette as much as Susan. They said so much.

The confession did not, in any way, alter Susan's determination to go to Australia. She had suffered too long from her mother's drunken behaviour to take it any more but knew that a feeling of duty would prevent her making a break if she were to remain in the area. Putting half the world between them was the only way she could see for her to find freedom.

'I'm truly sorry for your loss but, if you can face that fact, surely you can see that you've inflicted that same lack of a loving parent on us? If you didn't need a child's love, then why didn't you let us go and live with Daddy? He always gave us love. I don't understand why you didn't let us go to him.'

'It's the hardest thing in the world to give up a child!' Georgette responded distantly, her mind filling with thoughts of David and tears springing to her eyes. She could never have gone through that process again. If that was selfishness, then she had to admit she had been selfish.

'My being in business gave you children everything.'

'We didn't want "everything". We wanted love! Anyway Daddy could have given us all the material things we needed – he wanted to – and Granny would have helped him out if he hadn't enough money of his own. She loved us, too, and gave us anything we ever asked for.'

Georgette's hurt made her explode. 'You are an ungrateful wretch, Susan! Maybe if I didn't have you around things would be much easier for me. So go to Australia – the sooner the better!'

Within a month the Australian High Commission informed Susan of her departure date, and she had only ten days to sort herself out before she boarded her Qantas flight to Perth.

There were tears from both Georgette and Susan at the parting. The moment she was gone, everything got much worse for Georgette.

A letter from her bank, which informed her that they had just bounced several of her cheques, compelled Georgette to call on them one Friday lunch-time. She was deeply in the red and they had insisted she make an appointment to discuss her affairs.

Determined to look her best for the interview, she decided to wear one of her fur coats. But when she went to her wardrobe she could find only one – and that was a cheap imitation. Puzzled at first, she recalled finally that she had lost both her real furs – having left them in places where she had been drinking and then been totally unable to remember where those places had been. The imitation fur had been all she could afford by way of a replacement.

She was on time at the bank and was shown into the manager's airy room, lit by fluorescent light.

Mr Kellington, the manager, wore a grey suit that was well cut and flattered his portly frame. He had grey eyes and avuncular features, and his grey hair was sleeked back off his forehead.

'Mrs Barestone-Tailour, good day to you.' He shook her hand warmly and bade her take a seat before coming straight to the point. 'It's an awkward situation. You are badly overdrawn, despite our letters asking you to improve the condition and your previous promises to me to get your finances under control.'

'Mr Kellerton, I cannot pay off my overdraft, just like that. I must have more time!'

'We have given you more time, Mrs Barestone-Tailour, but you have not used it to pay us back. You have continued to live beyond your means and we have been very patient, but your debt continues to grow and I am afraid that our patience is exhausted. I have to answer to my head office, you know, and must take whatever action I see fit to ensure that my branch runs smoothly and at a profit. We are entitled to make arrangements for your assets to be seized and sold off, but I must tell you that you would be unlikely to get the full market value were we to take that course of action. However, if you agree to certain conditions, I am prepared to give you a further two months to sort out your affairs, and I shall also authorize payment of the cheques that we have just refused.'

'That sounds fair. ("Fair it's more than reasonable!") What are the conditions?'

'If you are able to raise the money by some other means, nobody will be happier than I but, if not, you must take immediate steps to dispose of enough assets to cover your debt to us. In the meantime, you may continue to write cheques for everyday necessities. We shall honour small amounts, by which I mean anything up to £25. If you need to withdraw more than that amount for any single transaction, you must ring the bank *before* you write out the cheque and obtain our permission to issue it. If any cheque for over £25 reaches us for which we have not given you clearance, it will be refused automatically and the privilege of writing small cheques will also be withdrawn without further warning. Is that agreed?'

'But, Mr Kellerton, your conditions mean that I will have to sell my car and the lease on my home!'

'I'm sorry, Mrs Barestone-Tailour, but you must do whatever is necessary. There will be no further concessions. So what is your answer?'

Georgette could not see that she had any real choice, and she agreed his terms.

She knew that she had no hope of raising the money unless she sold her flat but, when it came to it, she found that she didn't really mind. Now she was living alone she would really rather live somewhere smaller and less expensive, and if she rented a small apartment she wouldn't even have to worry about major bills for maintenance. As for the car, she hadn't much used it for months and was quite glad to see the back of it, as it was of an age when things were always going wrong. She didn't get much for it, but at least she wouldn't have any more garage bills.

She was very lucky with the flat, because she found a buyer very quickly. He not only paid her the asking price, without haggling, but said he loved her furniture and would be happy to pay a reasonable amount for anything she was prepared to leave behind in addition to the regular fixtures and fittings.

After clearing her indebtedness to the bank, she was still able to pay the fairly substantial key-money required to secure a small apartment at the top of a block of flats called 'The Regent Mansions'. The flat consisted of two medium-sized rooms and a bathroom, and the rent was payable monthly.

What upset Georgette more than losing her flat in Sparrow Hall Walk was having to let Daisy Brown go, but she really couldn't justify the expense of keeping her on for such a small flat; nor would the journey have been easy for Daisy, now in her sixties but, still full of life, she seemed very much younger. They promised to keep in touch.

Over the next few months, Georgette's sales dropped even further and she was now achieving below average results.

Most of her money continued to go on drink, but her new flat was cheap to run and, apart from food, she had few other major expenses, so she managed to stay out of debt.

On a Saturday, towards the end of March 1970, Georgette received a telephone call. It was Susan, ringing from Western Australia, where it was eight o'clock in the evening, and she was relieved that her careful timing had worked.

'Darling, what a lovely surprise!'

'Yes ... well ... I'm ringing for a reason, Mummy. I've decided you must know something.'

'Know what, dear?'

'I'm pregnant!'

'Oh, my poor darling!' Georgette was both shocked and full of concern.

Susan laughed happily. 'It's all right, Mummy. Roger's the father.' There was a slight Aussie twang in her voice, which Georgette found a little disconcerting.

'Roger?'

'You know who Roger is, Mummy. I told you all about him last year. I met him when I first got to Perth. I suppose you could say it was love at first sight – we've been together ever since!'

'Oh, darling, of course you told me! I'm sorry. I'm getting forgetful in my old age!'

Susan made no comment and Georgette hastened to break the silence.

'When is the baby due?'

'I can't be precise – around 20–23 October. We intend to fly to England with it, all being well some time next year – probably about February. We'll be staying with Daddy but we'll want to see you too, of course.'

Georgette was hurt that Dickie had been told the news first.

'And, in case you're wondering, we shall be getting married in the winter – summer your time. It'll probably be late July, but we haven't actually booked anything yet.'

'Well, congratulations. I'm very happy for you, darling!'

'We don't want a fancy wedding, only a registry office, but we'll send you an invitation when it's settled.'

'Do that, sweetie! Now this call must be costing you a fortune, so I'll say goodbye.'

Georgette poured herself a whisky, realizing as she did so, and for the first time, that she had not been talking to a child but to a grown woman, and one who had blossomed into a confident personality.

Georgette wept. She felt so detached from both her children. Now her daughter was going to make her a grandmother, and how marvellous, absolutely marvellous, it would be to hold that little child in her arms.

But when the wedding invitation arrived a few weeks later she put

188

it to one side, intending to answer, and promptly forgot it. She only remembered when, at the end of May, Dickie rang her – at Susan's request – to find out whether or not she was planning to be there.

Guilt-ridden, she pretended her reply must have gone astray, but she could tell Dickie didn't believe her. Dickie and Bridgitte were going with Joss and taking Alex, too; leaving the following week and spending a couple of weeks in Australia after the wedding.

Georgette asked Dickie to apologize to Susan on her behalf, and explained that she couldn't attend because she had to be at a GBE convention – the only excuse she could think of on the spur of the moment.

By some miracle, she did remember to send a telegram in time for the day itself, and another when she learned of the birth of Susan's son, Anthony Richard, on 23 October.

Chapter Twenty

Georgette was on her own more and more. Friends didn't call as once they did and invitations had dried up, while her own invitations met with few acceptances. Feeling absolutely rejected, she kept on drinking – at pubs if she could find there anyone she knew, and by herself at home if she couldn't – and all the time she was brooding more and more about her lack of promotion.

Matters came to a head in August.

She was alone in her flat and had worked herself into a real frenzy over GBE's refusal to train her for management. She wondered what Jack would have done and the answer came to her – he would have gone straight to the top. She decided to ring GBE's head office in New York. She had met the president, Hank B. Woodrow, several times, at the annual conventions. He had praised her salesmanship and she reckoned she knew him well enough to telephone him.

With the drink making her feel all-powerful, she worked out the time difference. If she rang him at eight o'clock in the evening it would be three o'clock in the afternoon in New York, and that should be a good time to get hold of him. She had a few more drinks while she waited.

'GBE good afternoon how can we help you?' The woman's voice was almost mechanical.

'I wish to speak to Hank Woodrow, please.'

'Yes, Ma'am. Who shall I say is calling?'

'Mrs Georgette Barestone-Tailour, speaking from England.'

'Please hold the line Ma'am, I'm connecting you.'

A pause.

'Thank you for waiting. I'm putting you through now.'

'Hello, may I help you?' It was another female voice, but this one sounded human.

'Yes, I hope so. I want to speak to Hank Woodrow personally. My name is Mrs Georgette Barestone-Tailour and I'm calling from England.'

'This is Mrs Treadgold. I'm afraid Mr Woodrow is out of the office right now.'

That deflated Georgette. 'That's not good enough!' she responded stupidly.

'I'm his personal assistant. May I help?'

'I think you must give him a message from me. It's not that I want heads to roll, but things are not going here the way Mr Woodrow meant them to go.'

'Oh, my! Could you give me some details, Mrs Barestone-Tailour?'

'Well, the ladder of opportunity is supposed to be equally open to men and women. That's what I was told when I joined the company, way back in the fifties. But that doesn't seem to be the case. I'm being deprived of a managership, just because I'm a woman, and it's jolly unfair!'

'I see.'

'Could Mr Woodrow please, please, come over and sort it out?'

Mrs Treadgold was silent for a moment. She couldn't fail to detect the slur in Georgette's speech and wondered if the caller could be slightly the worse for drink. She was used to diverting calls from dissatisfied employees, but she was also something of a feminist, and this particular complaint touched a nerve.

'I'll certainly pass on what you say, Mrs Barestone-Tailour.'

'You must. And he must act on it!'

'Leave it with me. I promise you that Mr Woodrow will be informed in full of your complaint, just as soon as he returns to the office. Have a nice day.'

'Well, now, there you are, that's done.' Georgette muttered proudly to herself as she rested the receiver, highly satisfied with her evening's work.

Georgette had no blackout that night and, in the cold light of the early morning, she suddenly came fully awake and remembered vividly what she had done. She was too worried to go back to sleep, so got up and made herself a coffee while she considered the possible repercussions. She realized that she might even lose her job.

'Who's my best advocate in the firm?' The answer was obvious – Les Dykes. She knew he was always in his office by eight-thirty and, today, she was waiting for him when he arrived. The confession poured out of her.

'My dear girl, what *will* you do next?'

'I know it's terrible, what I have done!'

'It certainly is not very ethical to go over everyone's head like that!

You'd been drinking, hadn't you? You know, Georgette, I've told you before, and I'll say it again: when you have had only one or two drinks, you are a splendid person, but more than that and you change.'

'I don't believe that!'

'Please take my word for it – don't you think you've just proved it? You would never have done such a thing when you were sober. I think I'll ring Lewisham and see what time Gareth Raistrick is expected in this morning. My guess is that he already knows what you've done!'

Even as Les made to act on his words, his phone trilled. 'Morning, Gareth . . . Yes, she has just told me . . . Right . . . Will do . . . Bye.'

'What's going to happen to me?' ventured a nervous Georgette.

With deliberation Les returned the receiver to its rest, then ran a hand over his chin.

'Gareth Raistrick is not best pleased with you, Georgette. Apparently Hank Woodrow rang him at home at about midnight. You're to see Gareth at Lewisham at ten-thirty today. Plenty of time to have a coffee and compose yourself before you go.'

GBE's admin building at Lewisham was a ten-storey structure of glass and pre-stressed concrete, with a wide imitation-glass canopy over the approach to the main entrance. It was not to Georgette's taste.

Gareth Raistrick's office was on the top floor, and very luxurious, a status symbol with wall-to-wall carpeting and furniture upholstered in blue leather. Raistrick had been appointed to the chairmanship of GBE in the UK only recently and Georgette had not met him before. She didn't like the look of the man, who had a top-heavy body supported by very short legs.

He bade Georgette take an easy chair in front of his desk, then came and sat in a similar one facing her, surveying her with interest. Her personnel file was on his large leather-topped desk.

To Georgette's surprise his manner was quite gentle.

'Well now – you know, my dear girl, this is not really the way to go about things, is it?'

She had decided that managers should not grovel and, since that was what she wanted to be, the best approach would be to stick to her guns.

'No, Mr Raistrick, maybe it isn't. But my action was taken out of desperation. I have been unable to get any satisfaction from anyone here in England. As you probably know, I want to be trained as a manager – and I believe I have earned that right. GBE was always supposed to offer an open door to the top positions to anyone, male or female, who proved worthy. My record with the company speaks for itself.'

'Nevertheless, ringing the president is not the way to go about things.'

'That may be, but it's got me this interview, hasn't it?'

'Did you ever ask for an interview with me, or my predecessor, and get refused?'

Georgette had not, and was silent.

As luck would have it, Raistrick had been reading Georgette's personnel file only the previous day and had come to the conclusion that, despite Les Dykes's warm support of the woman, the time had come to dispose of her services. It was quite clear to him that she was an alcoholic and that her work could only deteriorate. Then Hank Woodrow had telephoned to ask what was going on. Raistrick had explained the situation but, to his utter amazement, Woodrow had insisted that Georgette's services should be retained.

Thus Woodrow said he accepted Raistrick's judgement that Georgette was no longer capable of doing a good selling job, and could not be trusted as a manager, but his instructions were clear – his chairman must make it his personal business to find some position that would be suitable for her. What Raistrick could not have known was his thinking behind that decision. While he was still a small boy, Hank Woodrow's favourite aunt had become alcoholic – and *she* had been saved. And Georgette had made a good impression on him personally.

Having made his point about her behaviour, and with absolutely no idea what he could offer, Raistrick could only play for time. He said, 'I shall have to give this whole situation a lot more thought, Mrs Barestone-Tailour. In the meantime, I want you to see the company doctor.'

'Why?'

'You are obviously under stress, so I'm putting you on sick-leave for a while. You will be paid your full salary until you return to work, so you won't be out of pocket – I'm sure you will agree your commission is barely worth having these days. But it is necessary for Dr Baslord to provide medical back-up for my decision. Go home now, and rest. My secretary will telephone you this afternoon, after she has arranged an appointment for you with the doctor.'

The appointment was for the following day, at two o'clock. So Georgette returned to the same admin building, but this time only to the ground floor. She was shown into a little room where absolutely everything was white, the perfect impersonal setting for medical examinations. Dr Baslord was a silvery-haired gentleman of medium height and build. He was very kindly and charming, but had a knowing air.

He came forward, his spotless white coat buttoned neatly, and they shook hands.

'Hello, Mrs Barestone-Tailour. I've heard a lot about your spectacular sales record, and am very pleased to meet you at last. Come along in and take a seat.'

'Flannel!' thought Georgette, and remained silent.

'I'm here to help you, so please tell me what the problem is.' He knew, of course, but had to get his patient to admit it before he could do anything to help her. Her initial response was not encouraging.

'There is no problem, so far as I'm concerned, doctor. Mr Raistrick wanted me to come to you, so here I am. That's it.'

'But presumably Mr Raistrick had some reason for sending you?'

'He said he thought I was under stress.'

'And are you?'

'Not medically. I'm just fed up with GBE's attitude.'

'Please tell me why.'

For the next half-hour Georgette went through her catalogue of complaints, almost without pausing for breath, and the doctor said nothing. Simply listened with grave attention. Finally she came to a halt, feeling much better for having got everything off her chest.

'So, it boils down to the fact that you feel unappreciated?'

'Yes, doctor. And it was made worse by the fact that I couldn't talk to anyone about it. Whenever I tried I was offered a deaf ear.'

The doctor nodded sagely. 'I understand. I do understand. Do you drink at all?'

'Very little,' Georgette lied firmly, back on her guard.

'What is "very little", my dear? Do you, for example, have a sherry or something before dinner?'

'No, never a sherry. No sherry!' She didn't like the stuff, so that was the truth, but Dr Baslord noticed she did not deny the 'or something'.

'Well, after dinner, do you have a whisky or so?'

'Sometimes. Doesn't everyone?'

'I see.' The doctor's experience told him that he wasn't going to be able to make progress with Georgette in her present mood, and he was too wise to continue. To do so would probably alienate her forever whereas, if he stopped now there was a possibility she would return to him of her own accord when she needed to turn to someone.

He addressed his attention to the physical side, therefore, and gave her a thorough check-up. He made no comment when she admitted she went to an osteopath whenever she had trouble with her back. He asked her about bed-wetting but, embarrassed, she denied it. At last he told her she could get dressed.

'Thank you for coming, Mrs Barestone-Tailour. As this has been an official company examination, I'll be sending my report to Gareth Raistrick. But please do not hesitate to come and see me again if you feel I can be of help to you in any way at all. If the appointment is your idea, I can assure you of complete confidentiality.'

Next morning, just out of her bath, Georgette received a call from Godfrey Seely, the managing director. He was second only to Gareth Raistrick in the UK.

'Good morning to you, Mrs Barestone-Tailour. Can you call into my office. Perhaps this afternoon?' Georgette understood that the 'perhaps' was a courtesy, and did not demur.

'Two-thirty?' she suggested.

'Splendid! Bye for now.'

Georgette did not know Seely. Like Raistrick he, too, had only recently joined the company. He was short, late thirties and a snappy dresser. His face had a smug look, unfortunate because it was misleading.

His office, also on the top floor, was a haven for potted plants, some of which trailed off his modern wooden desk. Photographs of his wife and two children were prominently displayed.

'I hear you want to get away from selling?' Seely smiled.

'Yes.'

'You have done exceptionally well there.'

'Even so . . .'

'Have you thought about what you'd like to do instead?'

'I certainly have! I want a manager's job.'

'That's what I was told.' Seely drew out the words ponderously. 'But in which particular field of management?'

As Seely had gambled, Georgette was caught completely unprepared for this question. 'Well, I don't know. Just a manager. You know . . . managing a department. I mean . . .' she trailed off.

'Alright, Mrs Barestone-Tailour. I'm familiar with your record and I have something in mind which I think will suit you very well. But there are a few things to be done before I can tell you any more. Dr Baslord's report says that you are run-down and I want you to have a good rest. Consider yourself on sick-leave, with full pay, until we meet again. I would suggest that you come here again on Monday fortnight, let's say nine-thirty?'

Georgette returned home, feeling even more smug than Seely looked. Oh, the activity she had stirred up!

At nine-thirty on that Monday she reported to Godfrey Seely's office again, looking perky. She was well made-up and smartly dressed. Not a drop of alcohol had passed her lips for over twenty-four hours and, in that time, she had done some necessary running repairs to a suit that she had dry-cleaned especially for the occasion.

'Nice to see you again, Mrs Barestone-Tailour. I'm pleased to say that we have just the job for you. It's as head of a new department, one that's been needed for some time. It might be described as a sort of trouble-shooting department for the company.'

'How do you mean?' The expression meant nothing to Georgette.

'You will be aware that customer complaints and queries come into the office every day. The vast majority from users of our machines, who are having trouble understanding the instruction manuals – or, quite simply, can't be bothered to read them.

'What I propose to do is to set up a special department called "Customer Services". Customers will be put straight through to this department and they will be told precisely what to do in order to solve their problem. I believe that this one phone call will be sufficient in over ninety percent of cases. When there really is a problem of some kind with the machine, rather than the user, the Customer Services department will arrange an appointment for an engineer to call on the customer.

'And you, my dear, will be head of the Customer Services department. You know, from experience, the sort of problems that users have, and how they are best solved. You also have enough knowledge of every machine in our range to recognize a genuine fault when it is described to you. So you will be able to combine your unique knowledge of our products with your proven ability to deal with customers, and all without leaving the comfort of the office. No more walking for miles, and having to carry a heavy briefcase around all day. What do you think?'

Georgette was not fooled by the word 'head'. To be head of a one-person department was not to be a manager. But, manager or not, she saw at once that this job was absolutely right for her. 'Sounds wonderful to me, Mr Seely!'

Seely couldn't disguise his look of relief.

'You'll take the Customer Services job, then?'

'Oh, yes! It sounds ideal!' Her eagerness had betrayed her, and her next question was too late for negotiation. 'What will the salary be?'

Seely's answer was deliberately casual, for he hoped she would not explode when she found that it did not quite match a real manager's salary. He need not have worried. Although well aware of that fact, Georgette was thankful that her rash action had turned out so well and, after all, her new salary was noticeably more than she had been earning since her commission dropped.

'When do I start?' she asked.

'Would tomorrow morning be too soon?'

With her head held high, Georgette returned to the sales office. She knew her new position was not really promotion, rather a step sideways, but the mere fact that it had been created for her was a recognition of her abilities and she felt that it increased her status. Everyone at sales office dutifully congratulated her and Les Dykes organized a hasty 'Farewell from Sales' party for her that evening, as she was to be based in Lewisham on the fifth floor. She supposed that position meant she was halfway up the GBE ladder of importance.

The down-side of her new job was that, instead of being completely free to arrange her own working hours, she had to be at Lewisham by nine-thirty Monday to Friday, and could not leave before five-thirty. How could she drink the night before if she had to be up so early in the morning – and with what she thought of as a long journey to reach the office? She reasoned that she could drink on Friday and Saturday evenings, but she could not do so on Sunday evening, nor Monday, nor Tuesday, nor Wednesday, nor Thursday, because after those days she had to be at the office at the appointed time – and without a hangover. The thought was dreadful, but she was determined to justify GBE's faith in her, and she tried very hard to do so.

On the first Monday she went to work clear-headed. About four o'clock in the afternoon, she began to think 'no drinking until Friday' and it was all she could do to concentrate on her work. The same thing happened at about the same time on the Tuesday. On Wednesday morning she could still work all right, but her mind was not on her job at all during the afternoon and by Thursday she was obsessed with the thought that she still had over twenty-four hours to wait until she could have a drink.

Somewhat to her surprise, Friday was easier. The simple knowledge that there were only a few more hours to go made her less tense. Thus, she got through the day's work very easily. When five-thirty arrived, however, she had already cleared her desk, and by five-thirty-five she was in the Pig and Whistle, just along the road from her new office, ordering a drink. It restored her to life before she caught the train to Charing Cross and from there a cab back to 'The Regent Mansions'.

That first week set the pattern for the ones that were to follow: she had a good lunch in the GBE canteen, Monday to Friday, and snacks in the evening, and the weekend was, in the main, given over to drinking. At home and alone. In the sanctuary of her flat, she could lock the door, take the telephone off the hook (not that it was likely to ring), open her bottle of scotch and drink in peace. The rest of the evening was a blackout and Saturday, also, passed in an alcoholic haze. On Sunday she stopped drinking, and was in absolute torture knowing that it would be almost a week until she could find release again.

But she was a fighter, and she persevered.

One morning, Georgette found some grey in her hair, and started to dye it, but she ignored the increasing-amount of tell-tale puffiness of her face that was destroying her beauty and reflecting the fact that she was falling apart inside.

It was not as cold as February days can be, but nor was it comfortably warm, and Georgette wished she still had a fur coat. She had no intention of wearing an imitation fur on such an occasion, so she had to settle for the fairly new sheepskin swagger coat she had bought. At least it was warm, and it concealed her plumpness. She had had her hair done the previous day, and now checked her make-up with more than her usual care. Satisfied with her appearance, she went out to the waiting limousine that Dickie had arranged for her. Alex was passing-out from Mons Officer Cadet School today, and Dickie was taking no chances that Georgette would miss the ceremony.

Alex's big day was happening on a Friday, so Georgette was completely clear-headed: pleased that she had no need to make what she considered the supreme sacrifice, and keep away from her precious Friday evening drink, of which, after this day, she would surely have need.

She settled comfortably into the rear of the car and thoroughly enjoyed playing the 'great I am', a woman accustomed to having a uniformed chauffeur at her disposal.

They took the A3 and, before long, were near Cobham, but Georgette had fallen asleep and the drive aroused no painful memories of Jack.

When she awoke they had left the A3 and were held up at a railway crossing near North Camp Station, close to their destination.

'You've been asleep, Madam!' stated the chauffeur unnecessarily. 'We're almost there. I know the place myself. Did me National Service training here, Buller Barracks, twenty-odd years ago now. What regiment will your son be joining?'

'The Life Guards.'

'Oh, very nice! Royal Army Service Corps meself!'

Soon the car turned into Princes Avenue, and slowed to walking pace as a private indicated where it was to park. Another soldier came forward, opened the car door for Georgette, and ushered her to the parade-ground.

Dickie and Brigitte were already there with young Joss, now six and very interested in all the soldiers. Susan and her husband Roger were also there, having timed their visit to England to coincide with this great occasion. They had arrived from Perth a few days before, but Dickie had driven them straight to Grace Hall. So Georgette had not seen them, and thus today was the first time she had met Roger. Immediately, his presence brought to mind warm memories of Simon Tait – what a pity she had lost touch with him, sadly the way of life.

Roger was thirty years old. Tall lean and blond with steel blue eyes, he looked athletic, and Georgette understood at once why Susan had succumbed to his charms. Georgette knew that she might have fallen for him herself if she'd been younger. He had 'Australian' written all over him, and was decidedly uncomfortable in what, after the glorious sunshine of a Western Australia summer, he considered very cold weather.

Their greetings were warm. They had all been on tenterhooks in case Georgette should arrive drunk, or noticeably hung-over, despite her promises to Dickie, and they were intensely relieved to see that she had kept her word and was completely in control of herself. Georgette's pleasure at being able to see Alex's passing-out was real – she had been very afraid that she would not be invited – but it was overshadowed by the thought of meeting her little grandson, Anthony. She was greatly disappointed when she saw no sign of him.

'I didn't think it would be sensible to hang around this cold parade-ground with him,' said Susan. 'But don't worry, Mummy, he is here and you will meet him later. He's sleeping peacefully in the Rolls, with Daddy's chauffeur keeping an eye on him. He sleeps for hours.'

The friends and relations of those on parade were seated in a specially designated area at the perimeter of the vast asphalt square, actually an oblong, where the parade would take place. Some conifer trees shielded them from the worst of the wind that blew from across the playing-fields and the splendid running track that Alex, for one, had greatly enjoyed using.

Flag-poles around the square proudly bore the standards of all those nations who had cadets on parade today.

The ceremony itself was very impressive, Georgette thought. All the soldiers were in their best blues, a military band played. There was no mistaking Alex, either, because he was not just one of the crowd. He had achieved the rank of Under-Officer, and was standing in front of his fellows who, being the passing out troop, were stood right of the line. They carried rifles, but he carried a sword – and used it brilliantly to execute the obligatory ritual gestures as the cadets marched past the saluting base. If he wasn't to be awarded the silver stick for the best cadet, this was an excellent consolation prize.

The inspecting officer was a full-blown general in full dress uniform. He was acknowledged at the saluting base with a general salute then, with the band playing appropriate music, two officer cadets, acting as stick orderlies, escorted him through the assembled ranks. Next came the parade, as everyone marched past the general in quick time, then advanced in review order and gave another general salute.

The silver stick was presented to the deserving winner before a couple of equally deserving Training NCOs received good service awards. It was all very splendid and enjoyable to watch. And, oh, how proud Georgette was of Alex.

Tears came to her eyes, when, after a few more crisply executed manoeuvres, the officer commanding the parade brought everyone to attention and the band struck up 'Auld Lang Syne'. The adjutant, who was mounted on a horse, positioned himself at the rear of the passing-out troop and they marched off in slow time. They went up a short flight of low, wide steps that was cut into a grassy bank, turned right onto a road that ran parallel with the parade-ground and continued marching until they were out of sight of the spectators on the parade-ground.

A little later they returned, informally, to mingle with the spectators. Alex took his family to see his quarters at the officer cadet school and Georgette was quite shocked. While most of the school consisted of bungalow barrack blocks part brick built and pebble-dashed, Alex with the rest of his Company had lived most of his twenty weeks in a single-storey hut which formed one of the legs of a 'spider', the 'body' being the ablution block.

'It all looks dreadfully uncomfortable, darling!'

'No, Mummy, not really. I rather liked it actually. It was always very warm and friendly, a great place to come home to after a training exercise at somewhere like the Brecon Beacons or Dartmooor. I think I'll rather miss it!'

'If you say so, dear.' Georgette was not convinced. Alex had nine days of well-earned leave before he had to report for duty, but he was spending none of it with Georgette, so she thought this was the right time to give him Jack Grant's watch, and she was touched when she saw tears come to his eyes.

'Thank you, Mummy. I loved Jack, and I often think of him. I could not have asked for a better commissioning present!' He gave her a big hug and kiss, something he had not done for some years, and she knew that, for once, she'd done the right thing in his eyes.

A little later they all returned to the car-park and Susan, as promised, produced her son from the car, and handed him over to Georgette.

It was absolutely marvellous to hold little Anthony! Georgette felt so proud. Being a grandmother was wonderful, she thought.

'Oh, my darling, my little darling, how lovely you are! You are beautiful, yes you are!' And he was. With his very long eyelashes and longish fair hair, already plentiful, he looked almost feminine.

'Susan, are you sure he's warm enough, dressed as he is?'

'Yes, Mummy. He's fine.'

'What a little cherub! You must be proud, Roger?'

Roger merely smiled. He'd been warned by Susan about what Georgette could be like, and he was wary.

Georgette knew that she must make the most of today, for Susan and Roger had a full programme, and she would not be seeing them again on this trip. And who knew how long it would be until their next visit?

Eventually the time came for them to leave, and Georgette climbed slowly back into her hired limousine. As soon as she got home she poured herself a stiff drink.

PART FOUR

And the years go on . . .
March 1971–June 1983

Chapter Twenty One

Over the next several months Georgette became more and more tense. She was lonely, completely self-centred and a prisoner of her habit. She couldn't live with drink and she couldn't live without it: she no longer confined it to Friday and Saturday – just couldn't last that long without a 'pick-me-up'.

Sometimes she would stand by her window with her glass of whisky, looking at the street, at the people walking about, and think to herself 'what bloody fools!' though why they were fools she did not consider. They just were. As often as not, she'd drink through the night, then lay on her bed for an hour or two before work, and wet the bed.

Her ears were making funny noises, her eyes were not quite right, her knees ached like mad and her back gave her trouble more frequently than before. Then she found she couldn't take a bath, because she had become convinced that she would drown, so she washed in bits and pieces, standing at the hand-basin. Her life had indeed become miserable.

She considered suicide, but her childhood teaching came unbidden to her mind. She began to pray again, if a mixture of self-pity and accusation could be called praying.

'I want to die, God! Please let me die and get away from this misery you have brought me! I know it's not right to kill myself, but I can't go on living like this! Oh, Lord, if only you would make things nice for me! Why do you make me live this way? I am worthy of better things!'

She no longer cared about her appearance. She stopped dying her hair and couldn't be bothered to sew. Fallen hems stayed fallen, or were pinned up. Safety pins deputized for lost buttons or non-functioning zips. Tears remained torn. If a garment could not be worn without repair, she simply threw it on the floor of the wardrobe and didn't wear it again.

Then on some days she found she was too frightened to cross the road. She had to spend some time screwing up her courage and then wait until other people were crossing so that she could walk behind them, cowering away from the snarling traffic.

She became scared stiff, too, by the awesome dark of the Underground tunnels, while the gap that often appeared between the platform and the trains, especially on bends in the platform, was absolutely terrifying. She couldn't stand anywhere near the edge of the platform because she was sure she would fall onto the rails. She had to press her back hard against the wall until the train was stationary and then dive for the door without looking at the black void that was waiting for her beneath the train. If only she could afford taxis everywhere, as once she could, she wouldn't have to see the ghastly voids. But money for drink was more important so taking cabs couldn't be afforded every time, while if she didn't need to drink there would be no fear present of the gaps and she could meet the expense of taxis!

And always there were the blackouts. Sometimes she would even wake up to find someone in her bed: a man she couldn't recollect having ever met before, someone she must have met at the pub the previous day. She never saw any of them again.

Fortunately, her job meant that she no longer saw the customers, and there was nothing wrong with the way she sounded on the phone. She had heard all the questions and complaints countless times before in the course of her career and, drunk or sober, the solutions came to her easily. So the customers were satisfied and so (for the moment) were the top brass at GBE.

One Friday evening Georgette left her desk at five-thirty on the dot, caught the train to Charing Cross then headed for the bar on the station concourse. After only one drink she decided to go home. She emerged into the chill of the dark November evening, her imitation fur snug about her neck, and hailed a taxi.

The vehicle halted beside her and, at that exact moment, one of her blackouts descended. When she looked back on that evening, she could remember nothing between the taxi stopping and the moment she found herself being helped from the taxi by a policeman, who then walked her up the steps of a police station. She had no idea where she was, but recognized the man standing at the top of the steps as her cab driver. His expression was pitying, and she was suddenly afraid. She must have done something very wrong for him to have brought her here, but what? She had no idea, and her fear made her cover up her ignorance with a show of arrogance.

'Why am I here?' she demanded, as though she had been wronged.

'You are drunk, madam,' the desk sergeant said bluntly.

'Nonsense! I'm a respectable citizen, who was going home in a taxi after a hard week's work.'

'Then perhaps you would like to tell me your name, Madam? And your address?'

'None of your business!'

He sighed. 'Please take a seat over there, Madam.' He indicated a hard bench by a wall, shiny from much use. 'Someone will be with you shortly.' He turned to his next 'customer'.

Georgette went over to the bench, and lit a cigarette while she waited. The cigarette was finished and she was still waiting, so she lit another. When that was finished she decided that she had waited long enough and went back to the counter.

'Look, you know, this is ridiculous! I haven't done anything! You can't keep me here like some criminal! I want to go home!'

The desk sergeant was in the middle of a conversation with someone else, but he remained calm. 'Please sit down again, Madam.'

'There is freedom in this country, as I remember, and this is not freedom. I'll take this issue up with the Home Secretary!'

'Yes, Madam, I'm sure you will. But, in the meantime, I have work to do and I would appreciate it if you would return to your seat and let me get on with it. Besides, you don't want to say something you'll regret later, now do you?'

Georgette didn't and, somewhat to her own surprise, she meekly resumed her seat and puffed her way through another cigarette.

She was just finishing it when a thin-faced blond policewoman appeared. Her manner was friendly.

'Good evening, Madam. I'm sorry I've had to keep you waiting so long. I'm now going to take you into a little room, from where you can ring up a friend, anyone you like, and ask them to come and collect you.'

Georgette looked at the woman. 'An utter impossibility!' she snapped. How could she possibly admit she had no friends these days, none at all? There was absolutely nobody she could phone.

'Madam?'

'I don't know anyone who'd still be in town at this time on a Friday night. Most of my friends live miles from London. The ones who do live here go away at weekends.'

'I understand.' The woman officer disappeared and came back with another, older, male officer.

'You've no friends who can take you home, you say?'

'That is so, officer.'

'Then you will just have to stay with us, won't you?'

The first thing that happened was that her handbag was removed from her and every one of its contents was listed before being placed in a large brown envelope. The only jewellery she was wearing, a watch, joined the other things. Then she was asked to sign the list and did so, using her usual indecipherable signature. She was told that her belongings would be returned in the morning and led along a series of dreary corridors into the heart of the building.

Then she found herself in a small beige-brown tiled cell, with a bright light that could not be switched off from within the cell. There was no window. A lavatory in the corner of the cell, open to full view, was the only concession to hygiene. Along one of the walls was a bench bed with a vinyl-covered mattress. Too weary now to care, Georgette flopped onto the bed and watched numbly as her shoes were roughly taken off her feet by the hard-faced female warder, who then left the cell and flung the door shut with an almighty clang.

She cried for a while, then a desire to get out of this awful place seized her and she banged repeatedly at the steel door. No one came. She screamed, and banged again. Still no one came.

'My God, what have I come to? Is this it – prison for life?' Then she fell on her knees, and didn't bargain with her Maker, she simply said, 'Oh, God! Whatever I've done, I'm sorry. Please, please help me!'

Suddenly, very suddenly, she felt completely at peace. The effect of her single drink had worn off completely and she was sober. She could breathe deeply, easily, and felt quite calm.

She answered a call of nature, then wrapped her coat around herself and lay down on the bench bed. She fell asleep within seconds and did not stir until the cell door was flung open, at six-thirty in the morning, by the same horrible warder.

'Get up,' commanded the dragon, and she flung Georgette's shoes onto the bed. Why they had been taken from her in the first place Georgette hadn't a notion.

Georgette put them on, then stood up. The jailer took her by the shoulders and, with quite unnecessary roughness, pushed her out of the cell and back along corridors to reception.

A different sergeant was on duty. 'Can you now give us your name and address, Madam?' he asked politely. Georgette gave the details willingly, and her telephone number. The sergeant then filled in a piece of paper and pushed it towards her. 'Please sign this, Madam.'

'What is it?'

'Just a confirmation that you were found drunk and spent the night here.'

'I wasn't found drunk. I was in a taxi.'

'And I understand that taxi driver may wish to bring assault charges against you.'

'Assault charges? – That's ridiculous!'

'Madam, arguing achieves nothing. Do you want to go home now?'

'Of course I do!'

'In that case, you must sign the form. Then you can go to the police officer over there,' he indicated a constable at the other end of the counter, 'and reclaim your belongings.'

Georgette signed, and the constable duly gave her back her bits and pieces. She had to sign for those, too, but finally she walked back into the outside world.

Shocked by what had happened to her, she took a cab home and fell into her bed. It was mid-afternoon when she awoke, really refreshed – a feeling she had not experienced for some time. She felt different inside, but wasn't sure what had changed. She just knew that she didn't want a drink at that moment and that she had to give up drinking quite so much – and now – or destroy herself completely. The odd drink here and there would be all right, of course, but she must cut down enough to regain control of her life, was her thinking.

It was a while before she remembered that she may have to face charges of assault and then she shook from fear. She had no idea what the penalty would be for that conduct. Suddenly she had a brainwave – Nathan Carleigh – he would tell her what to do. In a panic, she telephoned him immediately, but the phone rang and rang and rang. Then it dawned on her that it was a Saturday, and his office was closed. She would have to wait until Monday – but, she determined, she would not touch alcohol at all before then.

She had two half-full bottles of scotch in the flat plus an unopened bottle of wine. She poured the lot down the drain before she could change her mind.

It was an effort, but her resolve held and she didn't touch a drop of alcohol the whole weekend.

First thing on Monday she rang Nathan Carleigh, and told him about her brush with the law. 'I still don't know what I've done, and I'm afraid that they'll come and arrest me at any minute!'

Carleigh laughed. 'I'm sure it's nothing heinous, Mrs Barestone-Tailour, or they wouldn't have released you!'

Georgette bristled. This was not the reaction she'd been expecting. 'I don't see what's funny, Mr Carleigh! But I'll tell you one thing – this sort of thing is not going to happen to me again!'

'Now that's a sensible resolve! Don't worry, Mrs Barestone-Tailour. Whatever you have done, I can assure you that nobody is going to arrest you. So you really needn't worry. I don't think it will take very long to establish the facts and I'll get back to you as soon as I've sorted the matter out.'

Despite his reassurances, Georgette was really jittery and did not consider she was in a fit state to work that day, so she rang in to say that she was unwell, which was, after all, nothing short of the truth.

The agony of waiting for Carleigh to ring back had to be endured, and the temptation to ring him for news had to be resisted. He'd said he'd phone as soon as he had some news, and she trusted him to do so, so she knew she just had to be patient. But she was so tense that, when the telephone did finally ring, its shrill note made her jump nearly out of her skin.

Carleigh's tone was light, 'I've found out what you've done.'

'Is it bad?'

'Er . . . The basic problem was that you gave the taxi driver two different addresses, neither one of them your own anymore.'

'I did?'

'The poor man went first to Dauphin Circus but before leaving the cab you said you didn't live there, and at the second address, you gave him, you struck him – that was at Sparrow Hall Walk. Then, unable to get anything else out of you, all he could think of doing was to take you to a police station convenient to himself. They were busy and not very keen on having to look after you, so he said he wanted to charge you with being drunk. Apparently they said that being drunk wasn't a crime, which is true, the sergeant at that station said that if they could find out your real address he'd have seen you taken there. But he thought it probable that, if you did answer, it would be yet another red herring, so he didn't pursue the matter very far when you got on your high horse and refused to answer. That sergeant is a very experienced and pragmatic man and, in the end, he thought everybody's interests would be best served if he kept you in for the night; no charge of being drunk and disorderly, and get the taxi-driver to think again about pressing the assault charge. I understand that you had nothing on you that gave either your name or your address – I would suggest that, in future, you do make sure you are carrying something that would identify you.'

'Yes, I will.'

'Forgetting where you live is not yet a crime, even if you are drunk at the time. The taxi driver is owed quite a lot, of course, but he doesn't now want to press charges, just asked that he should be paid as soon as possible. I took the liberty of contacting him, to ensure that was the case, and said that he would be paid twice the amount on the clock to compensate him for his trouble. I was sure you would approve that course of action?'

Georgette issued an almost audible sigh of relief. 'Of course! Thank you so much, Mr Carleigh! As always, you have handled everything perfectly!'

'Oh, it was no trouble – rather amusing, really, the whole thing. But do try to avoid this sort of incident becoming a habit, eh? The police get a little cross when the same faces keep turning up. I'd advise a bit of moderation with the old drink from now on.' The only time he had seen her in the last few years was when she had sold Sparrow Hall Walk, and she had been quite sober then, so he had no idea that she had a real problem in that respect.

Georgette laughed politely, but moderation was still precisely what she had in mind.

She felt she couldn't give up drinking completely, that she needed a bit of alcohol to keep going. But, on the other hand, she couldn't face a repetition of Friday night, and was sure that Nathan Carleigh had been right in implying that the police might not be so lenient again.

For the rest of that day, and much of the night, she thought about what had happened to her, fully facing up to reality for the first time. And she hated what she could now so clearly see herself to be – a drunkard. She still did not think of herself as an alcoholic, just a drunkard.

'Oh, dear God, what a mess I'm in!' she sighed heavily, forcing herself to look at what drink had been doing to her. How it was slowly destroying her, how its effects had gradually lost her all her friends, turned everyone against her, even her children. Tears of distress rolled down her cheeks and she wept until she fell into an exhausted sleep.

Her isolation was underlined when, the next morning, the hall porter brought her mail up. It was her birthday, her fiftieth birthday at that, surely a milestone in anyone's life, yet there was not a single card. She couldn't have expected to receive many but to get not one . . . Her mail consisted of an invoice and a circular-type invitation to support a charity.

She couldn't go to work, she just couldn't. Just getting through the morning would be impossible, her mind was troubled. She phoned the office and told them she was still unwell, then she went to her armchair to think things out. Her mind, alcohol-free for over three days now, began to work properly and came up with a possible solution.

Georgette did not know where the idea had come from but, despite the fact that she still did not consider herself a true alcoholic, she decided she would contact Alcoholics Anonymous. To her, alcoholics were tramps, homeless people who lived underneath the railway arches and begged for money to buy bottles of meths, not respectable ladies who had homes and good jobs, but AA would obviously know a lot about drink problems and should be able to give her some tips.

As soon as she got back to the flat, she got out the telephone directory and looked up the number.

A man answered.

'How can I help?'

'Are you Alcoholics Anonymous?'

'We are.'

'I think I'm on the slippery slope,' Georgette blurted out.

'Well, my name is Arthur and I am an alcoholic.'

Georgette started – those were the last words she had expected to hear. 'Oh! What is that to me? What do you mean?'

'I'm a recovering alcoholic,' the voice was very friendly and reassuring. 'I suggest you come along here this evening and we can have a little chat. Can you do that?'

If the person who answered her had not sounded so assured, so full of confidence, she would have been put off. As it was, she found the voice comforting, and said, 'I can, yes.'

'Would you like to give me your name?'

Georgette baulked. 'Er . . .'

'Just your first name, that's all I need, just so I know who you are when you come.'

'Georgette,' she admitted, just resisting the temptation to resort to her lesbian alter ego of Erica.

'Can you keep sober until then?'

'Oh, yes! I've not touched alcohol since Friday night.'

'That's very good!'

'I'm now going to make myself a coffee.'

'That's right, drink plenty of liquid with lots of sugar and also Vitamin B. Are you eating all right?'

'Yes.'

'Good.'

'Look, why don't you come along at about five o'clock. Then you can meet a couple of the ladies who work in the office here and have a little chat with them, too.'

'I'll do that,' agreed Georgette softly.

'Wonderful! I'll see you then. Have you got our address?'

Georgette read it out to him from the telephone directory.

'That's right. I look forward to meeting you and having a real chat!'

As she hung up, Georgette felt as if a great weight had been lifted from her shoulders.

She went into the bathroom to freshen up and, for the first time in ages, really looked at herself – and did not like what she saw. She thought she really looked awful, a real frumpy, dirty and unkempt.

'Oh, Jack!' she murmured, recalling his unusual endearment. 'Your absolute brick is desperately worn!'

At four o'clock, knowing she was going to the AA headquarters at five Georgette was too ashamed of her appearance, suddenly. Over the next hour she had a thorough top-to-toe wash – she was still unable to use her bath. Then she went through her wardrobe and found a skirt and blouse that were clean and in a reasonable state of repair. Both needed ironing, so she did that. She also found a new pair of tights and hastily polished some court shoes, amazed at the filth on every pair. Next she tidied her hair, put on fresh make-up and pulled on her imitation fur. All her gloves had holes, so she just carried a pair without putting them on. She still felt shabby, but at least she looked clean and tidy.

The AA offices were at 11 Redcliffe Gardens, just off the Fulham Road in West London. But she was afraid the cabbie would know that address and, even if he didn't, there must surely be a large sign of some kind, so she told him she wanted the Old Brompton Road end of Redcliffe Gardens, intending to walk the rest of the way – which was a fair distance. Fearful that the taxi driver might guess her destination, she began walking only after he had driven out of sight.

Darkness shrouded Georgette as she walked briskly, aware that she was late, along Redcliffe Gardens, which was lined by large terraced houses that reflected an age when Britain was still great.

A cold wind tugged at her all the way, and she wished she had left herself a shorter walk. She had not had so much exercise for a long time and her knees and back were feeling the strain. She was also nervous, sure that everyone walking past her must know she was making for number eleven. She kept looking around, wondering who was following her.

Tenseness engulfed her as she drew near to her destination and, as she reached it, she was amazed to find that there was no tell-tale 'AA' sign. She stood by the steps leading to the front door for some time, searching for some indication that this building did, indeed, house Alcoholics Anonymous. It looked just like all the other houses in the block, however, and she began to wonder if she had remembered the address correctly.

Lights were burning on the ground floor and a porch light threw its glare over her. Ornamental stone balustrades flanked the flight of five steps that led up to the porch, the canopy of which was supported by sturdy pillars. The black-painted door looked uninviting. Before she could change her mind, Georgette practically ran up the steps and rang the door-bell.

A middle-aged woman opened the door. She was tall and slim and looked very respectable: nicely made-up, very smartly dressed. Georgette was now sure she had got the wrong address, and prepared to apologize.

But the woman showed no surprise at confronting a stranger on her doorstep. She just smiled, very sweetly, and said, 'Hallo! Come in.'

'I'm Georgette.'

'Ah, yes! We have been expecting you. Come and meet Anne and Arthur. You spoke to Arthur on the phone, didn't you? I'm Judith, by the way.'

She led the way down a short corridor off right of the hall to a small room at the front of the house. The man and woman inside were introduced as Arthur and Anne. They shook hands.

'So, you are Georgette! I'm so glad you came!' said Arthur. He was relieved that she had shown up. Some people, despite crying for help, do not arrive and, when there had been no sign of Georgette at five o'clock, Arthur had been afraid that she had got cold feet. He was a short dapper man in his early sixties, with grey hair that, though it had thinned out, had not receded.

Anne, a little older than Arthur, Georgette guessed, was just as nice as Judith.

'So you think you have a drink problem?' Once they had taken seats, Anne broached the subject of Georgette's visit, her voice showing deep concern, but no condemnation.

'I don't know really. I mean, I would like to be able to continue to drink, but just to drink less – so I don't get into trouble, that's all.'

The three exchanged a knowing look.

Arthur spoke. 'Why not tell us what happened to bring you here, Georgette?'

Georgette fidgeted a little, but their manner was so encouraging and understanding that she did tell them about the previous Friday, in great detail.

'But that can't be the first time that you have been unaware of your own behaviour when you've been drinking?' said Arthur gently.

She admitted that it was not and, gradually, they drew out of her some other examples and began to get a picture of her life.

'It seems to us that, like us, you have a drinking problem,' stated Anne.

'But you all seem to be quite sober!'

'We are – and so are you,' pointed out Arthur. 'You told me that you haven't had a drink since Friday night. Is that true?'

'Well, yes.'

'Then you have been sober for nearly four days already. If you don't have a drink tomorrow, you will have been sober for nearly five days, and so on. Tomorrow is always a new day, however, so don't think about tomorrow at all. Just say to yourself that you will stay away from drink for the rest of today. I'm sure you can do that – it's only a few hours, after all.'

'Oh, yes. I'm sure I can get through this evening without having a drink,' she said confidently.

'Fine. And tomorrow morning, when you wake up, tell yourself that you will stay away from drink for that day – and only that day – don't think beyond that day at all. You must do that every day, but only think of "one day at a time".'

That made sense to Georgette. She remembered that, during the war, she used to think she, and all of them, should live just for that day, as they never knew what the next might bring and it was tempting fate to plan ahead.

'God gives us only twenty-four hours at a time,' continued Arthur, 'not three weeks, six months or eight years. Each morning yesterday is absolutely dead and gone, and there is nothing we can do to change it. If we did something evil yesterday, we can try to atone for it today, but we cannot undo it. We can only resolve not to do it again today.

215

Similarly, we can plan for tomorrow, but we can't actually do anything, good or bad, until tomorrow arrives – and it never does. Tomorrow becomes real only when it becomes today. So today is all we have, all we need to worry about – but we must worry about it every day.'

'It sounds simple.'

'It is simple,' said Arthur, 'but not necessarily easy.'

'That's what we do to stay sober – we stopped drinking "one day at a time",' put in Judith, 'but the days add up.'

'Of course, when you begin to practise sobriety, you find that you have to replace the drinking with something else.'

'What?'

'As I said on the 'phone,' came in Arthur. 'Food and plenty of liquids and sugar is usually the first answer, because it compensates for the sugar in the alcohol – sugar that the body has become used to, and craves. Secondly, it consists of learning how to change our way of life through going to AA meetings and applying the Programme of Recovery so that in time we know what to guard against if we want to stay sober and achieve peace of mind.'

'Are you working?' asked Judith.

'Yes.'

'Good! But work gently, don't get over-tired, avoid stressful situations, try to keep calm, eat regularly and get plenty of sleep.'

'Carry a packet of sweets or something with you at all times, so that you don't have to go out to buy something to eat,' advised Anne.

'And in the evenings,' said Arthur, 'every evening to begin with, have a meal and attend an AA meeting. There's one here tonight and there are plenty of other venues to choose from tomorrow. There's at least one every night, holidays not excepted, and we'll give you a list before you leave. It is important to get into the habit and we suggest you follow the routine for at least ninety days.'

'Ninety days!' Georgette gasped. That prospect didn't appeal to her one bit.

'At least!' confirmed Anne. 'It's very important to get into the habit of staying away from alcohol and you will need help to do that. Everyone at the meetings has the same problem, so you will be in the company of people who understand.'

'I have often stopped drinking without any help,' Georgette stated loftily.

'So did we before we came to AA,' Arthur came back lightly.

Judith said, 'Like you, we always started again. It's easy to stop – the trick of it is to stay stopped.'

216

'Any time you want to stop going to the meetings, you can – nobody will force you to attend if you want your misery back.'

'But I don't want to stop drinking altogether. I enjoy it. I just want to be able to drink a bit less.'

Arthur answered, his tone kind. 'Make your mind up, Georgette. You've got into trouble through drinking too much. You've just told us so. That is correct?'

'Yes, as I told you. By drinking too much.'

'If you don't want to get into trouble again, you are going to have to find some way of not touching alcohol at all.'

'But why?'

'A diabetic cannot take sugar, even in small doses. An alcoholic cannot take alcohol, even in small doses. It's as simple as that. It's not because you are a bad person or a good person that you become an alcoholic. It is because you are a sick person. You have an allergy to alcohol and alcoholism is merely the manifestation of that allergy.'

'But I'm not an alcoholic!'

'Not all drinkers are alcoholics. It's *how* it affects us that helps us to diagnose ourselves, and we do not say you are one.' Judith was firm, but gentle. 'But it appears that you have a drink problem of some kind and we believe that you may have the illness – and it is an illness, one for which there is no known cure, but one which can be arrested. Once you begin to understand that, it is easy to see that it is very much easier to tackle the illness in the early stages than to wait until it has taken you over completely, and the way to tackle it – the only way – is to abstain altogether. Would you be interested in hearing how I came to AA?'

Georgette said she would and Anne told her story, simply and without trying to make excuses. 'I finished up being certified, twice, because of drink. But it's not necessary to wait until you are in a strait-jacket, you still have the choice.'

A silence fell, while they let Georgette reflect on the horrible story she had just heard, then Arthur spoke. 'Judith's story and mine are somewhat similar.' He went on to relate his path to AA, then Judith followed with her story.

Georgette sat in horrified silence throughout the recital. Was it possible that she could go on to such dreadful experiences? 'But you've all managed to cure yourselves,' she said eventually.

'Oh no, Georgette. Never think that! We are *not* cured,' stressed Judith. 'We have simply learned that, no matter how long it has been since our last drink, we are still only one drink away from being drunk. We are alcoholics, and will remain alcoholics until the day we die. But we have become alcoholics who do not drink – alcoholics who seldom want a drink, but know how to resist on the occasions when we do. You see, we have too much to lose.'

'Remember, Georgette,' put in Arthur sagely, 'it's the first drink that does the damage. Or put another way, for the alcoholic the first drink is one too many, the sixth, seventh, eighth or more is never enough – if you don't have the first, you won't have the second.'

At that moment, Georgette saw the tiniest chink of light in her darkness. 'Will you help me? Will you tell me what to do to become like you?' All three of them said they would help her.

By now the hour was a quarter-to-seven o'clock and Arthur suggested that they should go out and get a quick bite to eat before the meeting began at eight. On their way out, Judith told the people manning the telephone service of their intention.

At the supper Georgette shared a carafe of water with her new friends, much enjoying their companionship, and finished off the meal with a cup of tea.

They returned to Redcliffe Gardens for the meeting. Georgette became nervous again, not knowing what to expect.

'Don't worry,' Anne said soothingly, 'you don't have to say anything at all. Just sit there and listen. You don't have to stay to the end if you don't want to. You can walk out at any time. It doesn't matter. Nobody is going to say anything to you, or shout at you, if you do.'

Georgette knew that she could never draw attention to herself by leaving in the middle of the meeting, but she still found the possibility of doing so comforting.

The meeting room was a through-room right next door to the small room where Georgette had had her initial chat with Anne, Judith and Arthur. It was quite large, and about seventy tubular canvas stacking chairs had been arranged in rows before a table which was set in front of the curtain drawn front windows. At the desk were seated a rather young, elegant woman – the guest speaker Arthur told her – and the secretary of the meeting, an elderly ex-naval type. Both smiled as she entered and, seeing her hesitate, the secretary told her to sit wherever she liked. The few people already seated smiled, too, then went back to their own thoughts, showing no curiosity at all.

Georgette felt more at ease. She took a seat three rows from the back and, while she waited, studied the wall posters, of which there were five:

EASY DOES IT
THINK, THINK, THINK
JUST FOR TODAY
LET GO, LET GOD
LIVE AND LET LIVE

Georgette was to remember these legends always in that order. After the earlier conversation, she understood the significance of 'JUST FOR TODAY' and she assumed that the others were equally significant, but had no idea what that significance was.

People were drifting in all the time and she behaved like everyone else, smiling and then ignoring them. It was obvious that none of them knew, or maybe just didn't care, that she was new, and she began to relax. What really surprised her was that they were all, without exception, decent-looking people, most of them men and many extremely smart. No one was drunk.

The secretary called the meeting to order, asking for a few moments to 'remember why we are here'.

In the silence that followed, Georgette thought, 'I'm not sure that I really know why I am here. I'm not really an alcoholic, after all. It's a bit pathetic, all this.'

Then the secretary introduced the young lady by his side as the evening's guest speaker. She remained seated. 'My name is Christine, and I am an alcoholic.' Her voice was cultured and she sounded stone-cold sober. 'I'm here to tell you my story . . .'

Georgette listened in absolute astonishment. It seemed this gentle young lady, while drunk, had beaten up her elderly parents so badly that she had only just been released from Holloway after serving a prison sentence of several years – and she didn't even remember doing the deed! She told the meeting that she had found AA whilst in prison and that she put down her recovery to going to many meetings and 'sticking with the winners'.

'My God!' mused Georgette. 'I do need to be here! I could have done something like that to Susan in one of my blackouts!'

She listened attentively to every speaker after that and realized, with horror, that she could identify with some part of every story – she had something in common with all of them. At the close of the meeting the 'pot' was passed around and the secretary suggested that the price of the 'first drink' might be a suitable amount of money to put into it, a comment that was greeted with many smiles.

While some people then left, many remained to chat over tea and biscuits. Judith, Anne and Arthur came over to Georgette. They looked at her and could see that she was, at last, beginning to admit the truth to herself. And that was the first step to recovery.

'You have every chance of making it,' Arthur said.

Judith gave Georgette her home phone number and so did Anne and Arthur.

'If you want to talk to me at any time, absolutely any time – day or night – just pick up the telephone,' Judith told her. 'Whether you are out somewhere or at home, any time you are tempted to pick up a drink, make yourself pick up the telephone instead.'

At that, Georgette smiled inwardly. For there was a time, was there not, when she had considered her telephone at home nothing but a nuisance. Now it was to be treated as a friend.

Armed with AA literature, none of which she intended to look at that night, Georgette took a taxi home. There she found a greetings telegram awaiting her from Australia. 'Happy birthday, Mummy. Love Susan, Roger and Tony.'

In her confused state, Georgette had actually forgotten that it was her birthday, that she was half a century old! What a dreadful thought – she broke down and cried. Even as she did, the telephone rang. It was Alex. 'Hello, Mummy. I've been trying to get you all evening to say Happy Birthday.'

'Oh, darling – I was out.'

'Had a good evening, then?'

'Yes, I rather think I did. I've made some new friends.'

'Oh, good. I forgot to post it yesterday, but your card is in the post, so you should get it in the morning. I'm sorry it'll arrive late.'

'Better late than never. Thank you, dear. All is going well with you?'

'Fine. I'm having to work hard, but I'm enjoying every minute of Army life.'

'That's good.'

'I'll be in touch at Christmas.'

The hall porter greeted her cheerily. 'Morning, Mrs Barestone-Tailour. Methinks it must be your birthday, all these cards!'

He'd brought to her door several envelopes, and they all proved to be birthday cards. The one from Alex was there, plus cards from Tom and Nancy, and Dickie, even dear Nanny, had remembered that it was a special birthday, and she was touched.

The fact that these cards, and others from friends in Belgium, had not arrived until after the day was a mystery. But Georgette was convinced that, had they arrived on time, she might not have been driven to ring AA. Could this be an example of God working in mysterious ways, she wondered.

She had a good day at work, more cheerful than she'd been for a long time. Five-thirty arrived and she wasn't interested in seeking a drink. She went straight home.

She had felt less nervous, so much better after yesterday's AA meeting, more hopeful about life in general and herself in particular, that she decided she would attend meetings every evening while she pulled herself together. Obviously she wouldn't need to go for the full ninety days, or bother to grasp the Twelve Steps they'd advised her to read and follow, as she wasn't a real alcoholic – just heading in that direction, but she would go for the next few weeks, up to Christmas seemed a reasonable compromise, and she'd be fine by then. She had been given a pamphlet, 'Where to find', which listed all the places she could go on different nights of the week, and she discovered that evening's venue nearest to her was in Shepherds Bush.

With still an hour to go before she need set off for the meeting, Georgette suddenly began to tremble, then to shake fiercely. Full of alarm, she was totally unable to stop what was happening to her.

To her mind there was nothing rational about it – except there was, of course. Having suffered so much misery of late, she'd built up a terrible amount of unconsciously denied nervous tension. And filled with prolonged distress, she had become vulnerable. She was on the edge, her body was screaming out for a drink. The balance of her mind had tipped and was telling her to go ahead.

'Go on, give way to drink.'

'No, don't! It's not the happy way, but it's the only way.'

'But it's only one drink you want, so have it. It'll steady your nerves. You know it will.'

'It won't! So don't! You're being tempted by the devil.'

Her self-preservation instinct cut in at that moment and she recognized what an absurd conversation she was having with herself. Then she was being reminded to heed what she had been told, avoid two pests – hurry and indecision. And right now it was indecision that had raised its ugly head.

'Right! Get yourself to the AA meeting, now,' she commanded herself forcefully.

A taxi took her to the meeting and she staggered into the hall relieved, to see the five AA legends posted on a wall, that immediately had her feeling strangely at home.

'I can't take it! I can't take it!' she blurted out to committee members, none of whom knew her, and fell to a chair, sobbing.

In fellowship, they rallied to her, anxious to comfort and revive a wounded warrior. They hugged her lovingly and held her hands, stroking them kindly, with care, each friend willing her to become calm, to be at ease with herself. And soon they knew her name.

Joe, that meeting's secretary, placed his hand on her forehead and allowed his thumb gently and continually to run across her temple. Georgette found the movement very soothing, gradually making her relax.

'You're at the right place, Georgette,' she heard Joe say over and over again. 'You're at the right place. You'll be all right. We're here for you. It's going to be all right. Fight through!'

And fight through, Georgette did. With her previous experience to aid her, she managed to beat the biggest battle of her life, well aware that to have yielded that night to that particular hiccup would have taken her over the edge and she couldn't have been brought back from it by anyone. Drink would have claimed her and death would have been her bed . . .

The true alcoholic can never give way to the temptation to drink. Not once. And she heeded that truth.

Georgette decided to change her daily pattern slightly, to save both time and bother: at the end of each day at the office she would leave dead at five-thirty, not go home for food, but eat at a cafe or restaurant near to that evening's meeting – she could not get there fast enough, for it was only when she was at AA meetings that she felt safe.

After a few days of sobriety she noticed the appalling state of her flat and most of her clothes and, on her first 'officially' dry weekend, she took a whole suitcase of clothes to the dry-cleaners and most of her other things she washed by hand. She would rather wear clean clothes than wash. She still couldn't bring herself to bath. She also stocked up on gloves and stockings and took several pairs of shoes to be heeled. The rest of that weekend, except when she went to the meetings, was spent cooking herself good meals, cleaning and, by Sunday evening, the place was habitable again.

Over the next couple of weeks Georgette spent all her spare time sewing and soon had a good range of presentable garments. She made a standing appointment for every Friday lunch-time with a Lewisham hairdresser, and had the grey in her hair concealed professionally. After a while she found she could bath again, and that made her feel like a new woman.

The AA meetings became the centre of her existence. Over and over again she resolved to speak but, when the moment came, she just could not bring herself to say: 'I am an alcoholic.' This troubled her greatly and she rang Judith expecting her to be at home. She wasn't there, so she rang Arthur. Blessedly, he was in and met her for a cup of tea before that evening's meeting, which was in Bloomsbury.

'Georgette, there's no need yet for you to say "I am an alcoholic". You'll find yourself saying that in you own good time. You are in too much of a hurry to get well, that's all.' Arthur was so reassuring. 'You're forgetting that it took you an awful long time to become alcoholic,' Georgette winced at this but said nothing, 'and it will take you time to get better. You're doing very well, and I'm sure you will find the need to speak soon, so don't get discouraged. You have been sober for only a couple of weeks, after all. And you can see that not everyone wants to speak at meetings. You have to learn to go easy on yourself, because you want to get better, but facing up to your problem is not the same thing as solving it. Just keep going to the meetings – your problems are not insurmountable, believe me, "Easy does it!"'

'It's three weeks since I last had a drink, Arthur and I do feel very much better now, under control again physically, but it seems to me that I think of nothing but drink and its effect on me – I really have become very self-centred.'

'You've got to be selfish, Georgette. At this stage you must think of yourself first. I know it's paradoxical, but concentration on yourself is the only way to keep on the right track. Once that's achieved you will be able to think of others as well, and they will reap the benefits of your recovery. In the meantime, try to avoid getting angry or tired or upset – that will put you under strain and make you need a drink. Take everything as calmly as you can and don't worry if you put on weight by eating instead of drinking – I put on over two stone, but I lost it again later.'

On the Monday of Christmas week, Georgette finally plucked up courage, after the guest speaker had finished.

'My name is Georgette and I am an alcoholic.' That out of the way, she found it quite easy to continue. Her fellows acknowledged her genuinely, then listened as she said how she felt and praised the way that AA was helping her. 'What I'll do now is to use my will-power,' she declared grandly, and sat down, feeling very pleased with herself.

But she was immediately deflated by a Scottish member, who did not mince his words. 'Aye, it's a grand thing, will-power, but it was your will-power that got you where you are, lassie – and me where I am. What you need rather than will-power is a genuine desire to stop drinking, and to go to any length to achieve sobriety. If you have that, the rest will follow, but I wouldn't rely too much on your will-power if I were you. I think you'll find that facing up to reality is more use.'

Another of the posters first seen in Redcliffe Gardens flashed through Georgette's mind, and she suddenly realised the meaning of 'THINK, THINK, THINK.'

She promptly decided to have 'a look' at those Twelve Steps at leisure come the weekend.

STEP 1. We admitted we were powerless over alcohol – that our lives had become unmanageable.

'Well, this one's true. I do admit that my life has become unmanageable.'

STEP 2. . . . Came to believe that a power greater than ourselves could restore us to sanity.

'That's all very well, but what has God done for me? I certainly haven't come to believe that!'

STEP 3. . . . Made a decision to turn our will and our lives over to the care of God as we understand Him.

' "as we understand him"? I don't understand that.'

STEP 4. . . . Made a searching and fearless moral inventory of ourselves.

'I am trying to understand myself, which I suppose is what they mean, but "fearless"? How can I be fearless? I'm full of fear!'

STEP 5. . . . Admitted to God, to ourselves, and to another human being the exact nature of our wrongs.

'I suppose by that they mean wrong-doings? Well, myself and God's one thing. But why should other people know my misdeeds?'

STEP 6. . . . Were entirely ready to have God remove all these defects of character.

'Yes, I'll go along with that. After all, He created me in the first place and it's fine by me if He wants to make some improvements. But He doesn't seem to be very interested in doing it.'

STEP 7. . . . Humbly asked Him to remove our shortcomings.

'That seems to me to be exactly the same as Step Six, except that I have to ask him to do it. All right, I'll ask – please God, humbly, I ask you to remove my shortcomings. There that's done.'

STEP 8. . . . Made a list of all persons we had harmed, and became willing to make amends to them all.

'That's easy, as I've never in my life hurt anyone – at least, not deliberately. Well, Phyllis Grant, I suppose, but I couldn't help that and, anyway, I can hardly make amends now – if only it were possible to bring Jack back!'

STEP 9. . . . Made direct amends to such people wherever possible, except when to do so would injure them or others.

'I can't see much difference between that and Step Eight.'

STEP 10. . . . Continued to take personal inventory and when we were wrong promptly admitted it.

'I don't see that I am wrong. Anyway, I consider that step is just a repetition of Step Four.'

STEP 11. . . . Sought through prayer and meditation to improve our conscious contact with God *as we understand Him*, praying only for the knowledge of His Will for us and the power to carry that out.

'There's that stupid "as we understand him" again. I wish they'd make their meaning clearer. Anyway, all this reference to God is getting on my wick!'

STEP 12. . . . Having had a spiritual awakening as the result of these Steps, we tried to carry this message to alcoholics, and to practise these principles in all our affairs.

'I don't think I have had a spiritual awakening, so that makes this Step meaningless for me.'

In fact, when Georgette went through the Twelve Steps again, she could see very little that was relevant to herself. She was prepared to accept Number one: that she was powerless over alcohol, because she had proved that to herself, and she was perfectly happy with Number Six: God removing all her defects of character. If she had any! But that was it . . . or did she need *someone* to explain them to her?

She had become such a compulsive liar that she found herself lying to herself and unable to differentiate between reality and fantasy. She knew she would need help to find the truth.

Chapter Twenty Two

Georgette had hoped to have the whole drink business out of the way by Christmas but, with only a few days to go, that obviously wasn't to be. She was living through days of wanting to drink, and determined to stay sober, but in such agony of mind that all the time she was wondering if it was worth it. Some demon seemed to be constantly perched on her shoulder, murmuring that one little drink would ease her pain. It took every ounce of her determination not to listen to the devil.

She had pinned up a little card: 'JUST FOR TODAY' where she would see it as she awoke, and she would lie reading it for a while every morning before she got up. Then she would read a list of nine recommendations that had been given to her to follow daily, such things as being happy, being agreeable, being unashamed, being more tolerant, keeping an open mind . . .

Once she had read the list, slowly, she would prepare for work, then read it again before she left the flat. Somehow it made her feel content. She kept another 'JUST FOR TODAY' card in her pocket and, whenever she found herself tensing up, which was often at first, she would shuffle off to the Ladies, lock herself in a cubicle and read the card until she felt better – she had no idea why, but it always worked. Sometimes her hands reflected her inner tension, then she would stretch them as she had been taught and gradually feel herself relaxing.

She had no life except AA. She no longer had any interest in anything else. She was hanging on by a thread. She had come to realize that she was not as clever, as important, as she had thought and her ego had not recovered from the shock of that discovery. 'Know your limitations' was one of the AA precepts and she felt she did know them, only too well. She had swung from over-confidence to a feeling that she could not exist at all away from the protection of AA. She was indeed changing. Turning on the radio one evening she heard 'Bridge Over Troubled Water' being played. 'How apt,' she thought. 'AA is *my* bridge over troubled water. May I cross it safely.'

She began to think seriously about Step Two of the Recovery

Programme: ' . . . a power greater than ourselves could restore us to sanity.' If that meant God, which she assumed it did, was His job done when He'd sent her to AA – or could she expect more help from Him? She hoped so, because she did feel that she had lost her sanity and could not find it again without help.

'God grant me the serenity to accept the things I cannot change, courage to change the things I can, and wisdom to know the difference.' Those words usually end the proceedings of AA meetings. Georgette knew them by heart, and said them fervently every day.

At the meeting on 23 December, however, the guest speaker, a man in his forties with longish curly hair and an air of piety about him, chose to end with the Lord's Prayer. He turned out to be a recovering alcoholic priest.

'As Christmas Eve is only a few hours away, let us welcome the Holy Season by saying it together. Our Father, which art in Heaven . . .'

While Georgette knew the prayer, she had never really considered the meaning of some of the words, and was suddenly struck by one sentence: 'Give us this day our daily bread.'

'What does that mean?' she asked Arthur, over the usual tea and biscuits.

'What do you think it means?' was his response.

'Well, I wondered if it was that, just as you desire to stay sober for today, you shouldn't pray for food – or anything else – beyond today.'

'That's right, Georgette!' He beamed his approval.

Colleagues at GBE noticed the change in Georgette. She always looked clean and presentable now, and her manner was much calmer. She no longer hit the roof over trivialities, or shouted at any engineer who told her he couldn't visit a customer that day. Word spread quickly and people stopped avoiding her. But she was worried.

Christmas Eve had fallen on a Friday and GBE's offices were closing to the public at one o'clock, but none of the staff was required to leave then because everyone was expected to attend the staff party at which the drink would flow freely before they went their separate ways.

Georgette had consulted Judith about this and she had been reassuring. 'You don't have to announce that you don't drink any more, merely say that, for this one round, you'd prefer to have something long and non-alcoholic – and say the same thing whenever anyone offers you a drink. Nobody will really bother. They'll assume that you've already had a "real" drink, or will be having one next time, and, after they've had a few jars themselves, they won't even notice that you are not drinking.'

Judith's forecast proved correct and Georgette wondered why she'd ever doubted it.

She was taking no chances though. Once armed with her long drink of lemonade, she kept hold of it, didn't dare put it down in case she accidentally picked someone else's up and found herself drinking alcohol.

Staff from the Sales Office were at the party and it was the first time Les Dykes had seen Georgette since she went to AA but he had heard rumours about the change in her. One look, and he felt sure she had stopped drinking. Thus, whenever her glass was becoming empty, he would appear with a lemonade refill. Georgette drank far more of the drink than she wanted, and began to feel rather bloated, but she was spared both the trouble of resisting temptation and embarrassment at asking for a soft drink.

The party broke up at about three o'clock and GBE closed its doors until 29 December. Christmas Day and Boxing Day had fallen at the weekend, so both Monday and Tuesday were official holidays and everyone was looking forward to the four-day break.

Georgette wrapped up well against the cold evening air, then went to a local supermarket to do her last-minute food shopping for the holiday. She was spending it entirely on her own and would, as usual, be attending AA meetings.

She didn't feel at all hungry after all that lemonade, but she made herself a savoury snack and ate a bit of fruit. The nearest evening's meeting was in Hampstead, and she didn't feel like making the journey. After her success in resisting alcohol at the party, for once, she did not feel the need of moral support, so she settled down to study some more AA literature.

After an hour or so of reading and thinking, Georgette looked again at the Twelve Steps and was surprised to find that they were no longer totally incomprehensible to her.

She decided that, yes, she could believe that 'a power greater than ourselves' had restored her to sanity. Something outside herself certainly had. She hadn't exactly 'found God' but it seemed to her that that wasn't the point – what was required was that she believe in some force outside herself, that she didn't believe herself to be all-powerful. And she didn't, not any more. So she had, in a way, turned her will and her life over to the care of 'God as we understand Him'. That is to say that she had submitted to whatever power it was that was directing her life.

So it seemed to Georgette that she had already accepted the first three Steps and was now ready for Step Four: to make a searching and fearless moral inventory of herself. She spent a while doing that and felt she was ready to face Step Five: she had already admitted to herself the exact nature of her wrongs, now she had to admit them to God and another human being.

Although she had never set foot in the place, she had noticed there was a Catholic church nearby, and she decided that she would go to Confession – that would surely constitute telling both God and another human being. The decision reached, she was impatient to see it through without further delay, so she put on her coat and set out for the church.

The place was in low light and seemed deserted, but as she neared the altar area, an elderly priest appeared from the vestry, attracted by the sound of her footsteps. He was tall and sparse of hair, and his blue eyes twinkled kindly.

'Hello, my dear. Can I help you?'

'Yes, Father. I've joined Alcoholics Anonymous and I've had a spiritual awakening.' The words struck her as odd now and she hoped the priest wouldn't smile. Had he done so, she might have fled.

But he didn't. 'Oh, how wonderfully brave!' he returned, without a trace of amusement.

'Yes, isn't it marvellous? I haven't been to confession for more years than I care to remember, Father – I'm a lapsed Catholic, I'm afraid. But now I'm desperate to clear my conscience. Will you please hear my confession now? Please, Father!'

The priest glanced at his watch. He had to conduct the Midnight Mass, but it was only a quarter-to-ten o'clock, so there was plenty of time and he did not want to turn away this penitent woman. He said, 'Of course, my dear. Just give me a moment.' He hastened into the vestry, wrote a quick note to his helpers to make the necessary preparations for the Mass without waiting for him, and emerged a few moments later, suitably garbed.

Once in the confessional, Georgette found the dark little cubicle released all her inhibitions, and the words poured out of her. She told the entire story of her life, dwelling on all the things which she saw as misdeeds: notably her affair with Gregoire, her failed marriages, her responsibility for the failure of Jack's marriage, her experience with Amanda, her affair with Martin and the abortion that followed, her abandonment of David and lack of love for Susan and Alex, the fact that she'd never been properly married in a church and her promiscuity before she contacted AA.

On and on she talked and the priest was in a dilemma. He had to prepare for the Midnight Mass – he could already hear people arriving – but it was unheard of to interrupt the flow of a Confession. But what choice did he have? He had just decided that he really would have to interrupt her when, to his enormous relief, she ground to a halt of her own accord. He muttered a few reassuring words, assigned her a hefty penance – to include her attendance at the Mass, gave her absolution and hastened back to the vestry to make his preparations.

Georgette made her penance and remained in the congregation for Midnight Mass. She was comforted by the familiar sights and sounds of her youth: the statues, the candles, the stained-glass windows, the Lady Chapel, the stations of the Cross, the rich smell of incense, the ritual at the altar and the half-forgotten Latin phrases. For a while she was utterly at peace. The service reached the stage where the priest prepares for Communion and she watched as he blessed the wine and drank from the chalice.

'Oh, he can drink, can't he?' and the thought did not hurt at all.

Then, to Georgette only, came the unexpected. Having received the Host (bread consecrated and representing the body of Christ) she noticed that, as yet, not one of her fellow communicants was returning to the congregational pews.

She soon saw why: Further down the line the priest was now offering the supplicants the 'blood of Christ', wine from the chalice. It was an action not in her memory, so clearly practices had changed since she was last in a Catholic church.

She looked away, and her eye was caught by a statue of Christ, his arms outstretched and with animals and children at his feet.

'Oh, you would, wouldn't you!' Georgette spoke silently to him. She saw the funny side and felt as if she were sharing a joke with God.

When the chalice reached her, she simply pretended to drink from it.

The Mass ended and she went home, light of heart and foot. In her mind, she had been tested in the presence of God and had not been found wanting!

The four-day Christmas break passed more easily than Georgette had anticipated. She went to AA meetings every other evening. The rest of the time she did housework, watched the TV, sewed, read AA literature.

She faced up to the fact that spending Christmas alone had not been entirely voluntary, because she had refused no invitations – there had been none to refuse – and no one had called on her. On Christmas Day both Susan and Alex telephoned but, apart from that, her phone was silent.

She still got Christmas Cards, but she knew she had wasted people, lost friends through her abuse of them when she was drinking.

Learning to live in the real world again was like trying to walk in mud: not easy, but it can be done with perseverance. Living with sobriety was strange. Georgette had embarked on a better way of living, but she felt very insecure and vulnerable, moving in a world that was often baffling and painful, and often seemed to urge her to reach for a glass to ease a difficult situation.

'Do not be discouraged,' her friends at AA urged. Easy to say that, but she was the one who had to do it. And what hard work it was! However, she knew that drinking solved *no* problems – just created more of them.

Despite the Scottish member's scepticism, staying away from alcohol required a lot of determination and placed a great strain on her. She had not gone back to Catholicism fully, but she did quite often pop into the church and offer up a prayer for strength. She could see the irony in the fact that the prize for her efforts was to be deprived of the drink she craved so much, and she derived a grim amusement from the paradox.

Membership of AA might cost nothing financially, she reflected, but certainly cost a lot of effort to stay sober and think soberly.

But as Georgette had read in the Big Book of AA: 'if you want what we have and are prepared to go to any length to get it, then you are ready to take certain steps . . . Half measures availed us nothing . . . we stood at the turning point . . .'

It was suggested to her that Step Meetings might help her, and as she was determined to make progress she decided she had to attend such meetings, where each week a particular step was high-lighted, explained and discussed.

This proved to be, for her, the turning point. For she realized she had misunderstood, misinterpreted or simply skimmed over the words of the Steps. Now their deeper meaning became apparent to her and gradually the scales fell from her eyes and she knew what sobriety was all about.

She began to recognize the difference between being 'dry' and being 'sober' and her gratitude to the fellowship grew in direct proportion to her progress in sobriety. She knew that she owed her life and her serenity to AA. Now she really knew she was part of it, that this was where she belonged. And in due course she lost all desire for drink. She was free!

A few days into 1972, Head Office announced that GBE's usual June convention was, this year, to be held in Spain's capital, Madrid. And for the first time in four years Georgette received an invitation. But the thought of going abroad and having no AA support for three whole days made her panic.

The AA meeting that evening was at Redcliffe Gardens and Judith, Arthur and Anne were all there. She saw Arthur first and tackled him. 'I don't think I can go. But I have to go – it's a duty. But it'll be just one long temptation and I don't know how I'll cope without AA help.'

'You won't have to, Georgette. That's not a problem. AA is international, you know, and you can go to AA meetings there in the same way as you do here. We'll give you contacts there and you can write to them with the details of when you're arriving and where you'll be staying. They'll get in touch not long after you arrive – and escort you to the meetings, as you won't know your way around. Then, if your colleagues ask you to do things with them, you can tell them truthfully that you have arranged to see some friends. We are a fellowship, remember, and that means we are all friends, wherever we go in the world.'

Georgette was reassured. For the next two months she continued to attend AA meetings every evening. She began to teach herself Spanish, in preparation for Madrid, and that helped her to occupy her mind. She really felt she was getting a grip on things, then disaster struck . . .

Chapter Twenty Three

The Life Guards were on a tour of duty in trouble-torn Northern Ireland, on policing duties in Belfast in support of the RUC. Ever since Alex's arrival there, Georgette had been plagued by the same nightmare, which culminated in an explosion of flesh. One night she had been jolted into sudden wakefulness by the cold conviction that something had, indeed, happened to her son – that he was no longer in this life, that *he* had just briefly visited her to say so.

Early daylight was filtering into the room through chinks in the curtains when the strident sound of her door-bell reverberated peremptorily round the room, waking her from a sleep that was only fitful. Instinctively, she knew it was bad news, the news that she had feared for weeks and had been actively expecting for some hours.

She stiffened, and a feeling of resignation came over her, effectively swamping a flutter of fear in her stomach, making her icily calm. She rose from her crumpled bedding and, struggling into her quilted dressing-gown, padded over to her front door.

'Hello, Dougie, come on in,' Georgette greeted the caller as if he'd come by arrangement, as if it was the most natural thing in the world for him to be standing there at the crack of dawn.

Dougie was dressed in a dark three-piece suit and wore the LG tie. His face was grim and he fiddled with a brown trilby as he tried to voice his carefully-rehearsed words.

'I know why you are here,' she told him softly, before he could find his tongue.

Dougie crossed the threshold, and Georgette bade him take a chair. He obeyed stiffly, and sat in silence while she moved to light the gas-fire, then threw back the curtains to let in the day.

'Please don't say anything for a moment. I think we will both be better off with a nice cup of tea.'

Dougie was uncomfortable and confused – he didn't know how to behave now. He had volunteered for this unpleasant duty, knowing Georgette would rather hear the bad news from someone who wasn't a stranger. But, somehow, she appeared to know already – could it really be that a mother's instinct could fathom such things?

'Two sugars?' he heard her ask.

'One.'

'Weight-watching?'

'Er – yes.' He had expected to be comforting her, making her tea, not indulging in small talk.

'Get to my size and then worry!' Georgette handed over a mug, stirring it even as she did so.

Dougie could be silent no longer. 'Georgette, you say you know why I'm here, but do you really know how serious my news is?' he blurted out.

'Oh, yes, Dougie! I really knew before I opened the door. But your look confirmed it. You've come to tell me that Alex is – dead?'

'I'm very sorry, Georgette! The whole Regiment sends its condolences.'

Georgette's eyes had brimmed with tears, but she held them back, the numbness within her increasing. She sipped at her tea. 'Did they send you all the way over from Belfast to tell me?' she asked, when she felt her voice was under control.

'No, I'm not based in Northern Ireland. I'm with the rear-guard at Windsor. I was in the Officers' House when the news came through, so I volunteered to come here. Another officer has gone to Titchfield to tell your . . . er . . . Mr Barestone-Tailour. We had to come early because there'll be a report of the incident on the news at six o'clock – no names, of course, until the BBC know that relatives have been informed.'

'I understand. How did it happen?'

Dougie cleared his throat. 'As I understand it, he was on a routine patrol which, sadly, was targeted to get a control-wire bomb. Alex took the full blast. He was killed instantly, Georgette, so at least he didn't suffer.'

'Just like my dream . . .Exactly like my dream!' Georgette responded distantly. 'He *was* the only casualty, wasn't he?'

Dougie was astonished. 'Actually he was. He'd gone ahead to check a suspect package. Wouldn't let his men near it. But that was the lure not the bomb. That was behind a garden wall, and the IRA must have realized he'd sussed 'em – so it was detonated, on the principle that it's better to get one Brit soldier than none.'

'So the IRA were watching them?'

'Yes, indeed. Very near. Probably it was only one man, who then legged it away.'

'Oh, my poor darling!' she said with feeling and fell into a reflective silence for a moment. 'It all makes me aware, Dougie, that

I did not know my son at all, what kind of man he had become.'

'A bloody good one! He was an excellent officer. His troop would have followed him anywhere, without hesitation. I don't suppose he had time to tell you, but he'd just been accepted for a regular commission. Apparently, he just walked into the CO's office and told him that's what he wanted, and the CO agreed on the spot. He was really cut out to be a soldier, and I believe he might well have gone on to command The Life Guards one day.'

'If he was such a good soldier, then why did he die?'

'It's an occupational hazard, my dear. He was a soldier and that's a dangerous occupation. It's not possible to avoid risks, and he was killed doing his duty – I'm sure that's the way he'd have chosen to go.' The comment was trite, but it was the truth and Dougie could think of nothing else to say.

It seemed to satisfy Georgette. She pointed to photographs of Alex on the mantelpiece. 'He was a lovely boy, you know. I knew he'd be handsome when he grew up.'

'He was popular with the girls, I can tell you that! Broke quite a few hearts by all accounts. But being a soldier was the only thing that really mattered to him. He was a natural.'

'Are you to command The Life Guards, one day?'

Dougie shook his head. 'Actually, I'm leaving The Life Guards. I'm to command a foot guards battalion, which apparently, has no officer suitable for that post at present.'

Dougie's Christmas cards had been keeping Georgette in touch with the Rusby family news, and she was aware that Ralph had died of a heart attack the previous year. 'Ralph would have been very proud. Your mother must be. And your wife, of course. How is Valerie?'

'Both are fine. I think Val has always seen herself as a colonel's lady!'

'I'd like some more tea. Will you join me?'

'I will, but I'll make it for us both.' He went over to the gas stove, still amazed at the way the conversation was going. Being asked about himself, at this time, was not what he was here for. Different people certainly behave in different ways when they were in stressful situations.

The reality was that Georgette had blanked out all emotion, afraid that giving way to her grief would lead to a drink.

'Just for today. I will live through this dreadful day without giving in!' The resolution ran through her mind over and over again. 'I've not been a very good mother, Dougie, you must know that.' Dougie knew that she was really talking more to herself than to him, and he did not comment. There was silence while he made a fresh pot of tea, then she said, 'What happens now, Dougie?'

'Alex's body will be flown home. Then, unless you or Alex's father object, we will organize a funeral with full military honours.'

'I don't object at all, and I'm sure Dickie will agree. It's very kind of the Army to spare us from having to cope with those kinds of arrangements. But, Dougie, it's such an unnecessary death – he was little more than a boy! How cruel life is! Now I have lost both my sons! I often wonder if I would have been a better mother to Alex and Susan if I had not had to give David up. Is he well? Is he happy? What is he up to? It seems so long since Christmas and my last news of him!'

'He's just been appointed a history don at Cambridge – he'll take up the position at the beginning of the next academic year. He's quite young for such a post and will obviously go a long way in academia. I believe I mentioned that he was going around with a girl called June, the daughter of the dean of his college? Well, they're madly in love and I understand that they are planning to marry this summer.'

'Oh, I'm so glad! He's twenty-seven in June, isn't he? It doesn't seem possible!'

'It does to me – I've just hit forty!'

'Then you must know I'm fifty-one this year?'

Dougie did.

Georgette's eyes returned to the colour photograph of Alex in full dress uniform, complete with gleaming helmet and shining cuirass

'I never deserved Alex, you know. I starved him of affection, as I was starved of affection. But the silly thing is this: I was planning to make amends to him for my bad ways. Now I can't! Why does life have to be such hell? He never knew if what I said was what I meant – I didn't myself half the time. But he was such a beautiful boy and I did love him – I just didn't know how to express my love when he was young. And then, when he was older, I was so wrapped up in my own problems that I had no time for his. Oh, Dougie, you might as well know it – I'm a reforming alcoholic!'

Before Dougie had time to come up with a suitable response to her confession Georgette caught the time. 'Look, it's six o'clock!'

The radio was by her side and, with a press of a button, she was just in time to hear the start of the news. 'Last night, in Belfast, another soldier . . .'

* * *

The next eight days made Georgette glad that she had the ability to blot out her emotions, or she would never have coped. A miracle had happened: she had not wanted to drink, she had coped without a drink. She just went to her meetings and was comforted.

From hundred's of people she and Dickie had never met came mail, from all over the world, all expressing their disgust, outrage, sympathy. Both were touched by their concern and astounded that the word of their loss had spread so far.

Letters for Georgette, personally, came from Nanny Trotter, from Don Kerr (the first time in ages she had heard from him), from Maurice (now living in Quebec), and from Hugo Adams, her good friend from those long ago days in Malta, who (to the surprise of Georgette and no doubt himself was now a married man working in Bahrain). Hugo had re-established contact when he had been paying a flying visit to London a few years before – three/four? Georgette couldn't quite remember, but she was sure it was when she had still been at Sparrow Hall Walk – and she had met his wife Angela. Since then he had sent Christmas cards.

Monique, who was working at a night-club in Germany, rang her from Berlin and was as supportive as ever. Madame Fourmeaux had died some months before and Georgette felt her grief was truly understood. She felt ashamed that she had not been sober enough at the time to have rung Monique.

Daisy Brown and Tom and Nancy Flowers neither wrote nor rang – they came round in person and provided welcome shoulders for Georgette to cry on. All three were deeply pleased to find no trace of alcohol on her. Despite her bereavement she was, once again, recognizable as the woman they had grown to like and care for before drink had changed her.

Dougie dutifully called every day, and kept her in touch with the progress of the funeral arrangements. It was to be held at Titchfield and Georgette was to spend two nights at Grace Hall.

With Dougie there to see her off, the day before the funeral Georgette boarded a train at Waterloo Station. She was still numb with grief.

Dickie met her at Fareham Station. Tactfully, Brigitte had told him to go alone. In the railway car-park they clung together in shared grief, the last trace of bitterness between them dissolved by their mutual loss. Georgette burst into tears, then Dickie cried, too, and it was some time before they drew apart, both feeling better for the outburst of emotion.

He was looking very much the country squire these days, his

tweed jacket and plus-fours contributing to the image. And older-looking, too, decidedly so, Georgette thought, but he was sixty-six now, she realized with a shock.

'I was afraid this would happen, Dickie, that it didn't even come as a surprise,' Georgette said sadly, but not wanting to admit her premonition.

'I know exactly what you mean,' agreed Dickie. 'You always half-expect the worst, don't you? Bridgitte is very cut up, too. She had become very close to Alex.' He swung open the car boot and dropped Georgette's two light suitcases into it. Then they drove for Grace Hall.

'Susan's coming over today,' Dickie said as they travelled. 'We'll go, meet her at Heathrow. She won't be arriving until mid-evening.'

'Poor soul! It's a long enough journey at the best of times, isn't it? I'm so glad that she can make it, though – the two children were so close, weren't they?'

Dickie nodded his head, reflectively. 'Roger's looking after young Tony, so she'll want to get back as soon as possible and will only be here for a couple of days. There's no time for socializing on this trip. Incidently, the Army sent me Alex's personal effects. That watch you gave him was among them. It still works. Would you like it back?'

'Oh, no, Dickie! No.' Georgette was quite emphatic in her refusal. She just knew she could never look upon it again without unbearable pain – two men close to her had worn that watch, and both were now dead . . . 'Maybe, Joss could be given it one day?' she concluded gently.

Bridgitte came to the front door to greet Georgette and was kindness itself, concealing her own distress. Little Joss, now seven, picked up the general pattern of behaviour and was very attentive to Georgette, too, though no one had asked him to be. His attention consisted largely of plying her with sweets and Coca Cola, but it was the thought that counted and she found herself smiling through her tears. Bless his little cotton socks!

Some of Dickie's relations were already occupying guest-rooms at Grace Hall and were very kind to her, too. Dickie had done a vast amount of work on the house and it was now very comfortable and homely – with everything in perfect taste, of course!

When Georgette and Dickie went to the airport, Bridgitte again left them to it. How could she have ever disliked someone with such sensitivity, Georgette asked herself. The plane landed and Georgette was shaken by Susan's appearance. The long flight hadn't helped, but Susan's features were moulded into a lined mask of mourning. Her eyes were hollow, her expression dazed.

She hugged her parents almost like an automaton, and uttered nothing but monosyllables all the way back to Grace Hall. Once there, she went straight to bed, but she looked a little better the next morning. She reminded Georgette of those soldiers she had looked after at the Gare du Nord in 1940.

No one who saw Susan at the funeral had any doubt about who had been worst hit by Alex's death. Even Georgette had to admit that her own suffering paled beside that of her daughter. The girl was almost bereft of speech, choking into silence after every banality, and with tears streaming unheeded down her pale cheeks from unseeing eyes.

It was a warm, sunny day, and hundreds of people lined the road to the little church. Most could not have known Alex personally but, thanks to the publicity his death had received, they knew of him and wanted to pay their respects.

In the church the congregation sang 'He who would valiant be'. It had been Alex's favourite hymn and was a suitable farewell to a brave man.

With the coffin draped in a Union Jack, the atmosphere was sombre as the procession moved along the picturesque main street to the strains of the 'Funeral March', played by a military band.

The burial itself was impressive. The coffin was lowered and a volley of shots was fired over Alex's grave while a bugler played the 'Last Post'. The plaintive notes got to Georgette and she could contain her tears no longer. They poured from her, and the press got their pictures: the bereaved father with one arm comfortingly around the shoulders of the sobbing mother and the other around the weeping daughter. Bridgitte, again, was self-effacing.

Georgette longed to take her daughter into her arms and comfort her but when, after the funeral service, she tried, she could not get close enough to do so. It was to Dickie that Susan automatically turned for solace.

The funeral over, Georgette went home and, within days, normality returned to her life. The phone ceased to ring and the letters of sympathy slowed to a trickle, then stopped altogether. The media circus moved on and she found herself alone again.

It was then the numbness vanished, to be replaced by rage at such a wasteful death. She found it difficult to accept that Alex was really dead, that she would never see him again, and his photographs became merely a cruel reminder that he had lived – and a constant reproach to her for not being a better mother. In the end she took them all down and hid them in a drawer.

Her misery was overwhelming. She threw herself into her work, often turning to her AA 'JUST FOR TODAY' card and urging herself to carry on, to try to live through that day only. And, one day at a time, she did struggle through. Each day seemed very long, but she got through it in the end. A great deal of her free time was spent at AA meetings, or reading their literature and following their advice. While thinking, she would sew or do some housework and every inch of her flat was soon sparkling clean.

The AA meetings did much to get her through that dreadful patch and she became a frequent speaker – but everything she said at the meetings was intended to convince herself as much as the listeners; sharing her thoughts eased her tension.

And she was winning. Gradually her grief and pain were subsiding. She was asked to become Secretary of the regular group she attended, and she agreed to do this. She was told that she was ready now to become involved in running a Group with the help of a Committee. She enjoyed this responsibility and learned much from it.

As time passed, soldiers returning from Northern Ireland would call on Georgette, Alex's brother officers, but also his men. They talked to her about her son, unconsciously showing by that very act, by everything they said about him, just how wonderful he had been in their eyes.

She found that talking about him was therapeutic, and got out the photographs again.

Would people ever be able to say such flattering things about her, Georgette wondered, and doubted it very much.

Chapter Twenty Four

One morning in late May, when her life was just about back to normal, the telephone in her office rang and Georgette was amazed to find that, instead of the customer query she was expecting, it was a personal call: from Hugo Adams!

'How lovely to hear from you, Hugo! Where are you?'

'In London.'

'Is Angela with you?'

'No, I'm quite alone. How about dinner? If you're free tonight, I can collect you from work – there must be places to eat round there?'

'There are, and I am free, but why not come to my flat? I'll cook something up and we can chat in comfort.'

'Perfect! I hoped you'd say that – I'll bring the wine.'

'Oh! No! I mean . . . I'm sure you'd rather have pink gin, and I've got plenty of that.'

'But I must make a contribution.'

'Not necessary, Hugo. Really. Just bring yourself. Do you have the address with you?'

Hugo rattled it off.

'Good, I'll see you at seven o'clock.'

He arrived punctually at seven, a bunch of flowers in one hand and a box of chocolates in the other. Georgette was quite overwhelmed by the sight of him, his bronzed face emphasising the blue of his eyes and his hair bleached almost white by the sun. His wrinkles were deeper but he hadn't an ounce of extra flesh on him and certainly didn't look his age, which was much the same as hers.

She settled him onto the sofa and told him to help himself to a drink. On the way home she had purchased a half-bottle of Gordon's and some angostura, which she had placed on a little silver tray, together with a glass – he didn't like ice. She had prepared herself a tumbler of ginger ale, knowing he would assume it was whisky. She didn't want to start talking about drink with someone she hadn't seen for so long.

'Georgette, you know how I feel about what happened to Alex,' he felt obliged to make reference while he was fixing his pink gin, and she arranged the flowers in a vase and added lemonade, for it did work, to keep them fresh!

'Your letter was so kind. Everyone was so kind,' Georgette responded automatically, but in a tone that he stopped on the subject there and then. 'There, that's that!' And with a flourish she placed the vase in a prominent position.

Hugo rose, clasping her round the waist and drew her to him. 'Thank God I'm here at last! How marvellous it is to see you again! Now, my love, we can pick up where we left off.'

Georgette's immediate thought was, 'My God! What on earth is going on here? Malta wasn't that important to him, surely?'

She eased herself free of his hold and settled into an armchair while Hugo sank back onto the settee. They chatted in general terms about his life in Bahrain and how Angela was, about Georgette's new job and how Hugo came to be in London. It was just small talk, but it was pleasant and it took them through dinner. Hugo helped her with the washing-up, then said, 'Come and sit beside me, Georgette.'

She did, but not too close, so he moved closer to her, his freshly charged glass in his hand. 'To us!'

Georgette raised her own glass, which she'd refilled with ginger ale while he was in the bathroom, and clinked it against his. He'd behaved like a perfect gentleman up to now, but she didn't have to be a genius to sense what was coming next. She was decidedly nervous, and it showed.

'What's the matter with you?' Hugo quizzed, putting his glass down and snuggling up to her, one arm going around her shoulders with the hand hanging casually down to rest against her breast, while the other hand turned her face towards him. His intention was unmistakeable and Georgette was terrified.

In other circumstances she could have coped easily but, at this stage of her recovery, she needed to concentrate on her prime aim in life – to stay sober. She could not afford to get into a situation that might result in further emotional hurt and she knew she must stay clear of romantic entanglements. Besides, this particular man was married – 'Oh why do they all have to be married men?' – so any relationship with him was quite impossible anyway. That was one path she was never going to take again!

'Hugo, behave yourself!' she said, rising to her feet.

Hugo's voice rose in astonishment. 'What are you talking about, Georgette? When I was over here last year, you promised that whenever I got over from Bahrain for more than a few hours we could be together again. You didn't behave like an outraged virgin then!'

Georgette's heart sank. She had no recollection whatsoever of having seen him last year and his words implied that she'd done more than see him, but she wanted to know what had happened between them. 'What do you mean "together again"?'

Hugo looked at her askance. 'Come on, Georgette, stop kidding! I'm here for three days this trip. And I can't wait for a repetition of the glorious fun we had last time.'

'I'm sorry Hugo, but I honestly don't remember last time.'

'You don't remember going to Wheelers with me – and what happened afterwards?'

She shook her head.

'Well, I suppose you were a bit pissed.'

'What did happen?'

'You really showed me how much you'd learned since Malta! My God, you were magnificent! I've never had such a night! It was quite unforgettable!' Suddenly he grinned. 'Oh, I get it! You're having me on! Very good, Georgette – you really had me going there, you little minx!'

Georgette looked at him blankly, then lowered her head. 'I'm sorry, Hugo, but it isn't a joke. I really don't remember!'

Now he was really angry and rose to his feet, shouting, 'You're lying, Georgette! You have to be! It isn't possible that you could have forgotten something that was so wonderful!'

Georgette flinched as he grabbed her arms and shook her. 'But Hugo, I am telling you the truth!'

'How can you be?' he shouted back.

She was frightened by his rage and saw she had no choice but to admit the truth, so blurted it out: 'Because . . . because . . . I'm a recovering alcoholic! Until last November I was an alcoholic and, after a few drinks, my mind would go blank. Great chunks of my life are missing and it appears that your last visit is one of them.'

'But you're drinking now,' Hugo sneered disbelievingly.

'No, I'm not – my glass contains nothing but ginger ale. If you don't believe me, taste it.'

Hugo practically snatched up the glass, and took a large gulp. To his surprise, it was unmistakeably neat ginger ale, as she had claimed, and his anger drained away.

'Oh, Lord! Georgette! Whatever happened to you?'

She told him the whole story, and he sank back onto the sofa and listened without interrupting, not quite believing this was happening to him. This sensual woman, with whom he'd had the best sexual experience of his life was not only rejecting him, but couldn't even remember being with him.

When Georgette had finished talking, he just sat there, feeling humiliated.

'It's not just you, Hugo. I'm finding myself in this situation with all sorts of people. Even my own children! Can you believe that I didn't even remember my own daughter telling me she was going to migrate to Australia, and that I'd signed the consent form for her to do so?'

Hugo was now totally bemused. He did believe her. He'd met alcoholics before and her story had the ring of truth. But it was plain that, whatever had happened between them in the past, he was getting the brush-off now, and he was offended. He stood up abruptly. 'I think I'd better go.'

'Won't you have another drink, one for the road?'

'I don't really think so, Georgette. Thank you for dinner. Goodnight.'

He stalked out, and she knew she would never see him again.

Confused by Hugo's visit, and shaking a little as reaction set in, Georgette rang Judith at home and poured out the story of her evening, feeling better for having done so.

'Did your friend finish the gin?' was Judith's first question.

Georgette was surprised to find she didn't know. She looked over at the tray. 'No.'

'I'll hang on while you pour it down the sink,' said Judith, and Georgette did so quite happily, then returned to the phone.

'Judith, I didn't care! When Hugo left I didn't even think about the gin, and I didn't mind pouring it away just now. I still don't! I'm cured!'

But Judith pulled her down to earth.

'No you aren't, Georgette! Don't ever think that – not for one second! We've told you before, an alcoholic is never cured. It is just that you are beginning to learn that life without alcohol is possible, that you can survive perfectly well without it.'

They talked for a while longer and Georgette went to bed feeling at peace with the world.

June arrived, and Georgette flew out to Madrid for the GBE convention. Knowing that she would be looked after by her AA contact while in Spain, she had decided to extend her stay there and have a real holiday – her first since Jack had died – so her return flight was booked for a week after the convention ended. Nice of GBE to pay the airfare for her holiday, she thought smugly. Nor did she have to worry about accommodation because, naturally, GBE paid for her hotel during the convention and, when that ended, she would transfer to a small villa on the outskirts of the city that belonged to Judith.

Her hotel was large, airy and comfortable, but it had a drinks cabinet. She didn't care for the temptation, so called room service to have it removed. The waiter who appeared did as he was bid, obviously a little surprised by her request.

Tingling with excitement at the thought of exploring a new city, Georgette changed into lightweight clothes and went for a walk with some of her colleagues. They strolled aimlessly through the ancient streets of what had once been a Moorish fortress, and enjoyed the clean air of the highest capital in Western Europe, Madrid being set at a little over two thousand feet above sea-level.

They returned to the hotel, and Georgette was admiring the view from her window when the telephone beside her bed rang.

'Hi! Is that Mrs Barestone-Tailour?' the accent was very American and she knew at once it was her AA contact, who was stationed at the local USAF base.

'You have to be Michael?'

'Right! And you're Georgette. Welcome to Madrid. How are you?'

'A little tired from the journey and a long walk, but happy to be here.'

'That's great. Just remember this: if you're happy, tell your face!'

Georgette laughed in delight.

'So, you will be coming along with me tonight, Georgette?'

'I thought I would.'

'Okay! I'll meet you in Reception at your place at twenty after seven, so we can get acquainted. Then we have only to walk three blocks down to a meeting at eight.'

'How will I know you?'

'Oh, just look for a typical American – I'll be wearing a Hawaiian shirt, I guess, and light slacks. I'm six feet tall, have a blond crew-cut and a bit of a moustache. And I'll come through the door exactly on the button!'

She knew him at once. He was a striking figure, and no more than forty years old. What he had failed to mention to Georgette was that he was spectacularly good-looking. She thought Hollywood had really missed out there, and found it almost impossible to believe he was an alcoholic. There were certainly no physical signs of the addiction. And he was charming, too, attentive to her needs from the first moment.

As for Michael, he was instantly attracted to Georgette. She was a little plumper than he'd envisaged from her voice, but not gross, and with a lovely face. But he was not a man who went on looks alone and what really caught his fancy was her total femininity and a hint of helplessness that he detected. That really brought out his protective instincts and he could feel a stirring in his nether regions. That seldom happened on first acquaintance with someone.

They shook hands and, obeying an impulse, he bent to kiss her cheek.

'So this is your "friend"?' A female member of the GBE staff teased good-naturedly, happening to be in the lobby at the time. There was a trace of envy in her voice and Georgette knew what she was thinking. The company gossips would soon be busy, but at least nobody would think twice when she refused invitations to socialize after the official functions.

'If only you knew!' thought Georgette, and decided to provide some fire to go with the smoke. She put a hand on Michael's neck, pulled his head down and kissed him warmly, if briefly, on the lips. She knew, instinctively, that he would understand and she was not disappointed – he returned the kiss with more than a little pleasure.

Then he grinned at her, revealing even white teeth that showed off his tan, and she thought he was absolutely gorgeous. So, obviously, did her colleague, and Georgette did not attempt to introduce him. 'Let's go, Michael,' she said, her tone possessive.

He put an arm round her waist and led her away from the hotel. When they were well out of earshot, he turned to business. 'The meeting tonight will be conducted in Spanish. Will that bother you? I can translate, of course.'

'I don't think it will be necessary. I always try to learn something of the language of any country I am going to visit, so I have been studying Spanish ever since I knew Madrid was to be the venue this year. I haven't had a chance to actually speak it yet, or not so's you'd notice – just a few words with the hotel staff – but I have a good ear and I expect I'll understand enough to follow the proceedings. It will be good practise.'

'Terrific, honey! I'm impressed – and relieved. I'm real dumb when I set my mind to it, you see, and it was only when I was on my way to the hotel that I realized there might be a problem. We do have meetings in English sometimes, but there isn't one tonight.'

Georgette classed it as a good meeting. She did, indeed, manage to follow most of the speeches, consulting Michael only once or twice during that part of the proceedings. Afterwards, over the tea, some English was spoken as a courtesy to three Spanish-speaking American ladies who were present.

Michael escorted her back to the hotel and kissed her goodnight.

On the following two evenings he was waiting for her when she got away from the official functions and they had a meal somewhere before going on to an AA meeting.

She learnt that he was a USAF major, a pilot who had been grounded for medical reasons and was waiting to hear about his next posting. She did not need to be told that the 'medical reasons' had some connection with drink. 'So, for now, I'm footloose and fancy free – and entirely yours! Do with me what you will!'

She laughed and the conversation turned to more impersonal matters.

'Have you any family?' she asked him, and his reply was succinct. 'My wife left me, because of my drinking. Usual story. No kids.'

The convention was a great success. Once it was out of the way, Michael helped Georgette move her things to Judith's villa, then they took a trip to Avilla and the Monasterio de Santo Tomas. It was situated on a very high plateau in the lovely Sierra de Gredos, and Georgette thought it must be the nearest place to heaven. They travelled there by a little mountain railway that provided marvellous views as it climbed up to the plateau.

'Saint Teresa use to confess here, did you know that?'

'I don't think I've heard of Saint Teresa.'

The only Theresa she knew was no saint!

'Then I recommend you learn something about her. Teresa of Avilla was a sixteenth century Spanish nun, who was also a mystic. She was a quite remarkable lady. I guess you've heard of the Carmelite Order?'

'Of course.'

'She reformed that, amongst other deeds, didn't think it was strict enough, it seems. You should read her autobiography – I think it might help you. "The Way of Perfection" is its title, but she wrote other things and you should try to get her collected writings. There'll be copies in England, for sure. You being a woman, you might learn something from them.'

'Then I must!' Georgette readily agreed, but had no such intention.

The rest of their sightseeing was of a less spiritual nature, and she thoroughly enjoyed every second, especially relishing Michael's sense of humour, which livened up the most mundane sights. They laughed a great deal and she felt like a girl again.

On her last full day in Spain, a bright and glorious day, Michael took Georgette south to Toledo, to see the beautiful and ancient cathedral that looks protectively down on the town's fulvous buildings and narrow streets. Once it had been the capital of Spain, and Georgette found it a fascinating place.

In the souvenir shop, Michael pointed out a picture postcard of St Teresa and Georgette bought one. She couldn't see how a saint she'd never even heard of before could possibly be of value to her, but she thought buying the card would please Michael.

At dinner that night, in an intimate little place Michael knew, he was particularly attentive. In different circumstances, both knew, they would almost certainly have made love. Their mutual desire was apparent in every look, every movement and there was genuine affection between them, too. But both knew that it could not be – there was no room for reckless romance in either of their lives at that time.

Their short friendship was, necessarily, coming to an end, and the feeling between them was too strong to allow for a casual affair, so adding a physical dimension to their relationship would almost certainly create a bond that would be very painful to break the following day. That would put them both under unnecessary emotional strain and might result in one, or both, of them seeking consolation in a bottle. So, with regret, they both held back.

Michael saw Georgette to the airport the following day and, knowing the surroundings provided a safeguard against things getting out of control, pulled her gently to him and kissed her fully on the lips, a lingering goodbye kiss that was full of love and tenderness but held passion in check. She clung to him weakly, unmoving, until her flight was called.

In that week he had brought her alive, made her feel like a woman again. She knew that, as long as she lived, she would never forget that sweet farewell embrace. Spain had been an uplifting experience for her in every possible way.

As her plane took off, she choked back tears for the man she had come to love. She knew it was unlikely that they would ever meet again, but there would always be a special place for him in her heart. For he had consolidated her position on the path back to normality. He had proved to her, conclusively, that it was possible to enjoy life without the aid of artificial stimulants – and she was looking forward to doing just that.

Chapter Twenty Five

'So I was in my car, wasn't I, and this sod in a van cuts me up. Know what I does? Me anger's up, so I gets out of me fuckin' car and runs after the bugger! How stupid can yer get? D'yer think I'd do that if I was sober? Never!'

Quite spontaneously, the AA meeting dissolved into fits of laughter and Victor, who'd delivered the statement from the floor, readily joined in.

Only a moment before these same people had been sitting in sombre silence while a young man had broken down in tears from the effort of relating his early attempts to achieve sobriety. No one had moved to put an arm about him, no one had expressed sympathy, but all of them had understood, for all of them could relate similar experiences.

It was late 1972 and Georgette had been invited to this East London meeting as the guest speaker. In front of this small audience, largely of tough-looking men she felt she should prove that she was not there under false pretences and deserved calling herself an 'alcoholic'. So she concentrated on the dreadful things that had happened to her which she thought had made her turn to drink, then she had moved on to describe how awful her own behaviour was when she was drinking. Half an hour was the usual length of such talks, but she was still at it after fifty minutes.

Suddenly the Secretary, a lively Cockney, intervened.

'Georgette, can I cut in 'ere? Yer tellin' us a lot about 'ow yer comes to be alcoholic. Could yer not come now to tellin' us somefink about yer recovery, as time is goin' on?'

Georgette wished the ground would open up and swallow her. In that moment she became acutely aware that, while she had been sober for a long time now, she had still not dispensed with the pride and self-pity that had led her to drink in the first place. She still expected everyone to consider her a poor misunderstood soul who was struggling bravely against impossible odds, a wonderful person who was constantly victimized by people far less worthy than herself. She was embarrassed and said, hastily, 'Yes, you are right,

Harry. But I think I've spoken long enough, so I'll just stop here.'

The meeting was given to the floor, and when that young man spoke, Georgette realized that the poor lad must have been in agony, waiting to open his heart while Georgette rambled on and on. The humour of Victor that followed had been much needed to lighten the atmosphere.

After that meeting, Georgette took a really honest look at herself, and she didn't like what she saw.

She went back to the Twelve Steps, and her weekly 'Step' meeting on Saturday afternoons and tried to keep pride and self-pity at bay while she considered them again. She accepted that she had made less progress than she had thought, and resolved to do better, thanking Harry mentally for having given her such a jolt. In retrospect, she understood that his motive had been helpful. What a marvellous way he had found to deflate an ego that was as large as Montgolfier's balloon!

At an AA meeting one night in September 1973, Judith took Georgette to one side to tell her the tragic news that she had just heard from friends in Spain that Michael was dead.

Georgette's knees gave way at the shock, and she half fell onto a nearby chair. 'But he was so young and fit! What happened?'

'Alcohol was given as the reason.'

'Oh, no! How did he die?'

'He was on leave in the USA when the news of his next posting came through. He had already been passed over once and, since he could no longer fly, he had been banking on promotion to make his life on the ground more worthwhile, but he was told that he was not being promoted and apparently felt that was his last chance. He bought a bottle of scotch to drown his sorrows! His body couldn't take it: he had some kind of fit, followed by a heart attack, and died five days later.'

'When did you hear?'

'I got the details yesterday, from mutual friends in Spain. It's taken a couple of weeks to filter through, but I thought you'd like to know.'

Georgette went home shortly afterwards. Once in the privacy of her own flat, she cried her heart out for Michael. She felt devastated – ever since she'd returned from Spain she had drawn comfort from the thought of his apparent strength and gaiety, his ability to find something amusing in almost every situation. If a man with his qualities could slide . . . Georgette's fears now turned to herself. She clung even more tightly to her AA lifeline, accepted that she would have to continue to grow in AA in order to stay sober; that she should never allow herself to relax her guard completely. She wasn't sure she had the strength, shaken to the depth of her being by Michael's failure, but she was determined to control her emotions at all times and she was very grateful – self-pity can lead to disaster. *Poor me. Pour me*, all too often!

Recalling those very special days they had spent together, Georgette sought the postcard of St Teresa that she'd bought to please him. She found it at the back of a drawer and placed it on her mantelpiece. She began to be curious about the saint and, the following Saturday morning, she went to Hatchards in Piccadilly and bought a copy of the lady's complete works.

The saint's quite remarkable writings revealed that she had been a woman of action, a very down-to-earth person who had surmounted problems far greater than those that Georgette felt were practically insurmountable.

As she read the meditations, Georgette became more and more impressed. She went on to read the prayers as well, and decided that Saint Teresa would understand her problems. So she went to church and prayed to the Saint to give her the strength to remain sober and to become a better person. She did feel that someone was listening to her prayers, and was comforted.

'Let go, let God' – another of the legends posted on the wall of the meeting room at her first ever AA visit now began to make sense to her . . . at last.

'I was reasonably happy with myself until that meeting pulled me down,' she confided Judith's news to Arthur at Redcliffe Gardens.

'How unhappy are you now?'

'I've been miserable for at least half the time today.'

'So you've been quite happy for fifty percent of the time?'

'Yes.'

'Good! Then you're not back to where you were when you started to come here. At that time you were miserable ninety-five percent of the time. Look at it that way and you will see that you are well on the road to recovery. But no road is free of setbacks and that knock was good for you!' The chastisement was lightly delivered.

'When you're happy, tell your face,' she caught herself uttering dear Michael's words.

'Exactly that!' laughed Arthur. Georgette clutched at that straw of hope, and decided to look for others. Maybe, one day, she'd have enough put together to make firm ground to follow on life's path.

During the months that followed, Georgette continued to attend AA meetings. But now she did miss them occasionally in order to see Daisy Brown or Nancy Flowers. They had kept in touch with her since Alex's death and gradually their friendship had recovered its warmth.

Tom, now in his late seventies, was not in the best of health, which meant that Nancy was more-or-less housebound. They had given up their Dauphin Circus flat when Tom had retired and were living at their house in the country. But, whenever she did come up to town, Nancy would ring Georgette and they would spend an evening together.

Daisy, still as fit as a fiddle, quite often popped in for a chat over 'a nice cuppa'. Her bright conversation always cheered Georgette up.

Georgette was now really determined to understand the AA bible. She went over and over the Twelve Steps, until she could hardly stand the sight of them on the page. Dealing with pride gave her the biggest headache. She had admitted to herself that pride, false pride, was at the root of all her problems, but knowing that did not help her to overcome it.

In the meantime she was back in GBE's good books. She had always been efficient and, these days, she was once more smart, punctual and pleasant to deal with. Gareth Raistrick began to understand the president's interest in Georgette and forgot his resentment at the way she had gone over his head. He gave her added responsibility and a rise.

Since she had stopped buying alcohol, Georgette had got her finances under control and, despite the fact that she was now spending quite a lot on her appearance, and on taxis all round London to attend the AA meetings, she was able to save a little.

'You're like your old self,' Les Dykes told her one day, while he was visiting Lewisham. 'Everyone is saying that. And you were lovely then!'

252

She was delighted with this compliment, knowing that Les never went in for false flattery.

Now Georgette began to feel a sense of achievement in her task of self-discovery, however painful some of it was. She would sit at home writing down everything that might be construed as having harmed her fellow man. She forced herself to be honest and, gradually, the list grew into a sizeable document – almost a dissertation on living, but one that arose from not knowing how to live.

Although her soul-searching routine became established, it grew no less difficult. Distractions were always welcome and progress was slow.

One day, in desperation, she rang Judith at home. She was relieved to find her there and poured out her problem.

'I keep coming back to Steps Four and Five,' she blurted out. 'My moral inventory just keeps growing and growing, and I know it's my pride that is to blame for most of my problems. I must be an absolutely dreadful person, but I just don't seem to be able to control my pride!'

'You think you've got problems with those Steps? Allright, let's meet tonight half an hour before the meeting and discuss it over a cup of coffee.'

They did. Judith encouraged Georgette to keep it simple. 'Do as I had to, work at yourself in small doses and rejoice at the good progress you have made to date without constantly harping on what you consider is lack of achievement. Keep going to your "Step" Meetings every week and think positive.'

Two years went by and, gradually, Georgette came to terms with herself. She had found a contentment in sobriety. By slowing down, and undertaking only what she could achieve without overtaxing herself, she avoided strain and was able to take a relaxed attitude to life in general. She fought to keep her ego under control and to put herself down when she felt pride encroaching on her. She tried to adopt a loving attitude towards everyone: that didn't always work, but it did make her responsive to other people's problems. Self-pity and anger were brought under control.

She became less dogmatic, more tolerant. For the first time in her life she could see the other person's point of view; in short she had joined the *human race*. And that felt good.

Chapter Twenty Six

The long hot summer of 1976 arrived, and Georgette knew the time had come to consider her future. She was nearly fifty-five, and it would not be all that long until she had to retire.

She was thinking now was the time to leave GBE and get the sort of job that would give her priority on a council housing list when the time came to retire. A 'little bird' at an AA meeting had put that notion into her mind and she nurtured it.

Her back still gave her trouble from time to time but, after a rest on her orthopaedic bed – she had never stopped being thankful to Jack for that gift – she always felt better and had not needed to consult an osteopath for years. So, as long as her new job did not involve her being on her feet for long periods, she was sure that her back wouldn't be a problem.

Les Dykes listened to what she had to say and suggested that she could take early retirement if she wished. 'It will, of course, reduce your company pension, but you could then take on a job where you will no longer have to struggle to keep up with much younger people – all men! And I don't mean that unkindly.'

'I know that!' Georgette assured him, and understood clearly that by acting as he suggested she could avoid the rat-race altogether. Consequently, she arranged to take out the maximum lump sum available, and agreed to the smaller pension that doing this meant, because her first priority, as ever these days, was to steer clear of debt, and have some savings.

The next Saturday, while doing her food shopping, Georgette bought a local paper and consulted the Jobs Vacant section. There was nothing to interest her, but the following week's issue was more productive.

The local hospital authority were looking for a resident administrator at a Nurses' Home. One of the perks of the job was rent-free accommodation, so she would be able to save even if the salary was less than she was getting at present, which she was fairly sure would be the case though the pay wasn't stated in the advertisement.

She applied for the job and was duly interviewed by a panel of three women. The chairman was a Mrs Harrington, a person well-used to being in command. On her right sat a wispy white-haired lady with a kindly countenance, the sort of soul who serves teas at garden fetes. On Mrs Harrington's left was a very thin-faced woman with straight black hair hanging down around her jowl. By a few years, she and Mrs Harrington were younger than Georgette.

The room was sparse, accommodating only a table and four chairs. Its cream walls were bare, except for a couple of pregnancy-testing posters.

Georgette smiled brightly with each introduction, and took the chair proffered.

Just when she thought the interview was going her way, Mrs Arbuthnot, the thin-faced woman, said, 'I see you are fifty-four, Mrs Barestone-Tailour?' She made the fact sound like a fatal illness. 'You do realize that you would be responsible for the welfare of around a hundred young nurses?'

Georgette bridled inwardly, but kept her face and tone pleasant. 'My age does not mean I am incapable of handling the job. In fact, I think my experience of life should be invaluable when it comes to looking after young and inexperienced nurses. I am very healthy and all my faculties are unimpaired. ('Oh, yes?' she was instantly self-mocking.) From the job description, it is one well within my capabilities – you have my CV and work references.'

'Yes, indeed, and the references are excellent,' said the chairman, quickly. Mrs Harrington's warmth towards Georgette had been growing throughout the meeting and Georgette knew she had a strong ally.

'Are there any questions you would like to ask us?' said Mrs Harrington, finally.

Georgette had several, for it was not just the job in which she was interested. 'My accommodation at the Nurses' Home, what would that consist of?'

'One room and your own bathroom.'

'Oh, dear!'

'You don't approve?' Mrs Arbuthnot seized on the possibility.

'I'm afraid I would have to insist on having two rooms, as well as the bathroom, of course: one for living in and one for a bedroom.'

'It would be quite a big room,' said the white-haired Mrs Greenaway, reassuringly.

'Nevertheless. I am not used to living in a bed-sit.'

Georgette's tone was friendly but made it clear that, so far as she was concerned, the point was not negotiable, though she knew she must be pushing her luck by stating it.

Mrs Arbuthnot made to say something, but Mrs Harrington cut her off. She was convinced that Georgette was ideal for the job. The other applicants they had seen were not, in her opinion, a patch on this candidate. She knew that it would not be difficult to comply with Georgette's requirement and saw no point in prolonging the interview. 'Would you mind returning to the ante-room now, Mrs Barestone-Tailour? We won't keep you long.'

Georgette did as bidden. Ten minutes later she was called back into the interview room. Two of the three faces were all smiles, Mrs Arbuthnot's face being the odd one out, of course. 'We would like to offer you the job,' said the chairman.

'Thank you. But will I get my two rooms, Mrs Harrington?'

'You will.'

'And they will be communicating?'

Mrs Harrington laughed. 'Very well, Mrs Barestone-Tailour. If that's what you want, they soon will be!'

'I have a certain amount of furniture of my own which I would like to keep, so I would prefer the rooms to be unfurnished, if possible.'

'That will be no problem at all.'

'In that case, I accept the position, and thank you very much.' The relief Georgette felt at that moment was just wonderful.

Georgette took up her post a month later, moving into her new quarters on the weekend before she started work. She smiled as she saw the tell-tale signs that showed the communicating door had been introduced very recently. The rooms were not very large, and were utilitarian rather than attractive, but by the time she'd arranged her personal belongings the little suite was quite homely.

Leaving GBE was not the wrench Georgette had expected. Though she had made friends there, they were not close, and she thought it likely that they would lose touch before long. The only person she would really miss, she concluded, would be Les Dykes – and he was due to retire the following year. She left the firm quietly, with the best wishes of all, and a Westminster-chimes gold carriage clock, suitably inscribed.

* * *

Within days of settling in behind her new desk, Georgette felt completely at home. She thoroughly enjoyed her job; it was no strain for her after so many years at GBE in Sales and Administration. Nor did it escape her mind that the reason she might be particularly good at the work she was now doing lay in her genes – after all what she was doing was nothing less than hotel-keeping, albeit on a much less grand-scale than when Henri had done the work!

Thus, she quickly proved beyond all doubt to herself, let alone her bosses that she was a good manager – GBE's loss had to be the Health Authority's gain. And she got on particularly well with lanky 'Shorty' Fred, the chief handiman, and Mr Rolfe whose firm supplied much of the Nurses' Home with furnishings.

She pleased herself as to when she worked, provided she did the hours. As long as everyone knew where she was to be found, or what time she would be back, her working hours were her own. This enabled her to go to some afternoon AA Meetings and even to get more involved in AA administration work; now that she had handed over her Secretaryship of her Friday meeting, she had plenty of time to do AA paperwork in her flat while remaining immediately available to her charges and superiors, if required. She continued to serve on various panels of AA Speakers in the Community.

Thus, apart from an occasional re-occurrence of her feelings of remorse and guilt (over her conduct to others when she had been a drinker) which needed immediate checking and 'talking out' with other AA Members, she was now far more relaxed; and she even managed to laugh at herself when she made mistakes, recognizing that she was 'only human', after all! And, yes, it did help a lot to 'promptly admit it' when she she was wrong . . . just like the Steps said. Indeed, it even felt good sometimes to take the blame for someone else's mistake simply to avoid an argument.

One day in 1977 Georgette received a letter from Susan enclosing a picture of the latest addition to the family: a chubby baby with big blue eyes and seemingly no hair at all. She was to be christened Ingrid. Georgette thought her granddaughter was enchanting, and longed to go to the christening, but her return airfare to Perth would have made such a large hole in her savings that she contented herself with sending a card and a little pink dress that she made specially.

The authorities were totally satisfied with Georgette's performance. The Nurses' Home now ran smoothly and cost-effectively and word reached them that the high level of morale among the nurses was, in part, due to the close relationship they had with Georgette. Newcomers who complained about her strictness were swiftly informed by their fellows that she was regarded as a universal mother, the fount of all compassion and wisdom, and countless tales circulated about the way she'd helped one person or another sort out a personal problem.

Mrs Harrington was given the pleasant job of telling Georgette that she could stay in her job for as long as she felt she could cope – beyond retirement age if she wished.

But the day came when Georgette felt she had had enough of working and wanted to retire. She had achieved all she could at the Nurses' Home and would be leaving a smooth-running, happy ship to her successor.

She had become more and more conscious of her age with every year that passed since she had turned sixty. Nowadays she became easily tired, and wanted less and less to get into arguments. It wasn't that she'd lost interest, simply that she didn't have the energy.

She'd had enough of confrontations and of being on call all the time. She wanted to take things easy for whatever time was left to her, to enjoy the leisure activities for which she'd had no time in recent years, to relax.

'How sorry I am to hear this, Mrs Barestone-Tailour!' There was no doubting the sincerity in the voice of her boss when Georgette told her that she wished to resign. 'Are you quite sure you mean it?'

'I am, Mrs Harrington. I'm sixty-two. I've done the job for nearly eight years now and I don't think I can achieve any more. I'm beginning to tire and to need the rest.'

Mrs Harrington slipped from behind her desk to take a chair by Georgette. 'You have done so well for us,' she said, and proffered her hand warmly, whilst almost begging Georgette to remember not to take it too firmly for, sadly, she now had arthritic fingers; and they looked very swollen and crippling. Georgette did remember, for it was why Mrs Harrington usually avoided shaking hands if she could. As she released her light grasp, Georgette thought that her boss must be coming up to retirement soon herself.

'I'll be in need of accommodation, Mrs Harrington. I have nowhere to go.'

'Yes, of course. I'll contact the Borough's Housing Department for you.'

Within a week, a housing officer was calling on Georgette in her office. An open-faced man in his mid-forties with thinning fair hair down over his forehead introduced himself as Neil Willows.

Georgette found him quite charming, despite a flaring boil on his nose; and the fact that he had need of pebble-glasses when taking down particulars. 'So you hail from Belgium, Mrs Barestone-Tailour?' Willows spoke rhetorically.

'Brussels.'

'Came here just after the war, eh?'

'Yes, with my first husband.'

'Quite!' Willows paused, then said: 'We hold one or two flats in country places and at the seaside. Would that be what you'd like?'

'I'm afraid that would not do for me!' Georgette's response was more adamant than intended.

'Oh, I see!'

'Maybe you don't. I really do not like the country, you see. I have to live in London, please. If I may.'

Recognizing that Georgette was an educated person, and would fit into the locality he had in mind, Willows named a desirable garden suburb. To his surprise, Georgette rejected that, too. He proposed another, less salubrious, area but Georgette wouldn't have that, either.

'You certainly know what you want, Mrs Barestone-Tailour, I can see that.' There was a chuckle in the man's voice, where there could have been exasperation.

'Forgive me, Mr Willows, but I do. You see, if I don't tell you, you won't know.'

'Quite!'

'I need to live centrally. I want to be only a short taxi ride from the theatre, and places like that. Visiting them more often is what I want to do in my retirement.'

Willows fell to pondering. Finally he said, 'I could offer you Mormill Green Estate. That's very central – about a mile from here.'

'I'll take it!'

Willows had his doubts that she would like the place, but she obviously knew her own mind and he was relieved that he'd found something she'd accept. 'Very well, Mrs Barestone-Tailour. I could probably let you have a one-bedroom flat, with kitchen and bathroom, fairly quickly.'

* * *

Three days later the noise made by a handful of hardback books tumbling to the floor right outside her bedroom jolted Georgette out of slumber. She issued a resigned sigh and forced herself fully awake, in time to catch nervous, girlish giggles coming under the door from two student nurses, as they hastily retrieved their fallen tomes.

The last echo of the culprits' footsteps died away down the passage, as they hurried to an early lecture at the hospital, and silence reigned.

Georgette yawned, then removed a lace-edged shade from her eyes and blinked in the daylight that was permeating through her summery curtains. The alarm clock on the bedside table stated eight-twenty and she decided to get up.

She performed her ablutions, then threw open her curtains, to look up at the sky, above the array of rooftops and backs of buildings that were her daily first sight of London. She was anxious, as ever, to determine the weather. On this June day, she saw it might not be that sunny.

'Well, that's not wanted!' she muttered to herself, and instinctively pulled tighter about her a blue quilted dressing-gown. She went into her living-room to prepare her morning mug of coffee, and while the coffee percolated, she sat at the dressing-table and carefully rubbed some still clinging sleep from the corners of her eyes before picking up her hairbrush. Thanks to regular visits to the hairdresser, her hair these days was light brown but allowed to show some grey. It was styled short and worn off her brow to add height to a face that was now rather round.

'You're gross!' she dismissed her appearance, in a voice devoid of dismay. In truth she wasn't over-fleshy, having lost some of her excess weight since she started work at the Nurses' Home, just pleasantly plump. She had welcomed the less-striking appearance that came with age but, for her years, she was still unusually good-looking.

By nine-thirty, half an hour later than usual, Georgette was neat and elegant in a classical dress of blue and white. She was ensconced in her office, a modest room with panelled windows that looked out onto the building's vestibule. She was sorting the mail when she found a letter for herself and recognized the franking logo – it was from the Housing Department and she hoped it would contain an offer of somewhere for her to live in her retirement.

But she dutifully finished sorting out the nurses' letters before opening her own. The letter offered the tenancy of No 48 Emhart House, Mormill Green, and to enable her to view the place the keys could be collected at the Housing Department . . .

* * *

The eight storey block of flats looked soulless and dispiriting in the way that only pre-stressed concrete buildings can. The taxi driver had looked surprised when she gave him the address, and now, as he drew up outside the flats, and told she might be living there, he said, 'This is a terrible place, there's always trouble round here. It's no place for a lady like yourself.'

Georgette said nothing. 'Mormill Green' had sounded quite cosy when Mr Willows of the Housing Department had said it! The letter offering her the flat had mentioned that the block had been named after a late, much-loved councillor, Emily Margaret Hart. She shuddered. 'Poor Councillor Hart, you must be turning in your grave knowing such a place is named after you! So much hideous concrete!' She took the lift to No 48. It groaned as if begrudging the fact that it had to carry her upwards. An overpowering smell of disinfectant barely covered something more unpleasant, and obscene graffiti had only partially been removed from its walls. As she stepped from the cage she was hit by a cold wind. She was standing on a walkway, open to the elements. Its view was towards central London and Georgette found that at least, reassuring. Below, she could see her taxi waiting patiently.

Ceiling lights were studded along the length of the corridor beyond a pair of glass doors but they were obviously only for night-time use. She scanned the numbers along the gloomy passageway and found the even numbers were on the right, which meant that she would have the view she had seen from the lift. At last a plus! Two numerals screwed to a white painted door proclaimed '48'.

'There is no one living there,' a gravelly voice informed her. 'Heard a sound. Came out to look,' the voice continued. An elderly man with thick grey hair and dull, button eyes was leaning against the door jamb of No 46. He smiled at her, revealing many missing teeth. 'They expect me to live here,' she said in a superior tone, as he began fiddling with his braces which were supporting baggy grey trousers whose turn-ups sagged over grimy carpet slippers. 'You've got keys then?' She held them out, and turned to let herself into the narrow hallway which led to a small room with a dirty window. The walls of the bedroom and the living room were covered with hideous green wallpaper with a pattern of vase-shaped swirls, and paintwork that could only be described as expletive-deleted brown.

They must be joking if they think I'm going to live here, she thought to herself. The open-plan kitchen's decor was slightly less gloomy but greasy dirt was engrained in every corner. But when she opened the bathroom door to her amazement she found it was both modern and charmingly decorated, and also clean! But the minuses by far outweighed the pluses and she couldn't wait to get out and get back to her waiting taxi.

'But we haven't anywhere else!' Mr Willows told Georgette some forty minutes later. He was sympathetic, but adamant. 'As I told you at our first interview, Mormill Green Estate is the only place that qualifies. You have been offered a place there, and if you refuse it then I'm afraid you will be crossed off our list altogether. Those are the rules, and there is nothing I can do about it.'

'That's stupid!' she retorted.

'You are entitled to think that,' he replied in a stubborn tone. 'Take my advice, Mrs Barestone-Tailour. Go back to Emhart House tomorrow, and have another look at it before you make a final decision. Our tenants there are all older people, mostly pensioners, so it's generally nice and quiet. I really don't think you'll be unhappy there.'

'But I know I *will* be unhappy!'

'Well, it's up to you. But I repeat, if you hand back those keys, that's all we can ever do for you.'

Shaken more than a little by that ultimatum, Georgette left, still clutching the keys to No 48. She recognized the unpalatable truth – it was Emhart House or nothing. She really had no choice.

PART FIVE

June 1983 and onwards

Chapter Twenty Seven

Georgette's mind came back to the present. Once more she became aware of rain hitting the windows, moving faster down the glass now for a strong wind had blown up to drive it so.

She wiped away her tears then, still sitting on her folding chair in the main room of the flat she had been offered in Emhart House, she gave herself a good talking to.

'Now come on, Georgette. There are only a couple of weeks left until you have to leave the Nurses' Home, so this is it and you might as well make the best of it. You won't be living on the landing, or in the corridor, so don't worry about them. You will be living in here and there's a lot that can be done to make it habitable. To start with, you are remarkably lucky because you have access to skilled decorators at the Health Authority who will put the decor right at a reasonable price. 'Shorty' Fred told you he and his mates would be happy to help out at way below their normal charges, didn't he? So take him at his word.

'And hasn't Mr Rolfe always said that he can pick up large pieces of carpet left over from big contracts and that all you had to do was let him know if you wanted some? So take him up on his offer, too. He said he can usually get any colour you like, so long as it isn't patterned, and that all you would have to pay would be the labour costs for laying it.

'The rest you can do yourself because, after they've done the major jobs, there won't be much wrong with the flat. So stop dithering and get on with it!'

That very weekend, Fred and his mates stripped off all the loathsome wallpaper, filled in various holes that were revealed by so doing and scrubbed down all the woodwork. Discovering the truly disgusting state of the kitchen cupboards, they scrubbed those down too, and Fred cleaned all the windows. They all liked Georgette, and wanted to see her comfortably settled, so they considered they were working for a friend rather than a Nurses' Home employee and put their hearts into it.

Over the next few days they put up the wallpaper Georgette had chosen and gave every wooden surface in the place at least two coats of good-quality white paint. One of them even brought in some adhesive drawer and shelf liner he happened to have at home and fitted it into all the kitchen cupboards. By the time they had finished the whole place was spotless and cheerful.

Then Mr Rolfe came and his men laid thick heavy-duty carpets in every room but the kitchen and bathroom. In these he used a good-quality carpet-tile. Georgette had purchased a new stove, a small refrigerator and a new washing machine that did the complete cycle.

Fred tightened the power points up and then did all the other odd jobs he could find that needed doing. By the end of the week the flat was transformed and ready for occupation – and all for a little over seven hundred pounds.

While the men were at work, Georgette had busied herself making curtains, for the first time in her life, for the quite large windows, and lampshades for the living-room, bedroom and hall. She had neon in the bathroom and kitchen.

She had worked out where she wanted to put her larger items of furniture and the removal man that Fred had recommended was very helpful. He and his son moved all her chattels into No 48, without damaging anything at all, and stayed to help her get them into some sort of order. They didn't unpack her tea-chests, of course, and she intended to take her time about that, spreading it over a few days so that she didn't get too tired. But they helped her position all the furniture, and did not complain when she suddenly changed her mind about where in the bedroom she wanted to place her orthopaedic bed – which meant moving her wardrobe, too.

Even with just the bare necessities in position, the flat was now very nice and Georgette was looking forward to settling in.

She returned to the Nurses' Home to attend a small farewell party Mrs Harrington had laid on for her. Nurses who were not on duty attended and she received many farewell cards and small gifts of appreciation. Knowing how hard up the students were, she was really touched by their generosity. Mrs Harrington presented her with a beautiful warm Icelandic scarf – it was of pure wool, but patterned, as the wool was of different colours.

Less touching than these personal presents, but of vital importance, was the fact that she would also receive a small monthly pension. It wasn't much but, with her GBE pension and the State pension, it would keep the wolf from the door.

Even after she moved in, at the end of June 1983, Georgette still felt that Mormill Green Estate was a bit beneath her! She was happy inside her flat but her heart sank every time she went out. For the first couple of weeks she had to keep reminding herself that she was extremely lucky – given the slope she had been on, she might well have ended up as a down-and-out with no roof at all over her head.

Once she was properly settled, surrounded by her photographs and other personal bits and pieces, she appreciated how very pleasant it was. The apartment building might look horrible from the outside, but she didn't have to look at it very often. Most of the time she was inside, and able to look out at a wonderful panoramic view of buildings. In summer the flat was very light and cheerful and, when winter came, she discovered that the central heating worked like a dream.

She soon got to know the two caretakers-cum-maintenance men who were responsible for her block, and got on with both very well, so they never kept her waiting long when she needed some small repair done. There were shops on the estate, and she found they were willing to save her a wasted journey by putting aside the things she wanted – she just had to phone and let them know what she needed.

There was also a hairdresser, but she only went to him occasionally, she didn't need that extra expense. She no longer cared if the grey showed and it was too short to need real styling, so she went to the hairdresser only when she required a cut and a perm.

It was all very convenient and, after a time, she honestly couldn't think of anything in particular that would add materially to her comfort – except a bit more money. Although there was no single thing that she needed, she would have liked to dispense with the necessity to watch every penny, would have liked to afford the odd luxury. She had her savings, but she was determined to keep them for emergencies.

Then the solution came to her: she was still blessed with good eyesight and firm hands, so why not offer her services as a needlewoman? Not only would that provide the extra money she desired, but it would also give her something to do with her hands while she listened to Radio Four.

Full of enthusiasm, she advertised in 'The Lady' and immediately received several replies. They all became regular customers and she did not need to spend her precious money on further advertisements as they, and their friends, produced as much work as she could handle. Another irony – all those dreadful years in childhood having to learn sewing were now working for her!

She no longer had to juggle with her fairly low household bills and she could afford to buy the necessary clothes she could not make for herself: a new mackintosh or sensible shoes. She even had enough left over to cover the luxuries she'd missed: a good meal out, a visit to the theatre, a taxi home when she was tired from walking round a museum or art gallery, a box of good chocolates, a train fare to visit the Flowers, or a fancy cake to offer Daisy when she called.

Daisy, who'd lost her husband for a few years now, was now eighty, and had slowed down a lot, but she had more vigour than many people half her age and Georgette marvelled at her undiminished enjoyment of life – no sign there of senility.

Tom Flowers, on the other hand, was almost ninety, bedridden and stone deaf. Nancy, beginning to feel her own age, had taken on a full-time nurse for him, but she did not like to leave the house for long as she felt that he could not possibly survive for very much longer.

If Georgette didn't socialize with her neighbours, it was less because she didn't care for them than because she didn't want to intrude. As she saw things, they were very much keep-to-themselves types, and she wanted her privacy, too, But if she got to hear that someone in her block was not well, or in need of help, she would always offer her services.

Sometimes her offer was refused, sometimes accepted, but word of her kindness spread through the grapevine and everyone was very pleasant and helpful towards her – even the few rough-looking youngsters that hung around the estate for want of anywhere more interesting to go. Despite the dire warnings she had received before she moved in, Georgette never saw the least sign of violence on the estate, and very few signs of racial prejudice.

Georgette even grew to like the old man next door, whom she had met on her first visit, who had a heart of gold despite his unpromising exterior – rather like the flats, she thought. She no longer saw him as beneath her.

She has finally learned to 'live and let live' – the fifth and last of the aphorisms that she had seen posted on the walls at her first ever AA Meeting, and she was always to see displayed at every subsequent meeting, whether at home or abroad.

In 1987 Georgette heard the sad news that Nanny Trotter had died and, shortly afterwards, poor Tom Flowers finally gave up his tenuous hold on life. Nancy, now in her mid-seventies, seemed to acquire a new lease of life and came up to town regularly to take Georgette to the theatre or out for a really good meal.

'Goodness, my dear, I can afford it!' she said, when Georgette tried to pay her way. 'I don't suppose I've got long to go myself and whatever's left over will then go to some distant relations of Tom's – I hardly know them, but that's what he wanted and I don't have relations of my own any more. So I intend to enjoy it while I can – and I like your company.' That was the end of that argument and Georgette settled for repaying Nancy's hospitality by cooking her a lovely meal from time to time.

Photographs stood or hung in frames all round Georgette's living-room and bedroom. Of her father and mother, of Beatrice and Albert, of Andre – very faded, those three, of Alex, of Susan, of Anthony – now a bright-looking teenager with long blond hair and the finely chiselled nose so characteristic of the Barestone-Tailours, and of Ingrid – Georgette often wondered if she would ever meet her grand-daughter. A picture taken at a night-club during her last visit to Brussels showed herself flanked by Monique and Maurice. There was even a press-photo of her and Monique taken on Liberation Day in Brussels. Maurice had taken the trouble to get a copy after Georgette's last visit to him.

She regretted that she did not have one of Michael. Or of Simon Tait, of whom she thought about a lot of late – she should have slept with him, they'd both wanted sex. They would have been good together, she was sure of that. He was so sexy, so desirable, so delightful.

Nevertheless, all in all, Georgette was happier now than she had been at most periods of her life, relaxed and benign. There had been good times, certainly, but not for all the tea in China would she have wanted to turn back the clock and re-live the bad ones.

She felt she was no longer climbing slopes in life because, obviously, she didn't have to anymore. Well, that is how she saw things. Who would be interested to know that? Dear, sweet, Amanda Freshwood, of course, who, Georgette had learned through a chance meeting with an acquaintance at the theatre a year ago, was now doing missionary work in Africa – at her age!

Deeper consideration of her conclusions would have told Georgette that, as she felt herself to be on a 'high', if she wasn't on a slope now then she must be on a plateau of some kind. And if it were the one with paradise at its end she might hope that she wasn't due to reach it quite yet . . .

Whilst sewing a frayed skirt one afternoon for a customer, Georgette was thinking of Susan and that it had been a while since she had heard from her. The very next day, the post brought a letter from Perth – Susan and Roger and the children were coming to England the following month. Their parents could now afford for Tony and Ingrid to make such a trip, glad for them to meet 'Grandma B-T.' Roger was now a senior partner with a successful insurance broker and, over the past few years, he had made occasional business trips to London. At Susan's request, he had made a point of looking in on Georgette each time, if only for half an hour. So they knew that her drinking really was a thing of the past, and Roger had got over his wariness and come to like Georgette.

'We'll be staying at a London hotel for a couple of nights, and I'll ring you as soon as we arrive,' the letter said.

Georgette could hardly wait.

A month later, as promised, Susan rang Georgette to tell her they had arrived safely and were at a hotel off Great Portland Street. It was just after ten o'clock in the morning.

'We're all totally exhausted, Mummy. We know we must try to keep going until a reasonable hour: if we go to bed now, we'll never get over the jet-lag. But we'll be rotten company today, so we thought we'd just take a river trip to Greenwich – interesting without being too strenuous and the river breeze should keep us awake. Then we'll get a really early night and see you tomorrow – may we come for lunch?'

The next day the four arrived absolutely on time. Georgette had fussed about all morning to make sure the place was looking its best and the meal she had prepared, a simple roast, would be done to perfection. She was surprised to realize that she was very nervous.

Ingrid was the first to step into the flat. She was a very pretty child of ten, her dark hair held back by a wide red ribbon and her brown eyes bright and inquisitive as she looked at Georgette. She was wearing jeans and a T-shirt under a light wind-cheater, though it was not windy. 'Hallo, Granny,' she smiled, 'I've been longing to meet you!' Georgette thought that sounded a bit rehearsed and wasn't sure it was true.

'And me you, sweetie!' Georgette leaned down and kissed her firmly on both cheeks.

Tony, now five feet ten inches tall and still growing, hastily held out his hand in greeting and Georgette sensed he was dreading that she might kiss him, too. A little hurt, she spared his blushes. He looked very grown-up. He wore bleached jeans with a broad black belt, an open-at-the-neck cream shirt under a dark jacket, just beginning to be too short in the sleeve, and a pair of trendy trainers. Having shaken hands, Tony self-consciously gathered a handful of his straight long hair and shot it lazily back off his brow. The action revealed a cluster of adolescent spots.

While Tony and Ingrid looked round the living-room, Georgette turned to Susan and Roger. She was uncomfortably aware that her nervousness was making her welcome gushings sound false.

'Well, what are your plans during your stay?' Georgette asked, as she served the lamb a while later.

It was Susan who answered. 'Tomorrow Roger is taking the kids to watch the Changing of the Guard, then they want to see the dinosaurs at the Natural History Museum.'

'And the Tower of London!' prompted Ingrid.

'And Madame Tussauds and the Planetarium as well, if there's time. I'm going to be busy!' laughed Roger.

'Meanwhile, I thought I'd come and see you,' stated Susan.

Georgette was a bit surprised at that. 'Well, yes, of course, dear. That would be lovely. But don't make it too early, please – I'm a late riser normally, remember.'

'I intended coming about one o'clock, Mummy, after I've done a bit of shopping. I'll grab a snack while I'm at it, so don't bother about feeding me.'

'Then we're going to Grandpa's,' Ingrid piped in again. 'That'll be beaut!'

'Too right!' Tony agreed, his mouth full of lamb. 'He's promised to take me onto *HMS Victory*!'

'The kids and Susan will stay with Dickie while I clear up an odd bit of business,' said Roger. 'Then we head for Stratford-upon-Avon and will see whatever's on at the Shakespeare theatre – the hotel are arranging seats for us. After that it's a leisurely drive up to the Scottish Highlands. Susan wants the kids to see a bit of the English countryside, and we're likely to make a few detours en route, because I want to see the graves of some of my forefathers. When we've finished exploring, we dump the car at Glasgow and fly back to London – just in time to connect with our flight back to Oz.'

'I can see you'll all need a couple of months to recover from this holiday!' said Georgette with a laugh.

* * *

The next day Susan bought two dresses in Harrods and was well pleased with them. 'I think Roger will have a fit at the prices, though!' she chuckled, as she showed them to Georgette.

'But you enjoyed yourself buying them,' concluded Georgette, offering her daughter a large mug of fresh-ground Kenyan coffee.

'Oh, absolutely! And it's so nice to get away from the kids for a while!'

'So what's bothering you?' Georgette suddenly asked.

'Mummy?'

'Darling, you wouldn't be here by yourself if you didn't want to talk to me about something in particular.' Her tone was slightly abrasive – she knew her daughter would not be spending time with her entirely out of pleasure.

'That's true. Mummy, I've got fibroids!'

'Well, that's not uncommon!'

'I've been advised to have a hysterectomy.'

'That's not uncommon, either.'

'But we'd like to try for one more child, you see. What do you think I should do?'

'We'd like a lot of things we can't have, darling! You have two lovely healthy children, already. You're nearly forty and the next one might not be so perfect. If I were you, I'd count my blessings and leave well alone. You have to use sanitary towels, I take it?'

'Yes.'

'Then I suggest you have the hysterectomy. You'll feel much better afterwards.'

'But it'll affect my sex life with Roger!'

'That's not necessarily true, and you'll find a way round any problems. I'm afraid that you'll probably put on weight, but that's part of the price – and a bit of extra flesh will suit you, in my opinion. Remember this, too, babies and small children take a lot of energy – and that's something you have less of as you get older. Believe me, I know. Surely you're finding that already, aren't you?'

'I must admit I do seem to have less stamina these days, so I think you're probably right. But that wasn't the only reason I wanted to see you, Mummy.'

There was a long pause, so Georgette murmured encouragingly, 'Go on, dear.'

'Well, it's just that I now understand a lot of things that I didn't understand when I was younger, but there's still a lot I don't understand and I thought it would be nice to have a little time alone to talk.' She paused again, then blurted out, 'I was so unhappy when

I was a child! I was always beating myself up mentally, wanting things to be different! It was the same for Alex. We both loved you, but we felt that you didn't return our love and we didn't know why, what we were doing wrong. I still don't – and I'd like to.'

'It wasn't you that was doing something wrong, darling, it was me, but I couldn't help it. I was brought up by parents who seldom spoke to each other and didn't know how to demonstrate their affection for me. So I grew up starved of affection and self-trained to hold back my own feelings. I have always felt very awkward when in a position where I was expected to express my emotions, and have never been able to get over the inhibitions that became so deep-rooted in me. It was only after I grew up that I began to understand that my parents actually did care for each other, and for me. By then it was too late for me to change. I tried very hard to show you that I did love you and Alex, but I just didn't seem to have the knack and everything came out the wrong way.'

'I see. Thank you for telling me. At the time I thought there must be something wrong with me, something that stopped you loving me in the way that my friends' mothers loved them. Later on, I thought that, in some way, I must be responsible for your drinking! I tried to help, but your constant fault-finding just convinced me even more that everything was my fault! So I had to get away. I was so lucky to find Roger! He was so understanding, and gradually built up my self-confidence. His love helped me to find myself and become a whole person. Now I can look back on the wretched period dispassionately and, if it's not too late, I would like us to become friends.'

'My darling, I'd like nothing better. I'm so very glad that you found Roger, and that he stopped you from making the same mistakes with your children as I did with you. My solution was in AA, not nearly so pleasant. But I think I have at last become a real person. I'm at peace with myself now and that enables me, for the first time in my life, to look forwards.'

Susan gulped at her cooling coffee, then said gently, 'Mummy, why don't you come to Australia to visit us? You can stay as long as you like and we'll have plenty of time to get to know each other properly.'

Georgette's immediate reaction was not 'How wonderful!' but rather that she might meet Simon Tait if she did. After all, he'd been living in Western Australia last she knew, she was sure of that. 'Was it Kalgoorlie? Oh, why can't I remember?' continually antagonized her. And the tremor of delight that spread warmly through her at the prospect of being with Simon again finally convinced her of something she had long suspected – he had always remained in her consciousness because she loved him. She was now sure that deep down she had loved him from day-one – more than forty years ago. He'd been much more self-assured than either of her husbands or any of her lovers; with Simon in her life she might have been a different person altogether . . .

Then reality came to Georgette, brought her back to earth. 'That's sweet of you, Susan, darling, but I couldn't possibly afford the fare! I'll save up, though!'

'How stupid of me! I hadn't even considered that,' said Susan. 'I suppose I'm so used to Daddy popping over that I never saw it as a problem. I know the firm paid Ralph's and my air fare, but we've used all our spare cash to fund this trip.' She brightened again. 'Never mind – I'll start saving, too, as soon as we get back – a few dollars every week will soon mount up. I've made up my mind, Mummy – you shall spend your seventieth birthday with us, down under!'

That was a good three years away, so Georgette reckoned that both she and Susan had plenty of time to change their minds, and she accepted gracefully. The talk turned to lighter subjects until Susan left, in the early evening, to rejoin her family.

Chapter Twenty Eight

Over the next two years Georgette's health deteriorated noticeably as old age began to take its toll. She was so tired that she began to have daily naps in the afternoon and often experienced a touch of giddiness. Her feet were a little swollen most of the time, making walking a bit painful, and arthritis had begun to attack her fingers. That, combined with failing eyesight, forced her to give up her needlework, and thus her pin money, but she didn't mind, because she no longer desired the outings which that money had provided. She had enough, from her pensions, to buy food and pay her household bills, and that was all she needed. She was perfectly happy to stay in her cosy flat, watching the television and reading her favourite magazines – with the aid of glasses, her eyesight was still good enough to do that. She kept in close touch with AA and went to day-time meetings once a week.

Her closest friends, Daisy Brown and Nancy Flowers, had both passed on, Daisy's death coming as rather a shock since, right to the end, she had been healthy and active. If Georgette had no desire to pursue a social life she was not lonely. Since their chat on Susan's last visit to London, her daughter's letters had become fairly frequent and loving. The children had taken to writing to her, also, chatty letters about how each was getting on at school and what each had been up to in the holiday. Like Georgette, Susan was still saving for Georgette's visit to Australia the following year. Georgette was, all in all, more than content; and the 'glow' from getting nearer to Simon Tait, too, was still within her.

She might have gone on being satisfied with her lot had she not chanced to pick up not her usual woman's magazine at her newsagent.

When she realized what she had done she couldn't be bothered to return to the shop, so she gave a light sigh and settled down to read the unfamiliar magazine. One illustrated feature included mention of a series of forthcoming lectures on natural disasters which was to be given in Cambridge during February and March. A small coloured panel in the centre of the article gave the precise details and

Georgette froze as she caught the word 'Rusby'.

She looked more closely, and her coffee cup went down so heavily that the liquid splashed into the saucer. Giving the lecture on Wednesday 14 March, 1990, was a history faculty doctor, one David Rusby!

The conversation she had had with Dougie had said that her son had just been made a history don – surely there couldn't be two David Rusbys at Cambridge with such a distinction? The lecturer had to be 'her' David.

For the first time a chance had arisen for her to see him anonymously at close quarters. As a member of the public ostensibly interested solely in his lecture, she could watch him, listen to him – and he would not even know she was there! That was important, because Dougie had said that David regarded Thelma as his mother and not for the world would she wish to upset his life by making a reappearance at this late stage. Dougie had kept her informed of major events, and she knew that David had married his June and, a year later, had a son named Peter. The boy would be sixteen now, Georgette realized, and obviously he would think of Thelma as his grandmother.

Now, suddenly, God was giving her a chance to see her son again without upsetting his life, and she regarded that a reward for her self-sacrifice. Or was it a temptation that could put her sobriety at risk . . .?

To see David again was what she had longed for ever since he had been torn from her by the court's decision. The ache in her heart grew, as she remembered the pain of that time, and she began to cry. But the tears were of happiness – her greatest wish, but one suppressed, was now within her reach.

'Oh, God! I thank you!' she sobbed freely. 'I shall see my boy!'

Her cup rattled against the saucer, as she made to raise it to her lips, and she saw her hands were shaking. Quickly she took a swallow of her coffee and told herself to calm down. She decided to speak to Judith at AA about it, seeking advice before making a decision. She told Anne and Arthur, too, and other members she had known for years, and they all agreed that if she felt strong enough to resist the temptation of approaching David she would be safe and all would be well.

David's lecture did not sound at all Georgette's cup of tea – 'Starvation in Late Seventeenth Century Northumberland', but she longed for the day, still more than a month away. She was pleased to note that the talk was not due to start until five p.m., and that none of the lectures in the package was scheduled to last longer than one hour. That meant she could get up at her usual late hour and still not have to hurry to be there on time and, afterwards, she would not have to rush to get home at a reasonable hour, so she could plan a pleasant day's outing.

That very afternoon, she rang British Rail to ask about train times. The 13.35 from King's Cross sounded admirable, as it would get her into Cambridge in time to have afternoon tea there before the lecture. She was sure there would be somewhere suitable not far from the DPMMA ('whatever those initials, stand for!') Lecture Hall in Mill Lane.

The return fare came as a nasty shock, till she appreciated she could get a concessionary fare! But she would have paid whatever, and she was glad that she had her nest-egg to draw on.

Time dragged as she waited for the big day. Georgette's mood varied from listlessness to impatience, from anticipation to doubt. Maybe she had leapt to the wrong conclusion and the lecturer was not her son, at all. Should she try to contact Dougie (who was now a retired brigadier) and check with him? She had his address. But Dougie might try to dissuade her from going. And that would never do! Worse he might tell David to expect her, and that would never do, either!

Then came a thought that, at the last minute, David would be unable to give the lecture for some reason and someone else would deliver it for him. Would she be able to stand the disappointment if that happened?

'Should I go at all? How will I behave when I see him?' She feared that she might behave uncharacteristically, and make a fool of herself in some way, since we are all unfathomable, even to ourselves. The sight of David might unlock such deep-seated emotions that she would lose control and disgrace herself in front of him. 'Stop projecting,' she told herself. 'Keep calm and take it easy.'

She had to discipline herself. 'Just for today' was as hard as ever it had been, but she still read it daily, and applied it to her life to the best of her ability. She was sure that it would give her strength when that particular 'today' came, but the wait was agonizing. She went to many AA Meetings to gather strength and curb her emotions.

At last 14 March arrived. Most of the country was to have a cold day but in the south the winter sun came out early and lifted the temperature.

Georgette woke earlier than usual, tingling with excitement.

As she threw back the curtain and opened her top window to let the fresh air in while she was in her bath, she heard the contented sound of chirping birds. She considered that a good omen and it perked her up. Yesterday the weather had been in keeping with the season, and she considered the spring-like feel of today as another good sign. 'God must think I deserve cheerful weather for such a special occasion!' she told herself.

She had made an appointment for a cut, shampoo and set with the hairdresser on the estate and, after she'd had a cup of coffee and her usual croissant, she enjoyed the short walk there.

'So where are we off to today, Mrs Barestone-Tailour – somewhere special?' asked Neville, the young coiffeur, as, having washed her hair, he snipped skilfully at her locks. 'Mind you, one should always look one's best, I say. You never know who you are going to meet by the day's end.'

That innocently delivered comment sent a weird sensation through Georgette, for she did know, only too well.

'Off to see your sugar daddy, I expect!' Neville laughed.

'Keep it a secret, Neville!' Georgette joined him in laughter. 'No, I'm off to see my oldest son. He's a don at Cambridge!'

'A schoolmaster, like?' It didn't matter to Neville what the actual truth was, he was but humouring a customer, part of his job, he considered.

Georgette came away from the salon feeling very good for, like most women, she seldom felt so prepared to face life as when her hairdresser had done a good job.

She returned to her flat and put on her smartest outfit, adjusting the hat, that best complimented it, carefully so that she did not disturb Neville's work more than necessary. Then she considered her reflection with satisfaction. She felt she looked much younger than she was, and definitely a woman of taste.

As she was about to leave for the station, her eye was caught by one of the photographs of Alex and a sudden impulse came over her. She went over to the picture and kissed the face within it, repeating the process with photographs of Susan, Anthony and Ingrid.

'Never done that before!' she thought, and concluded that it was some sort of reassurance to them that she loved them even if she was going, with a singing heart, to see her first-born.

The sun was now at its peak and Georgette enjoyed the warmth while she waited for a passing taxi to take her to King's Cross.

She reached the station early and had time to purchase some

cigarettes and matches and then find the smoking carriage. She could no longer afford to save for Australia and smoke regularly, and had given up in principle. But she had found that she was able to enjoy the occasional cigarette without the addiction returning – and today certainly qualified as a special occasion.

She wanted a window seat facing the direction of travel, and that proved to be no problem as she had the compartment almost to herself, a reflection on modern society's attitude towards smoking. Feeling very excited, Georgette really needed a cigarette to calm her down, and she drew heavily on it as the train pulled away from the platform.

She enjoyed the journey, as the Cambridge train was routed through much beautiful countryside. There were cows grazing in some meadows and horses in others. The placid sheep were accompanied by little lambs that frisked around them like children at play. What a delight! Georgette giggled at their antics and, suddenly, liked the world.

Her cigarette finished, Georgette took from her handbag a sandwich she had prepared for her lunch, to keep her going until it was time for the big afternoon tea she had promised herself – a treat that she had not enjoyed for some years. She visualized little cucumber sandwiches, followed by scones and a cream cake, and looked forward to the spread.

Soon a burly taxi driver was dropping Georgette off in Mill Lane. 'There's a restaurant along there, lady,' he pointed down the street, 'I'm told they do a good afternoon tea. And this is the lecture hall – I hope the lecture's not as boring as the place looks!'

Georgette gave him a good tip. It was too early for tea, so she wandered past the restaurant and down to the end of the lane. And there was the River Cam. She stood on a small bridge that crossed a weir and looked out over the water towards the bridge by Silver Street.

Ducks paddled sedately, weeping willows bordered the weir and students punted along, chatting and laughing. Everything here exuded an air of gentle leisure, pleasantness and peace, and Georgette appreciated it fully. David must enjoy such sights every day, she reflected.

Then two mallards went skittering noisily over the water, their agitated quacking indicating some dispute. Georgette became aware of a cold breeze sweeping along the Cam, and shivered a little under its caress. She could feel her feet beginning to swell, too, and decided it was time for tea, so she strolled back up the lane and entered the restaurant.

She took a seat thankfully and studied the menu for afternoon tea. It offered all her favourite delicacies but, now that the moment had arrived, she found she was not very hungry. Her anticipation of seeing David again was making her nervous. She put down the menu and drew the packet of cigarettes out of her handbag. There was an ashtray on the table and there were no customers near enough to her to be affected, so she lit up.

'Yes, Madam?' A friendly-voiced waitress was standing by her table, pad and pencil at the ready, and Georgette knew she must order something, so she settled for a pot of tea and some scones.

'Butter or cream?'

'Cream – with strawberry jam, please.' She was just extinguishing her cigarette, and remembering by association the Cressingboroughs, when the order arrived, not just the one or two that she had been expecting, there were four large scones. They looked delicious, but she still wasn't hungry and didn't think she would be able to eat so many. But they were very light and, as soon as she took the first mouthful, her doubts vanished. All four vanished, with pleasure, and Georgette really enjoyed the tea, too, and intended to ask the blend. Service was included, so she put the exact money on the table and went off to the cloakroom to freshen up before the lecture. By the time she returned the waitress was serving someone else and Georgette forgot to ask about the tea.

'You want No 3,' a courteous porter said, 'That's just along the corridor there, on the right. The lecture's not until five, you know.'

'I do, but I want a good seat,' Georgette explained, and she set off along the wide corridor, busy with students and others moving with familiarity about the place. Then, there it was, written up, 'Lecture Room No 3'. Georgette had, at long last, arrived at her destination, and an hour of seeing her son. Her heart was thumping and her stomach churning with anticipation. She entered the room from the back. Just when she badly wanted to, she couldn't smoke, because 'NO SMOKING' notices were about, but she did not want to leave the room now she was finally here.

She looked around. It was a large, high-ceilinged room, with an ornate interior and a sky-light. At the far end was a dais, with a lectern, and all the rows of seats were slightly curved, with the dais as their focal point. The seating was in bench form, with fairly high back-rests, and reminded Georgette of church pews. She estimated that it must seat about three hundred people. Would David get that many? How awful it would be if no one but her came along!

The walls were covered in wood panelling to about half their height, then what seemed to be some kind of canvas material took over the rest of the job. A blackboard devoid of chalkings stood on the dais beside an unravelled film screen, so perhaps there were to be slides?

The floor sloped down from where Georgette stood to the dais, so the seats were staggered and everyone would be able to see the lecturer, but Georgette wanted to be close enough to see him in detail. She was the only person in the room, as yet, so could pick any seat she liked. Making up her mind, she walked down towards the dais and took a seat in the centre section of the third row from the front.

It was four-thirty. The clock on the side wall said so and a glance at her wristwatch confirmed it. Even as she entered her chosen pew, one of the doors behind her swung open and the chatter of young voices filled the room.

She slipped off her coat and scarf and settled down to wait, resolving to keep a check on her emotions when David appeared.

Within a few moments of the first group's arrival, the trickle of newcomers grew to a steady stream and the room began to fill rapidly with people of all ages. Glancing back, Georgette saw that most seemed to know someone, as many hands were waved to people a distance away and hallos mouthed across the room.

But, to Georgette's dismay, people seemed to prefer to be at the back of the room, and that filled first. It was only in the last few minutes that some took seats in her row, and they were some distance from her. She hoped she wasn't too conspicuous. Nobody could know that the solitary woman was here to see the lecturer, rather than listen to the lecture, so she wasn't worried about the rest of the audience. But surely she was isolated enough for David to notice her? She considered moving, but she had left it too late.

The chat suddenly tailed off, to be replaced by an expectant hush which was, in turn, followed by applause. Georgette turned her head. Coming through the door was the guest speaker, and there could be no mistake at all about his identity – he was a male version of Georgette in her younger days! Dougie had never mentioned the likeness and it took her completely by surprise. A head of thick dark hair, not yet streaked with grey, was parted at the side but tended naturally to cascade over his brow. He regularly, and quite subconsciously, threw it back with a sweep of his left hand, something he did even as he entered.

Though David was gowned for the occasion, he was not in the robes of his doctorate. Preceded by two younger academics, he was followed in by a fair-haired slim woman in a neat two-piece suit. Beside her was a narrow-faced youth with thick black hair, who looked a trifle self-conscious. Of course David had brought his family, why wouldn't he? Georgette had considered the possibility and now studied the youth who must be her grandson, Peter. Though less striking, a Delire family resemblance was there, too. An elderly, distinguished-looking, gentleman brought up the rear.

As the procession progressed down the aisle towards the dais, the applause was acknowledged by slightly embarrassed smiles.

David's wife was very attractive, but Georgette thought her demeanour a little haughty and wondered if that could be a front for shyness. With the two young academics and Peter, June took the front central seat by the aisle.

The elderly academic in the party proved to be the head of the history faculty, and it was he who introduced David.

'Ladies and gentlemen, I should like to welcome you to the third lecture in this series on ecological problems of the past. Our lecture this evening is given by Dr David Rusby. Some of you already know Dr Rusby, others will be familiar with his work through his books ("My! I must read them, get them through the library!") and articles and talks on Radio 3. ("Oh, if only I'd known!") He is . . .'

As David rose and took the lectern, Georgette was proud. She had done much that she considered wrong in her life, but transparently giving up her sweet little boy had worked out well for him, and she knew she need have no further guilt on that account.

'I'm not sure I'm worthy of all those superlatives!' David modestly dismissed the glitter the professor had sprinkled over his achievements. His voice was smooth, mellifluous, and his manner assured and friendly; a man who, without vanity, knew his own worth.

Georgette tingled as she listened to her son begin his speech on Starvation in 17 century Northumberland. 'In this remote corner of England, with its coastline battered by contrary tides and winds, the failure of provision ships to arrive could have devastating results . . .'

At that moment something utterly unexpected happened. All Georgette could see at the lectern was a little bundle of babyhood,

David as she had last seen him, her darling first-born. She was no longer in the lecture hall: she was back in his nursing home, undressing him for his bath, patting him dry with a soft towel, sprinkling him with baby powder and putting on his nappy, then dressing him and holding him in her arms.

Tears sprang to Georgette's eyes, misting her vision. She came back to reality and rummaged in her handbag for a handkerchief, then dabbed at her eyes, hoping no one was looking her way and that, if they were, they would assume that she had been moved to tears by the appalling picture of world poverty that the lecturer was painting. For she now became aware of his words again, and he was describing a pattern of starvation which, he suggested, could be visited upon any country in the world in the twenty-first century. He described it graphically and insisted that it would come to pass if the ecologists' warnings were ignored. Then he returned to his parallel in the past.

'. . . As hunger mounted, the death toll rose and, as always in such famines, it was the children and the elderly who suffered most.' With those words, quietly delivered, David ended his talk.

There was a moment of thoughtful silence from the floor, then enthusiastic applause. A short question-and-answer session followed, then the faculty head thanked David and there was more applause as both men left the dais. They joined June and Peter, who had risen to their feet. Before they could move towards the exit, however, a few members of the audience went up and engaged them in conversation.

The audience began to drift away, stimulated by what they had heard. Georgette was among those who retained their seats, waiting for the main crowd to leave before making their own move. She sat watching the people who had gathered about David to congratulate him, and wishing she could be among them. The other people in her row had left, so she moved along to the end and, now barely feet from her son, took her time putting on her coat and fiddling around with her scarf – straining to catch snatches of his conversation as she did so.

'You're so right, David! If we don't listen to the ecologists surely we will all starve, too,' an elderly woman twittered.

'And you, young Peter,' asked her florid husband. 'Are you planning to follow in your father's footsteps and become a don?'

Peter laughed shyly. 'Oh, I'm not clever enough for that, Major Baillie.'

'That's not really true, you know,' David said, his tone affectionate and proud. 'He's never failed an exam in his life. The truth is that he thinks the academic life is rather dull. It's The Life Guards for you, isn't it, Peter?'

'Now that's a grand regiment,' said the major, ex-Royal Army Educational Corps, himself.

'His Uncle Dougie's old Regiment,' mentioned Mrs Rusby.

'His Uncle Alex's Regiment too, if he did but know it,' thought Georgette, finding it odd to hear Dougie mentioned by people she didn't know.

At that moment she became aware that David was looking at her. It was her peripheral vision that caught the direction of his look, and against all her instincts, Georgette hastily turned away and finished buttoning her coat. She could feel his eyes still on her and strained to hear anything he might say.

'June, that lady, the one in the third row – do we know her?'

Georgette's heart almost stopped – how could she have been so stupid as to draw attention to herself by lingering for so long?

'I don't think so dear. No, I'm sure we don't. I think it must be simply that you've seen her around the town, maybe.'

Georgette, afraid that they might approach her, forced herself to head for the exit and only heard the beginning of David's reply.

'Yes, dear, I'm sure you're right. It's very strange but, all through the lecture, I had the oddest feeling that I knew her.'

As he uttered that statement, what David had noticed subconsciously suddenly rose to the surface of his mind and he knew exactly what had been bothering him. He knew, without a shadow of a doubt, that he had just seen his real mother: that was why it had felt as if some kind of magnet kept drawing his eyes back to her – she was somehow reaching out to him, compelling his attention however unintentionally.

He controlled an impulse to run after her, respecting her obvious desire of anonymity, but he knew he could like her, maybe even love her. As long as he could remember he had tried to keep her out of his mind, puzzled and hurt because she had not loved him, and hating her for her callous act of abandoning him.

But her mere presence at the lecture was proof positive that she *had* loved him, still did, even after all these years, and he realized that her leaving could have had nothing to do with her feelings for him. Something dreadful must have happened to her, to make her walk out of his life, and it must have taken great courage to come here today without making herself known to him.

Then Major Baillie spoke again, and David's thoughts returned to the present.

* * *

Georgette found the same kindly porter she'd spoken to on entering the lecture hall and he readily rang for a cab. It seemed to take an age to arrive and Georgette was desperately afraid that David would emerge from the lecture room before she could escape. Her mind was in a turmoil: she had seen her son and, for the second time in her life, she had let him go forever, reassured he was happy. She had seen her grandson, and she had let him go, too. And she had loved everything about both of them. She prayed that both would continue to have full lives and be happy.

They seemed to be content at the moment and she felt oddly elated by this second sacrifice. It was as if her purpose in life had been fully achieved.

Her cab finally arrived and she climbed in quickly. Darkness had fallen by the time the taxi reached Cambridge Station, and Georgette had about ten minutes to spare before her train was due.

Seeing David so well and happy had exorcised the load of guilt she had been carrying since that dreadful day when she had walked out on his life, and she was feeling oddly elated.

Alex had gone forever, of course, but next year she would be spending her seventieth birthday with Susan 'down under', as she'd put it, so all was well. She was content, happy and at peace.

Suddenly she felt strangely enervated and not a touch giddy, and was glad to find a platform seat while she waited. She took the 'turn' with surprising calm.

The day had wrung a gambit of emotions from her – and this had to be a reaction, she concluded.

The train pulled into the station exactly on time, and smoothly. Georgette stood up and, again giddiness invaded her. With the distress fully upon her, she made for the nearest carriage. As she pulled the door open, she felt really vertiginous, as if she were spinning into oblivion. And it required a conscious effort to haul herself aboard. She half-fell onto a seat and a passing railway official slammed her door shut without glancing into the carriage. She wasn't well, and she knew it, but at least the dizziness had passed and, once she was back in London . . .

A whistle blew and the train drew gently away from the station. As it built up speed, clicketty-clicketty over the joins in the line, Georgette, alone in her compartment, settled herself comfortably into a corner seat, leant her head back on the cushion and closed her eyes.

Something within her knew that David had forgiven her, and a contented smile was on her lips as she drifted off to sleep.